A Note Before Dying

A Ghostwriter Mystery
(Book 6)

C. A. LARMER

Larmer Media
ISBN: 978-0-9942608-1-9
Cover design: Stuart Eadie

To the musicians in my life,
may your music live on

ALSO BY C.A. LARMER

The Ghostwriter Mystery series:
Killer Twist (Book 1)
A Plot to Die For (Book 2)
Last Writes (Book 3)
Dying Words (Book 4)
Words Can Kill (Book 5)
Without a Word (Book 7)

The Murder Mystery Book Club series:
The Murder Mystery Book Club (Book 1)
Danger On the SS Orient (Book 2)
Death Under the Stars (Book 3)
When There Were 9 (Book 4)
The Widow on the Honeymoon Cruise (Book 5)
Gone Guest (Book 6)

The Posthumous Mystery series:
Do Not Go Gentle
Do Not Go Alone

The Sleuths of Last Resort:
Blind Men Don't Dial Zero
Smart Girls Don't Trust Strangers
Good Girls Don't Drink Vodka

PLUS
*After the Ferry: A Gripping
Psychological Novel*

An Island Lost

CONTENTS

C.A. LARMER

ACKNOWLEDGEMENTS

A big thank you to Michelle Sim for doing such a thorough edit with such a gentle hand. Thanks also to US reader Elaine Rivers for her unwavering support, and to musician Christian Pyle for the technical advice (and for not taking this story to heart!). Finally, thank you to my beloved Byron Shire community—you are a daily source of wonder and delight. Remember, guys, this is a work of fiction and any similarities to those living or dead, earthly or celestial, is pure coincidence (or a case of wishful thinking, perhaps?).

PROLOGUE

The young woman looked up at the figure in the distance, her pale blue eyes widening with surprise. It had been raining solidly for three full days and she had a classic case of cabin fever, eager to get out and return to his arms. But this was not who she was expecting. Feeling disappointed and somewhat caught off guard, the woman still managed a wave as her shoulders relaxed beneath her soggy poncho.

"You're not going to lecture me again, are you?" she asked, turning back to the creek to search out the shiny red Coolamon leaf she had thrown in earlier. She spotted it now, still trying to snake its way through the rapids and out towards the clearing before becoming snagged between two rocks. She watched the leaf for a few more seconds, wondering if she should try to free it. Her clothes were already sodden from the rain and she had stupidly donned her new suede boots, eager to impress him, but she was damned if she was going to ruin them after just one wear.

Besides, Sam would probably accuse her of cheating. He had such suffocating standards it drove her berserk.

"Wanna race me?" she asked, as the sound of branches crackled underfoot just behind her. "These Coolamons can really move." She bent over to grab another leaf from the muddy bank, turning back just in time to see a flash of brown before something thick and wet smacked her in the face.

She should have been shocked, outraged even, but she was too busy trying to stop from toppling into that frigid, rushing water. Too late, another "thwack" and she was down this time, head first into the creek and caught up against the same rocks that held her leaf prisoner. She had to get up; she knew that very clearly but she was feeling heavy, as though she'd just taken a shot of heroin, and there were black sparkles in front of her eyes.

As she tried to stand, the woman felt something rough wedge into her cheek. *A wooden plank? A boot, perhaps?* Whatever it was, it pushed down hard and unrelenting until her face was fully submerged in the icy depths.

'This is what happens when you play with fire,' she thought with quiet despair. *'This is what happens when you defy your brother.'*

Then, as the last bubbles of oxygen escaped from her paling lips, the young woman spotted her tiny racer dislodge and make a bid for freedom, and she felt a momentary sense of jubilation before darkness finally descended.

CHAPTER 1

Roxy Parker stared hard at her reflection and frowned. The tailored black jacket and blue and white striped scarf looked okay, so, too, the oversized baggy T-shirt, slipping down ever so slightly on one shoulder, cutting in close to her hips, then across her skinny blue jeans, just enough to hide the fact that she wasn't quite so skinny anymore.

When on earth had that happened?

She tugged the T-shirt lower, then glanced down to her maroon ankle boots and up to her dangly earrings, all the while chewing mercilessly on her lower lip.

Something was still not right.

Leaning into the mirror, she squinted at her face. Too much makeup, perhaps? Grabbing a tissue, she blotted back the red lipstick, dampened down the eyeliner and stared hard again. Nope, still wasn't working; she looked ridiculous. That was it. She was trying too hard. Roxy groaned and tugged at the scarf, pulling it off, then ripped out the earrings and reached for a delicate silver necklace. As she dropped it around her neck, she smiled. That was better. Less try-hard, she thought.

The phone rang shrilly and she grabbed it, then tried to

sound casual: "Hello, Roxy Parker speaking."

"Ready for your hot date?" It was her friend and agent Oliver Horowitz and he had that trademark smirk in his tone, the one that boiled her blood.

"It's an interview, Olie, not a date."

"Sure it is. So why're you stressing over your outfit?"

Roxy's eyes swept around the room. Had she left her front door open? Did he have a telescopic lens peering in through her fourth-floor apartment window?

Olie chuckled. "I know you, Rox, I know your every neurosis. I know you've spent all morning trying to work out what to wear, and before that, half the night trying to come up with questions that make you sound like an uber-cool rock chick."

She relaxed. "You are the polar opposite of cool, Olie. You know that, right?"

"Are you saying I'm hot, Roxy?"

"I most certainly am not! You have an atrocious way of twisting words," she said.

Oliver laughed. "That's why I'm the literary agent and you're the one doing the interviews."

Roxy felt her stomach clench again. It had been doing that for the past week, ever since Oliver had announced her latest ghostwriting gig; an autobiography for one of Australia's hottest musicians, Jed Moody, of the infamous Moody Roos. The band had been Australia's premier rock act in the 1990s, and while their star had faded of late—thanks to encroaching middle age, a spate of mediocre albums and the frontman's dodgy dye job (why, Roxy often lamented, did older men think faux black hair suited them?)—Jed, at least, was still a household name. Several solo albums, the odd arrest for drug possession and a sexy swagger that hadn't diminished all these years later, made sure of that. And despite the bad hair, Jed had kept her heart rate at rocket speed for the past week. Roxy didn't normally worship false idols, and found most celebrities boring at best, but there was *something* about Jed.

She took a few deep breaths and eye rolled Oliver.

"What do you want, Olie? I'm a very important person and I've got to get off the phone. I have a plane to catch."

"Not before brunch with your literary agent, you don't. Haven't forgotten that, have you? We're all waiting."

"Well, I'd be there now if you let me get off the phone and finish getting ready."

"By 'getting ready' you mean 'tarting yourself up'?"

"By 'literary agent' you mean 'the guy who takes 15 percent for being a smart arse'?"

He laughed again and hung up.

Roxy's local, Peeps Café, was bursting to the brim and out onto the sidewalk. She had to take a good look around before spotting her friends, just inside, wedged together against the coffee bar, deep in conversation.

She smiled and made her way through the queue. They had managed to save her a stool, and she dropped onto it, stealing quick kisses from the group as she went.

"I can't believe you all made it," she said, waving off the menu Oliver was holding out. "I am only going for a week, you know that, right?"

Gilda Maltin scoffed. "You've barely been back a fortnight and you're off again. I had to take the day off work just to see you."

"Really, you took a day off for me?" Roxy blinked incredulously. Gilda was one of the state's finest detectives and had been working virtually nonstop since being promoted to the Homicide Serious Crime Squad.

"Well, how else am I supposed to catch up with my best mate?"

"You could bring out the cuffs and chain her to her apartment bed," suggested Oliver, and Gilda stared at him, her top lip curled up.

"You'd like that, wouldn't you?"

His beady little eyes narrowed and he nudged his chunky eyebrows up and down.

"Urrgh, you guys are disgusting," said Caroline, her button nose wrinkling. "Well, I've seen more than enough of Roxy over the past month, thank you very much. I'm just here for the coffee, if it ever comes." Her big brown eyes glared at the waiter who was usually more attentive but was now busily sweating over a hot espresso machine. Caroline was the youngest in the group, the pretty blonde one, and she wasn't used to being ignored, didn't like it one bit.

"Give him a chance, Caro," said Lockie, their Scottish café owner friend whose many years in Sydney had not diminished his thick accent. "It's hard work when ye café gets a five-star rating in the *Herald*. Bet the crowds have been coming thick 'n' fast ever since."

"Yeah." Oliver groaned. "It's been the curse of this place. We used to have it to ourselves, eh, Rox? Maybe we should have met up at your caf', Lockie."

He mock shuddered. "Noooo way, I needed a break. Place has been a wee bi' stressful of late."

"Why?" Roxy asked. "What's going on?"

Gilda held a hand in the air. "Hold it right there. Sorry, Lockie, but we're here to catch up with Roxy. Are you all packed? Excited about meeting Juicy Jed?" Her smile was smarmy.

Roxy shook her head. "What is it with everyone? I'm interviewing the man, for a book. I'm a professional, okay? This is a *ghostwriting* assignment. I am not going to Byron Bay to hook up."

"Well you can't, the guy's married," said Olie, and Caroline snorted.

"Like that's ever stopped anyone."

"Least of all Jed Moody," added Lockie. In response to everyone's raised eyebrows, he added, "What? I scan the gossip mags while I'm at the supermarket, too, ye know." He turned to Roxy. "Besides, I thought Max was the only man for you."

The very mention of photographer Max Farrell's name brought the group to an awkward silence and Gilda and

Caroline began shooting death stares at the Scotsman. He looked at them bemused, then back at Roxy who just sighed.

"You clearly aren't as switched on as you think, Lockie. Max and I have broken up. For good this time. It's over. We've both agreed, and we're happy with that. Right, Caroline?"

Max's sister gave a noncommittal shoulder shrug and, sensing Roxy's growing discomfort, Gilda quickly jumped in. "Rightio then, let's drop that tender subject and get back to Juicy Jed, shall we?"

"No," said Roxy. "This needs to be made clear, once and for all." Roxy took a deep breath and spoke very slowly, as if addressing a group of dimwits. "Max. And. I. Are. Not … I repeat *not* … An. Item. Got it? We're best mates. He's in Berlin, where he works, I'm heading to Byron Bay—"

"To interview a rock god, no less," said Gilda, trying to lighten the mood, and Roxy nodded.

"Exactly. And that's all there is to it."

Yet, as she got up to order a latté, she couldn't help wondering why her heart still felt like it had been pummelled with a sledgehammer.

When Roxy returned, Oliver had a plastic folder out in front of him. He was wading through what looked like press clippings and website printouts while Caroline and Lockie keenly watched on. Gilda had stepped outside to take a phone call, and Roxy stole her stool, closer to Oliver, and raised questioning eyebrows at him.

"The Moody Roos' publicist couriered this over late yesterday. Says it might help."

"Anything interesting?"

"Nah, just stuff about past albums, a few interviews, nothing sensational. You're in for a treat, though, the house looks like a stunner."

He handed over a glossy six-page spread, clearly ripped from the pages of a luxury home living magazine, which featured an enormous white timber Queenslander-style mansion. The photos were mostly of the interior and revealed expansive polished wooden floorboards and expensive designer furniture. In several shots, the blurred image of a thin, black-haired woman could be seen striding, first through a gleaming silver kitchen, then along a tapestry lined hallway, like a ghostly presence, just beyond the camera's grasp. It sent Roxy's memory barrelling through time.

She had an immediate flashback. It was circa 1998, she was wearing her favourite ripped denim jeans and tight Stussy T-shirt, standing, wedged to one side of a smoky inner-city pub, watching a late-night gig by the Moody Roos. The bass player, Alistair Avery, was on the right-hand side of the stage, his body barely moving as he plucked at his bass and stared out at the crowd through black-rimmed glasses, a look of utter boredom on his face. The drummer, Doug someone-or-other, was up the back, hammering away with his sticks, a goofy smile on his lips and his long blonde curls flying about as he played. In front of them both and eclipsing the band with sheer energy and pizzazz, was the eternally sexy Jed Moody, the real reason everyone had showed. Back then he was already getting long in the tooth, and was no longer filling concert halls, but that night the place was packed. Roxy remembered a gaggle of groupies hanging out at the front of the stage, clinging to his every word, ogling him lasciviously as he strutted the stage as if he owned it.

And to the side of the stage, just behind an enormous speaker, was a woman who looked like she owned him. She was tall and thin with chiselled cheekbones and dark, almond-shaped eyes, which kept darting from Jed to those groupies and back again. Roxy had been surprised by her intensity and had wondered back then if she was Jed's girlfriend or the manager, perhaps? Whoever she was then, the magazine spread revealed that she was now Jed Moody's wife.

"Oooh, she looks a wee bi' scary," said Lockie.

Oliver scoffed. "Nothing our Writer Extraordinaire can't handle."

Roxy just smiled, hoping he was right.

"Bloody Chief Houlihan," Gilda snarled, returning to the group. "He's nagging me to take some of my accrued time off and suggested I don't come back to work today."

"Why would he say that?" asked Roxy.

"Something to do with budgets, being over them. That's the third phone call today. He's worse than your mother."

Roxy shuddered, and they all shuddered along with her. "No one's worse than my mother," she said, and no one had the heart to disagree.

"How is Ms Control Freak?" asked Gilda. "She must be cranky you're not hanging around."

Roxy grimaced. It was worse than that. When Roxy broke the news over dinner a few days ago, her mother, Lorraine Jones had stared at her daughter with the facial equivalent of a sigh—head tilted, slackened features, pure disappointment in her eyes.

"What?" Roxy had asked, her shoulders tense and ready for battle.

"Nothing, darling, it's just … well, I can't help wondering if you're trying to avoid me. Is this all about not having to spend any time with your mother at all?"

"Mum, it's work, it's not personal."

Lorraine sighed, verbally this time. "I thought you said you were going to stay put for a while. You've only been back in the country ten minutes."

"Actually, I've been back ten days and I'm only going up the coast. Not all the way to Germany."

"Might as well be Europe, darling. *Byron Bay*." Lorraine turned her nose up like she had just smelt something bad and Roxy knew exactly what she thought of that idea. "Isn't it full of hippies, and feral people that don't bathe?"

Roxy laughed. "Hardly. More like TV executives and rock stars these days, hence the reason for the trip. I'm actually doing a book on Jed Moody, and there's nothing feral about him."

Glancing back at the photos in the file, Roxy couldn't help smiling. Jed was not only a rock star; he had a stunning home and lived in a glorious part of the world. Despite her nerves, this was one ghostwriting assignment she was really going to enjoy.

She said as much to the group as they finished up their coffees and they all burst into laughter.

"What?" she said and Olie shook his head.

"Just don't stumble across any dead bodies this time, okay?"

able in these parts. It was also true that she was

CHAPTER 2

"So how does it feel, glorifying a murderer?"

The harsh tone took Roxy by surprise and she looked up from her iPad-mini and towards a man standing by her table, wide sunglasses covering the top half his face, the beginnings of a beard covering the rest. It wasn't the kind of beard the young hipsters were all donning these days, thick and meticulously coiffed. This was more the 'fallen-out-of-bed', 'forgotten-to-shave' look. He was older, too, maybe early forties, judging from the tuft of greyish-brown hair on his head and the soft lines across his forehead. He was wearing blue jeans and a red and blue checked shirt, which had been rolled up at the sleeves to reveal lean, muscled arms, the kind that came from hard yakka, not the gym. He would have been handsome if it wasn't for the ugly scowl.

"Sorry?" Roxy said, blinking her emerald green eyes at him.

"Are you the Sydney chick doing the Jed Moody book?"

She hesitated. It was true, she was a "Sydney chick" and there was no avoiding that charge. Her tailored jacket, Ray-Ban glasses and coiffed black hair were all dead giveaways, especially in these parts. It was also true that she was ghostwriting a book for Jed Moody, but how did he know that? She'd only just arrived.

Roxy's flight from Sydney had taken an hour and a half. And despite getting lost twice, as she steered her hire car along the winding roads of the Byron hinterland where the Moody's property was located, she realised she was running early—she wasn't due for another twenty minutes—so she decided to stop for coffee. Luckily, Roxy had noticed a few signs on the side of the road advertising The Goddess Café ("A vegetarian café with bite!"), and she was delighted to find it right on the corner of the turnoff to Jed's road.

Roxy promptly pulled her car into the muddy parking lot and switched the engine off. The café was more of a convenience store than anything else, a weathered old wooden shop with a post office, bottle shop and petrol station thrown in. She lingered out the front for a few minutes, reading a notice board which was plastered with handwritten pleas for work—"any work"—as well as For Sale signs (one VW Kombi van, several items of "preloved" furniture, a range of chickens, aka "chooks", and a vintage Vox Amp). She also saw ads for Hatha Yoga classes, pottery and something called "The Art of Mindfulness".

To the left of the shop was a weathered old shed with a sign that read "Trev's Motor Mechanic", although the padlocked doors and undisturbed cobwebs suggested Trev hadn't checked anyone's motor for some time. To the right of the shop, a cluster of wooden tables and chairs were perched under mouldy umbrellas on the lawn, and below a large Poinciana was a soggy sandpit with some faded plastic buckets and spades. Apart from a heavyset man in a baggy Quicksilver hoodie and dark sunglasses reading a newspaper, the place was deserted.

"You right, chook?"

Roxy swung around to find a woman standing at the front door of the shop, one hand on her tanned hip, her big blue eyes open wide. She had a full head of dirty blonde dreadlocks, many of them interwoven with multicoloured ribbons and beads; a small belly button ring on her bulging tummy, several rings on each ear, and a wrist full of silver bangles which were jangling now as she held onto what turned out to be a young child hiding inside her flowing, gypsy-style skirt. The woman was probably in her early thirties and, despite the chill in the hinterland air, was wearing the skimpiest of tops, her enormous breasts about an inch away from toppling out.

"I'll have a latté, thanks."

"Soy milk? Goats? Skim?"

Roxy hesitated. "Do you have normal milk?"

The woman paused for a moment as though Roxy had just spoken French. "Yep. Anything else? I've got gluten-free brownies, raw carrot cake, a few energy bars left."

Roxy shook her head. "Just the coffee, thanks."

"Take a seat, hon. I'll bring it out." She jingled a hand towards the tables then disappeared inside the darkened shop, the small child vanishing with her.

Roxy chose a seat in the sun and stretched her legs out under the table, then checked her mobile phone. There were no missed calls so she retrieved her iPad from her handbag. It was still in airplane mode so she switched back and began trawling for the WiFi. Her nerves were still skittish from the drive and she needed the distraction.

"No coverage out here, sweetheart," said the man from the other table. He pushed his wraparound glasses up onto his head and squinted at her with smudged brown eyes, a sly smile on his lips. He was well into his fifties with a receding hairline and a straggly greyish brown plait down his back; his face a ripple of deep wrinkles and fresh sunburn. He had a tabloid newspaper spread out in front of him and a packet of cigarettes close by.

Roxy closed the lid of her iPad case feeling like a goose. "Oh well, thought I'd try my luck."

He watched her for a bit longer then returned to his newspaper just as a white Jeep came rattling to a stop in front of the shop. Roxy hadn't paid it much heed so she was stunned when the driver leapt out and charged straight up to her table, accusing her of glorifying a murderer.

"Well? How does it feel, glorifying someone that evil? I bet you're not going to mention that in your fancy book."

"I... I don't know what you're talking about," she stammered.

He stared at her for a few more seconds then his scowl softened and his voice cracked a little. "Just ask him about Sunny. Ask him what really happened."

Before Roxy could demand to know what he was on about, he had turned away and was striding back to his vehicle. As he cranked his door open and jumped inside, Roxy noticed a large black and white dog in the passenger seat, staring back at her with wide, curious eyes.

The older man at the café had seen all this and was now watching Roxy curiously, his smile widening. She blinked at him confused before turning back to the road where the Jeep was spitting up dust as it rounded the bend and disappeared from sight. The waitress had also witnessed the incident and was shaking her dreadlocks slowly as she placed a recycled coffee cup in front of Roxy.

"Don't let Sambo worry you, chook. He's carrying a lot of dark energy these days." She glanced down the road. "'Course, you can't blame him, after what happened to Sunny."

"Sunny?"

"His sister, sweet young soul. Showed up dead on the Moody property about eighteen months back. All very innocent, but he seems to think otherwise." She sighed heavily. "I've tried to soothe him, everyone has, but nothing's worked. He just can't seem to let it go."

Roxy wasn't listening now, all she could hear were the words "dead" and "Moody property" and they were ricocheting around her brain. "Dead?" she repeated now. "What happened?"

"Sambo's sister drowned trying to cross a swollen creek;

silly, silly kitten."

"And he blames Jed Moody?"

She smiled sadly. "Better than blaming yourself, hey?"

The waitress twirled around and headed back into the café, her beaded skirt jangling as she went. Roxy's insides did a little jangle of their own. Before she could give it any more thought, the man with the wraparound glasses loomed over her, blocking out the sunlight.

"Wanna make some easy cash?"

"Sorry?"

He dropped a business card in front of her, leaned in and said, "Let me know where and when, you get 10 percent."

Then he, too, strode away, this time around the back of the shop and towards a rusty white Commodore station wagon.

Roxy looked at the card, saw the words "Macker Maroney Photographer" printed beside a mobile phone number and website. He must be paparazzi she thought, looking up just in time to see him wave as he drove off.

Roxy slumped back in her seat and stared forlornly at her coffee.

"*Bloody hell, Roxy Parker,*" she thought, echoing the words of her agent many, many times before. "What have you got yourself into this time?".

CHAPTER 3

The shop was surprisingly dark when Roxy stepped inside to pay for her coffee and make her escape. She had been in the Byron Shire less than an hour, had not even met Jed Moody yet, and already she felt wrung out. What had started as harmless anticipation at meeting her teenage idol had turned to deep apprehension. This job wasn't going to be as straightforward as she'd anticipated. Already, one man was trying to steal pictures of her client and another was accusing him of murder.

Olie and her friends were right. It had become a recurring theme in Roxy's life.

"That'll be three bucks, thanks," the waitress said, one hand on the cash register, the other wrapped around the toddler who clung to her hip like a baby koala. The child had a tangle of long, blonde curls and a strand of tiny amber beads around her neck, although she could easily have been a he, it was hard to tell.

Roxy smiled at the child, a girl she decided, and then realised with a start that she was suckling on her mother's breast, which had now spilled out of her top. Both mother and child seemed perfectly at ease with this arrangement, the girl even watching Roxy intensely as she drank, her wide, yellow-green eyes twinkling with mischief, and Roxy couldn't help blushing despite herself.

She was all for breastfeeding in public, admired it in fact, but it wasn't something you encountered very often in the city, at least not at the cash register while paying your bill.

The woman deftly snatched Roxy's cash, opened the till and handed her some change, all without causing any disturbance to the child. Roxy had to admire her skills. This woman took multitasking to a new level.

As Roxy turned to leave the cafe, the waitress called after her, "Say hi to Jed for me. Tell him Govinda sends her love."

Roxy's eyes widened. "You know Jed then?"

She jiggled her daughter higher on her hip. "Everybody knows everybody around here chook!"

As Roxy left the shop, she felt a sudden yearning for the overcrowded anonymity of the big smoke.

It was now just before 5:00 p.m., Roxy's designated arrival time, and she stared at the publicist's scribbled directions to the Moody property. "Moody Views" was located on Jasper Road; a good hour's drive southwest from the airport, forty kilometres inland from the popular coastal town of Byron Bay. It had all seemed simple enough when she read the directions, but no sooner had Roxy turned down Jasper Road when she found herself hopelessly lost.

"This is ridiculous!" she hissed, pulling the car over so she could read the directions again.

"Moody Views, 88 Jasper Road, just down from the Goddess Café."

That had to be the only Goddess Café in the area, surely? And this had to be Jasper Road. She hadn't taken any unexpected turns. The problem was the numbers, which seemed to be all over the place. Lot 102 on one side, No 45 on the other, and there wasn't a number 88 or a "Moody Views" to be found. Eventually, after turning back for the third time, Roxy decided to take a punt on the only driveway along the entire stretch of road that boasted a lock-up gate (currently open) and fresh, sealed tar. She figured if anyone had the means and motivation, it had to be the local celebrity.

Slowly, carefully, she manoeuvred her tiny red hatchback through the gate and across the bumpy cattle grid, then continued driving past a wide, open field. The road seemed to stretch for kilometres before plunging into thick, subtropical rainforest, which extinguished the remainder of the day's light and forced Roxy to grapple with the controls to locate the car's headlights. The canopy overhead was lush, but she soon drove out into a clearing where a historical timber mansion managed to dwarf what would otherwise have been an impressive fig tree beside it. The house resembled the pictures in Oliver's press clippings and Roxy felt a flood of relief. She glanced at her watch and her relief evaporated.

She was fifteen minutes late. *Damn it!*

Several structures sat on either side of the main house, including what looked like horse stables, a sizeable polyethylene water tank, and a large timber shed with an extremely high roof and a vintage Ford Valiant parked out the front.

Roxy turned towards the main house and rolled her car to a stop in front of the fig when a tall, painfully thin woman appeared from the stables. The woman was wearing tight jodhpurs and riding boots and she had the same dark colouring and the same haughty expression as the woman in the magazine. It had to be the wife, Annika Moody, Roxy decided.

As Roxy switched the engine off and got out, she spotted someone else exiting the stables, a man with dark glasses and a goatee. He was pulling his hoodie down over his face as he walked away from Roxy's car and towards the high shed. He looked vaguely familiar but it wasn't Jed Moody. She knew that much.

Annika was now walking swiftly towards Roxy, tapping

one sinewy thigh with what looked like a horsewhip, her long black hair swishing from side to side, her frown intensifying. She wore a low, V-neck sweater, which emphasised her bony décolletage, and around her neck hung a thin gold chain with a tiny crystal attached.

"Houghton was supposed to be here before you," she exclaimed. "I was expecting him first."

She sounded extremely annoyed, and Roxy wasn't quite sure how to respond. Did Annika want her to bugger off until the band's publicist arrived?

"He *did* tell you I was arriving around five, right?"

"Houghton says lots of things, most don't amount to much." Now she sounded more weary than indignant. "Oh well, you're here now. Might as well come in."

Annika began crunching down the pebbled driveway towards the house where a tiny, fluffy white dog appeared, belatedly yapping at Roxy.

"Oh shut up, Coco!" Annika cried out.

"Should I bring my bags?" Roxy called after her.

Annika continued walking, "No, you should not. You're staying the night in the bails."

The bails? Roxy's jaw dropped. Wasn't that a barn where they milked dairy cows? She tried not to think the worst as she grabbed her oversized handbag from the passenger seat and locked up, before wondering why she bothered. It wasn't likely anyone was going to pinch it out here. Burglars would be hard pressed finding the place.

Annika hung her whip on a hook by the front door and slipped her polished brown R.M. William's riding boots off. Roxy noticed a pile of muddy shoes on either side of the enormous Balinese-style wooden doors and took this as her cue to unzip her boots. She hoped desperately that she was wearing a decent pair of socks.

Annika had already pushed open one of the doors and was padding softly down the long hallway, the dog one step behind. Roxy had to rush to catch up, her mismatched blue socks now on full display.

The hallway broke off into various different rooms, but Annika swept past them all and towards the back half of the house where the hall ended and a wide, curved doorway opened into a spacious living area. At one end of the room Roxy could see the opening to what looked like a kitchen and at the other end, a rather impressive bar complete with chrome and leather stools, and a staggering array of liquor bottles. Glasses of various shapes and sizes were hanging from an overhead railing, and there was an ornate mirror against the wall. Beside it were several gold and platinum albums that had been framed and hung up, loot collected during the Moody Roos' heyday, no doubt. Just to the left of the bar was a side door that appeared to lead outside.

Annika was now behind the bar, Coco still at her feet, and she was holding a bottle of Stolichnaya vodka in one hand, a pair of silver tongs in the other.

"So, you found us okay," she said.

Roxy wondered for a moment if she was talking about the trip from the airport or the trek down the hallway. In any case, it wasn't put as a question so she decided not to mention her many wrong turns.

"We're not on the GPS," Annika continued, "which is just the way we like it. I suppose you need a drink?"

"Yes, thanks, that was certainly a long drive."

Annika snorted. "How long did it take you?"

"About an hour."

"And how many hours have you wasted sitting in Sydney traffic?" Before Roxy could reply, Annika was shaking her head. "I find it bizarre the way stupid city folk get so stressed the second they get on a country road. I'd much rather drive along a few dirt roads past koalas and rainforest than sit in the smog of the city waiting for the lights to go green. Wouldn't you? Vodka cocktail?"

She was still waving the bottle in the air and Roxy nodded. It wasn't her favourite tipple, but it would do the job. As she watched Annika mix the cocktail like a professional barmaid, splashing pomegranate juice,

Cointreau and lime into the vodka, Roxy wondered whether to take her to task on her comment or quietly concede that she was right.

Roxy loved her city life, but there was no denying she had lost plenty of precious hours stuck in the middle of bumper-to-bumper traffic. The woman had a point, but it still riled her a little. Did she have to be so aggressive about it?

Choosing to avoid the bait, Roxy stepped away from the bar and towards the centre of the living room, which was as beautiful as the magazine spreads had promised, and then some. The main feature wall had been plastered with luscious Florence Broadhurst wallpaper, a decorative palm and vine design, and in front sat a plush purple velvet sofa, with matching armchairs on either side. An enormous TV set, stereo system and turntable dominated a second wall while the third was made up of pretty French doors that were currently closed but still revealed a dazzling green view beyond.

"Bottoms up," Annika said, handing her a martini glass with the lurid orange concoction inside. She took a good gulp of her drink, sighing after she did so, before pushing open two of the French doors and stepping out onto the veranda.

The living room was stunning, but the veranda was clearly the heart of the house. Typical of a historical home, it had hardwood floorboards that wrapped right around the structure, and extended so deep there was room to hold several leather lounges and an entire dining suite. The railings had all been painted white and many were dripping with wisteria, small Chinese lanterns hanging at random intervals between tinkling chimes and fairy lights above. There was a wide set of stairs in the centre of the veranda leading down to the rolling green lawn, and beyond that a magnificent view that included the lush rainforest in the foreground and hazy valleys that dipped and dived as far as the eye could see.

At one end of the lawn, Roxy spotted part of the tall

timber building she had noticed when she drove up, and at the other end an old shed on stilts with a wide timber deck that was strewn with party lights. A pebble pathway led back from the shed to a smaller set of stairs on the east side of the veranda that appeared to lead directly to the bar inside.

To the left of the main staircase sat a long wooden dining table, cluttered with dripping candles and what looked like detritus from the previous night—empty beer bottles, wine glasses, an old cheese platter and several ashtrays full to overflowing.

Annika had now positioned herself on one of the leather lounges, her long legs spread out in front of her, her little dog coiled into a ball beside her.

Roxy waved a hand to the view and said, "I'd tell you it was breathtaking, but you don't need 'stupid city folk' to state the bleeding obvious."

Annika looked up at her and was about to say something then appeared to change her mind. She smiled, her features softening a little. "I'll drink to that." She held her glass high.

Roxy held her own glass up. "Cheers," she replied, wondering if this was a truce of sorts, or if they were just toasting the end of round one.

CHAPTER 4

As she leaned against the railing, looking out at that seemingly endless view, Roxy wondered whether Jed was around and how soon she could get started.

As if reading her thoughts, Annika said, "He's in the studio. Could be there for hours, even days, so you might as well settle in."

"Days?"

She stared into her glass. "He comes up for air eventually. It'll give us time to have a chat first." Then she pointed her glass at the chair beside her.

Roxy took a fortifying gulp of her cocktail and sat down. She knew how these things went. This would be no idle "chat". This was Annika's chance to interrogate the writer before her husband showed up. Annika was not just Jed's wife, she was also the band's manager and she called the shots. At least, that's what Roxy was led to believe from the press clippings she had devoured on the flight up, and nothing Annika had done thus far gave her cause to dispute this. The woman was clearly bold and outspoken, but that wasn't unusual in Roxy's line of work. While she'd never written a book on a musician before, she'd done plenty of magazine interviews and she knew how these things worked. No manager worth her weight in gold would let a journalist loose on their client without a few road rules first. That must go doubly so for a manager/wife.

This time, however, Roxy was in for a surprise.

"Tell me about yourself," Annika said, one hand now softly stroking Coco's head.

"You mean, my credentials as a writer?"

She stopped stroking. "Oh, I don't give a crap about that. That's Houghton's business. I want to know where you were you born and bred, where you live now, that kind of thing."

It was a strange request. Roxy wasn't used to discussing her personal life in interviews; that was considered a no-no amongst good journalists. It was also the reason she had become a journo in the first place. She didn't *like* talking about herself; was not interested in being in the spotlight. It was other people's lives she wanted to illuminate, not her own.

Annika had other ideas. "Are you married? Any kids?" she persisted.

Okay, thought Roxy. *I can play along.* "I'm Sydney born and bred, have a little pad in Elizabeth Bay that's about the size of your bar fridge." She paused, but Annika did not laugh. "Um, I'm not married and don't intend to be any time soon, much to my mother's disappointment, and there are no kids to speak of."

"Not even a dog?" It sounded as though she was equating the two, and Roxy shook her head.

"As I said, my place is tiny, wouldn't really be fair to a dog." She glanced at Coco who only had eyes for her mistress. It'd be nice though, all that unequivocal love. "Still, I do have some very loyal friends and a pretty sweet life." *If you didn't count the stream of dead bodies that had been showing up lately.* She decided not to mention that. "Anyway, it's my work that really drives me. I've had the chance to interview some amazing people in my time."

"Ever written a book about a musician before?" Roxy

shook her head again. "They're a unique breed, let me tell you that." Annika placed her glass down on a wrought iron table to the side of the lounge and leaned towards Roxy, her voice dropping to almost a whisper. "When I first met Jeddie, I was a photographer-slash-model. He had a lot of women in his life back then, too many women." She stopped, choked out a half laugh that didn't reach the eyes. "You could say he had a different girl in every port. It took me a while but I eventually got their little claws out of him and brushed them out of our life. He's with me now."

"Yes, I realise—"

Annika held a long finger up to quieten her, clearly unaccustomed to being interrupted. "You need to hear this, Roxy, and I don't want to have to say it again, so please listen up. Jed Moody is a very friendly guy, he'll flirt with you, make you feel very, *very* special. It's what he does, it's why his music just, well, *works*. You're going to come away feeling like the centre of the universe, one very desirable woman, but it won't last and it's not real, so try not to take it personally or flatter yourself. He does it to all the girls."

Roxy's cheeks were now burning and her knuckles were white around her glass. "Annika, I'm not—"

She held her finger up again. "*Of course* you're not, darling! They never are." Her eyes glazed over briefly as she looked past Roxy towards the horizon and her anguish was now obvious in the deep groove between her eyes and the hardened downward turn of her mouth. When she looked back, though, her tone was acidic. "Jed Moody is *my* husband and he won't be leaving me for anyone. Not now, not ever. He knows that, I know that, so I think it's helpful that you know that, too. It'll just save us all a lot of time and grief in the long run." She had been stroking her crystal necklace and now sighed heavily, wearily, before picking up her martini glass again. "Just do the dreaded book and leave us in peace. Okay?" Then she closed her eyes and polished off her drink.

Roxy was stunned, mortified, too, and she wanted to rail against what Annika was saying. She'd never slept with a client, let alone a married one, and she didn't intend to start now, but then she remembered how long she had dithered in front of the mirror that morning, how keen she had been to get her look "just right". And she recalled the way her friends had all joked about "Juicy Jed" over breakfast, as though any rock star, married or otherwise, was fair game.

"You giving this journo a hard time, Annie?" A squeaky voice cut through the tension and both women looked up to find a man standing just inside the French doors, a plump smile on his lips. The strain on Annika's face dissolved instantly and Roxy, too, felt a sense of relief.

This man was clearly not Jed, and she was glad of that. Thanks to Annika's warning words, Roxy's nerves were fluttering like bunting in the wind; it was not how she wanted to present herself to her client. She smiled at the man who was stepping out towards them. He was the antithesis of Jed: short and plump with baggy clothes and thick, fuzzy orange hair—half Ronald McDonald, half Sideshow Bob.

To Annika he was more like Santa Claus and she jumped up to greet him, squealing with delight, causing Coco to leap off the lounge and start yapping again.

"Of course I am, darling!" she said throwing herself into his arms. "That's what I'm here for, you know that!" She remained coiled around him as she turned back to look at Roxy. "You had to send him a pretty one, didn't you?"

"Hey, I did you a service, at least she's not blonde."

"Ouch," she said, throwing her head back and laughing for the first time, unleashing what sounded like rapid machine-gun fire.

Roxy watched all this in a state of perplexity. Annika's animosity had completely thrown her, and she struggled to regain her equilibrium, to channel her cocky sense of self, the one that usually helped her slap down the antagonists in her life. She realised now as she sat blinking up at them like a deer caught in the headlights, that her self-confidence must have gone AWOL somewhere between angry Beard Man's outburst and Annika's condescending lecture.

"Awww, don't mind us," said the short, fat man as he extricated himself from Annika's embrace and shuffled towards her, his arm reaching out to shake her hand. "We're just mucking about. Don't mean anything by it! I'm Harry Houghton, the band's publicist. Welcome to the sticks."

"Thanks," Roxy managed.

"You found the place okay?"

"Yes." She took a deep breath and steadied her nerves. "It's very beautiful out here."

"Yeah, but who'd wanna live here, right?" He laughed loudly, his fuzzy hair wobbling as he did so. Then he wedged a fat forefinger to his lips and whispered, "Just don't tell Annie. She thinks it's paradise."

"Oh, you love it here!" Annika hissed, flinging herself back onto the lounge.

"Only when you're around." The look they gave each other then almost smouldered. The man was half Annika's height and twice her size, but there was definite chemistry between them. "Speaking of which, where's the grump?"

Annika nudged her head towards the tall timber building to the left of the veranda.

"Where else? Been at it for days. I'm bored beyond belief. Get yourself a drink, darling, and replenish ours while you're there."

Houghton turned to Roxy. "Annie will be a very generous host, Roxy, but you'll notice there's always an ulterior motive."

"I'm just asking for a vodka cocktail, darling, not your life blood."

"You've already sucked that dry, hey?"

She barked with laughter again. "In your dreams, Mr. Naughty Houghty."

Once again they seemed to forget that Roxy was there and simply stared at each other as though under some spell. Eventually Houghton coughed and she smiled and shook her head. "You are such a wicked man."

There was some sort of private joke between them, that

much was obvious, and Roxy watched them closely, wondering about it and feeling suddenly peeved. If anyone was doing the flirting around here, it was Annika and the publicist.

"Another cocktail, Roxy?" Houghton asked and she nodded.

She had a feeling she was going to need it.

CHAPTER 5

No sooner had Houghton returned with fresh drinks than Annika leapt back to her feet and declared it was time "to fetch us some goddamn grub". As she stepped inside, Houghton took her place on the lounge and smiled warmly at Roxy.

"Annie have a bit of a chat about the rules, did she?"

"The only rule I heard was 'no flirting with the talent'."

He chuckled. "Don't worry about that, hey, don't give it another thought. Annie's little green monster is on heightened alert these days, that's all."

"Why?"

"Ohhh, there was a bit of an incident not long ago, nothing for you to concern yourself with. No, no. This is a feel-good book, am I right or am I right?"

"It's whatever you want it to be, you're the boss."

"Nah, love, that'd be Annika, just don't tell Jed that." He chuckled again. "Rightio, so I'd best go through some of the basics, you know, just to make sure we're all on the same page, that kind of thing."

"Go ahead." She didn't bother bracing herself this time, just took a good gulp of her cocktail. She was already on heightened alert.

"Rightio, so…" He took a swig of the beer in his hand then said in his strange, squeaky voice, "First point, an important one: please don't give out any detail about the house and contents, or where it's located, that kind of thing. Too many nutters out there, not to mention paparazzi, don't wanna give them the heads-up."

"You might be too late for that. Some photographer already nabbed me at the local café, gave me his business card."

His eyes narrowed. "Beefy bloke, bad ponytail, mid-fifties?" She nodded and he frowned. "That'd be bloody Macker Maroney, I'd say, local pap. Tries his luck from time to time, the bugger. A bloody hopeless photographer, too—specialises in far away, fuzzy shots. Let me know if he tries it on you again, otherwise just keep your distance, okay? Oh, and tell me if you see him on the property, I'll call the cops." He found his smile. "Right, so, what else? Um, try not to bring up the wife and kids if you can help it."

Roxy blinked, surprised. "I didn't think they had kids."

"Exactly. That's off-limits."

"Is it a sore point?"

"Bitterly sore, just leave it alone, hey?"

"Have they struggled for a long time?" He gave her a sideways look that suggested, "Good try, lady", so she said, "Okay, I get that, but his *wife*? Really? Isn't Annika a huge part of Jed's life? How do I *not* mention her?"

"You mention her, of course you do, but strictly as the band's manager. We try not to emphasise the fact Jed has a wife." He grinned. "The groupies have got to have something to hope for. Let's just stick to the music, hey? Leave the domestic stuff out of it."

Roxy stared at him. "I have an entire book to write, Houghton. Usually the client's home life comes into it. I'm going to need to ask him something."

"Yeah, 'course you are! Music, ask him about his music."

"Right, but—"

"Except his first band, Horror Story. They're off-limits, too." He leaned in closer and half covered his mouth with his hand saying, "They *were* a horror story—but don't quote me on that!" Then he sat back chuckling at himself again before taking another good swig of his beer. "We're going to need to see the full manuscript draft by draft, if that's all right with you. Best not to give it all to us at the end, hey? Might be a bit of a shock when we have to chop it and change things around."

"Chop? Change?"

"Yeah, yeah, Annika's got full editing rights. Your agent told you that, right?" *No,* she thought, *he did not.* "So," he rubbed his hands together. "How long do you think you're going to need? I'm thinking three days tops?"

"*Three*?! That's going to be a bit tricky. Annika just told me Jed could be locked away in the studio for days."

"I hear ya, I hear ya, and I know what you're saying. Let's just see how it goes, eh? Just take it day by day. But let's not try to drag it out too long. The boys have got an album to finish and lots of work to do before the tour."

"And what if Jed can't give me much time?"

"Then you might just have to work with what you've got." He shrugged, slugged the Crown Lager again. "We don't need a lot anyway, will fill half of it with photos. Just get the general gist—childhood background of the three guys, early bands—"

"Except Horror Story."

He chuckled and pointed his beer at her. "You're a quick learner, I can see that about you. I think this is going to work really well, really looking forward to it." He smacked his lips together. "Rightio then, any questions or concerns, leave Annika out of it, if you don't mind. Just come see me directly."

"I thought you said Annika was in charge."

"Yeah, but the book idea was mine, not hers. So, well, let's not bog her down with all that. If you need to see me, just check out here." He glanced around the veranda. "This is usually where I set up camp when I'm in town. Otherwise, you can find me in the cottage behind yours."

"So, you're not staying in the main house either?"

"We're the hired help, love, we stay where we're told."

He went to stand up and Roxy grabbed one of his arms and drew him back down.

"Actually, there was something."

She was determined to find out more about the drowning that occurred on the Moody property, but she never got a chance. Houghton was now staring past her and towards the sweeping staircase where something caught his attention and made his whole demeanour change. He sat up straight, ran a hand through his hair and cleared his throat.

"Well, well," he squeaked, stumbling back to his feet and towards the stairs, one arm extended, "look who the cat dragged in!"

Roxy turned to find a man stepping up onto the veranda, an iconic Akubra slouch hat on his head. It was Juicy Jed, in the flesh.

CHAPTER 6

Think of every stereotype you have of the aging rock star and you've got Jed Moody in a nutshell. Tall, lanky and larger than life, he had a battered, beaten-up look that suggested a life lived fast. Too fast. His face was as craggy as his hat, deeply lined with a tufty, goatee-style beard and there were tousles of hair falling down around his chiselled cheekbones, unwashed and streaked with grey (he'd ditched the dye at last, hurrah!). He was wearing a crumpled black cowboy shirt, black jeans and cowboy boots, and she could just make out a tattoo under one rolled up sleeve. Was that a set of naked breasts? To top it off he had a cigarette dangling from one corner of his mouth. *Of course.*

Despite the crumpled exterior, or perhaps because of it, he was as sexy as ever and when he pulled the ciggie out and let his lips open into a smile, his sunflower-coloured eyes—a curious shade of goldish-green—sparkled mischievously, and it was like every light in the house had suddenly switched on.

"You must be my Ghostie," he said, his voice slow and deep as he extended a large hand for Roxy to shake. "I'm Jed Moody."

Like he had to say it.

Much to Roxy's horror, she found herself blushing crimson red, her heartbeat accelerating, her legs turning to jelly as she struggled to get up and return the handshake.

"Sorry to keep you waiting," he added, filling her quivering silence as though he was used to that, and she giggled.

Yep, she *giggled*, then tried to swallow it back down as she said, "Oh, no, don't be silly, that's perfectly fine." Then she giggled again.

Roxy was grateful that Annika had not witnessed this embarrassing spectacle, but Jed didn't seem at all surprised. In fact, he acted as though this was situation normal and was already turning back to his publicist.

"How's tricks?"

Houghton appeared to be blushing, too, as though Jed's presence was sending his own emotions into a tailspin, and Roxy didn't feel quite so foolish. Surely he'd be used to the rock legend by now.

"Yeah, good, mate," Houghton chuckled after each word. "Real, real good."

"That's the way." Jed paused. "You settle that issue for me? Give that prick his marching orders?"

Houghton nodded, flickering glances at Roxy as if to say, "Not now, mate, let's discuss it later," but Jed didn't seem to care.

"I'm not giving that asshole one more cent, got it? Tell him he can go shove it up his—"

"Okay, food's ready inside!" Annika sang out as she stepped through the French doors towards them. She was about to say something else when she spotted her husband standing there and she stopped, also appearing flummoxed.

There was an intense silence as the husband and wife stared at each other, like two wildebeests sizing each other up.

"So," Annika said eventually, crossing her arms over her bony chest and narrowing her eyes considerably. "You're alive after all."

Jed grinned. "Yeah, sorry to disappoint you." He winked at Roxy and glanced back at his wife. "So what's cookin', good lookin'?"

Annika appeared to bristle then and took a step back. "For you? F* all. You can find your own damn food. This is for my guests."

Jed's smile tightened. "I think you mean *my* guests, don't you, babe? Or have I got that wrong again?" Then he turned to Roxy, who was pretending to be engrossed in her empty martini glass. "Annie always gets a bit pissy when I spend too much time in the studio. She thinks I love my Strat more than I love her."

"At least someone's getting some loving," she shot back and he plunged a fist to his chest as though shot in the heart.

Roxy didn't know what to say or where to look, but Houghton had clearly seen enough of their banter to know when to cut in.

"I'm sure there's enough for all of us," he squeaked. "Come on, folks, let's go inside and eat."

Jed swept his eyes from his wife to Houghton and snarled, "Who the hell died and made you boss?"

Houghton blanched white as the railing posts then and seemed to recoil a little before Jed mock punched him in the stomach and laughed.

"Shit, man, I'm just playing with ya, you know that!" He turned back to Annika. "Can't stay anyway, babe, I'm in the middle of a take. Just gonna load up and run."

His tone was suddenly light and carefree as though he had not just had a spat with his wife in front of a journalist. He tugged off his boots then held his hand out to Roxy.

"Come on, Ghostie, let's be obedient children and go inside."

Roxy felt her stomach lurch as he took her hand and pulled her to her feet, and she couldn't help stealing a glance towards Annika, expecting an "I told you so" sneer. But the rock star's wife was staring towards Houghton with what looked like immense relief across her face.

Had a massive fight just been averted? Roxy wondered. *Or was this business as usual in the Moody household?*

True to his word, Jed simply piled his plate with food—a selection of cold cuts that Annika had assembled on a platter—then plucked a beer from the bar fridge and winked at Roxy again before heading back down the veranda stairs and across the lawn to the recording studio.

"Back to the grindstone," Houghton explained as Roxy's shoulders drooped.

"Maybe I could grab him in the morning?"

Annika barked with laughter at this then filled up her own plate and promptly vanished, this time deep inside the house somewhere, Coco clipping along beside her. Roxy heard a television crank on and a door slam shut.

Houghton handed Roxy an empty plate, then the two of them helped themselves to some antipasto before settling into matching velvet armchairs in the living room. The French doors were now closed to the encroaching chill, and they ate quickly, making small talk as they went. Roxy was eager to ask Houghton about the angry bearded man who had berated her at the Goddess Café, the one whose sister had drowned on Moody land, yet something made her resist. Perhaps it was because there was more than enough tension in the air already, or perhaps she simply didn't have the energy tonight.

"Come on," Houghton said, as they took their plates into the kitchen. "Let's call it a night, eh? Get you settled into the bails."

"Should we just clean up first?" She indicated the stack of dirty dishes that were now threatening to topple over into the large, double sink. He shook his head.

"Cleaner'll take care of it in the morning," he said, also sounding weary. He glanced down at her socks. "You might wanna chuck your shoes back on, though, it's a bit of a trek."

The old bails were, in fact, an easy stroll along a leafy

pathway that ran around to the front of the house and back towards the main road. Roxy had not noticed the path or the bails when she first drove in but was relieved to be putting some distance between herself and the Moodys.

Annika had not exactly been the most welcoming of hosts, and Jed had given her little more than a cute nickname and a cold shoulder. Was it always like this? Perhaps things would improve in the morning.

"Hey, listen, I'm really sorry about earlier on," said Houghton as they stumbled along the path, torches in one hand, overnight bags in the other. "Annie might be a bit prickly, but he can also be a total prick when he wants to be."

Roxy snuck a quick look at Houghton through the torchlight. He was being oddly candid for a publicist.

"But don't quote me on that, eh?" he said, as though he'd just realised that himself.

"You get to edit it anyway, right?"

He chuckled. "Yeah, right."

"So what is it with those two? Going through a rough patch, or is it always like that?"

"Bit of both, I'd say. He's really focused on his music, which is great, but he forgets he's got a wife sometimes. His wandering eye doesn't help. It can make her a bit, you know, tetchy."

Bitchy, more like, Roxy thought, but kept that to herself.

"Just don't read too much into it, eh? They always make up eventually and then the cycle starts all over again." He sounded exhausted by it all.

Roxy shook her head. She just couldn't understand it. Annika might rail against other women and their attempts to destroy her marriage, but Roxy wasn't sure there was much of a marriage there to start with. They didn't want to publicise their union to the world, and she wondered now why they even stayed together, especially if Jed was preoccupied with his music and pretty women? It's not like there were children to protect, unless, of course you counted

Annika's faithful pup, which Annika clearly did.

And why, more importantly, did Jed stay? He was still a renowned "Rock God", could have any woman he wanted.

As if reading her thoughts, Houghton added, "You know they've been together nearly twenty years. I guess it counts for something."

"Wow," Roxy said. She'd barely lasted two years with Max Farrell before she'd pulled the plug. And he'd been as faithful as poor old Coco.

"Must be some kind of record for any celebrity couple," Houghton was saying, and Roxy laughed.

"I dunno. I think Sting and Trudie have been together almost thirty years. Oh, and Bowie and Iman must be getting up there somewhere."

"Bloody hell, Jed'd be thrilled to hear you put him in the same company as that mob. Ah, here we are. Your own private Idaho."

They had reached a fork in the path and he was shining his torch to the left, towards a small wooden structure with a short, wide door and a pot of what looked like lavender out the front. A sensor light switched on and Roxy flicked her torch off and bid him good night.

"Where are you staying?" she asked, and he flashed his torch back down the path to the right. She could just make out a timber and corrugated iron cottage sitting in the shadows of a large Poinciana.

"Not quite as slick as yours, but it'll do the job. G'night."

As he shuffled off down the path and was swallowed up by the darkness, Roxy continued on to the bails, pushed the door open and stepped inside.

Houghton had not been exaggerating. Common old milking barn it may once have been, but today the bails looked like something out of *Vogue Living*, albeit in miniature; all crisp white walls, and shabby chic furnishings. She pulled the front door shut and switched on a low lamp, casting the room in a warm orange glow. It did little to improve her mood and as she dropped her bag by the wrought iron bed and began searching through it for her bath bag and pyjamas, she couldn't help feeling an encroaching sense of dread.

Shaking it off, she brushed her teeth, changed into her pyjamas and slipped under the thick white duvet. Things will look better in the morning, she told herself as her eyelids began to droop. They're just having a bad night, but everything will be okay.

Still, it didn't stop her dreams from turning into a warzone—Annika in fatigues, Houghton close behind driving a cross between a military tank and an old white Jeep, the angry bearded man beside him, a look of rage on his face. Beyond them all, completely out of reach, was Jed Moody. He was standing bare-chested in an open field, hands beckoning them towards him while he mocked them with his sexy, slouchy smile.

CHAPTER 7

Roxy woke up with a start.

She fumbled first for her glasses, then for her iPhone, which she'd placed beside the bed the night before, even though it had absolutely no network coverage.

"Shit. Shit. Shit!"

It was 9:45 a.m. *How the hell had that happened?!*

Jumping out of bed, she frantically looked around. The bathroom, where was the bloody bathroom? Towel, was there even a towel? She flung herself towards the only other door in the small cottage and spotted the gleaming shower vestibule. In her exhaustion she hadn't even noticed it last night. To one side of the shower hung an enormous fluffy white towel and beside that an even fluffier-looking bathrobe.

She whipped on the shower, discarded her pyjamas and jumped in.

Fifteen minutes later Roxy was dressed and stumbling back down the pebbled pathway towards the main house, her trusty digital recorder and notebook in the handbag over her shoulder. Unlike the day before, there was no time to dally over her outfit. She'd just pulled on some skinny jeans, a crumpled top and a creamy blue cardigan, then slipped into the same boots and necklace, and swept a strip of red lipstick across both lips. It would have to do.

As she reached the main house, she pulled some fingers through the back of her hair and straightened her fringe down. The front door was locked, and this surprised her. She'd been led to believe country folk didn't need to lock their doors. Perhaps burglars had a better sense of direction than she did?

Roxy continued around the veranda to the back of the house where all the action seemed to happen, but there wasn't a soul about.

Had she missed Jed altogether? Was he already hard at it in the studio?

"Still snoring," came a voice from below the veranda, and Roxy spotted Houghton perched at the bottom of the staircase, a cigarette in one hand, a cup of coffee on the step beside him. She walked down the stairs to join him.

"There's food inside if you're hungry," said Houghton. "The cook does a mean omelette."

"There's a cook as well as a cleaner?"

"Oh, only when there's guests about." He chuckled. "You weren't expecting Annika to cook for you, were you? Last night's spread was an anomaly, I can tell you that."

"So when does Jed normally get up?"

"Whenever he wants. Did a late one in the studio again, I believe. Probably best to chill out for a few hours, just hang back, okay?"

Roxy's shoulders slumped again. Okay, this was new. Her previous clients had been almost exclusively elderly. The elderly were the ones who generally commissioned someone to write their life story, not only because they had actually lived a life, but because they were usually the only ones who had the spare cash to splurge on something so self-indulgent.

And with the elderly came early mornings. She'd learned that one the hard way. Being a classic night owl, Roxy had struggled with the early hours but had learned to adapt in the interests of her clients and her endlessly hungry mortgage. Many of the interviews had started at dawn. One client even liked Roxy to show up *before* dawn, so they could be well on the way when the sun showed up.

Roxy liked to start late, preferred it in fact, but midday was probably stretching it, especially considering the deadline she was on.

"I spotted Al earlier, you can always speak to him," Houghton said, noticing her disappointment.

"Alistair, the bass player?"

"That'd be the one."

"Great, that's a start."

"But fetch some breaky first, eh?" He went to wave his hand then dropped it back. "Just before you go, a quick word." She turned to look at him. "The boys are putting on a bit of a jam tonight, just working out some of the chinks in their new tunes. You'll wanna hang around for that one."

Roxy's eyes lit up at the thought of watching the Moody Roos in action. "So the drummer's here, too?"

"Not at the property yet, he lives down in Byron, but he'll be here soon. We'll crank the barbeque up about five-ish, sink a few brews. Should be a bit of fun, they always are."

"Do they get together and jam often?"

His smile deflated slightly. "Not often enough, nah. Try to grab Jed before then if you can. He'll be back in the studio this arvo."

"That's the tall shed over there, right?" She pointed to where the blue Valiant was still parked. "And Alistair, where can I find him?"

"Getting up to no good as always." He said it so quietly she wasn't sure she had heard right. He looked up at her and said, more clearly, "Try the stables, round the front."

With a full plate of omelette and a cup of strong coffee under her belt, Roxy made her way back around the front of the house towards a large timber barn painted mission brown with white fringing and a pine fence around the perimeter. The Moody Roos bassist was standing outside the open barn door when Roxy approached, deep in conversation with a young, redheaded woman barely out of her teens. Roxy recognised Alistair this time. He was still wearing the thick black glasses of his youth, his goatee a new addition, no doubt compensating for his rapidly receding hairline.

He was holding the young woman's hand and whispering something in her ear, and she giggled briefly before spotting Roxy. The young woman quickly snatched her hand back, plunging it into the pocket of her jeans, and strode off towards a small silver car parked behind Roxy's hatchback.

Alistair turned to see what had startled her.

"Alistair Avery?" she called out and he blinked a few times as if trying to place her. There was an almost overwhelming stench of manure lingering in the air. "I'm Roxy Parker," she said, holding out a hand to shake. "Jed's ghostwriter."

He looked confused for a moment and then said, "Yeah, right, how you doin'?" He shook her hand. "My turn now, is it?"

"In fact, you're the first. Haven't spoken to anyone else yet."

"Guitar Hero still sleeping, is he?"

She smiled. "Apparently. Can you spare me an hour or two? Just some background questions?" When he hesitated, she quickly added, "I'll try and make it as painless as possible, I promise."

"Sure, where do you want to do it?"

She looked around. "Wherever you like."

He led her around to one side of the stables where several horses were feeding in a fenced-off paddock. There was a wooden park bench beside a water trough and he strode across to it and they sat down. As Roxy pulled her recorder out from her bag and placed it between them on the bench, Alistair tapped at the top pocket of his leather jacket and pulled out a packet of loose tobacco and some cigarette papers.

"You mind?" he said, pointing to the tobacco.

When she shook her head, he crossed one leg over the other and got to work rolling his own cigarette, delicately placing the tobacco in the paper and gently rolling it until it was thin enough to lick closed, before lighting it up. As he did this, Roxy took the opportunity to study him close up.

Alistair Avery was never considered the good-looking one; that honour went to Jed, naturally enough. But even the drummer, Doug Campbell, with his unruly blonde curls and wide, goofy smile, managed to steal more hearts than Al ever did. Al always seemed a little too serious, a little too dull, and it wasn't just because of the specs, Roxy realised now. He was a very ordinary-looking bloke, medium height, slightly on the plump side. Almost forgettable if it wasn't for the fact that he was one third of Australia's hottest rock act. If anything, middle age had improved his looks, the goatee and deepening wrinkles adding some much needed character to his otherwise bland face. But only just.

"So how long have you been waiting to interview Jed?" he asked before leaning back on the seat and sucking on his rollie.

"Oh, not long. Only got here yesterday afternoon."

He exhaled. "Long enough, selfish prick."

Roxy was caught off guard. That was the second time in less than a day that Jed Moody had been referred to so derogatorily. *With friends like these...* Roxy thought, but she would never say that out loud. "Really. I don't mind."

"Well, you should. Your time's just as precious as his. Who the hell does he think he is?"

"Jed Moody," she replied, cocking her head to one side, and he stared at her blankly for a moment before nudging his lips into a smile.

"That's right, I keep forgetting, he's the one and only, the formidable, Mr. Jed 'Come on Down' Moody!" He mimicked the sound of an audience roaring, laughed and then dragged on his rollie again.

"So, no love lost between you two, then?" Roxy asked.

"Oh, Jed's all right. So long as he gets worshipped, he's under control. It's when the attention goes elsewhere that he turns into an asshole."

"Harsh words." She darted a glance towards the digital recorder, which was already on.

He followed her glance and pretended to laugh. "Just kidding, of course. Jed's a top bloke. True superstar." But there was no sincerity in his tone, just a hissing on that last word.

Roxy wondered how to take this. If she were writing a freelance article, she'd be in journalism heaven about now, already envisaging the headline: *Moody Roos at Breaking Point!* She would be keen to probe further, find out what Al's beef with the lead singer was all about. But this was nothing of the sort. This was a book commissioned by that lead singer and it had to be gushing. There would be no discussion of Alistair's obvious disdain. And even if she did include it, Annika and Houghton would be sure to edit it out. She knew it, and perhaps Al did too, which was why he was being so forthright.

Still, Roxy had a book to write and no time to waste, so she gently steered the conversation into safer territory. Over the two hours she asked Al about his own background and participation in the band. Yet all the answers seemed to lead back to Jed, and when Roxy made the error of asking what Al thought was the secret of the band's success, his tone turned snarly again.

"We're a successful band because I know how to write shit-hot melodies and Doug knows how to keep a drum beat."

"And Jed? Surely Jed's got something to do with it."

Alistair looked at her like she was speaking nonsense, then shrugged, dropped his third rollie to the ground and stood on it as he got up. "Yeah, you're right. Jed knows how to strut like a peacock. Every good band needs one of those—think Mick Jagger, Jim Morrison, Freddie Mercury. And you can put that in your book."

Then he scooped up his tobacco pouch and marched off towards the studio

CHAPTER 8

"So did you get the wounded bass player act or was he behaving himself this time?"

Houghton was still on the veranda when Roxy reappeared and she sat down beside him again.

"Bit of both."

He nodded his head, his fuzzy hair flopping about. "Sorry about that. It's just hard, you know, playing second fiddle to a guy like Jed."

"Why? Because Jed gets all the glory?"

"*And* most of the groupies, or at least first dibs on them. Poor old Al just gets sloppy seconds. Thirds even, if Doug's about."

Roxy winced. "Really, is that *all* it's about? Groupies?"

He scratched his stubbled neck. "Well, there is the small matter of writing all the songs and only getting half the royalties. That kinda pisses him off, too."

"I thought Jed cowrote."

"That's what you're supposed to think. Al's the brains behind it, always was. But, you know how it is, without a sexy frontman Al's songs were going nowhere, fast. Al writes, Jed shares the royalties, it's the only way to keep the band together."

"And Doug? What does he get?"

"Oh, he gets enough, if you count proceeds from gigs and merch."

"Merch?"

"Merchandise—T-shirts, posters, that kinda shit. He's just happy to play along. Besides, he knows he's expendable, he just keeps the beat; it's not rocket science. Could be replaced like that." He clicked his pudgy fingers.

Roxy looked at Houghton sideways. She still couldn't get over his candour. For a publicist, he was extraordinarily frank. Wasn't he supposed to be telling her how legendary they all were? Her face must have said as much because he cackled with laughter.

"Listen, I love the Moody Roos, you gotta know that, right? They're the best band this country ever produced, and I'm not being disingenuous. I mean it. Hell, I'm not slogging it out here in boonsville for nothing, lady!" He scratched his stubbly neck again as he glanced around. "But things are always complicated where bands are concerned. There's always a little friction, a little history. It's what makes the music so raw, gives it the edge we all love. Am I right or am I right?"

"But I can't imagine you want me to talk about that friction in the book?"

"Christ no! Your job is to—"

"Whitewash history?" she suggested and he looked back at her.

"Just talk 'em up, eh? We wanna sell books, tickets to the reunion tour, albums, merch. This is one big happy family, it's all his fans wanna hear and it's all they need to know."

She sighed. It would be easier said than done, if early indications were anything to go by. No one seemed to have a nice word to say about Jed Moody, and already she could feel her own admiration waning. Was that really all Jed was, a prancing peacock looking for his next conquest? Were women really that stupid?

Was she?

Sadly, Roxy never got a chance to find out. Before she knew it, morning had turned into afternoon and Jed Moody was still nowhere to be found. And despite asking Houghton to help, he seemed reluctant to seek Jed out, so it wasn't until late afternoon, as the sun began to descend towards the horizon, that she first spotted the lead singer meandering along the footpath, towards the studio.

He was wearing dark blue jeans today and another western-style, long-sleeved shirt, this one a creamy white colour. Dark sunglasses were covering his eyes.

Roxy grabbed her recorder and chased after him.

"Hi, Jed, hello!" she called out just as he reached the front door of the studio.

He turned back and looked at her blankly for a moment before his thick lips broke into another of those dazzling smiles. He pushed his sunnies up onto his head where they got tangled in his wet grey mop, and she saw that his greenish-yellow eyes were now bloodshot.

"My gorgeous Ghostie!" he said, stepping towards her. "You're still here? Annie hasn't scared you away yet?"

She laughed and was relieved it didn't sound like yesterday's girlish giggle. "I'm not going anywhere, Jed Moody, not until you give me an interview. Got some time now?"

He looked towards the studio and back to her. "Not the best time, hey? We're doin' a jam later, need to get the gear ready."

"Can I talk to you while you do that?"

"Nah, not gonna work for me. Tomorrow, I promise. Tomorrow, my gorgeous Ghostie, I am *all* yours." Then he bowed before her, almost toppling over, before flashing her one of his 1000-kilowatt smiles and disappearing into the studio.

****

As she watched from a distance, Mr. Millionaire Pop Star did his pathetic little dance, bowing down and causing Little Miss Four Eyes to blush like an idiotic schoolgirl, the woman couldn't help feeling a ferocious sense of rage. It had been creeping up on her lately, getting stronger and stronger until she almost couldn't breathe, almost couldn't think straight.

How long was this going to go on? She thought. *How much more must I endure before I put my foot down, before I make it all stop? Before I force some action!*

She spotted Alistair sitting on the side steps of the studio, restringing his bass while sucking on a cigarette like it was an oxygen tank and her brain began to click into gear. The fog finally lifted. She knew now what she had to do.

It was time, she decided. *Oh yes indeed, it was time.*

CHAPTER 9

It was just after 5:00 p.m.

As she walked towards the sound of music, down the pebbled pathway between the main house and the bails where she'd just vamped herself up, Roxy couldn't help frowning. If this was the sound of the Moody Roos screeching through the gum trees and across the sprawling lawn, then she was Diane Sawyer.

The drum beat was sloppy, there was a wailing sound that she assumed was a guitar, but if it was, it needed tuning, desperately, and—horror of horrors—what sounded a lot like a squealing fiddle, one of her least favourite instruments, second only to the flute which she could also just make out amongst the din.

As Roxy got closer, though, she felt a wave of relief. A stage had been set up in the open shed at the farthest end of the lawn in front of the veranda. A black curtain had been strung up and, in front of that, was a merry band of men who were definitely *not* the Moody Roos. More like a local hippie act. These blokes were even older and scruffier, most wearing flared trousers, some in woollen vests, others in open peasant-style shirts. Not one of them appeared to know how to play a note. Yet it didn't seem to put the crowd off.

There was already a gathering of similarly dressed people dancing in front of them, arms in the air, heads back, dazed smiles on their faces as though they were in some kind of trance. Perhaps they had been hypnotised, Roxy thought, or, more likely, smoking some of the local weed. It would certainly explain why they didn't find the music as offensive as she did.

A large bonfire had been set up in the centre of the lawn and it was crackling away, a wide circle of hay bales around it where several other hippies were seated, chatting and smoking what looked and smelt a lot like pot. That explained that, then. An elderly couple sat together on a hay-bale, looking more stony- faced than stoned, and about as comfortable as chicks in a snake pit. Roxy wondered momentarily who they could be before she noticed Houghton waving to her from the other side of the fire.

"When do the Roos go on?" she asked, seating herself down beside him.

"Oh, Jed'll tell this mob to bugger off when he's ready." He held his hands out towards the flames as though attempting to toast his fingers.

Roxy looked around. "Who *are* all these people?"

He followed her eyes. "Just the local riffraff. Jed always invites them to his jams. Keeps the natives happy."

Roxy spotted Govinda then, the woman from the Goddess Café. She was in the middle of the crowd, childless this time and twirling around in circles to the music, her eyes closed. She was surrounded by a swirl of other women, some blonde, some brunette, one with cherry red hair that fell about her face in long, luscious locks. It might have been the same woman Roxy had spotted earlier with Alistair at the stables. All of them were wearing the standard hippie garb— long skirts, feathers hanging from their ears and hair, velvet vests and tinkling silver beads that looked straight out of an Indian marketplace.

"And who is that band? Please tell me they're going to stop."

He chuckled. "Local lads called the Cloudchasers. Again, it's all about keeping the peasants happy. Let 'em have their moment in the sun, then they let Jed and Annika get on with their shit."

"What 'shit', exactly? Recording albums?"

"And the rest." He lowered his voice slightly. "Got big plans to turn this property into a festival site. Got a development application in with the local council now." He pulled a piece of hay from beneath him and began chewing on it. "Some of the locals aren't happy about it, been trying to make waves. Jed keeps throwing bones out to them, trying to woo them all back."

"Who's against the DA?"

"Just your usual greenies, a few councillors, some of the neighbours. It's nothing Annie can't sort out."

"What sort of festival are they planning?"

He spat the hay out. "*Festivals*, actually. Plural. Want to put at least ten on a year, bring in top rock acts; maybe do a jazz fest. Take advantage of the growing yuppie crowd down in Byron. Anyway, as I say, it's early days. Still jumping through hoops with Council at this stage." He shrugged. "They have to do something if they want to start making money."

"I thought Jed was raking it in." He did have a cleaner and a cook, after all.

"Oh, he's doing all right. You and I wouldn't complain, but he's not getting the record sales he used to get. The cash ain't flowing like the old days."

"Hence the book and tour?"

He grinned. "Got it in one. Hey, here's the High Priestess herself."

Roxy looked up to find Annika strutting across the lawn towards them, an enormous goblet of red wine in one hand, a plate laden with some kind of brownish white meat in the other. She looked breathtaking, in a long, white halter neck dress that billowed out as she walked, accentuating her chiselled shoulders and long black hair. She stopped to offer the plate of food to the surly older couple who brightened up when she approached, then to several others before she reached Roxy, a wide smile on her face.

"Hello, my darlings!" she said, bending down to plant a thick kiss on Houghton's lips, followed by a sly wink.

The jealous wife had transformed into a zealous hostess and she was now holding the plate out to Roxy who still couldn't work out what it was.

"Freerange pork! Just off the spit."

"There's a spit?"

"We *always* do a spit. It's not a Moody jam without one!"

Houghton was already plucking several slices of oily meat from the plate and shoving them into his mouth.

"No, thanks," Roxy said. "I'm not real hungry yet."

"Well, don't wait too long." Annika glanced around surreptitiously then leaned in closer and said, "With this lot there'll be nothing left within the hour. Vegetarians my arse!" She stepped back, flinging her long hair behind her as she did so. "Didn't get a chance to chat to Jeddie, I hear?"

Roxy shook her head. "He thinks tomorrow will work better."

"I'm sorry about that. I've kept him a bit busy today." The look she gave Roxy reminded her of the cat who'd just swallowed the cream. Clearly Mr. and Mrs. Moody had made up for last night. "If you need a drink, just help yourself. You should know where the bar is by now."

Roxy nodded and glanced around the crowd. Several people were nursing beers and glasses of wine. Did they all just help themselves? It seemed considerably gracious of her.

"I can*not* believe it!" Annika exclaimed, staring across the fire. "The Green Brigade has shown up!" She turned to Houghton and dropped the plate into his lap. "Here, hide that, quick. If Joe sees it, he'll start lecturing me again. I don't think I could bear it, not tonight."

She took a large mouthful of wine, then said, "Wish me

luck!" before striding in the direction of a small group who were just entering the party from one side of the house.

There were two men, an older one, short and slightly beefy with curly white hair and a brown woollen poncho, and another half his age, taller, leaner with a swishing ponytail and linen drawstring pants. Behind them Roxy could just make out a young woman, a teenager perhaps.

Both Roxy and Houghton watched as Annika rushed up and gave the two men an air kiss then said something before breaking into her trademark machine-gun laughter. The ponytailed man laughed along with her but the older man did not.

"A couple of the greenies I was telling you about," Houghton said, picking up another piece of pork. "The young one's one of the councillors, can't remember his name; other one's the mayor."

"The *mayor*? At a rock jam?"

He chuckled. "This is Byron Bay, Roxy. That's situation normal." He made a whistling sound. "It's also a good sign for Annie. Maybe Mayor Kidlong is coming on board after all."

Roxy stared at the short, white-haired man who was now deep in conversation with Annika. "He's against the festivals?"

"Kidlong's against everything. Typical bloody NIMBY."

She looked back at Houghton, a confused look in her eye.

"It stands for Not In My Back Yard," he explained. "There's thousands of NIMBYs in these parts and it's all very well for them. They've moved here, set up homes and businesses, but don't want anyone else to have a crack. Selfish bastards." He chuckled but there was no laughter in it.

"You'd think, being a greenie, he'd be into music and the arts. It's not like it's a shopping development. What's his beef with the whole idea?"

"Shh, don't say beef, not around that bloke." He laughed

more genuinely this time. "Guy's a vegan from way back. Says it's all about the marsupials."

"Marsupials?"

"Yeah, reckons any kind of development here will destroy their natural habitat. Make sure you don't get stuck talking to him, eh? Will bore you senseless with lectures about koala corridors, threatened quolls, even cares about bloody bush rats, would you believe?" Houghton looked around. "Listen, I'm as big on animals as the next bloke, but there's 250 freakin' acres here, Roxy. How much more room do the furry little critters need?"

He thrust some more pork into his mouth.

"Who's the girl?" Roxy asked, nodding towards the teenager who was still standing just behind them, a bored look on her face as she chomped away on a candy-coloured string of beads that were hung around her neck.

"That's the mayor's daughter, Asha I think it is. Now, she's a hottie."

"She looks about fifteen," Roxy said, thinking she also looked out of place. Apart from Roxy and Houghton, she was the only other person not dressed like she was heading to Woodstock. Asha had a short, '50s style white lacy dress on with black leggings underneath and Dock Martin stomper boots on her feet. Her white-blonde hair had been pulled up into a high ponytail and her eyes smudged with so much black eyeliner, it was a wonder she could pry them open.

"Oh, she's older than that, but only just. Finished school last year I think. Must be at least seventeen or eighteen by now."

"Perfect age for Jed then."

He stared at her horrified, then across to Annika. "Why? What have you heard?"

She quickly backpedalled. "Nothing, Houghton, I was just having a joke."

He didn't appear to hear her. "You know, that is one rumour doing the rounds that is total bullshit. I don't know who started it, but it's got to stop. He is not sleeping with

Asha Kidlong, he's promised me he's not. He's mended his ways."

"I believe you, Houghton. Seriously, it was just a joke." But she could clearly see he didn't have a sense of humour where this was concerned. "Anyway, it looks like Annika and Jed are back on track. They obviously made up for their little tiff last night."

He nodded. "Always do. Those fights are what keeps the passion alive."

She thought about that. Perhaps that's where she and Max went wrong, both too damn polite and accommodating.

After watching the fire for a few minutes, Roxy said, "If I'm going to listen to more of this noise pollution, I think I'm going to need a drink." She stood up. "Can I get you anything?"

"I'll be right." He produced what looked like a joint from his shirt pocket. "You want?"

She shook her head and weaved her way around the hay bales towards the thin set of stairs on the side of the veranda, which she knew led straight to the bar. The living room was empty when she stepped inside, and almost dark with only a selection of candles scattered at various intervals to light the place up. Roxy walked behind the bar and kneeled down to inspect a large wire rack full of dusty bottles of mostly red. There was plenty of Shiraz and a few Cabernet Sauvignons, but she struggled to find a Merlot amongst the blends. She was just giving up and reaching for a cab-sav when she heard a door creak and a familiar voice filtered across the room.

"Come on then, but we have to be quick. He'll be on stage soon."

It sounded exactly like Annika, and Roxy wondered how she'd managed to get away from the Greens Party councillors so fast. Roxy was about to stand up and identify herself, when a man's voice broke through the silence. He was whispering and it made Roxy hesitate. It did not sound like Jed.

"What if he catches us?"

"Who's afraid of the big bad wolf then?" Annika giggled.

"You can joke all you want woman, but he'll have my balls if he knows what we're up to!"

Annika giggled a little more flirtatiously, "Not if I have them fiiiiirst."

Roxy heard Annika's voice trail off, as though she was moving deeper into the house. "… Keep telling you … we have to act now. It's time, babe… it's time."

Although Roxy was struggling now to hear them, she could just make out the faint sound of laughter before a door slammed and the room returned to silence. Roxy stood up slowly, making sure she was alone. The room was empty again.

Hurriedly, she cracked open the bottle, poured herself a hefty glass, and slunk back out the side door. She wasn't exactly sure what she'd just overheard but it didn't sound anything like a faithful wife.

What a piece of work, Roxy thought as she descended the staircase. *And she has the gall to lecture me about flirting!*

"You okay?"

Roxy looked up with a start to find Angry Beard Man standing at the bottom of the staircase, an empty bottle of Coopers Green in his hand. She felt a sudden shot of adrenaline.

What was he doing here?

As if reading her concerns, he smiled and said, "It's okay I got invited."

"*Really?*" She couldn't mask the disbelief in her voice as she glanced around, hoping to spot Houghton.

"Listen," he said, taking a step towards her. "I was hoping I might see you."

"Oh?" She stepped back.

"Yeah, just wanted to say how sorry I am about yesterday, about biting your head off at the café."

"Oh, right." She took another step back.

"I was just having a really bad day, that's all. Shouldn't've taken it out on you. I'm Sam, by the way."

"Roxy," she said, her back now up against the bar door.

"Anyway, I can't imagine how you felt. I was a bit rough." His eyes narrowed slightly and he leaned back a little. "I'm not going to hurt you, you know?"

She attempted to laugh him off, but her voice sounded strained, nervous even. Sensing this, he took several steps back down the staircase and waved a hand as if permitting her to pass. Tonight he was wearing a dark dress shirt, rolled up at the sleeves, and deep blue jeans, muddy boots on his feet. His three-day growth was still present but it looked like he'd clipped his hair shorter and it tufted up just slightly at the front. His eyes were softer and less angry than the day before.

Roxy smiled and continued descending the stairs again. She wondered why this man left her feeling so jittery. It's not like he'd ever actually threatened her. He was clearly just a loving brother, traumatised by his sister's death. Roxy had a sudden thought. She stopped just as she was level with him and said, "You should get someone to look into it, you know."

"What?"

"Your sister's death. The woman at the café told me about it."

The man's face clouded over then and his eyes began to swell. She had a dreadful feeling he was about to cry.

She quickly said, "It's just that if you think it's suspicious, you can always ask for a second opinion. Take your suspicions to the police. If you believe it wasn't an accident, that is."

"It *wasn't* an accident."

"Then speak to the police."

He flicked her a scathing look. "Round here? They're like a pack of groupies, all in Jed's pocket. He's the big superstar, no one will investigate."

"Then take it higher, insist that it get looked at properly."

"Like that's gonna happen. It's too late. It's over with."

"Not if you don't want it to be."

He stared hard at her. "What do you know about that?"

"I know that if you feel strongly about it, you can force change. You just have to speak up."

"Oh, and that's worked for you, has it?"

There was deep sarcasm dripping from his voice and she felt her defences rise again. "Yes, *actually*, several times." He was still looking skeptical. "I've come across several mysterious deaths in my time, I'll have you know, and I didn't just moan about them. I've got a friend, who also happens to be a top detective in Sydney; I got her to take another look. We were able to prove that justice wasn't being done. The police aren't the enemy, you know? At least, not all of them are. You just have to know who to speak to and you need to find the courage to speak up. You can fight for justice."

"Can you ask her for me?"

"Sorry?"

"Your detective friend, can she look into my sister's death for me?"

Roxy hesitated. *That's not what I'm trying to say.* "No. I mean, she's based in Sydney. You need to find someone local, someone in Byron or Tweed Heads, that's the biggest town around here, right?"

Sam's thick eyebrows nudged together like he was about to say something when a high-pitched voice called out to them from across the yard: "Hey, you two!"

They both looked around to find Govinda swirling on the grass between the stage and the bonfire. At some point the band had finally given up and someone was playing bad dance tracks from a turntable on one side. Govinda held both hands out beckoning them over.

"Come on!" she cried out. "Come boogie!"

Sam glanced back at Roxy and rolled his eyes. "God, I hate hippies."

She smiled, not sure whether he was being serious, and went to walk past him, but he caught her arm and held her close. "Thanks for the advice, but if you ask me, the only way Jed is ever going to get justice, is when karma comes and bites him on the bum."

Then he released her arm and stepped past her up the stairs and into the house.

CHAPTER 10

Roxy took a fortifying mouthful of wine and returned to the bonfire where Govinda was now whirling like a dervish, her full skirt flying up to reveal shapely legs and Ugg boots. Roxy hoped she wasn't wearing anything synthetic. One wrong step and she'd be alight.

"Come!" Govinda implored again, going to grab Roxy's hand, but she ducked back.

"No way, Govinda, I'm not nearly drunk enough for that. You're on your own."

"We're all on our own, chook, no matter who we think we're dancing with." Then she twirled in a half circle and jangled away.

The backing music came to an unceremonious stop and Roxy looked up to the makeshift stage to see Houghton standing in front of the microphone, tapping it silently with one finger. The black curtain had been pulled back to reveal what looked like a cosy living room—a glowing orange lamp on a side table, fairy lights hanging down, and a plush Persian carpet on which several guitars, amplifiers and a drum kit had been set up.

Suddenly a burst of feedback screeched through the air

62

and everyone cringed. "Oh, shit, sorry, guys!" Houghton's voice bellowed through the PA and across the lawn. "It's workin' now!"

"Get off!" called someone from the back and Houghton held a hand up.

"Don't worry, I'm not here for long. Just wanna say a quick thanks for coming. The guys just wanna try out a few new tracks and it'd be good to get your feedback afterwards."

"Who gives a rat's what this pack of losers think?" came a booming voice from the side and Roxy spotted Jed walking up onto the stage, still wearing the same cowboy shirt, jeans and hat, only he was now barefoot.

The drummer, who had already dropped down behind the drum kit, did a quick comedic drum roll—*ba dump dump chshshshshshshsh.* And the crowd cheered wildly, clearly not offended by their local rocker's rebuff.

Houghton laughed nervously. "Yeah, well, you're gonna love this new stuff. I'll leave the boys to it."

As Houghton scurried offstage, Roxy watched Jed step towards the centre microphone where several guitars were positioned on stands, a lead dangling from one of them. He bent down to adjust an effects pedal attached to an amplifier. He straightened up and looked around then back out at the audience before leaning towards his microphone and snarling, "Where is that useless freakin' bass player of mine?"

The crowd laughed uproariously and the drummer did another comedic drum roll. Several faces turned to look around and when Alistair still didn't appear, Jed said, "Anyone here play bass? We're looking for a new bass player. Can't be much worse than Alistair bloody Avery. Tosser."

Again the crowd laughed and at least two of the hippies held their hands up, waving them about as if to indicate they were up for the job, when Alistair appeared from the back of the stage looking flushed.

"Sorry!" he called out as he raced across to the right-hand

side where a five-string Pedula bass was resting on its stand. He hoisted it up and over his white shirt while Jed gave him a look of utter contempt. Clearly, his apology was not accepted. Alistair ignored Jed's glare and for a moment Roxy wondered whether Jed was going to start a fight; the tension between them was palpable. It must have lasted at least a full minute—Jed staring darkly at Alistair, Alistair inspecting his strings, tuning his bass, not meeting his eyes—before Doug started playing a steady groove. Perhaps he was just trying to dissolve the tension, or perhaps he hadn't noticed. In any case, Jed managed to tear his eyes away from his bassist and back to the audience who had now all deserted the warm fire to gather closer to the stage.

Amongst them, Roxy spotted the mayor's pretty young daughter fighting her way through to the middle of the crowd, as well as Govinda, swirling to the beat of her own drum, and the gaggle of gorgeous young things. They were staring up at their idol, entranced, the redhead even holding her arms out as though trying to reach him. Only the farmer couple was nowhere to be seen and Roxy guessed they'd taken the opportunity to sneak off. It was hardly their scene.

Jed picked up one guitar, a classic, candy apple red Fender Stratocaster, and stepped towards the microphone.

"Here's a little tune I've written for the love of my life."

He paused and stared straight into the crowd and Roxy could not tell who he was looking at, but she knew one thing for certain. It was not his wife. Annika was standing to the side of the stage, just in front of Houghton, her face inscrutable in the dark.

"This song's called, 'It's time, baby, it's time'."

He paused again as the crowd whooped loudly, then adjusted his guitar strap and slammed one hand down across his strings with a harsh stroke, just as someone screamed out from the crowd.

There was another piercing cry, then an almighty crack filled the night sky, followed quickly by a booming crash and a spray of bright white sparks. Roxy gasped along with the crowd and for a few moments assumed this was all part of the act. She continued watching, mesmerised, as Jed's body began pulsating back and forth. Sparks flickered from his fingers and his hair seemed to glow as though eclipsed by the sun. That's when she realised something was not right. Thick smoke and a sharp stench filled the air and finally the audience began to scream, like the backing vocals had just kicked in; but this was no stage act.

Jed Moody was burning alive.

CHAPTER 11

"Nobody touch anything!"

The voice came loud and fast from one side of the audience and it took Roxy a few seconds to realise who was speaking. Sam was frantically pushing through the crowd who were now surging forwards, screaming and crying out as Jed's body hit the floor of the stage and continued pulsating, his guitar still stuck to his hands.

"You'll electrocute yourself!" Sam called out again, and the crowd suddenly surged back.

Roxy spotted Alistair then, still clutching his bass and staring open-mouthed at Jed, a look of horror on his face. The drummer, too, seemed in shock and was now standing behind the drum kit, his sticks held like a cross in front of him as though for protection or prayer.

Only Sam was moving now, shoving people out of his way before leaping up onto the stage towards Jed. Roxy noticed that Houghton and Annika had also stayed in place, holding one another in a tight, protective embrace.

Sam lifted what looked like a guitar case from the side of the stage and threw it at Jed's hands, attempting to dislodge the guitar. It did not work and he turned to look offstage.

"Annika!" he yelled. "We need to shut the power off!" Annika appeared to be in a daze and was still clinging onto Houghton as though refusing to let go, so he yelled more loudly this time, "Annnnnika! Now!"

Finally she snapped out of it, pushed free of Houghton and began running down the stage steps and towards the house, to the side staircase near the bar, then beneath the stairs to where the fuse box was located. Sam was close behind, yelling something to Houghton as he raced to catch up.

"People, people!" Houghton suddenly cried out, making his way to the edge of the stage, his pudgy hands waving madly in the air. "Stay where you are! We don't want anyone else getting hurt. Stay back!"

A minute later, every light on the property snapped off and the entire place descended into darkness.

The rest of the night played out like a horror movie in slow motion. Roxy recalled a woman shrieking, over and over again, hopelessly out of control. Others were sobbing quietly or simply standing on the lawn, arms crossed staring up at the stage in disbelief. Jed was no longer convulsing and someone was shining a torch down upon him while an older man administered CPR. Annika, Sam and Houghton were all hovering close by; Houghton with his mobile phone fixed to one ear, but Roxy couldn't read any of their faces in the dark. She felt like a third nostril, suddenly, useless and out of place.

Eventually, after what seemed like an hour but was probably closer to twenty minutes, an ambulance came wailing down the long driveway and around to the back of the house, cutting across the lawn and towards the bonfire. The crowd parted as two paramedics jumped out and swiftly strode towards the stage. A young female paramedic commenced mouth-to-mouth while the male began working on Jed's heart. It seemed an interminable period of time again before they finally stopped and sat back on their heels.

The male paramedic looked up at Annika solemnly and shook his head.

Then, and only then, did Annika burst into tears; turning back towards Houghton where she bent over and sobbed into his chest. Some people in the crowd dropped to the ground, shocked and distraught, others moved slowly back to the bonfire, which was now almost out. As some set about stoking it back to life, others dropped onto the hay bales and hugged each other close. There was no more dancing or smoking joints now, just a deep sense of melancholy and despair.

Almost nobody spoke, although an acoustic guitar appeared from somewhere and an elderly man began strumming a mournful tune. It was the same guy who'd first administered CPR.

Soon after, a police patrol car arrived, also cutting across the lawn, and two uniformed officers got out. Both were short, one plump with a shaved head and the other with an odd little Hitler moustache. They looked around open-mouthed, as if shocked by the whole scene, then made their way to the stage where the paramedics were now talking with Houghton and Sam. The police officers joined the conversation, then one of them walked with Sam back towards the house while the other stepped towards the front of the stage and addressed the crowd.

"We need to get everyone's details then we'll let you get home!" A small cheer erupted as the lights suddenly came back on and several people began clapping as Jed's body, which had now been placed on a stretcher and covered with a sheet, was slowly carried down the stage stairs and towards the ambulance.

The redheaded groupie yelled out, "We love ya, Jeddie, we love ya, mate!"

But he could no longer hear her, would no longer savour the unequivocal adoration of his fans. Jed Moody was officially leaving the stage for the final time.

Roxy watched on in stunned silence from the bottom of the veranda, perched on one step, head in her cupped hands. She felt chilled to the bone, her body shaking beneath her too-thin coat, but she couldn't bring herself to move towards the fire, or seek out the warmth of the living room where, she guessed, the remaining band members had now retreated.

Another patrol vehicle soon arrived, and a third uniformed officer appeared walking just behind a short, nuggety man in a crumpled blue suit. He was clearly the guy in charge and strode directly across the lawn towards Annika, who was still being comforted by Houghton on the stage.

Shakily she moved away and into the officer's arms, sobbing into his chest as he stroked her hair and spoke softly into her ear. They looked almost like lovers, certainly close friends, and for a few minutes no one dared interrupt them. Even the other officers stood back, heads bowed, quietly waiting for instructions from their boss, while the man in charge continued to soothe the grieving widow.

Eventually, Annika pulled back, said something to the man in the crumpled suit, and then let Houghton lead her slowly away from the stage and towards the veranda. Not wanting to intrude, Roxy pulled herself up and fled inside, to the warmth of the living room and the panacea of the bar. As suspected, she found Alistair and Doug slumped on stools, nursing tumblers of whisky, a near-empty bottle of Jack Daniels close by. Alistair nodded at her and then towards the bottle, but she shook her head.

"I just need a glass of red."

She stepped behind the bar and found the bottle she had opened earlier, then filled her glass to the brim before taking the vacant stool on Alistair's left.

"You meet Dougie earlier?" Al said, his voice croaky, and Roxy glanced across to the drummer who was now staring towards her, a blank expression on his face.

"Hi," she said offering him a wave and thinking how

immaterial introductions seemed now.

He seemed to think the same thing, batting his thick blonde eyelashes a few times before staring back into his glass.

"Pigs finally arrive?" Al asked, and she nodded. "What is the freakin' point?"

"They have to find out what happened."

"I'll tell you what happened." His tone was surprisingly bitter. "Jed got murdered by his own guitar."

Doug cackled suddenly as though the whole thing was hilarious and said, "Someone put out an all systems bulletin for Fender Strat. *Asap.*" Then he stopped cackling and slumped lower over his glass.

"You think it was an accident?" Roxy asked.

"Of course it was, happens all the time. Faulty equipment, that kind of thing. If it wasn't the guitar, it'll be the amp or mic." Al shot her a sharp look. "Jesus, what else?"

She shrugged and looked away, not willing to go there.

"Oh Roxy, there you are, how are you holding up?" Houghton was shuffling through the living room from the direction of the veranda; his cheeks flushed bright red, almost matching his hair. She tried to give him a reassuring smile. "I'm so sorry you had to see that. Bit of a shock, hey?"

"How's Annika going?"

He sighed. "Not good, no, she's in her room. I took her via the ambulance, got them to give her something strong, to calm her down, you know?"

Roxy didn't recall Annika being particularly hysterical. There had been wailing women, but Annika was not one of them.

"I'll have what Annie's having, thanks," Doug said, cackling again. *He* must have been hysterical, Roxy decided. No one could be that flippant.

Houghton ignored him and said, "Cops will talk to Annie tomorrow, when she's feeling better." He lowered his voice a little. "Listen, sorry, they seem to want to talk to you now.

You okay to have a quick word?"

"Me?"

"Just a few details, that's all."

"Oooh, maybe it was the Ghost in the machine!" goaded the drummer and Houghton scowled at him this time.

"Pull your head in, Dougie," he said, then to Roxy added, "Nothing to worry about, come on."

He led Roxy back out to the veranda and towards the middle-aged man in the wrinkled blue suit who was, as Roxy suspected, the guy in charge, a Detective Sergeant Rodney Quick. He had short, shaggy blonde hair and bronzed skin. The tan seemed to accentuate the colour of his eyes, which even in the low light looked like glassy blue rock pools as they stared keenly at her now.

"Hey, how you going? I'm Detective Sergeant Quick from the Tweed-Byron Local Area Command."

She shook his hand, noting it was rough and craggy, before letting him direct her into a chair at the main table. He remained standing, Houghton hovering close by.

"Houghton tells me you got here yesterday," he said. "All the way from Sydney?"

"That's right. I was invited up, to write Jed's autobiography."

"You written about any other rock stars before?" She shook her head no. "Anybody really famous?"

Roxy looked at him, bemused. *What did that have to do with anything?*

As if working it out for himself, he didn't wait for an answer, just pulled a chair out, sat down and said, "Hopefully I won't have to keep you too long."

He pulled a notepad from his pocket and began flicking through it as if looking for something to ask, so she took the opportunity and asked a question herself. "Jed was obviously electrocuted, right?"

He kept flicking as he said, "Looks that way."

"Was it deliberate?"

He glanced up at her. "Why? Have you got some

information for me?"

"No," she said quickly. "I was just wondering."

He stared at her for a few silent seconds then said, "Can you tell me where you were standing when it happened and what exactly you saw?"

Roxy had a flashback of fire and could still smell the burning flesh. She fought back the revulsion, then slowly went through the events of the night as she recalled them—explaining how Jed had simply spoken a few words to the crowd, picked up his guitar and gave it one quick strum.

"And that's when all hell broke out?" She nodded. "You were seen conversing with Samson Forrest just before the band went on stage. Can you tell me what you were conversing about?"

Roxy stared at him, confused by the subject change. "Samson Forrest?" It took her a second to work out who he meant. *Oh, Angry Beard Man.* "Um, just some stuff about his sister, that's all." *What did that have to do with Jed's death?*

"What 'stuff' exactly?"

She tried to think back. "He was just apologising for something he'd said to me the day before. It's not important now."

"I'll determine what's important, thanks, ma'am. What exactly were you discussing?"

There was an earnest, almost menacing edge to his voice, and she hesitated. What was with this line of questioning? Did he think Sam had something to do with Jed's death? "Um, Sam had been upset that I was writing Jed's book. He seemed to think Jed had something to do with his sister's death."

The glance the detective gave Houghton seemed to confirm her suspicions and she felt suddenly complicit, as though she was securing the noose around Sam Forrest's neck. "But, you know, he seemed fine tonight, he really did. He even apologised to me, said he'd just been having a bad day."

"Did you see where Mr. Forrest went after your

conversation ended?"

"He went into the house, I assume to the bar."

"Did you see him at the bar?" She shook her head. "Did you see him again at any time between your conversation on the steps and the moment Jed Moody was electrocuted? Do you have any idea where he might have gone in that ten-minute period?"

Again she shook her head. "But he must have returned to the audience at some stage because I did see him after it happened, he called out and—"

"Told everyone to get back, yeah, yeah. Quite the hero, I'm told." Detective Sergeant Quick's voice was as flat as a pancake.

"Sam probably saved a few lives," Roxy said, feeling a strange need to rise to his defense. "People were pretty hysterical and it looked like they were going to run up onto the stage. If Sam hadn't stopped them, there might have been more people electrocuted."

Quick closed his pad and pushed his chair out. "Thank you, ma'am. That'll do for now. You'll be hanging around here tomorrow?"

Roxy glanced at Houghton who had been watching the conversation quietly, leaning against a railing, brushing his stubble. "I guess that's up to the band. So you do think his death is suspicious, then?"

Quick didn't even bother to answer her as he strode down the stairs and back in the direction of the stage, which was now being taped up by the officer with the small moustache.

Roxy watched them for a moment, noticing that several more people were now mulling around up there, some inspecting the musical instruments, one holding a lead up to the light. She guessed they were part of the forensics team.

"Everything okay?" Houghton asked, and she glanced back at him, frowning.

"Do you guys suspect Sam had something to do with this?"

He shrugged. "You know what he's like."

Not at all, she thought, but she hadn't picked him for a killer. An angry man certainly, but not a callous murderer. Still, after she said good night to Houghton and was making her way down the path to the bails, she couldn't help recalling the words Sam had used on the staircase, just ten minutes before Jed hit the stage:

"The only way Jed is ever going to get justice, is when karma comes and bites him on the bum."

Had karma finally come calling for Jed Moody? And had it been given a helping hand by a vengeful brother?

CHAPTER 12

It was not yet 8:00 a.m. when Roxy awoke, and at first she had no idea where she was and what was going on. Then it hit her with a force that made her cringe beneath the sheets, her eyes scrunched up as Jed's burning body began flashing over and over in her mind like a bad YouTube video stuck on a loop.

She kept seeing Jed strum his guitar, his hand going down hard and fast across the strings just as the piercing crack rang out and the smell of burning flesh filled the air. But something else was niggling at her brain. There had been a cry, just a millisecond before his hand hit the strings. She was sure of it. It was as though someone was crying out to warn him, but it all came too late.

Roxy flung the sheets off and jumped up, trying to shake the horrendous memories away. The cry must have come afterwards, she was getting confused; she was disoriented and traumatised. What she needed was a strong coffee, and fast. Yet Roxy was reluctant to return to the main house. It wasn't just that she was scared of running into the grieving widow—what could she say to the woman who didn't want her there in the first place? Roxy also felt like the worst kind of intruder now. No one wants to worry about a houseguest in the middle of a crisis. Maybe she should just pack up and go home?

"Not before you get some decent coffee!" she told herself, stepping into the tiny bathroom.

Roxy stood under the gushing shower for many long, blistering minutes trying to erase the sights and smells and horror of last night. She knew she should get out soon, they were on tank water, after all, but she really didn't care about that, and she doubted they would either. Conserving water would be the last thing on anyone's mind today.

Eventually, Roxy gave up and got out, then riffled through her luggage for black gym leggings, an oversized sweater and her joggers. She'd thrown them in on a whim, not really expecting time to exercise, but now she was grateful for them. A long speed walk was just what she needed.

Since returning from Germany, Roxy had done no physical activity and both her brain and body were crying out for some, especially after last night. She slipped a blue cap over her black hair, put on her dark prescription Gucci sunglasses and stepped out of the bails.

If she was lucky, the Goddess Café would be open.

Despite getting badly lost only two days before, Roxy calculated that the café couldn't be more than a few kilometres away. If she headed down the driveway then stuck to the main road, she had to come across it. And she was right. Within twenty minutes, she spotted the shop just off Jasper Road and, as she got closer, was relieved to find several patrons at outdoor tables, the front door wide open. Most of the patrons looked up as she approached, but she kept her cap down and headed straight for the shop.

Sunnies still in place, Roxy looked around. Govinda was nowhere to be seen, but there was a tall, sinewy man of indiscriminate age with dark curly hair pulled into a thick bun at the top of his head and a tribal tattoo on one arm. He was wearing the hippie uniform—lots of felt and velvet and the customary flares—and might have been in the local band last night. He looked vaguely familiar as he piled avocadoes into a crate at the back of the shop where a small selection of largely bruised fruit and vegetables marked "Organic" were displayed.

"Hey there!" he called out. "I'm Hans."

"Hi, Roxy Parker."

His face crinkled into a smile. "I know who you are. You'll be needing a coffee then?"

She stared at him, stunned. This really was a small town. "Thanks, yes, latté with cow's milk please."

"I'll bring it out to you, just pop your three bucks on the counter if you like." He then turned back to the crate and continued unloading, so she did as suggested before heading to a spare table out near the road. It had just one chair and she was glad of that. Several people were staring at her again and she didn't meet their eyes. She didn't know if they'd heard the news about Jed, but she didn't want to engage with anyone. Not yet, not before her caffeine fix.

Unfortunately for Roxy, Macker Maroney had other ideas.

"Hell of a night, hey?"

Roxy looked up to find the photographer looming over her, his dark glasses on.

"Were you there?" she asked, trying not to scowl.

"I heard the goss. Can I hear your version of it?"

Now she let the scowl have full rein. "Not a chance."

Roxy looked away but it didn't perturb him. He pulled a chair from another table and plonked it across from her, then sat down.

"Look, I'm really not interested—"

"Oi, just hear me out first, love, no need to shoot me down in flames."

Roxy's scowl deepened and she looked around. The same patrons were still watching, some now frowning, and she hoped they did not think she was about to spill the beans to the local paparazzi. She felt grubby again all of a sudden.

Macker did not seem to notice her discomfort, simply reached for the cigarette packet in his shirt pocket and held it out to her. She shook her head and he said, "I don't know what you've heard, but I work for the local paper, the *Valley Times*. It's a legit newspaper, and I'm just trying to get the facts straight."

He was now lighting his cigarette with a plastic lighter, holding one large hand around it to shade it from the breeze. "I just want to know what happened, that's all, how it went down. I think we all owe it to Jed. We just want to do justice to Jed's memory."

Roxy felt a wave of nausea. *What a sleazebag.*

She was about to say as much when the shopkeeper appeared with her coffee. He handed it to her, glanced from Roxy to Macker and back again before leaving them to it. She felt even grubbier and wanted to race after him, to explain that she didn't know this guy and she didn't intend to help him out.

Sighing heavily, she reached for the sugar dispenser and poured several teaspoonfuls into her cup, then gave it a little swish while Macker continued dragging on his smoke, watching her intensely. After a good sip of her brew, she decided there was no point arguing with him; she had encountered paparazzi before. Best to just shake him off.

Keeping her tone as casual as she could, she said, "I understand you have a job to do, and I'm glad you want to get the story straight. But I'm not the person to speak to. You should try calling the house or maybe contact the police directly."

He blew smoke up into the air, then leaned forward, his nicotine breath stale; his eyes just visible behind his dark glasses. "I just want to hear your side of the story, love, it won't take you long."

Roxy smiled stiffly. "I don't think so."

He sat back. "I'll pay you well for it. You're without a book now, you're going to want my money."

"I don't need your money, book or no book."

"Too good for that, huh?"

Roxy groaned audibly and placed her hands on the table to push her chair back, but he grabbed hold of one wrist and held her down.

"You think you're better than me, don't ya?"

Roxy shook her wrist free and glared at him. "I *know* I'm better than you."

"Why, because they let you in the front door? That makes you worse, sweetheart, because you're the one peddling their lies. At least I'm putting some truth out there, setting the record straight."

"What?" Roxy's jaw dropped. "You call sneaking photos behind bushes and repeating gossip in trash mags the truth? Are you serious?"

"Oh, so you've never read any of those 'trash mags' before? Of course you have! You all do. And who do you think puts that stuff in there? It doesn't write itself, you know."

"That's funny. I was under the impression that's exactly what happened. All bullshit, no substance."

He exhaled smoke again, this time straight at her. "You don't need to be a bitch about it. I'm just saying we can work together."

"And she's telling you to bugger off!" It was Sam's voice again, and he was now standing behind Roxy, hands on his hips, a deep frown etched into his forehead. His dog, a large, black and white border collie-Alsatian-cross, was beside him, looking almost as angry as his master, his eyes trained on Macker, the hair on his back standing on end.

Macker looked from Sam to his dog and back again; a sliver of a smile on his chapped lips.

"Well, if it isn't Big Brother Sam. Haven't you got a little sis to be sobbing about?"

"Piss off, Macker."

The dog growled sensing Sam's anger, and Macker held his hands up defensively. "Hey, take a chill pill, mate. I'm just having a friendly conversation with a fellow journo, that's all."

Roxy recoiled at this, but before she could say otherwise, Sam stepped towards Macker, hands now by his side, fisted into balls. "She doesn't look too friendly to me," he said, "and don't call me mate. I'm no mate of yours." Then to Roxy he said, "You okay?"

She shook her head, but she wasn't sure she needed Sam Forrest to rescue her either. The man had other ideas.

"How about I get you out of here." He tilted his head in the direction of his Jeep, parked in the café parking lot. He must have already been here when she walked up.

Roxy hesitated, loath to play the damsel in distress, yet a quick glance at Macker told her the slimeball was going nowhere fast. He was now leaning back in his chair, arms crossed over, smug smile barely able to hold his cigarette in place. Without her own wheels, she might struggle to shake him off. What if he followed her all the way back to the Moody property? That was the last thing anyone wanted.

"Go on then," Macker said. "Run away with Sooky Sam."

Roxy railed. "Hey, he lost his sister, you don't need to be so rude about it."

"You think *that's* what he's crying about?" Macker snorted. "He's sooky because his sister was a slut who got her kit off for kicks—"

Sam roared with anger and lurched at Macker who ducked out of his seat, his fists up. He was laughing. "Come on, then, you stupid sop. You've been wanting to do this for months." He was pointing to one side of his jaw now. "Come on, give me your best shot."

"That's enough!" Roxy yelled, reaching out to Sam, trying to stop him from throwing himself across the table at the photographer. The entire café was now watching them, and now Hans was approaching, a grim look on his face.

"Come on, Sam," Roxy said, grabbing his arm and pulling him away. "Let's get out of here. I could do with the fresh air anyway. This place was starting to stink."

She flashed Macker a furious glare then pulled Sam in the direction of his Jeep.

"You are an arsehole, Macker Maroney, and I will get you one day!" Sam was yelling, his dog bouncing around his feet yelping along with him. "You are history, you hear me, history!"

Sam shook Roxy off and began striding towards his vehicle, his dog dashing ahead to stand by the driver's door as if waiting for it to open. Sam whistled once and the dog looked around then ran to the back of the truck and leapt up into the tray where he positioned himself into a corner and sat down. Sam held the passenger door open for Roxy and she got in. Without saying a word, he then slipped into his side, cranked the engine to life, checked his rear-vision mirror, and pulled out onto the main road in a hail of dust.

Neither of them gave Macker so much as a second glance.

After a few minutes driving along, the wind whipping Roxy's hair up through the open window and cooling down Sam's temper, he glanced across at her and said, "I'm really sorry about that. The guy's a lowlife. But I shouldn't've lost it with him."

"Don't worry about it. He was out of line." She glanced around then, suddenly aware they had not taken the Jasper Road turn off. "Hate to break it to you, but you missed my turn."

He looked at her briefly then back at the road. "You said you wanted fresh air. I know just the place."

Roxy smiled. "Oh. I was just referring to Macker's bad breath. I actually just want to return to the Moody property, thanks. I need to get back and talk to Houghton, see how things are going with Annika."

Sam's hands tightened around the steering wheel. "I can't do that, sorry, not just yet."

"What?" Roxy glanced across at him and he shot her a quick look then returned his eyes to the road.

"Just need you to come with me for a bit. It won't take long."

A flutter of trepidation hit Roxy's stomach, and she shook it away and half laughed. "Oh, I see, kidnapping me now, are you?"

"Something like that."

There was no trace of humour in Sam's voice and Roxy's smile sunk like a lump of cement. "You're kidding, right?"

He shook his head. No, he was not. She turned her whole body to face him now.

"What's going on, Sam? Where are you taking me?"

This time he didn't look at her and he didn't speak; his jaw was tense, his knuckles were white, and she felt the flutter in her stomach turn into a gale.

"I really don't know what you think you're doing," she said, "but I'm not impressed. You need to turn this car around and take me back to the Moody property please. Immediately!"

Again, Sam ignored her and kept right on driving, and the blood drained to her feet. *Oh God,* she thought, *what the hell was I thinking?*

In her haste to escape the sleazy paparazzi, she had just gotten into the car of a man she knew nothing about, the same man the police had been asking pointed questions of the night before. The man who'd just, minutes earlier, threatened to kill a photographer.

It was as though she had willingly jumped out of the frying pan and into the fire.

CHAPTER 13

As the Jeep rattled along at breakneck speed, Roxy wondered whether she should try to make a break for it. The "breakneck speed" thing gave her pause for thought, though, and she simply shifted in her seat, flinging glances every which way and hoping that a car would come past and she could scream out.

Yet they did not pass a single vehicle and the road quickly turned from sealed tar to loose gravel and then to badly potholed dirt. When he eventually slowed down to take a left turn at a road marked Grears Crossing, Roxy felt her apprehension intensify.

"You can't do this!" she blurted. "Kidnapping's a serious crime."

He finally responded and looked across at her before saying, "Kidnapping's the least of my worries right at this time."

"What do you mean?"

Again he did not respond, so she tried pleading a second time: "Look, Sam, I don't know what's going on, but I just want you to take me back to the Moody property, please. And let's leave it at that."

He shook his head. "I can't, I'm really sorry."

"Why not? What's going on? What do you want?"

Once again he said nothing.

Roxy thought then of her mobile phone and instantly her heart plummeted. In her quest for coffee, she had left it behind in the bails; had no way of calling for help. She considered punching the guy, grabbing the steering wheel, putting an end to this, but she didn't do any of those things; she simply sat back with a huff, arms folded, her anger now edging out her fear.

Who did Sam Forrest think he was, kidnapping her in broad daylight!

Her thoughts turned to Macker Maroney. Would he alert the police or had she just burned her bridges with him? The sleazy photographer no longer seemed like the enemy. She glanced across at Sam who was driving more carefully now, concentrating on the badly kept roads, his eyes straight ahead.

What did he want?

The Jeep dropped down a few gears and Sam took another left turn, this time at an old metal milk barrel labelled Lot 21. It led down a long, winding driveway, past a forest of towering eucalypts and camphor laurels and into a clearing beside a small timber cottage.

This is when Roxy's fear returned, her head swinging from side to side trying to look for signs of life, but apart from a few swooping black cockatoos, there was none. The place was deserted.

"Where are we? Where have you taken me?" she demanded as he brought the vehicle to a stop.

Sam ignored this and simply opened his door and stepped out. He then whistled and began striding towards the cottage, the dog leaping out of the back tray and catching up to him in seconds. Roxy took a quick look at the steering wheel, hoping he'd left the keys behind. But of course he hadn't. *Damn it.* She slowly opened her own car door and looked around. Sam had disappeared into the house and she swept her eyes back down the driveway towards the direction from which they'd come. Maybe she should try to make a run for it? She heard a tap running and glanced back to find Sam filling up a water bowl for his dog, who watched patiently, waiting for a signal before leaping on it and slurping it up.

Sam stood up and looked across at her. He called out, "I don't bite, you know." Then he stopped, smiled and added, "Unless that's what you're into, of course."

He chuckled and she bristled even further. *The hide of the man!* Wrapping her arms around herself, Roxy strode towards him. Fear wasn't going to help; it was time to feed into her indignation.

"How do I know you don't bite?" she yelled back. "I don't know who you are or what the hell you think you're doing! First you rant at me like a lunatic, now you drag me to this secluded spot and scare the shit out of me!"

He looked affronted suddenly. "Sorry. I didn't mean to scare you. I won't hurt you, I promise."

"What about your dog?"

He laughed. "Lunar? Wouldn't hurt a fly, would you, boy?" He gave the dog's fluffy black and white head a rough tussle.

Then he stood up, pulled a crumbling wicker chair off the deck and dragged it out into the sunshine just near a tall ghost gum. He waved a hand at it, offering her the seat before retrieving a second chair and placing it nearby. He sat down, spread his legs out in front of him and crossed them over.

Roxy watched him for a few minutes, glancing back at the driveway, then sighed dramatically and walked towards him, still keeping her distance.

"I'm really sorry I had to do that," he said.

"What? Threaten to beat the living shit out of someone, or kidnap me? Which one are you sorry about this time?"

"Hey, you got in my car willingly. Even that scumbag Maroney will testify to that."

"You said you were giving me a lift back to the Moody place."

"Ah, no I did not. I never mentioned the Moody property. I said, 'How about we get out of here?' and you said, 'Okay'."

There was laughter in his eyes and she glared at him, went to object, then sighed heavily again and took the seat beside him. "This is ridiculous. What exactly do you want, Sam? And don't tell me you brought me here for the fresh air."

He leaned forward and clasped his hands together, prayer-like in front of him, his expression now serious. "I need your help. I don't know where else to turn."

"Help? What do you mean?"

"I mean Jed's murder."

"Murder? We don't know that for sure yet. The band-mates seem to think it was a terrible accident."

He scoffed. "That was no accident. I saw the fuse box. Someone had jammed a nail into it. The wiring on his gear also looked dodgy. He was deliberately electrocuted."

She sat back with a thud. "Oh shit," she said and then, "Oh right."

"I know the way those cops think and they're going to try to pin it on me."

Roxy thought of all the questions Detective Quick had been asking about Sam, and suddenly she couldn't meet his eyes.

He didn't seem to notice. "I hated Jed Moody, everybody knows that. You don't have to read crime novels to know that puts me at the top of the suspect list. They're probably issuing my arrest warrant right now. I need your help."

"What were you even doing there last night, if you hate the guy so much?"

"He invited me."

"Yeah, you said that already, but excuse me if I don't believe you."

He shrugged. "Believe what you want. Jed and I went to

high school together. Friends from way back." The way he said the word "friends" spoke volumes. There was no love there. "He never told you that, hey?"

"No, he did not." Roxy thought then of the interview that never happened, of the life story that now would not be told.

"Jed always invited me to his gigs. Trying to make amends."

"Why would he do that if you keep accusing him of killing your sister?"

He shrugged. "Guilt, perhaps, or maybe just a lack of conscience. Jed Moody didn't really have one. His ego was so mammoth, he never even noticed I had grown to hate him. Still thought the whole world was in love with him. Hell, if he'd survived that electrocution, he would've thought it was all just a silly accident."

"And it definitely wasn't?"

"That nail didn't find its own way into that fuse box, Roxy. No, it wasn't. And it had nothing to do with me."

"That's what this is about? You want to declare your innocence to me? I'm not the person you need to convince, Sam. You need to speak to the police, or Annika, Houghton, anyone but me. I'm just a ghostwriter who turned up at the wrong time."

He shook his head firmly. "You said you had a cop friend. Someone who could help me."

"Er, no, I said I have a cop friend who helped *me* a couple of times. I wasn't talking about helping you."

"But she can, right? Help me?"

"No! She works in Sydney. You need to find someone closer. Besides, I was talking about your sister's death, that has nothing to do with this." She paused. "Does it?" He sat back, not answering. "Either way," Roxy continued, "you could have just asked for my help without kidnapping me, you know?"

"I did ask for your help last night, and you couldn't be bothered. Told me to find my own contacts." He frowned.

"And you gotta stop saying that. I didn't really kidnap you. I just took you on a nice drive. We can head back anytime you like."

Roxy stood up. "Good, let's go now then."

The dog, who had been sitting patiently at his master's feet, jumped up, as if hoping for some action, but when Sam did not budge, he sat back down and dropped his head into his paws.

Roxy, too, returned to her seat. "How am I supposed to help? What am I supposed to do about all this?"

She wondered if he had Googled her and discovered her bad habit of meddling in other people's murder enquiries. It didn't seem to be the case, though; he seemed more interested in Gilda Maltin.

"I need you to call your cop friend, the one you mentioned last night. I need you to ask her to look into my sister's case."

"Why do you keep bringing up your sister? What's she got to do with—"

"Sunny's case was never investigated properly. The idiot detective in charge barely gave it an hour of his time. Asked Jed Moody a few questions then called it 'bad luck'. Even worse than that, he hushed it all up."

"Are you talking about Detective Quick? Why would he do that?"

"Because he's a groupie dickhead, enthralled with Jed just like everyone else in this godforsaken place."

Roxy's memory shot back to the evening before, to the way Detective Quick had headed straight for Annika, soothing her with hugs and platitudes. Perhaps it was the wife he was more enthralled with. "How long have they known each other? Quick and the Moodys?"

"Wouldn't have a clue, but I do know they're thick. When Jed says, 'Jump', Quick asks, 'How high?'" He growled. "It's the same for all of them. It's like Jed can do no wrong. Abuses them all, shows up to gigs hours late, tells them all to bugger off when he's had enough, and they all just bow and scrape like he's some kind of god. It makes me furious."

Furious enough to kill? she wondered. "Okay, but what's that got to do with all this, or me, for that matter?"

"If you could just ask your cop friend to take a quick look at my sister's case, she'll see that the investigation was a joke, Quick didn't do his job, and then maybe he'll get taken off this case. If he stays on it, I'm screwed."

"Why?"

"Because he's got it in for me. Reckons I'm unduly badgering poor little Jed, like he's some innocent child. He's pulled me up on it a few times." He sighed. "Quick's not going to investigate Jed's death properly, he's just going to pin it all on me." He stared at her stunned expression. "Look, I know I'm sounding really paranoid."

"You think?"

He half smiled. "I just need Quick out of the equation or I'm screwed. The guy is as good as useless. He jumps at the first logical conclusion to anything. My sister looked like she'd drowned in a creek so he just assumed she'd drowned in a creek. Never bothered looking into it. And now, well…" He broke off.

"Now it looks like you were the one with the beef against Jed Moody, so he's going to jump to the conclusion that you did it?"

He didn't answer that, instead he said, "I'm just asking, very nicely, please, if you could get your copper friend to take a look at the case."

"But she's in Sydney."

"So? They don't have access to the files?"

Roxy chewed her lower lip. "I don't know."

"Can you find out?" He held out his mobile phone. "If your mate says it's all above board, I'll give it up, put my faith in the system. Hell, I'll even hand myself over to Quick if she thinks he's up for the job."

"He'll probably come for you sooner than that."

"He'll have to find me first. This place isn't exactly on

Google Maps."

Roxy glanced around and felt a small shiver. She wasn't too thrilled to hear that.

"Okay," she said at last, holding out one hand, "give me your phone then."

CHAPTER 14

Gilda Maltin was midway through a bowl of nutritiously tasteless cereal when her mobile phone rang. She glanced down at the number, which was foreign to her, and was about to ignore it when instinct forced her to pick it up. Very few people had her personal mobile number and she had the feeling it was someone from work, dragging her back in. She wasn't sure if she dreaded the idea or had been secretly longing for it since yesterday.

There was a slight pause on the other end before a familiar voice said, "Hey, there."

Gilda's face lit up. "Ms Parker! You're calling from a strange number. How's Juicy Jed treating you?"

"You haven't heard then?"

"Heard? What?"

It was still early morning, but Roxy couldn't believe it hadn't made the national news yet. "He died last night. Electrocuted while on stage."

Gilda gasped. "Oh God, no, I hadn't heard. I've got the day off; well actually they're trying to get me to take a week off. They owe me so much overtime, so I've been hanging at home all morning, bored to my eyeballs, haven't even put the radio on. So what happened? Are you okay?"

There was another pause before Roxy said, "I'm fine. But I need your help."

"Of course, anything. What's going on?"

Roxy cleared her throat. "I need you to look into something for me."

"Sure, but, Roxy," Gilda frowned, "you're not trying to take over the investigation again, are you?"

She would have laughed if she were in a better mood. "No, it's not about that. At least I don't think it is."

"What are you talking about?"

"Listen, I can't talk for long. He's..." She hesitated. "I just need to know whether you can look into a death that occurred on Jed Moody's property last..." She paused again and spoke in a muffled tone to someone out of earshot before saying, "January 25, last year."

"Death? What kind of death?"

There was another pause and then Roxy said, "A young woman called Sunny Forrest. Drowned in a creek on the Moody property, it was deemed an accident. Investigating officer was a guy called Rodney Quick. We don't think he investigated properly, we just want you to check it was all above board."

"Who's 'we', Roxy? Who's there with you? Whose phone is this?"

"That's all I can say for now, Gilda. Can you do it or not?"

"Yes, but listen." Gilda hesitated, choosing her words carefully. "You want to tell me what's really going on?" There was no sound from the other end. "Roxy, what—"

"Please, Gilda," she interrupted, "can you just take a look and get back to me on this number when you find something. It's important."

"Fine, yes, I can. But Roxy—"

The phone abruptly hung up and Gilda stared at it, astounded. That was Roxy Parker, but not as she knew her. Something very strange was going on. She went to call the number straight back but then reconsidered, trawled through her mobile address book, and tapped in a different number.

"Hey, Johnno, it's Gilda Maltin here. Have you got a second? I need you to look into something for me."

CHAPTER 15

Back at the old cottage, Roxy relaxed into her seat and watched Sam for a few moments as he threw a stick to his dog. Sam had stepped away, out of earshot, entrusting her to make the call, and as she dialled the number Roxy knew she should be alerting Gilda to her situation. She should have told Gilda she was being held captive and begged her to summon the local police to Grears Crossing pronto, preferably with a psychiatrist in tow, but as she glanced across at Sam, something stopped her. Perhaps it was the loving way he played with Lunar, so gentle, so unlike a crazed kidnapping murderer, or any she'd ever met. Or perhaps it was simply her endless need to be the one doing the rescuing that stilled her tongue. And so she had simply followed through on his request and hung up.

He walked over, his dark eyebrows arched high, and she nodded, holding the phone out.

"Keep it," he said. "She'll call you back."

"And in the meantime?"

"In the meantime, I'm sorry, but we stay put."

"Figured you'd say that."

"You do know I won't hurt you, right?"

She shrugged. She didn't really know that, not at all, but her instincts told her she would be okay. For some reason, one she couldn't quite articulate, she trusted the guy. Maybe it was simply because he'd given her a mobile phone. "Thanks to you I never finished my latté. Got any coffee in that hovel of yours?"

His face lit up. "Best coffee in the shire."

As Sam set about making a brew, Roxy took a look around. The cottage was neater than she expected and had been cosily decorated. Despite being little more than a large slab hut made from local timbers with a corrugated iron roof and a chimney at one end, the inside was surprisingly plush—more quaint, English village than Aussie rural outback. The furniture was mostly vintage antique, the furnishings fading but still charming. One timber wall had been plastered with floral wallpaper, the others left bare, and a deep, fraying sofa, half covered with a large crocheted rug, sat in the middle of the living room, in front of an old woodburner. There wasn't a television set in sight.

"It was my Grandma's place," Sam explained. "Sunny was living here before..." He broke off.

"It's pretty."

He looked around as though only just noticing that himself. "So was Sunny. Too pretty, that was the problem. Jed couldn't help himself."

Roxy leaned against the kitchen bench and asked, "So they were having an affair?" He seemed to shrink at the words but still nodded. "Did Annika know?"

"Probably. I don't think Jed was all that discreet. It wasn't his first, won't be his last." He blinked. "Well, I guess it will be now."

"Were you really friends? You and Jed."

"Friends? We were best mates."

"Really?"

"Yeah, long time ago. Before fame and fortune turned him into a tosser. Even then, I forgave him all his bullshit, because he was likeable, you know? A charmer. But then he got his hands on my sister and, well, I could never forgive him for that."

"She was a lot younger than you both by the sound of it."

"Seventeen years younger. Different dad but that's pretty typical around here. I have two other half siblings, different dad again, they shot off years ago."

"What do they think of Sunny's death? What does your mum think?"

He let out a puff of air. "Mum's in lala land, just wants to grow her organic veggies and pretend the real world doesn't exist. Saffron and Siena have washed their hands of the rest of us. Saffie lives in New York, Siena's married some Sydney wanker and we rarely speak."

Roxy tried not to smile. "Saffron, Siena, Sunny and Samson?"

He laughed. "Yeah, I got off lightly, huh? Mum's your classic old hippie. Couldn't help herself."

Roxy thought then of Max and Caroline's parents. They lived around here, were hippies, too. She wondered if they knew Sam's mum.

"Sugar?"

"Yes, thanks, lots."

He looked at her with inquisitive eyes. "Now that's not like a woman."

"Let me guess, they keep telling you they're sweet enough." She laughed. "There's nothing sweet about me, keep piling it in." She was watching as he spooned the sugar into her cup then stopped him before he started on the fourth teaspoon. "So you've lived here all your life?"

"In the general area. Mum moved a lot back then." He handed her a knobbly handmade ceramic mug and she thanked him, cupping it in both hands and soaking up the earthy smell of fresh coffee. "I eventually escaped." He glanced around. "Not that I don't love this place. I do with a passion, but I'm only here temporarily. The place can send you mad, everybody in everybody else's business."

She nodded. She'd already worked that out. It was funny the way people talked of the countryside as an escape, a private hideaway, when the truth was it was so much easier to hide in a city. There were more people to get lost amongst.

Sam stepped out of the tiny kitchen and made his way back outside to the ratty old chairs in the open sunshine, and Roxy followed. She suspected this was where he spent most of his time. He didn't seem like the indoor type.

"So where did you move to?" she asked.

"Sydney."

"Really?" She didn't peg him for a Sydney guy, either. "Where?"

He looked across at her with a smirk. "Nowhere you'd hang out." Then his eyes flickered down to her black leggings and Nike trainers.

She bristled a little. "Try me."

"Newtown. The grungy part."

"I don't live that far from there. Elizabeth Bay."

He scoffed. "Far enough."

Roxy decided to let that one slide and said, "Did you come back after your sister died?"

"Few months before, when Gran died. Came back to help Sunny clean the place up, sort out Gran's stuff. We were thinking of putting the place on the market, Sunny was supposed to come back to Sydney with me." His face clouded over and he looked down into his cup. "It was my fault."

"You can't blame yourself."

His eyes shot back to her. "How can I not? I introduced them; like waving candy in front of a child."

"They'd never met before?"

"Oh sure, years earlier, when she was just a scrawny kid. Jed didn't have much time for her back then, but this time… well…" He took a gulp of his coffee. "I ran into Jed one day down at the café. He told me they were having one of their infamous jams, said to come along. Sunny begged to come with me and I thought nothing of it. She was twenty-one then. Thought she'd be bored stupid around us older buggers, but I wasn't counting on Jed's charm. I should've known he couldn't help himself. He always did have a thing for young groupies, especially the blonde ones."

Roxy recalled Annika being relieved she was not a blonde. "Sunny was a groupie?"

"Not until that night. Suddenly she couldn't get enough of the band. Bought all their albums, put all Jed's posters up, even got one of those stupid Moody Rings."

"Moody Rings?"

He scoffed. "You've heard of mood rings, right? Got a crystal that's supposed to reflect the state of your emotions or some crap. The Moody Roos had a bunch of stupid merchandise like that, although the Moody Rings were supposed to be 'collectables'. Limited edition and all that. Anyway, she flashed it about, kept begging me to take her back to see the band play. Of course I never clicked that it was *Jed* she wanted to see."

"They started seeing each other?"

"I guess so. I didn't catch the details, but I caught them out. A few weeks later I was supposed to be driving back to Sydney. Sunny was originally coming with me, but she made up some excuse about a job interview and said she'd come down later. I stupidly believed her." His eyes clouded over again as he shook a dark thought away. "Anyway, it was raining something fierce that night and I only got as far as the highway turn off when I realised it was a bloody stupid idea, way too dangerous to drive. I decided to return to the cottage and head off the next morning. When I got back, Jed was here." Sam's voice cracked a little then and his jaw tensed. "He was in my grandmother's bed, for God's sake." He tossed the remainder of his coffee out onto the dry earth as if the taste was no longer palatable.

Roxy didn't know what to say. It had to be hard to find your baby sister in the arms of a much older guy, let alone a married rock star, someone you once called a friend. "What happened then?"

"I was fuming, I got straight back in the car and pissed off. Two weeks later she was dead." He leaned over, his head in his hands, and Roxy didn't say a thing, just let him work through the haunting memories. Eventually he said, "I should have packed her up and taken her with me. I should have punched him out. I should have done *something*."

"Oh Sam, they were both adults."

He sat back up, his eyes fiery. "No! He was an adult; she was still a kid, at least at heart. She was so naïve, so innocent and pure, you know? Ate only organic food, was a yoga maniac and really anti-technology. You know, she didn't even own an iPad or a mobile phone, unlike every other Gen Y in the universe. Said they gave you cancer, refused to have one." He half smiled. "Which was a pain in the arse, actually, 'cause there's no landline here. I could never get in touch with her." His smile deflated. "Jed would've loved all that about her, would've thought it was 'quaint'." He turned to meet her eyes. "It was his pattern, see? He always got them young, promised them the world, and then returned to Annika. Always. He broke my sister's heart."

Roxy sipped her coffee. It was very good, strong, just as she liked it. "I get why you're angry," she said after a few minutes. "Perhaps he did break your sister's heart and sure, that's unforgivable, but did he kill her?" Roxy wasn't convinced. "His pattern was to sleep with them and leave them, not kill them. There's no logic there, no reason why he should. Annika obviously knew about his affairs and she was still married to him. He had no obvious motive, Sam."

"Well, if he didn't do it, somebody did. That wasn't an accident, Roxy, she was held down in that water and she was drowned."

"How can you be so sure? Accidents happen, Sam. I'm sorry, but they do."

From the recesses of her brain a grisly memory reached towards her: an entire family drowned in a creek, still strapped to the seatbelts inside their car. She tried to recall the details now as he blinked back at her, not looking convinced.

It had been a long and rather macabre habit of Roxy's to cut out newspaper articles of suspicious deaths and paste them into a growing series of scrapbooks she dubbed her Crime Catalogues, which both enthralled and appalled her friends and family. Max had been in the appalled camp and she had found herself cutting out fewer and fewer articles after they hooked up. This particular story was older than their relationship, yet she still remembered some of the details now. It had been a dreary, rain-swept night. A young couple and their three small children had tried to drive across a swollen creek, to check in on the in-laws, or something like that. She couldn't quite remember what they were doing out on such a woeful night. She knew one thing for sure, though: they had never made it. The couple's car was eventually found several kilometres down river from the creek's causeway, all five souls dead inside.

Roxy wondered now why she'd even pasted that story into her Crime Catalogues. It wasn't exactly suspicious; just a dreadful, tragic waste. Sam was shaking his head furiously. "Not my people; no way. Sunny would *never* have drowned in a bloody creek, I know that much." He stood up and whistled for Lunar who came racing from the back of the house, stick still firmly in his mouth. Sam pulled it from his jaws and threw it as far as he could, out past the line of gum trees and Lunar galloped after it. "We grew up in these parts, Roxy. There is no way Sunny crossed raging waters. None of us would. It was rule number one. You just didn't do it. But that's not the only thing."

She looked up at him, her eyebrows high.

"After I heard … after Quick called me about Sunny, I got straight in the car and came back here." He nodded his head towards the house. "The house had been trashed."

"Trashed?"

"All of Sunny's posters, the ones of Jed and the Moody Roos, had been ripped down and torn to shreds. His albums and DVDs had been smashed."

Roxy's eyebrows dropped. "Could Sunny have done that, before she drowned? Maybe they'd had a fight." It was sounding suddenly like suicide, but Roxy didn't want to say that, not yet. Sam's emotions were too volatile to hear it.

He was shaking his head furiously. "That's not all. I had to go down and…" He choked again. "I had to … identify her body." A long pause, a weary sigh. "She wasn't wearing the Moody Ring. It was missing. I came back here, couldn't find it anywhere. It's gone."

"Okay," said Roxy, thinking, *that still doesn't prove anything.* "Could it have washed off in the creek?"

He ignored this. "Here's what I think happened. I think maybe you're right, maybe they had a fight, Jed and Sunny. Maybe Sunny finally woke up to herself, realised she shouldn't be sleeping with a married man, maybe he dumped her, or maybe it was over something bloody trivial, I don't know. Either way, they might have had a fight, she ripped up his shit then arranged to meet him at the creek to throw his ring in his face, but he couldn't handle it. Jed wasn't used to being rejected. He was the great Jed Moody. That would've stung. So he lashed out."

She cocked her head to the side. She wasn't buying it.

"How about this then?" He shifted in his seat and turned his whole body towards her, his eyes boring into hers. "Maybe Annika found out about the affair and *she's* the one who came here and ripped Jed's shit up. Then she followed my sister to the creek, or lured her there, who knows, ripped the ring off her finger and killed her. Revenge."

"You've really thought this through, haven't you?"

"It's been seventeen months, one week and two days. A lot of time to think."

Sam's phone rang then and they both jumped, Roxy almost spilling her coffee. Glancing at the screen, she spotted Gilda's number and felt a stab of relief. "It's my detective friend," she said and he nodded before getting to his feet and stepping away.

"Hi, Gilda," Roxy said.

"Hi, sweetie, are you okay?"

"Sure, what have you got for me?"

Gilda hesitated. "You want to tell me what this is all about? What it's got to do with Jed Moody?"

"No I don't, not yet."

"Right, well, I had a word with Detective Brent Wiles. You remember him? He was the lead investigator on the Gordon Reilly homicide last year."

Roxy's brain shot back to a dreadful series of murders that all linked in to the death of an old surveyor and his missing photograph. It was one of several cases Roxy had helped solve over the past few years and it still saddened her to think of it, which she didn't want to do, not now.

She pushed the memory away and said, "What about Detective Wiles?"

"Wiles is fairly high up at the NSW Homicide Squad and is usually the first one to get on a plane and investigate suspicious deaths around the state."

Roxy flashed a glance at Sam who was watching her eagerly. "So you guys *do* investigate homicides outside of Sydney then?"

"Only when the local area command aren't sufficiently resourced or specifically request our help. Many just don't have the skills and expertise. It's a point of contention, but it's all to do with funding, or lack thereof. I won't bore you with the politics now but Tweed/Byron is usually one area command that does need our help, whether they like it or not. In this case, Wiles says he never got the call. In fact, he didn't know anything about Sunny Forrest's death, not until I gave him a buzz. He was able to take a look at the case file for me, which was really nice of him." She paused. "You know, I'm surprised he could find the time, to be honest, he's usually so—"

"What did it say, Gilda?" Roxy's patience was wafer-thin.

"What? Oh, right, um, I hate to say this, but you might be right. There are some obvious clangers."

Roxy glanced at Sam again and this time she nodded, then watched as his jaw tightened and he abruptly turned away. "How so?" she said.

"Well, judging from the report, the local detective there put it down to an accident, and never ordered a post-mortem."

"Is that unusual?"

"Yes and no. Death by drowning is quite a common cause of death."

"But in a creek?"

"Yes, funnily enough. About 90 percent of all drownings occur in freshwater, Rox. We usually think of the surf when we think of dangerous water, but it gets a bad rap. You're more likely to drown in creeks, rivers, dams, swimming pools, hell even the bathtub can be bad news, at least for little kids."

"Okay, so what about a grown woman who knew never to cross a swollen creek?"

"Yet one more reason to order a post-mortem, which the local area commander, Quick, never bothered with."

"You think he should have?"

"Yes I do. Looking at it now, so does Wiles. It's like your local bloke made no effort. One brief witness report, but no last sightings and nobody canvassed the area. Plus, she had a fairly suspicious head wound that might have been explained by the drowning, but it might not have. Who knows, it was never investigated further. On the advice of Detective Sergeant Quick, the coroner ruled it an 'accidental death' and left it at that."

Roxy lowered her voice. "Could it have been suicide?"

"Maybe, maybe not. As I say, the head wound is suspicious. In any case, it's rare for a coroner to rule suicide without strong evidence to support that. And as we know, there wasn't any evidence."

"And the cop in charge?"

"Detective Sergeant Quick? I asked about him. Wiles has worked with him once or twice before. Reckons he's okay, at least he didn't want to bitch about him to me, but I could read between the lines. It sounds like Quick is one of those slacker cops, looking to ride out the rest of his career in a cushy job in a quiet part of the world. He got posted to the Tweed Heads command about four years ago, probably more for the surf than anything else. Apparently he used to be a pro surfer, before he entered the force. Look, you have to tell me what all this has to do with Jed Moody."

Roxy explained, "It's actually more to do with Quick. He's the one about to look into Jed's death and I'm just wondering whether he's up for the job."

"*You're* wondering?"

"Well, let's just say someone I know has got his reservations."

"His? Who is this someone?"

Roxy hesitated; Sam was watching her again. "Just someone I've met."

Gilda cleared her throat. "I know something's up, Roxy, and you don't seem to want to tell me about it." Still Roxy remained silent. "I've already got my mate Johnno trying to trace this number, but it looks like a 'prepaid', which doesn't help. Just say the words 'okeydokey' if you're in trouble. Just say it."

Roxy nearly did, she wanted to, but again Sam's doe eyes seemed to hold her back, and it didn't help that his gorgeous, faithful dog was also staring at her with his big, wet eyes. She said, "I'm okay, Gilda, really. But I'd be better if I knew this idiot Quick was off the case. Is there anything you can do from there?"

"Not really. As I say, Wiles is the one who usually gets the call when the death is ruled suspicious."

"But what if Quick rules Jed's death an accident? Drops it."

"Oh, he's not gonna do that! There's no way they can fudge this one. I've finally logged in to the outside world and it's all over the press. Every celebrity, politician, news groupie is tweeting about it."

Roxy said, "There's another problem with Quick. He seems very friendly with Jed Moody's wife."

"Friendly as in, 'seen-her-around' friendly?"

"More 'cuddle-and-stroke-hair' friendly. They were almost intimate. Made me wonder whether they're best mates, maybe ex-lovers."

Gilda considered this for a moment. "Okay, well, that might naturally preclude him from the investigation, then again it might not. In small towns, if you prohibit the top cops from investigating their mates, you leave them twiddling their thumbs all day. It's a bit impractical."

"Yes, but if it is murder, Annika could be a suspect. Quick can't be seen to be doing her any favours."

"Or doing your mate any disfavours, right?" When Roxy didn't answer, Gilda said, "Look, no matter what happens, the Powers That Be are not going to let this one get swept under the carpet. No way. Judging from the police buzz, it's sounding increasingly suspicious."

Roxy glanced back at Sam. She wasn't sure whether that was good news or not. "What are they saying?"

"I haven't got all the details yet. I can look into it further for you, if you like."

"Thank you, that would be great. And I'm sorry for ruining your day off."

"Nah, I was bored to tears anyway. I'm not real flash at entertaining myself. Was even considering watching *Bold & the Beautiful* reruns when you rang."

"So I saved you from a fate worse than death then?"

"I think you did. And I'd like to repay the favour. You have to tell me what's going on. Are you really okay?"

"Really, I'm fine But I have to go. Thanks again, Gilda. I owe you one."

"You owe me more than that, Missy. You owe me the truth."

"One day," she said softly, then hung up.

Sam made his way back over, his hands shoved into his

pockets, his eyes hopeful, so she relayed what Gilda had said.

"You were right about your sister. Accident or not, it was never investigated properly. Gilda thinks Quick's a joke."

His whole mood lightened. It was as though a heavy weight had been lifted and he pumped a fist in the air. "I bloody knew it! I knew it!" He turned back to her. "Now what do we do?"

Roxy held both palms up. "Hey, I don't do anything, this is your fight, Sam, your case, remember?"

"Yeah, right, of course." He did not look discouraged.

"Whatever happens, regarding Jed Moody, Gilda says it's very unlikely Quick will be in charge of the case, at least not for long. She says someone from Sydney will probably be sent up to investigate, most likely a detective called Brent Wiles."

"Good, then hopefully he'll look at it with fresh eyes, won't jump to any conclusions."

She nodded but wasn't as mollified by this. Despite her instincts, Roxy had to concede that things looked pretty grim for Sam Forrest. And she remembered Detective Inspector Brent Wiles well. He was smart and he was efficient. In anyone's books, the disgruntled brother Sam was a pretty obvious suspect.

Sam seemed to be considering this too as his shoulders slumped and his face clouded over again. "Want me to drive you back?"

For the life of her Roxy did not. She liked it here and she liked this burly guy with the sad eyes and the faithful mutt. But she nodded anyway and stood up. It was time to get back to the Moody property, to pack her bags and head home. The book was clearly off now and she had lost her taste for it anyway. The more she knew about Jed Moody, the less she seemed to care, and it saddened her.

Roxy had once been so impressed with the rock star and his music. Now, Jed Moody seemed little more than a cliché character from Gilda's favourite soap opera.

CHAPTER 16

Roxy and Sam did not say a word to each other the entire trip back. Lunar was seated between them and had taken a sudden liking to the ghostwriter, dropping his soft head onto her lap and blinking up at her with his big dark eyes. She stroked his head gently, not looking forward to returning to Moody Views. She wondered whom she would find there and what would happen next. For ten minutes they simply drove in silence, Sam watching the road, Roxy stealing glances at him from time to time trying to work out what his story really was.

She had always been a softie for the brooding type, but this was one brooder she needed to stay clear of. Despite his declarations of innocence, she had to wonder. Sam had said it himself. He had both motive—a deep hatred for Jed Moody—and opportunity—he was there on the night.

She had also witnessed his anger in full flight, and it was not pretty.

How did she know he was not a killer? How could she be sure of that?

Eventually Sam's vehicle turned down the long Moody

driveway and into the clearing near the house. Roxy noticed that several police cars were still present, as well as two vehicles she did not recognise. The plump officer with the shaved head was hauling boxes out of an unmarked car while the officer with the Hitler mo' was wading through the garden beneath the veranda, clearly looking for evidence. Two other officers were scouring the ground around the stables.

The plump officer glanced up as they approached then dropped the boxes back into the boot and started speaking into what looked like a walkie-talkie attached to his jacket. Just then, Houghton appeared from the side of the house and came rushing across the grass, arms in the air, as Sam brought the car to a halt beside one of the squad cars.

"I was wondering where you'd disappeared to!" Houghton called, shooting Sam a frown. He opened Roxy's door. "Everything okay?"

"Yes," she said, "I'm fine."

"It's just that I brought you some breakfast this morning and you'd vanished. But your car's still here. Your agent's been calling; he's got me all worried. I didn't know what had happened to you."

"Sorry, Houghton, I just went for a walk. Thought you guys needed your space."

"Well, Annie hasn't even appeared yet, and I wanted to a have a quick word with you, you know, before she gets up. Got a minute?" He stared at Sam again, his disapproval now obvious.

Sam opened his door and got out. "I'll see you round, Roxy. And thanks again."

She looked back at him, wondering what to say, how to help. *"It's not your problem, Roxy,"* she told herself and simply nodded at him and let Houghton lead her away. She thought he'd take her up to the veranda but they only got as far as her hire car which was still parked beneath the fig tree, and was now splattered with bat droppings and seeds.

"What's going on there?" Houghton asked, shrugging

one shoulder back towards Sam who was leaning against his car while one of the officers strode swiftly towards him.

She shrugged back. "Nothing, I walked to the café, Sam gave me a lift back."

"Okay, sure, but you know, you've been gone for hours, Roxy."

"It was a long walk."

He stared at her. "You know he's a bit of a nutter, right? You do understand that?"

Roxy glanced back to Sam who was now talking with the officer.

"He's okay," she said, her tone wavering a little.

Houghton sensed this. "Just be careful, there, hey? He's not who you think he is, I can tell you that much." Before she could say anything, Houghton took a step closer and said, "Listen, about Annika." He glanced around again as if checking she wasn't loitering close by. "Last night, well, she was ranting about the book being off, wanting you to head home."

"Of course, I understand that. I'll pack up and—"

"No! No, no, no, that's nonsense. She's just under a lot of stress, that's all. She's not thinking straight."

"But surely, with Jed gone…"

"Now's the perfect time to bring the book out. In honour of him."

In honour of your bank account more likely, Roxy wanted to say. "In any case, I'm not sure I'm the girl for the job. I never even got to interview Jed, remember?" Her stomach sank at that. Sure, he might be an unfaithful fool, but he was still one of Australia's hottest musicians, and she had liked his work. She would have enjoyed interviewing him, sharing his life story with the world. Instead, they never even shared more than a few sentences and a plate of antipasto.

"You're the perfect person for the job. You were here when Jed died, that's going to be a great selling point. Terrific for marketing."

Roxy cringed. Perhaps Macker Maroney was right. Was

Jed's publicist any less sleazy than him?

"I've just got to convince Annie of that," he was saying. "It might take some time. Can you hang around?"

She looked across at the sprawling timber mansion and the lush rainforest beyond. "Well, there's worse places to hang, I guess."

He blushed. "Ahh, actually, it'd be better if you... I dunno... went for a drive today or, if you don't feel like that, maybe just lob in the bails for a bit. Just until I get a chance to talk to Annie."

"You want me to hide in the bails?"

"Not hide so much as hang out, chill. I'll get some food sent across and you can just relax; hey, that'll be fun!" He brushed his frizzy hair off his face. "It's just that, well, you know what she's like? Bit territorial, bit tricky. I think it'd help if you stayed out of sight. Just for a night or so, until I get her on side."

"You want me to hide in the bails all day *and* all night?"

He blushed deeper. "If that's okay."

"You can stay at my place."

Roxy swung around to find Sam standing there again, hands by his side, eyes wide. He had a bad habit of sneaking up on her, she thought, and trying to steal her away.

"I thought you buggered off," Houghton said, his tone indignant.

Sam ignored him and kept his eyes on Roxy. "Quick wants me to come down to the station, got some 'questions' apparently." He gave her a pointed look. "You'd be doing me a big favour if you could take Lunar back to the cottage, give him a feed. I could be a while, don't want him sitting in the car the whole time."

"Lunar? Your *dog*?" Houghton retorted, like he'd never heard anything so ridiculous. "Why should she? She doesn't know you from—"

"That's fine," Roxy said, looking down at Lunar who was standing by his master, tongue out, tail wagging. She knew it was a strange request, but the idea of canine company seemed preferable to hiding away from a grieving widow in an old milking shed, even if the shed was incredibly glamorous.

Sam looked relieved. "Thank you. You are a lifesaver. His food is in the pantry, bottom shelf. Just give him a good feed this evening, and keep his water filled up. I should be back later, hopefully not too late. Help yourself to whatever, use the bed if you want, there's fresh sheets in the cupboard near the bathroom. Should be enough wood for the fire, but if you need more, there's a stack of logs at the back of the house, just near the chook shed. You might need to split them; the axe is on the chopping block." He didn't bother handing her a house key, as he never locked the place. "You can find your way back? Lot 21, Grears Crossing."

She nodded, thinking, *"What the hell am I doing? I don't even know this guy."*

As if reading her mind, Sam said, "It's okay, you already know I don't bite." He smiled, tilting his head to one side. "And you know I'll always bring you back in one piece."

Then he bent down, gave Lunar a quick hug before staring into the dog's eyes and saying in a deep, firm voice: "Lunar, stay!"

Lunar didn't look like he wanted to obey that order, glancing between Roxy and Sam, but he did as instructed anyway, now watching his master worriedly as Sam strode back to his vehicle, got in and drove away. Roxy, too, watched on, wondering what she was thinking. Max had tried for years to convince her to move in and here she was moving into a virtual stranger's place after just one afternoon together.

Was she having an early midlife crisis?

CHAPTER 17

"Are you completely nuts?" It was Oliver's voice on the other end of the line and he sounded as stunned as Houghton by the turn of events.

Roxy's mobile phone had no network coverage and she had borrowed the Moodys' landline, a portable phone that Houghton had insisted she use just outside the front door, clearly terrified Annika would stumble across her. Roxy found his behaviour infuriating and it only hardened her resolve to get off the property. Oliver did not sound so convinced.

"You are seriously going to stay at some strange guy's place looking after his *dog*. You don't even like dogs."

"I love dogs, how can you say that?"

"Because you don't have one."

"I don't have one because my apartment is the size of a porta-loo, not because I don't like dogs. It's no big deal, Oliver. I'm just doing the guy a favour."

"This is the same guy you just told me is being hauled in for questioning over Jed Moody's death?"

She hesitated, scrunched her eyes up. "Yep, that'd be the one."

"Mary, Jesus, Mother of Christ!" Oliver whistled loudly. "Just when I thought you couldn't surprise me anymore, you go and move in with a murderer!"

"He's not a murderer."

"And you know this, how?"

"I just know."

He scoffed. "You getting soft in your old age, Roxy?"

"Just around the middle. Listen, I'm not calling you to get a lecture. I'm just telling you where I'll be, in case…" She hesitated again.

"In case we find you chopped up into little pieces?"

"That won't happen." She repeated Sam's address again. "I can't seem to get through to Gilda's mobile. Know where she is?"

"No, I don't. Should I call your mother, tell her you've finally flipped?"

"God, no, leave her out of it."

"So what's the story then with Jed? You know this is going to be the last ghostwriting job you ever get? The way your clients bite the dust, who'd want you?"

"Hey, it's not my fault Jed's equipment was faulty."

"Is that what they say happened?"

She thought about this. "At this point they're not saying. He was clearly electrocuted, and it looked suspicious, at least that's according to my friend Sam."

"The weirdo with the dog?"

"That's the one. And he's not weird. He's just hurting after his sister's death."

"Huh? His sister died as well?"

"Yeah, was found drowned in a creek about eighteen months ago."

"How do you know he didn't do her in?"

"Oh, come on, that's ridiculous."

"Yeah, right, because family members never kill each other." He paused. "Jesus, you're not smitten with the guy, are you?"

She tsked loudly. A little too loudly "For goodness sake,

Olie. I'm feeding his dog, not marrying him. Jeesh!"

"Yeah right, sure. Okay, well, what can I do from here? Need anything?"

"No, thank you. Although I do have to work out what happens now with the book."

"Yeah, I was trying to sort that out with Houghton, but he can't give me any answers yet. If it doesn't go ahead, they'll owe you a kill fee." He chuckled. "Excuse the pun."

"That's just woeful, Oliver. I mean, poor Jed."

"I know, Juicy Jed, up in flames. Who woulda thought? And you say the wife wants you out?"

"Yeah, it's the publicist who wants to keep it alive." She winced at her own pun then spotted Houghton just outside the studio, chatting animatedly into his mobile phone, one hand gesticulating wildly as he spoke. She wondered about his motivation. Did he care at all for his old client, or was it all about making a buck?

"Well, tell Houghton he needs to call me directly. He shouldn't be speaking with you about this. He has to confer with me. I'm your agent. That's what you pay me the tiny bickies for. You're gonna want a bigger commission, by the way. A tell-all bio is a very different kettle of fish. More work for you, more people to interview, more facts to check, especially now the poor bastard's dead."

"I'm not even sure I want to do it."

"I'm not even sure you've got much choice, my dear. There's nothing else lined up. Everybody thinks they're a writer these days, you know that. Everyone has a bloody blog. I think you should try to make it happen whether you want it or not."

She sighed. "I better go, I've got a dog to feed."

"Try to knock some sense into yourself while you're at it!"

****

An icy chill descended quickly at the small cottage at

Grears Crossing. The tall trees blocked out most of the afternoon light and it was just on 5:25 p.m. when Roxy knelt in front of the rusty old woodburner to start the fire.

Fortunately, the metal bin beside it was overflowing with twigs and other kindling, and beside that was a stack of old newspapers and half a dozen split logs. Good, she thought. While she admired Sam's confidence in her, she wasn't keen to channel her inner woodchopper tonight. She could manage with what she had.

It had been a long time since Roxy had made a fire, but she was determined to get one started, could tell this old cottage with its gaping timber walls and floorboards would become unbearable without it. She could even see faint strands of late afternoon light filtering in through sections of the ceiling; clearly there was no insulation above.

Roxy had brought her overnight bag and when she placed her iPad and mobile phone on the kitchen bench, she noticed neither was functioning. Clearly she was using the wrong provider for this part of the world. Sam's mobile phone had worked perfectly well earlier today, and she felt eerily isolated. A quick survey of the cottage confirmed there was no landline telephone. She had a momentary panic before she reminded herself that humans once survived perfectly well without these contraptions, and she would survive too.

If she could just get the blasted fire going.

Roxy scrunched up sheets of newspaper and tossed them over last night's ash, then snapped twigs and placed them on top. She thought about Houghton and how he, too, had tried to talk her out of staying at Sam's place.

"He really is a nutcase, you know, the things he's been saying about Jed."

"He's just hurting; after what happened to his sister, he's looking for someone to blame."

"He blamed Jed, Roxy. And look what happened to Jed. He's not to be trusted."

"Do you honestly think Sam's responsible? For what

happened to Jed?"

Houghton had stopped short then, had just shrugged. "I'm just saying, you'd be better off staying here tonight."

She scoffed. "What, hiding out in the bails, waiting for Annika to invite me to the big house?"

"Hey, she just lost her husband, you know."

"I know, I'm sorry. But hiding out is not my style."

He looked chastened. "I'm sorry about that, yeah? It's not that you need to hide so much, it's just that, well, I just want to give Annie her space for now, you understand? She'll need some time to work through what's happened. He was the love of her life, after all. God, we all loved him, dearly. He'll be sorely, sorely missed."

Roxy placed a larger log over the top of the kindling and lit a match. She had to wonder if Houghton was right. She could think of several people who wouldn't exactly be weeping over Jed's casket. Sure, Annika would be anguished and Roxy didn't doubt her love for the guy, but this was a man who had cheated on her over and over again, and who, in the short time she was there, seemed to give more attention to his music than his muse. Wasn't his death a kind of freedom? A chance to keep Jed Moody to herself forever?

She thought, too, of Jed's bandmates, Alistair and Doug. They had seemed pretty shocked the night of his death, drowning themselves in Jack Daniels, but were they heartbroken? Really? Roxy wasn't convinced. She didn't really know Doug, but he seemed to find the whole thing more amusing than upsetting. And Al had already made it clear to Roxy that he was no fan of the "selfish prick".

Even Houghton had agreed there was little love lost between Jed and Al, and Roxy had noticed that herself, up on stage. Would Al weep? Or would he now flourish? If what Houghton had said was true, Al was the brains' behind the Moody Roos. Maybe this was his chance to take centre stage.

Nah. She shrugged that thought away. Few famous bands ever pulled that off. Roxy had seen it happen from time to time when lead singers died. Some bands ploughed on regardless, others recruited a new frontman, but very few made a real go of it. AC/DC and Pink Floyd were rare exceptions. Most of the time, if you replaced the lead singer, everything turned to shite—just ask the boys from INXS.

Besides, in rock and roll terms, these guys were ancient. Their current success relied mostly on nostalgia. Without Jed, what was the point? He was the only one anyone ever remembered. No one was going to get nostalgic over Al and Doug.

As the kindling burned out and the logs began to power away, the fire intensified and Roxy glanced around to find Lunar had taken off. She spotted him fossicking near the run of gum trees in the distance, so she left the front door slightly ajar then did a little fossicking of her own.

There was only one bedroom and it was positioned just on the other side of the kitchen. A quick peek inside revealed a small double bed decorated with a bright coloured quilt. Beside the bed was a mismatched timber cupboard, bedside table and chest of drawers. The tiny bathroom was situated on the other side of the kitchen, and had clearly been added on some time after the house had been built. She guessed there was an outhouse somewhere, probably by the chicken pen, and was glad for the luxury of an indoor toilet. Beside the toilet was a tiny shower cubicle with a bright green shower curtain, and one of those old-fashioned ceramic sinks with separate hot and cold taps.

After locating a towel, she had a quick shower and changed into fresh black leggings and a baggy red jumper from her overnight bag. Back in the living room, Roxy combed her wet hair and glanced around. She could still find no television set, but she did see a relatively modern stereo sitting beside a cluttered bookcase. She stepped across and pressed "Play" on the CD player. Soon the soft dulcet tones of Nick Drake began to stream through the air, and she smiled. Sam Forrest also had good taste in music.

As she let the song wash over her, Roxy continued

poking around, knowing she should be minding her own business but intrigued nonetheless. There were no pictures on the walls but a few photos had been clustered together on a sideboard that she hadn't noticed the first time she'd been here, and she took a closer look. There were several photos of an elderly lady with a soft mop of long, white hair. In one of them, she was standing by a horse, a wide smile on her face and a small hibiscus flower poked out above her ear. In another, she was reaching down to pick up a small child wearing an enormous cloth nappy. That had to be Sam's grandmother, she decided, judging from the photo quality and the woman's age. A larger frame displayed a picture of three children, circa 1980s. The boy, just on the cusp of puberty, wore a pair of Stubbie shorts and a worried smile; the two girls were older and wore matching terry toweling dresses. They both had mousy brown hair, and faces crammed with freckles. Sam and his older sisters, thought Roxy, surely?

Then she spotted the picture of Sunny. It had to be Sunny; this girl was young and breathtakingly beautiful, and she was clearly taking a selfie, her arms reaching out and getting lost behind the lens. That was something her older siblings would never have done. So much for Miss Anti-technology, Roxy thought. She might not own a mobile device, but she clearly had access to a digital camera of some sort.

Roxy picked up the photo and studied it. Sunny had long, cashmere-blonde hair that draped over her eyes provocatively, and a face that was tanned and blemish-free. Her nose was small and perfect, her teeth straight and gleaming white, and the smile she was offering the camera was coy, even a little cheeky, and it choked at Roxy's heartstrings. She wondered now if Sam was right. Had someone deliberately put an end to that beautiful smile? And if so, why?

Perhaps it was time to get a few things straight. Roxy placed the photo back on the shelf then returned to her overnight bag and located her journal, a small, leather-bound book that went everywhere she did. Catching the pen before it fell out, she opened it to a blank page before settling onto the couch and quickly beginning to write.

As the fire crackled away, Roxy scribbled down every event she could remember of the past two days. It had been a while since she'd last written in her journal, but she felt the need now to get it all down, every detail from Jed's final night. As she did so, it suddenly hit her, something she had completely forgotten about—she recalled crouching behind the bar, bottle of red wine in her hand, as Annika talked suggestively to a man who was not Jed.

She underlined those last two words and gave it some thought. Who had she been talking to? What did they say? Most of it was now a blur—it seemed so long ago—but one thing Annika said stood out very clearly and now sent shivers down Roxy's spine.

"We have to act. It's time, babe, it's time."

Wasn't that the same thing Jed called his new song, the one he was about to sing before he was electrocuted? The one he dedicated to the "love of his life" while staring out at the crowd, away from his wife?

Had Jed Moody fallen in love with someone else? Was he planning to leave Annika, and did she know that? The way Annika had talked in that darkened living room had sounded intimate to Roxy, though her words could almost have been an instruction, a directive to a secret lover. She shuddered. Could Annika have killed her husband? Or ordered someone to do it?

"Stop it!" Roxy said aloud. "You're letting your imagination run wild again!" Oliver would be so disappointed with her. So, too, would Max.

As if hearing her voice, Lunar reappeared, trotting inside then straight up to Roxy, planting his head in her lap again.

"I've already fed you, boy," she said, watching his eyes droop. "Is this about Sam? If so, I'm worried too."

She glanced at the clock on the wall above the stove. An

hour had vanished and she'd barely noticed the time. She wondered if Sam would be home soon, or if she and Lunar were in for a long night. Her stomach growled then and Lunar blinked up at her, surprised.

She laughed and stood up. "Come on, then, let's see what else is in that pantry."

After throwing some more wood on the fire, Roxy wandered into the kitchen to start searching the fridge and cupboards. Lunar had been fed, but she was famished. There was an onion, some zucchini and packaged pasta. She could work with that. She recalled seeing tomatoes and parsley growing in the veggie patch around the back and she pulled on some oversized gumboots and trotted outside before it got too dark, Lunar bounding ahead.

Twenty minutes later, Roxy had the pasta bubbling away and the tomato sauce simmering on the old gas stove. It smelled delicious. Was that the fresh ingredients, or was she just plain starving? Roxy realised that, apart from a few coffees, she hadn't eaten a thing all day. No wonder it was so appealing.

Leaving a generous portion in the pan for Sam just in case he hadn't eaten, Roxy scooped some pasta into a bowl then returned to the sofa, watching the fire burn as she ate. Lunar turned in a circle a few times then dumped himself close to Roxy's feet, and she dropped one hand to stroke him as she ate. She'd never had a pet, not even as a child. Her mother had detested animals, felt they were too smelly and took too much of her precious (albeit idle) time. Roxy would love a dog now, but her tiny apartment would be torture to a dog of this size. And she wasn't interested in small breeds like Coco. Might as well get a cat, she thought.

"Or a rodent, eh, Lunar?"

Lunar thudded his tail hard against the rug, ears twitching in response to her voice.

Just as Roxy was scooping the last of the pasta from her bowl, the dog's ears pricked up again and he leapt to his feet and started barking. A car was approaching.

Roxy jumped up too, not sure whether to be happy or alarmed. It had to be Sam. *Didn't it?* But Lunar's response said otherwise. His tail was no longer wagging and the hair on his back was standing up again.

Roxy placed her bowl aside, swallowed hard then stepped towards a front window, pulling the curtain aside. She could just make out a dark-coloured vehicle, a sedan of some sort, pulling up to the house. It wasn't Sam's Jeep. Roxy's stomach dropped. She looked back at Lunar who was now barking like a watchdog, pacing up and down in front of the door. Never before had she longed so much for a working telephone.

Roxy leaned down to calm Lunar, or perhaps she was just holding onto him for her dear life. Roxy heard the slam of a car door followed by the muffled crunch of gravel, then a loud banging on the front door that made her jump and Lunar launch into another round of barking. Her stomach now in her throat, Roxy glanced at the dog and then at the door, wondering whether to open it. Was it even locked?

Finally, rediscovering her vocal chords, she yelled out, "Who's there?"

There was an interminable pause before a familiar voice boomed back, "It's your fairy godmother, let me in!"

CHAPTER 18

Gilda Maltin was standing just on the edge of the front deck exhaling thick plumes of condensation, her eyebrows knotted together, her arms wrapped tightly around herself. The second Roxy opened the door Gilda burst forward, grabbed her in a hug and didn't seem to want to let go.

"My God, woman, you gave me the scare of my life!" She pushed Roxy back and began to check her over. "Are you okay? He didn't hurt you, did he?"

Roxy stared at her spellbound, still not sure if Gilda was really here or if it was just a mirage. She was clad in her usual city getup—tailored pants, silk shirt, heeled boots and a creamy cashmere coat that would stand out in these parts like dreadlocks in the Upper East Side of Manhattan.

"Come on, then," said Gilda, "let's get inside, it's bloody freezing out here."

Gilda dragged Roxy back in, one hand still holding onto her as though afraid she might vanish, the other slamming the door shut. Lunar had stopped barking and was now glancing from Roxy to Gilda and back, clearly not sure whether to slobber on this strange woman or attack. Roxy finally came to her senses and bent down towards the dog.

"She's okay, Lunar, she doesn't bite."

Gilda's eyes narrowed. "Yeah, but does she? That's the question."

"She's a he, actually."

"Whatever." Gilda stared at the dog suspiciously. She had never been much of a pet person and didn't intend to start now. She lifted her eyes to the living room and began to look around, first poking her head in the bedroom, then the kitchen, and finally, with a crinkled brow she peered into the tiny bathroom.

"There's no one else here," Roxy told her, but Gilda needed to see it for herself.

Finally, she relaxed a little and said, "What are you doing out here, shacking up in the sticks?"

Roxy turned to the woodburner and bent down to stoke the fire. "I'm not shacking up; you sound like Oliver. I'm just looking after a man's dog."

"A man you barely know, who's held you hostage all morning, and is currently being questioned over Jed Moody's murder."

Roxy swung back. "They don't really think he did it, surely?"

"Yes, I think they do. They've cautioned him, he's asked for a lawyer."

"But he didn't do it, Gilda. He's not the type."

Gilda pulled off her coat and collapsed on the sofa with an exaggerated sigh. "Here we go again."

"What?"

"You, trying to save somebody from themselves. How well do you know this guy?"

Roxy turned back to the fire, deciding not to answer that. She secured the glass door and then stood up, hands on her hips. "Why are you even here, Gilda? How did you find me?"

"Your new boyfriend gave me directions."

"He's not my boyfriend."

"Yeah, well, lucky for you I just ran into him at the

Tweed Heads station—*while he was being read his rights*. Did I mention that?" She rubbed a hand through her tousled blonde hair then cocked her head to one side. "Are you going to offer me a drink or do I have to fend for myself?"

Roxy smiled at last. "Come on, I spotted a bottle of Merlot in the back of the pantry, was wondering whether to open it."

"The only good Merlot's an open Merlot." Gilda followed her through and then watched as Roxy dragged the bottle from a top shelf. "So he's got your crap taste in wine, has he? No wonder you've moved in. And the same slit-your-wrist taste in music, I hear."

Roxy realised the Nick Drake album must have been on repeat the whole time; she had been so lost in her thoughts she hadn't even noticed.

"Why don't you find something more cheerful then, and I'll find some glasses. Are you hungry? There's some pasta left."

"No, I had a Byron Bay Cookie and gin and tonic on the plane. So all the important food groups have been covered."

Gilda returned to the living room and began studying the small selection of CDs that were scattered around the stereo, some in their cases, most out. She settled on a Motown compilation CD while Roxy gave up on wine glasses and, struggling to find a water glass that wasn't badly cracked, settled on two coffee cups that looked new and clean. She gave them a rinse anyway then filled them up.

As she handed one over, Gilda frowned at the cup but stayed silent, then they both took a seat on the couch as the detective told Roxy how worried she had been after their phone conversation that morning.

"I knew something was up. You were not yourself at all, but you didn't seem to want to admit it, you cheeky bugger."

"Because I knew you'd do exactly what you've just done and try and rescue me!"

"Well, someone's got to look out for you. Besides, your mother would never forgive me if I didn't."

"She doesn't know, does she?"

"God no, I'm no masochist! My mate Johnno tried to track down an address for that mobile number but failed miserably, so I rang the Tweed/Byron area command. That's when I got put through to that idiot, Quick." She took a good gulp of her wine. "Your boyfriend's right about him, total knob."

"He's not my boyfriend."

"Yeah, yeah, you already said that. Anyway, Quick refused to listen to my concerns, said your whereabouts were the 'least of his worries', quote unquote, so I decided to get on the first plane up and find you for myself. The last time we let you loose in these parts you were locked in a haunted house, left to starve. Remember that?"

Roxy did remember that, it was yet one more case where murder seemed to land in her lap. "This is very different, Gilda, I'm not being held against my will. At least, not anymore."

"A-ha! So you admit you were kidnapped!"

"Sam just needed my help, that's all."

"Don't they always?"

"So, what, you went straight to the police station from the airport?"

"Yep, headed to the copshop and found Quick in the middle of questioning your boyfr—I mean mate."

"Is Sam okay?"

She shrugged. "Is anyone when they're being accused of murder? He kept saying he had nothing to do with it, that all we needed to do was look into his sister's death to get the real story. *Blah, blah, blah.* I just wanted to know where you were and, luckily, Sam was happy to oblige. That made me think you might just be fine, but until I saw it for myself, I wasn't taking any chances." She swatted Roxy across one arm, almost spilling her wine in the process. "You gave me such a bloody scare! He could have been a homicidal maniac, what were you thinking?"

"Hey, he kidnapped me, remember? I didn't have any

choice at the time."

"Yeah, then he took you back and you returned. Willingly! Like a boomerang. What is *that* about?"

"That's about me believing him. I just don't think he killed Jed. He just doesn't seem the type."

Gilda eyeballed her friend, went to rebuke her, and then thought better of it. She leaned back and watched the fire for a moment. Eventually she said, "Okay, Roxy, history tells me you've got good instincts, so I will believe you. At least until my better judgment kicks in. But you have to accept that you really don't know this guy and have no idea what he is capable of. Can you at least accept that?"

Roxy shrugged. "Fine."

"Good. So try and keep an open mind, no matter what your instincts tell you. Now, you'd better tell me exactly what's happened, and let's start at the beginning, shall we? Don't leave anything out. Oh, but before you do." She placed her cup down, then jumped up and disappeared outside, returning a minute later with a large bag of chocolate-coated peanuts and a family block of Rocky Road. "Let's get sugared up!"

Over the next hour, as they devoured chocolate and cheap red wine, Lunar snoring at Roxy's feet just near the fire, she told her good friend all about the past forty-eight hours which sounded increasingly like a B-grade movie plot. When Roxy had finished, she stood up, stretched like a cat then poured the remainder of the wine into their cups while Gilda digested everything.

Eventually Gilda said, "So you think this is all connected to the first death, to Sunny's supposed drowning?"

"I don't think anything. That's what *Sam* thinks, and he seems convinced of it. You said yourself it wasn't investigated properly."

"And it wasn't. That doesn't automatically make it murder, could just be sloppy police work. And it certainly doesn't mean it's connected to Jed's murder."

"You keep calling it a murder. So that's official then?"

She nodded. "The fuse box had been tampered with and so had his equipment, or at least that's what I could glean from the very brief chat I had with Quick. He was being a bit cagey, but I can read between the lines. Looks to me like somebody wanted Jed Moody dead and they made doubly sure it happened."

"Pretty lucky they didn't kill someone else in the process. What if someone else had picked up that guitar? Or touched Jed before the power went out." Roxy shivered. "Who would do such a thing? It's so theatrical."

"And so technical. Not your run of the mill murder. Whoever did this knew exactly what they were doing. And they had to have been there on the night of the murder because the wiring was perfectly fine during the tune-up, which was about an hour before the gig." Gilda hesitated before asking, "Did your friend Sam happen to mention he's a sparkie?"

"Um, no, he didn't."

"He's got his electrician's license. That's how he makes his money around these parts."

Roxy shifted in her seat and wondered why Sam hadn't mentioned it. Of course, it did explain why he had acted so quickly when Jed was electrocuted, how he knew not to touch anything and to switch off the fuse box. But why hadn't he told her that? She wondered. Had he deliberately misled her?

"Still," Roxy said, feeling some strange compulsion to defend the man, "there must have been other people who knew their way around a fuse box. There was quite a crowd there, plus the guys in the band must have an idea about how it all works."

"Do any of them have it in for Jed Moody?"

"Yes, at least one. The bass player wasn't exactly his biggest fan. And we don't know who it was Annika was flirting with that night. Maybe that man's a sparkie too?"

"Quick says Sam was the only sparkie at the gig and is

determined to lay the blame firmly at his feet. I got that much out of him before he turned all tight-lipped. Seems quite annoyed by my presence." She chuckled again. "I love stirring up the local lads."

"Are you allowed to look into it? Surely they have to send in some big guns."

"I don't *want* to look into it, Roxy. I'm not here to investigate. I'm here to bring you home."

"I don't need a chaperone, Gilda. I'm not twelve."

"And you're also not a detective, although you seem to think you've morphed into one."

"What's your point?"

"My point is, you don't need to be sticking your nose into this case. It has nothing to do with you." When Roxy looked away from her then, her jaw clenched shut, she added, "I'm right, you know."

Roxy walked into the kitchen and dumped her cup in the sink, causing Lunar to leap to his feet, alert now, and looking a little alarmed. Roxy stared out of the kitchen window to the dark night sky. She could just make out the silhouette of the chicken shed beneath the gum trees. Something swooped down low. Was it an owl? A flying fox? "I never said I was going to stick my nose in. I never said that."

Gilda followed her in. "That's the impression I got. I'm sorry, Roxy, but I know what you're like, trying to fight other people's battles." She reached out and touched Roxy's back. "This is one fight that you need to leave well alone. I know you pity Sam Forrest and I get that. He's kind of like a big puppy dog. Cute, if you like them rough around the edges, but this has nothing to do with you and it's time you came home."

Roxy's back stiffened. "I might not have much choice. Jed's publicist has asked me to hang around in case they still go ahead with the book, and quite frankly, Gilda, I need the money."

Gilda dropped her hand. "Fine, do the book. But just keep out of the investigation, okay?"

"Okay." Gilda took Roxy by the arms and turned her around so they were eyeballing each other. Roxy smiled then and repeated herself: "Okay, okay, I promise!"

"Good! Then get your things, let's go."

"Where are we going?"

"Somewhere with internal heating and a functioning bar would be a good start."

Roxy pushed past her friend and returned to the sofa. "No can do. I'm staying put. Besides, I like this place."

"But it's so…" Gilda looked around as she followed her back to the fire, "primitive. It's like we've time traveled to the *Little House on the Prairie.*"

Roxy laughed. "I think it's more *Midsomer Murders,* myself."

"Well, you got the murder part right."

Roxy grabbed a cushion and hugged it tight. "You're welcome to go, Gilda, but I promised Sam I'd watch his dog tonight and I intend to keep that promise."

Gilda's eyes dropped to the dog, who had also returned to the sofa and was now settling onto the rug, close to Roxy's feet again.

She sighed. "A handsome rogue and his cute dog. How am I supposed to compete with that?"

CHAPTER 19

A melodic kookaburra laughed Roxy's sleep away and she
sat up with a start. She looked across to the other side of the
bed where Lunar was lying huddled in a ball, his tail now
thumping; one eye open.

Roxy smiled and dropped back onto the pillow, turning
onto her side to face Lunar and reaching a hand out to pat
him. The warm sunshine was streaming in through the
bedroom window and there was a distinctive smell of freshly
ground coffee in the air. She could get used to this. She
thought then of Sam and sat back up.

Had he returned overnight?

Roxy leapt out of bed, Lunar following suit, then grabbed
a baggy cardigan from her bag and covered herself up. They
both wandered out to the kitchen where they found Gilda
leaning against the old cooker, watching the coffee maker
splutter to life.

She had slept on the sofa the night before, but you would
never have known it, the sheets and blanket were already
packed away and she looked as fresh as the hinterland air. At
some stage she had changed into a different silk blouse and
her wispy blonde hair had been tousled back to life. She even

had a lick of lip-gloss and eyeliner in place.

"Don't look so disappointed, guys," Gilda said, grinning at them both. "Sam will be back before you know it."

Roxy stepped towards Gilda and gave her a hug. "Sorry I was so stroppy last night."

"Ah, don't worry about it. You just watched a man get electrocuted, then you got kidnapped, then lumbered with the kidnapper's dog!" She laughed. "You've had a lot on your plate. Speaking of which, I couldn't find much in the way of cereal in that dusty cupboard of his."

"There's a chook shed outside. I'll go and see if I can rustle up something for breakfast."

Half an hour later they were seated out in the dappled sunshine on the wicker chairs in front of the cottage, nursing plates of fresh scrambled eggs with parsley and tomatoes, mugs of warm coffee at their feet.

"I could get used to these fresh organic ingredients," Roxy said, and Gilda shrugged.

"I dunno. It's missing Peep's smoky oil flavour with the carburetor aftertaste." She looked around, waving her fork as she said, "You're really digging this rural life, aren't you? I would never have picked you for a country girl."

Roxy laughed. "Me neither. I'm as surprised with myself as you are." She gave it some thought. "Maybe, after the year I've had—breaking up with Max, then thinking he'd been kidnapped, traipsing across Europe trying to find him— maybe this is just what I needed."

"You mean another murder or another man?"

Roxy looked at her sideways. "There is no other man, Gilda."

"So Sam Forrest, who's he again?"

"He's just a guy who needed my help." She was beginning to get annoyed by this broken record of a conversation.

"Okay, so it's another murder that's brought this glow to your cheeks then?"

Roxy swept a hand to her face. "Of course not. Although

dead people do have a habit of cropping up around me, don't they?"

"It's business as usual for you these days, that's true. We'll have to start calling you Jessica Fletcher, or Miss Marple. Which one would you prefer?"

"Can't I be Hercule Poirot? He's so much more interesting."

"Ah, but he's a *professional* detective. You, my dear, are just a lowly ghostwriter."

"A Ghostie. That's what Jed called me." She sighed wistfully thinking of the few exchanges they'd had, of the missed opportunity.

Gilda took a sip of her coffee. "What was he like, Juicy Jed? Sexy as ever?"

"Sexier. But not without fault, clearly had a mega ego, although he was very polite to me. Definitely a lot of tension between him and his wife, and he had a mean streak in him, too. Was even a little nasty to his bass player and his publicist now I think about it."

"Plenty of suspects for his murder then?"

She shrugged one shoulder. "So why are they keeping Sam so long? Do you think they have something on him?"

"Nothing that Quick was willing to reveal to me, apart from Sam's electrical credentials, of course. He seemed to think that made it an open and shut case, but of course it proves nothing." Gilda chewed quietly on her breakfast for a while. Eventually she placed her half-eaten egg aside and said, "So what are your plans, then, Missy? Are you really going to hang around here, playing dutiful dogsitter? I mean, I like him, he's super cool, but I'm not sure I'd desert my fab city life for him."

Roxy wondered if they were still talking about the dog. "I'm not deserting anything. I'm just doing a guy a favour. Besides, I may still have to hang around to write Jed's biography, remember? Oliver's sorting that out with the publicist today."

"And in the meantime?"

She shrugged, not knowing the answer to that question.

Gilda edged a foot towards hers and gave her toe a nudge. "I know I'm going to live to regret this, but I was thinking I might try to take a sneaky peek at Sunny Forrest's file while I'm here. See what Quick's got to say about that."

Roxy was mid-mouthful of coffee when she said it and nearly spluttered it everywhere. "Really?! I thought you didn't want to know about it. What happened to chaperoning me home?"

"Well, if you're staying to write this bloody book, I might as well hang around, too. And quite frankly, bushwalking and dogminding ain't my thing. Would rather get productive."

"Will they let you investigate?"

"Not sure yet. As I said before, Wiles is usually the man for the job, but I know from our chat yesterday that he's snowed under and if he gets appointed to the Moody investigation he's definitely not going to have time to look into a cold case as well. Whereas I have very little on my plate right now, unless you count that extraordinarily orange egg! What is it with the colour? Is that even healthy?"

Roxy laughed. "It's free range, Gilda, the healthiest egg you're ever going to eat."

"Looks scary to me. I like my food beige and bland, thanks very much. Anyway, before you get too excited, I still have to call the Powers That Be to see if I can wangle it." She squinted her eyes a little. "Better check with Wiles first, too. Make sure I'm not treading on his handsome toes."

"Sam would really appreciate that."

"He may not, you know. I may end up coming to the same conclusion as Quick. I may decide there is no case to answer, that the poor girl did just drown. Or worse, killed herself."

"Then so be it," said Roxy. "Maybe then he'll be able to let it go."

Lunar's ears twitched and he barked suddenly again, his every nerve on end, and Roxy knew that someone else was coming up the driveway. She smiled at the dog. Who needed an expensive security system with Lunar about?

This time, however, she had a hunch who it was as Lunar was already bounding down the road, his tail wagging maniacally. A minute later Roxy heard the roar of an engine and saw a flash of white through the gum trees.

Roxy felt her own heart lift then looked around guiltily for Gilda, who had taken the plates back inside. As the Jeep drew near, Gilda returned to the deck and the two women watched as Sam came to a dusty halt in front of the cottage. At some point he must have stopped and let Lunar in, because the dog was now beside him in the passenger seat, tongue hanging out, grinning like all his Christmases had come at once.

"Hey there!" Sam called out, his smile now visible, and Roxy tried to look indifferent as she waved back.

Gilda just snorted beside her. "So they finally let you out," she yelled.

He jumped down from the front seat and laughed. "Had no choice. Got nothing on me." He looked across to Roxy. "Of course. I didn't do it, you know that?"

Gilda wondered why he needed Roxy to believe that so much and felt protective of her friend. "We know nothing of the sort, Mr. Forrest, we're reserving our judgment for now. Aren't we, Roxy?"

Roxy remained silent and Sam's smile widened.

"Anyway," Gilda said, growing uncomfortable with the situation, "Roxy and I have to head back to the Moody property now. Don't we, Rox?" Roxy was still staring at Sam, as if mesmerised, and she gave her a little nudge.

"Huh?"

"You need to see whether you're still doing the book, right?"

Roxy seemed to snap out of it then. "Yes, right. Of course."

Sam's smile deflated. "You're still writing the book?"

"I don't know yet."

He went to say something but stopped, swallowed hard. "Well, thanks for looking after Lunar. He been okay?"

She nodded. "He's been great. My protector."

"No, no, no," interjected Gilda. "That's *my* job. Come on then, Missy, let's get your things and give Sam his space back."

Sam stepped towards Roxy. "You're welcome to stay here, you know. If you do end up writing the book." He paused, rubbed a hand through his shaggy short hair. "It's just that it didn't sound like Annika wanted you there and … well … it'll be cheaper than a hotel room. Closer to Moody Views, too."

Roxy glanced from Sam to Gilda then back to Sam again. "Oh thanks, but Gilda's right. We should probably give you some space."

He laughed. "I've got eleven acres here, Roxy. I don't need all of it."

Gilda wasn't having any of it. "And where exactly do you propose she sleeps, hey? Out in the chook shed?"

"She can have my bed, of course, I'll take the sofa."

"No thanks, we'll be fine." Gilda pulled Roxy towards the door. "Come on then. Let's get your stuff and get going."

Sam shrugged. "Suit yourself. I'll be feeding the chooks."

As he strode off towards the chicken coop, Gilda grabbed Roxy's arm and dragged her back inside. "Okay, so who the hell are you and what the hell have you done with my best friend?"

Roxy pushed her away. "What are you talking about?"

"I'm talking about Miss Gooey Eyes back there. Who was *that*?"

"I wasn't gooey. That's ridiculous." She strode into the bedroom and began thrusting her clothes back into her bag.

Gilda watched her for a moment and let it drop. She just wanted to get Roxy out of Sam's cottage and back to the Moody property pronto. There was something about Sam Forrest that put Gilda's nerves on edge, and she couldn't yet decide what it was. Roxy may have developed a soft spot for the guy, but Gilda did not trust him one bit.

CHAPTER 20

As Roxy steered her hatchback past the Goddess Café and back onto Jasper Road, she hoped she would not miss the turn onto the Moody property as she had done last time. Gilda had been following close behind in her own hire car since they left Sam's property, and Roxy didn't want to lead her astray.

This time, however, there was no chance. A large group had gathered by the Moodys' front gate, some standing arm in arm, others seated on the ground around a collection of flowers, old guitars and djembe drums, as though this had become a kind of makeshift memorial site.

Roxy slowed her car down as she took the turn and noticed that the crowd was mostly made up of women in their late thirties and forties, old groupies, she suspected. She wondered, somewhat bitterly, how many of these women Jed Moody had slept with. Several of them cheered as she drove past, others just stared at her, their eyes wide with sadness and curiosity.

For all his sins, Jed Moody had certainly touched a lot of hearts.

When they reached the main house, Roxy noticed several more unfamiliar vehicles parked beneath the fig tree but no police cars, or at least none that she recognised. She pulled up to the side of the stables this time, and directed Gilda to do the same, then was just getting out when her mobile phone began to beep wildly. She stared at it, stunned. She hadn't heard it make a sound in three days. There were eleven missed calls, including one from Caroline, two from Gilda, four from her mother, and the rest from her agent.

She rolled her eyes and glanced back at Gilda who was pointing her keys at her vehicle about to press the remote control lock.

"Don't bother!" Roxy called out, but Gilda pressed it anyway.

"Can't help myself," she yelled back.

Roxy was about to suggest they walk around the side of the house to the back veranda when Houghton appeared at the front door, waving frantically. He had clearly been looking out for Roxy's car and ushered her inside, nodding quickly at Gilda as Roxy did the introductions. For now they had decided not to mention Gilda's police credentials, and if Houghton was curious about why Roxy's "good friend" had suddenly appeared out of nowhere, he didn't show it. He simply shook her hand quickly then indicated they should remove their shoes before following him down the corridor.

Gilda looked horrified at the thought but Roxy just dumped her boots by the growing pile of dusty gumboots, Crocs and trainers then followed Houghton along the hallway. It was amazing, she thought, staring down at her socks, how quickly one adjusted to country life.

"How's Annika doing today?" Roxy asked as they stopped at the entrance to the living room, waiting for Gilda to catch up. She was still pulling off her heeled boots, a look of irritation on her face.

"She's good, yeah, she's up and about." He nodded his head in the direction of the veranda where, through the French doors, Roxy could just make out Annika's back, her dark hair arranged in an elaborate bun, a spangly kaftan on. There was a small crowd around her, seated on chairs, at her feet, several leaning against the railing, and Roxy recognised a few familiar faces from the night of Jed's death.

Annika's machine-gun laughter suddenly echoed through the house and it seemed incongruous with the events of the past few days. "They're swapping old war stories about Jed," he explained as Gilda approached, leading them through the door to the velvet couch. "A kind of early wake, if you will."

Roxy nodded. She bet they had plenty of stories to swap. Glancing back out to the veranda, she spotted the same elderly couple from the night of the gig, sitting grim faced and silent on one side. "Who is that older couple? Family?"

He followed her line of sight and frowned just slightly. "Oh, that's the farmer from next door and his wife. They've come to pay their respects, which is, you know, bloody decent of them, considering."

"Considering what?" asked Gilda, but he waved her off.

"Listen, Roxy, I'm really close, I promise I am, but I'm still waiting on the final approval from Annie for the book." He rubbed a hand through his scruffy red hair. "She's coming around, I know that much. I know the signs. I can read 'em. She's starting to see some sense." His face scrunched up. "Is there any way you can give us another twenty-four hours?"

Roxy frowned. "Look, Houghton, if Annika's not interested, there's really no point pushing her into it. That just makes my job a lot harder, and it's not really fair to her."

"Yeah, I know what you're saying, but what about Al and Doug? What's fair for them?"

"*They* want me to write the book?"

"We all do, we're just trying to get Annie on board that's all. We want it to be a group effort and we need to get it happening before the tour."

"The tour?" Roxy blinked. "You're still doing the tour?"

"Yeah, well, it won't be the same tour, of course, but we're thinking a set of memorial gigs might be just the ticket, might see if Barnsey or maybe the bloke who took over for INXS could stand in for Jed. I think we can make it work."

"You're kidding, right?" said Gilda, one eyebrow cocked high.

"Not at all. No. I mean, it's the songs that make the band, and you saw the fans out the front. People love this band, they loved Jed, and they want to hear those songs one more time, at least. Am I right or am I right?"

"What about Jed's new material?" Roxy asked. "What about the new album?"

He waved a hand at that. "Not so important now. I mean, sure, we'll put that stuff out later, but I think it's his greatest hits that people want. I'm negotiating with the record company to rerelease his entire back catalogue then, with the memorial tour—and your book, of course—we'll rake it in." He caught himself and had the decency to blush. "And more importantly, of course, we'll honour poor Jeddie's memory, eh?"

Roxy was aghast. She didn't know if she wanted to be part of this money making machine, but then her agent was right. What choice did she have? Her next mortgage payment was beckoning and it wasn't like there were any other clients beating a path to her door.

"Look, I just need another twenty-four hours," Houghton said. "Just a bit of extra time to get Annie on board. She's close; she's just got to get her head around it, that's all. If not, I reckon we can still do it, but we're going to need some financing. That could take a bit longer."

Roxy held a finger up to stall him. "You can discuss all that stuff with my agent. I stay out of that."

"I have been discussing it with your agent, but we haven't firmed it up as yet. Oh, and he says to call him, by the way. Says he's left you a few messages."

Roxy cringed. "That's an understatement. Okay, I'll give him a call now."

"But can you hang around? Just in case? Got somewhere you can stay?"

Roxy's mind went straight to Sam's cottage, but the glare she was getting from Gilda put paid to that. She turned to Houghton and said, "Know any good hotels in town?"

As Gilda returned to her car to make a few calls, Roxy remained in the lounge and logged into the Moodys' WiFi. She needed to e-mail Caroline, Oliver and her mother to let them all know she was safe and would call when she got a chance. She knew the e-mails were a cop-out, but it was all she could muster. She then began scanning the Internet for hotels in Byron Bay. The three places Houghton had suggested had no vacancies, and she was reluctant to ask Annika for advice.

The grieving widow was still holding court on the veranda and she looked like she was in her element, hugging, air kissing and laughing a lot. Roxy wondered about that. Was she lapping up all the attention now that the spotlight had finally fallen her way?

"Don't be a bitch, Roxy," she scolded herself silently. Wasn't that the whole point of a wake—comfort and support for the ones left behind?

Houghton had some phone calls to make and had left Roxy with the promise that he'd get a final word on the book by the following morning. Until then, she needed to find backup accommodation, so she tried to concentrate on that but was struggling to find anything that was both available and within her price range.

"That one's okay," Gilda said, suddenly glancing over her shoulder.

"Too pricy," Roxy replied. "And way too white."

"Is there such a thing? Beach pads must always be white, *darlink*."

"Yeah, but you don't want to be blinded by it. Anyway, I'm not convinced we should be staying at the beach. I mean it's a long drive from here. Shouldn't we be looking for something closer, something in the hinterland?"

"What, like Grears Crossing?"

Roxy ignored this and reset her Google accommodation search to include the words "Byron Hinterland." As she typed, Roxy asked Gilda, "So how'd you go, with your boss?"

"I've got good news and bad news, which do you want first?"

Roxy scowled. She loathed this question. It was like being offered ice cream in a cone of dried dog vomit. The bad always seemed to ruin the good. "Go on then, let's start with the good."

"The good news is they are sending Wiles to lead the Moody investigation. He's flying up as we speak. Should be here by close of day. He'll take over from Quick."

"Good." As far as Roxy knew, Wiles had no association with the Moody family and would at least investigate the case without prejudice. "And the bad news?"

"The bad news is, the boss says we're way over budget and there's no way he can divert funds towards Sunny Forrest's case when he's about to fork it out big time for Jed Moody."

Roxy's shoulders slumped. "That's a pity. Can't he see what a botch up it was? Surely it's in the public interest?"

She smiled. "Which is what I said, so he's come 'round. Well, to a point. He's given me forty-eight hours to make my case."

"Really?"

"Yep, I get two days—off the books—to look into it, probe a little deeper and convince him and the Public Prosecutor that it's worth the money and manpower to reopen the case. Until then, I'm on my own. I've got authorisation but not funds."

"Do you need funds?"

"Not if we choose wisely," she said, glancing back at the iPad screen.

"And you'd do that? You'd investigate for nothing?"

"Well, it's hardly for nothing. I'm on paid leave for the rest of the week, and it's not like hanging out in the Byron

Shire is any great effort. Plus, I'm not prepared to head back to Sydney with you hovering around, getting your nose stuck where it needn't get stuck. I think it's in everyone's best interests, most of all yours, that I stay and snoop."

"Sam is going to be thrilled."

Gilda shook her head. "I'm not doing this for Sam. I'm doing it for Sunny. And I only have two days to prove there's a case to answer. I may come up with nothing, and if I do, that has to be the end of it. Sam has to let it go."

"I'm sure he will. He just wants a second opinion; you can't blame him for that. So what happens now?"

"We find cheap digs, my darling, and we start digging! Ooooh, that one looks lovely."

Gilda was pointing to a leafy picture of a small red cottage that had sprung up on Roxy's screen. Roxy clicked on the link and opened it to find the details for a bed and breakfast called Bindi's Eco Hideaway, which was nestled in lush rainforest. She double- clicked on its location and smiled. "And only a few kilometres from here!"

"From Sam's place, you mean?"

Roxy decided to ignore that comment.

CHAPTER 21

As the crow flies, Bindi's Eco Hideaway would have been an easy five-minute trip from Moody Views, but there were few direct roads in these parts. Instead, it took the women a good fifteen-minute drive, past the Goddess Café and down several winding gravel roads, through gullies and across two causeways before they reached their destination. Bindi's was really just another timber homestead, a two-storey structure that had been meticulously renovated, painted a deep red with pretty yellow trimming and towering Bangalow palms planted beside a wide deck out the front.

There were enormous glass windows on both sides, which looked out over a leafy pond in the middle of a recently mowed lawn, and beyond that a patch of old-growth forest. A rainbow-coloured hammock hung between two mango trees and several freshly painted rattan chairs sat underneath another.

It was very pretty and Roxy fell in love with it instantly. Gilda was not so convinced.

"I still think it would have been more fun to be down in Byron, near the beach, where all the action is."

"I thought you were here to look into a suspicious death,

not hang out with the tourists."

"A girl's allowed to have fun, isn't she?"

"Namaste, welcome," came a soft, melodic voice as they stepped through the front door and into the front room-lobby. The room featured a small, bubbling water fountain below a large framed photo of an elderly Indian man with a ragged white beard and flowing orange garbs.

A woman in her sixties was standing behind the front desk, round glasses propped on her nose, her hair grey and soft around her face. She, too, was wearing a flowing outfit, all white with an orange trim, and she had a bright red bindi smudge between her eyes. She was clearly not Indian, although her whole getup and the way she held her hands, prayer like in front of her face, suggested she wished she was.

"Welcome to my humble haven. I'm Bindi Harbor. You must be Roxy Parker and friend?"

Roxy had e-mailed to make sure there was a vacancy, and she nodded as she handed over her credit card.

"The stars must be in alignment for you, young lady," Bindi said, taking the card from her. "We had two cancellations just this morning, otherwise we would have been full."

"Oh lucky, lucky us," said Gilda, who clearly still had her heart set on the beach.

Roxy scowled at her friend then thanked Bindi. "You've got such a beautiful place here."

The older woman smiled. "We built it with love and blessings and we wish that for your stay. This is an eco-resort and a native animal sanctuary, so you may come across koalas if you take a walk through the forest, and you will certainly see plenty of birds and wallabies at dusk."

Roxy thought of the local Greens Party councillors. They should make this their headquarters.

Bindi turned and pulled two keys from a rack behind her, then waved a hand in the air motioning them to follow. She led the way up the wooden staircase to the next level then handed one key to Roxy and the other to Gilda.

"Rooms 4 and 5. Please help yourself. Breakfast is served at 7:00 a.m., just after yoga with Chaitanya by the pond. Chaitanya is also holding a meditation session this evening at five, should you want to join us for an hour of mindfulness in the living room, downstairs, to your right. Just wear something comfy. If you can." She glanced at Roxy's skinny jeans then down to Gilda's high-heeled boots. "No shoes, please."

"Thank you," Roxy said, stifling a smile as the woman swept back down the stairs.

"Mindfulness?" Gilda hissed. "I'll give her a piece of my mind. I haven't got time for that kind of nonsense."

"Don't be so harsh, Gilda. The woman means well, besides, it might do you some good. Might be just what you need to crack the case wide open."

Gilda snorted. "Good old-fashioned police work is what's going to crack this case open, if indeed there is a case." She snorted again. "Bloody hippies."

Now Roxy laughed. "You sound just like Sam."

"Do I? I'm starting to like the sound of him, then." She plunged her key into the door and opened it. "Okay, you've got five minutes to dump your stuff and freshen up, then let's meet back out here and get going. We can take my car, it's bigger than yours."

"Bigger is better?"

"On those bloody potholes, you bet it is."

"Where are we going?"

"I've got a suspicious death to investigate, remember?"

"And you want me to come with you? I thought I had to stay out of it."

"Well, what else are you going to do until Houghton calls? Meditate?"

Roxy narrowed her eyes. "You're really letting me help you investigate?"

"Nobody said anything about helping. You can just tag

along. For now." She winked then disappeared inside.

Roxy unlocked her own door and swung it wide open. The room was small but had a high ceiling and was brightly decorated. There was a double bed in the centre of the room and a wide window looking out over the pond. A ceramic Buddha sat on the windowsill and above the window, colourful Tibetan flags hung down.

Roxy headed for the bathroom, which was small but adequate, and stared at her reflection, a little startled. She'd forgotten to put makeup on that morning, and her overgrown black bob looked more like a beehive. She quickly ran a comb through her hair, straightening it down, then whisked her glasses off, gave them a rinse and placed them back on top of her head. Next she applied some tinted moisturiser and lipstick from her handbag and repaired the damage before inspecting herself again. Okay, that was better; the old Roxy had returned.

"So where first?" Roxy asked as Gilda keyed in the quickest route to Tweed Heads on her vehicle's GPS.

"Copshop first. I want to get hold of Sunny's file and take a really good look at it." She chuckled as she started the car. "Quick is going to be overjoyed to see my ugly mug again."

In fact Detective Quick was nowhere to be seen when the two women were buzzed into the Command headquarters, an old weatherboard building situated behind a fence at one end of the Tweed Heads township.

"So where is he?" asked Gilda, speaking directly to the duty officer seated at the front desk.

"He's gone to the airport to collect the detective from Sydney."

"Rightio. Did he tell you I was to be given free access to the Sunny Forrest case?"

"No, but Chief Commissioner Houlihan just sent authorisation through."

"Great. If you'll point me in the direction of the file, I'll get onto it."

The officer looked at Roxy. "And who might this be?"

"This is Roxanne Parker, she's with me." Gilda's tone indicated this was nonnegotiable and in case he was thinking of questioning it further, clapped her hands together and said, "Come on then, I haven't got all day."

Five minutes later, the two women were seated in plastic bucket seats under harsh fluorescent lighting, peering into a relatively empty cardboard box that had been dumped on the Formica tabletop. It was marked Forrest. S.A.

"This is it?" Roxy said. "This is all they've got?"

"Looks like it." Gilda said, pulling out a folder. She spent a few minutes reading through various pieces of paper including a police statement and a crime scene analysis report, none of which shed any more light on the subject.

The witness statement, however, was more enlightening. After studying it briefly, Gilda handed it across to Roxy saying, "FYI."

Roxy took the page and began to read it to herself. It had been handwritten with shaky, old-fashioned loops, and signed by a Mr. John Holloway as well as two police witnesses, one of whom was R.J. Quick.

"Holloway must have been the one who discovered Sunny's body," Roxy said. "He describes finding her lying in the Wilson's River at around dusk on the same day they believed she died."

Roxy proceeded to read the statement out loud now to Gilda.

"It had been raining heavily all day and I would not have gone that way except that my dog kept barking and I wondered whether some of the cattle had strayed. I was shocked to find the girl. She had her face half under the water and she was not moving. She had one arm twisted up behind her back, and she looked fully clothed. I went to get her out and then realised she had passed, so thought I should best leave her be. I walked straight back home and got Deidre, my wife, to call 000. I did not see the body again. I did not know who it was at the time."

Beneath the statement, in red ink, someone had added the words, "*No suspicious circumstances.*"

A typed copy of the statement had been stapled to the back of the original and also signed.

"You ready for this?"

Roxy looked up to find Gilda holding a plastic sheet with what looked like an A4-size print inside. It was a photo taken at the scene. Roxy nodded and Gilda handed it across. Bracing herself, she looked down and saw what must have been Sunny's lifeless body, lying as the witness had described, face down in the creek, one arm twisted up. She was dressed in a long flowing skirt, pinkish brown jumper and knee-high boots. There were twigs and leaves all over her, through her clothes and entwined in her knotted blonde hair. You could not see her face and she looked just like a Barbie doll that had been left out in the rain, weathered and broken. It was a miserable image and Roxy handed it straight back.

"I have more," Gilda said, "but you don't need to see these. Her face is pretty swollen, there's lots of bruising and discoloration. Looks like her nose has been broken and she's missing some teeth."

Roxy shuddered. "Done after she drowned, I hope."

Gilda plunged her hand back into the box. She pulled out the only remaining item, a copy of the *Valley Times* with a yellow Post-it note stuck to one page. Spreading that page open on the desk, they both leaned in to take a closer look. The free local newspaper had scored a scoop of sorts, and the item featured a grainy photo of the same creek bed where Sunny's body had been found. Thankfully Sunny had been removed, but you could still make out the indentation on one side of the bank where she had lain, and there were two paddlepop sticks with numbers on them, which were clearly used to identify forensic evidence. Beside the photo was a small snippet that bore no byline.

The body of a young woman was found washed up in a creek on rock star Jed Moody's property last Wednesday. The woman, a twenty-

one-year-old local from Byron Shire, is believed to have drowned while attempting to cross the swollen Wilson's River during the recent downpour. Jed Moody, of the legendary rock band the Moody Roos, was not available for comment; however, Local Area Commander Rodney Quick said, 'This is a timely reminder to everyone to avoid crossing creeks and causeways during heavy rain.' The woman's family has been notified and have requested privacy at this time."

Roxy reread Quick's quote and stared up at Gilda. "That's all he had to say?"

She nodded then glanced back into the box. "And that's all there is on the case. The rest of the file is empty."

"Nothing about her missing Moody Ring? The Moody Roos posters and stuff being ripped up back at her cottage?"

"Quick probably never got that far or didn't think it was relevant."

"So one witness statement, a couple of dreadful photos and a small newspaper article. That's all her death amounted to? So what do we … I mean *you* do now?"

Gilda stood up. "I'd like to have a chat with this witness," she glanced back at the sheet. "John Holloway."

Roxy smiled. "Luckily for you then, I know just where to find him."

CHAPTER 22

Annika Moody was no longer holding court on her spacious veranda when Gilda and Roxy returned to the house but Houghton was there. He informed them that farmer John Holloway and his wife, Deidre, had departed hours earlier.

"Probably milking cows or something," he said, dismissively, as he flicked through various pages on a silver laptop he'd set up on the cluttered table. Roxy caught sight of a webpage for the Sydney Entertainment Centre before he whooshed it away.

"You're aiming high," she said, nodding her head towards the screen and he chuckled, almost nervously.

Gilda ignored this and said, "I doubt anyone would be milking cows this late in the day. I'm no expert, but I'm pretty sure milking is a morning enterprise." She glanced across the lawn. "Which is the quickest way to his place?"

"How would I know?"

"Who're you looking for?" Alistair Avery had just stepped out onto the veranda and was looking a lot more relaxed than he had two days earlier. His white cotton shirt was opened to reveal a small beer belly, and he was nursing

151

what looked like a glass of iced tea, although it could have been a large whisky for all Roxy knew.

She introduced him to Gilda, adding, "Gilda's a detective from Sydney, she's looking into Sunny Forrest's death."

Both men appeared to recoil at those words, and Houghton said, "You never told me you were a copper."

Gilda smiled. "Yep, guilty as charged."

"But why Sunny?" asked Al. "Isn't Jed the priority here?"

"Absolutely he is. Another more senior detective, Inspector Brent Wiles, has been assigned that case. I'm just here to look over Sunny Forrest's death and make sure that was all in order."

"She drowned in the creek, didn't she?"

"That's what I'm here to find out. You're Alistair Avery?" He nodded warily. "Were you around at that time?"

"Me?" Al looked stunned. He began doing up his shirt buttons. "Yeah, but it had nothing to do with me. I mean I barely knew the chick."

"But you did know her?"

"Yeah, blonde bimbo, had a hard-on for Jed."

"That 'blonde bimbo' was somebody's sister," Roxy snapped, and he glanced at her then back to Gilda.

"Oh, I see what this is about. Sam's tantrums have finally worked. Forced you to reopen the case, has he?"

Gilda stepped towards him. "Is there any reason why we shouldn't, Mr. Avery?"

He shook his head quickly and reached for a cigarette packet that was sitting on a wicker table. "I don't give a shit about that," he said, plucking out a cigarette. "Like I said, I barely knew her, nothing to do with me."

"Good, then you won't mind telling me how to get to farmer John's place. The neighbour."

"I can tell you how to get there."

They all swung around to find Annika standing at the French doors. She looked like she'd just crawled out of bed, her bun now tufted up to one side, her kaftan heavily wrinkled.

She stepped out and towards Alistair who was just handing her his lit cigarette. She took it without so much as a thank you and dragged on it for a few seconds, before throwing herself on the lounge beside Houghton.

"Give us a foot rub, darling. Feet are *killing* me."

He promptly obliged, pushing his laptop aside and focusing on her right foot. Roxy noticed a tattoo on her ankle with two letters that looked like JM in cursive script.

"So, you're a detective?" she said, and before Roxy could do the introductions, added, "My husband has just died, and all the police are worried about is a case that's what, two years old? Three?" She dragged on the cigarette again.

"It was less than eighteen months ago, actually, and the police are very interested in your husband's death, Mrs. Moody. But unfortunately, that's not my case. I'm Detective Gilda Maltin. Chief Detective Brent Wiles is running your husband's investigation and will no doubt be calling in on you this afternoon when he arrives. I'm just trying to get directions to the Holloways' property."

Annika exhaled a long plume of smoke and looked for a moment like she wasn't going to oblige. Finally she said, "Go back to the main road, turn right, next driveway on your right. It's about a kilometre along from us. Or you could take the shortcut across our property, everyone else does. You go past Jed's studio, through the trees and across to the creek. Just follow the sound of bubbling water. I hear it's quite blissful out there. Quite *romantic*."

There was an edge in her tone, something accusatory, too, and Roxy noticed Houghton and Alistair share a glance.

"Thanks, but I think we'll take the main road," Gilda said.

Annika's eyes narrowed. "You obviously think Sunny's death is linked to my husband's?"

"I think nothing, Mrs. Moody, until I get all the facts. Now, if you'll excuse me."

Gilda nodded at Roxy and they were about to make their exit when Annika pointed her cigarette in Roxy's direction.

"I'm sorry if I'm a little dim these days, darling—you can blame Jed for that—but what's all this got to do with our ghostwriter?"

Roxy felt a blush rise in her cheeks and stumbled for an answer. "Well, I…"

"Roxy is assisting with my enquiries," Gilda interjected. "That's all I can say at this point in time. I trust you understand?"

She directed this at both Annika and at Houghton who had stopped massaging Annika's foot and was now staring suspiciously at Roxy.

Annika waved her cigarette in the air dismissively, as though she really didn't care one way or the other, so they took this as their cue and left.

"She's a piece of work," Gilda said as she steered the vehicle back down the Moodys' driveway and towards the Holloways'. "Did you see the way the guys fawned over her? I'd be disgusted if I wasn't so bloody envious. How does she do it?"

Roxy laughed. "I think having a famous husband, and now a fabulous inheritance, might have something to do with it. I should have been fawning, too, now I think about it. I need her approval to write this book. You probably shouldn't have been quite so dismissive."

"Oh, she'll approve it," Gilda said, slapping Roxy on one leg. "How else is she going to stay relevant now Rock Star Hubby is kaput? She probably needs that book more than any of you."

Roxy hoped she was right. Now that Gilda was hanging around to look into Sunny's death, she felt like staying, too. And the book was as good an excuse as any.

"Did you catch that strange comment, about the shortcut being 'romantic'?" Gilda said and Roxy's eyes widened.

"Yes, I did. Wonder what that was about."

Gilda clicked her tongue. "I wonder, indeed!"

The Holloway driveway could not be in greater contrast to the Moodys', and the cattle grid was about the only thing they had in common. Their front fence was rundown, the wooden fence posts looking dilapidated and so termite-riddled, it was a wonder they held the old rusty wiring in place. There was a rickety gate open, just before the cattle grille, but it looked as though it hadn't been shut in decades and was leaning so far to the right, it was likely to never shut again. The driveway itself went for just a few hundred meters before it reached the main house, but it was all loose gravel and heavily grooved in places where the rain had wreaked havoc, causing Gilda to drive so slowly in parts, they would have made faster progress on foot.

Unlike the Moodys' property, this one was considerably more barren, with far fewer trees, and dozens of cattle as far as the eye could see. Roxy also spotted several old sheds that looked like they too would topple over if you sneezed on them. There was nothing of the Yuppie-style "hobby farm" about the place. It was definitely a working property, although not a prosperous one judging by the dilapidation.

The main house, too, was aching for some TLC. Built far too close to the main road and painted white too many moons ago, the house looked unwashed and unloved, and the tinned roof was so rusty Roxy wondered how many leaks they suffered during the wet season.

There was not a tree anywhere near the house, but a pretty garden had been created just below the front steps of the veranda, and bright pink and lilac hydrangeas helped pep things up a little, as did the lacey curtains that were now billowing from the open windows.

"Wouldn't want any privacy," Gilda said as she manoeuvred the car to a stop at the side of the house between a rusty red tractor and a large cement tank.

"Wouldn't want any shade either," Roxy added, staring across to the Moody property, which looked like a lush oasis by comparison.

Deidre Holloway was already standing on her veranda

when they approached, wiping her hands on her faded apron, her eyes squinting out through round silver spectacles as though trying to work out if she knew them.

Gilda stepped forward, one hand waving. "Hello, Mrs. Holloway?" The woman nodded, her eyes widening a little. "I'm Detective Gilda Maltin, and this is my associate Roxy Parker."

The older woman's eyes settled on Roxy. "Yes, I remember you. You're a friend of the Moodys." Close enough, Roxy thought, nodding her head. "Good oh, in ye come then."

Deidre turned and disappeared into the old house while the two friends swapped looks of surprise before following her. They found her in the first room, a dusty living area cluttered with so much furniture, they could barely squeeze in.

"Take a seat, girls. I'll fetch us some tea."

Before they had a chance to reply, she was off again, out the door and disappearing up the creaky hallway. They did as instructed and sat down in two patchy arm chairs that had been placed directly in front of a small television set in the centre of the room. There were dozens of framed family photos, wedged on side tables, along the mantelpiece and even on the coffee table. Some showed naked babies basking on a lawn, others were clearly official school photos and revealed children of all ages and dental stages, smiling, smirking and looking beyond embarrassed. A particular shot caught Roxy's eyes—the face of a beautiful young woman with long, golden locks and freckly tanned skin. Her eyes were glowing green and she had a stunning smile. She seemed to epitomise healthy country living, and she reminded Roxy of Sunny, although a little more country, a little less rock 'n' roll. Behind her and just out of focus, was a young man wearing a large cowboy hat and wraparound sunglasses. He wasn't smiling.

"She never even asked us what we wanted," Gilda whispered.

"Probably just happy to get visitors out here in the sticks," Roxy whispered back.

"Ah, here we are then," said Deidre reentering the room. She had a tin tray with a china teapot, three matching cups, a jug of milk and a sugar pot and she placed it on the coffee table, toppling a photo frame over as she did so. "I'll just fetch the tea cake."

"Really, you mustn't go to any bother," Gilda said, picking the frame up, but Deidre looked appalled.

"Can't have our tea without cake, love." Then she disappeared again.

A few minutes later, the tea was poured and the apple teacake dished out. Gilda said, "We really appreciate your time, Mrs. Holloway."

"Deidre, please. Call me Deidre."

"Of course, Deidre." Gilda smiled warmly. "You've got a lovely house here."

The older woman looked around at her cluttered furnishings and numerous photographs, then said, "Well, we're not millionaire pop stars, but we do our best."

Roxy sensed a little bitterness in her tone but her expression remained light and friendly.

Gilda said, "I'll try not to take up much of your time. We were actually hoping to speak with your husband. John, is it?" Deidre nodded. "I actually wanted to talk to him about Sunny Forrest's death, in January last year."

Deidre's cup rattled. "Oh, dear. I thought you were here about Mr. Moody."

"A separate detective will be speaking to you about that."

"You were at the Moody's place that night?" Roxy said, knowing she should be butting out but unable to help herself. Deidre looked at her and her eyes narrowed.

"Yes, dear, as were you, I believe."

Roxy nodded. "Were you there when Jed—"

"Goodness me, no!" Deidre said, cutting her off, a spindly hand reaching up to her neck. "Thank goodness we had left by then. Oh dear, that would have been most upsetting, most upsetting indeed." She glanced at Gilda. "Not our style of music, of course. But well, they keep inviting us and one can't be rude. They are the neighbours, after all. Even if they are a little noisy."

"You can hear the studio from here?"

"Not so much the studio, my dear. More the parties they keep having, and the crowds that keep coming." She placed her cup down and folded her hands in her lap. "But that's neither here nor there. What is it you want to know about that poor girl? Sunny, was it?"

Gilda nodded. "Your husband found her body."

"Yes, it was quite a shock. He came running in, white as a ghost, told me to call the ambulance, goodness knows why, the poor thing was long gone. Still, you've got to give it a go, haven't you? You've got to have hope."

"Yes, of course. Is your husband around? Can we talk to him?"

She looked scandalised again. "He's working the land, my dear. Best not to disturb him."

"When does he get back in?"

Deidre squinted across at the clock on the mantelpiece. "Usually comes in for his tea around five-ish, but, well, we spent some of the morning over at the Moody place, making sure Annika was all right. So he may want to make up for lost time. May not get back until six, I'd say, in time for his tea."

Gilda glanced at her watch. It was 4:45 p.m. She stood up and handed across her business card. "If you could ask your husband to call me, on that mobile number, that would be very helpful."

"Yes, dear."

Gilda smiled. "Before we go, do you mind if we walk the track between your place and where Sunny's body was found? I'm keen to understand the terrain. I know Annika is fine with it."

Deidre hesitated. "Well … it might be better if you wait until John comes back, I think."

"Ah but you said he'd be ages." Gilda tapped her watch. "We're on a bit of a tight schedule. You don't mind, do you?"

The older woman looked like she did mind, very much, but couldn't quite bring herself to say it. She was "old school", had been brought up to be polite, so simply smiled stiffly and led them out of the living room, down the narrow hallway to the small kitchen at the back. She creaked open the back door and waved them out.

"You follow the path to the east end of the fence line, just over there, beyond John's shed. There's a small gate, was put in years ago when the old neighbours were there."

"The Moodys haven't been here long?"

Her eyes clouded over. "No, the Thomas family used to live there, back when it was still a working dairy. They were good people, the Thomases. Quiet folk. Honest, too. You always knew where you stood with them." She gave her head a little shake. "Anyway, go through the gate and you'll find yourself at the back of the Moody property, the creek is a bit of a trek from there. And you'll struggle in those lovely city shoes." She was glancing down at Gilda's boots.

These boots seemed to be having quite an effect on this country crowd, Gilda thought, and said, "I'm sure I'll be fine."

Roxy had seen Gilda chase down criminals in much higher stilettos and didn't doubt it for a moment.

"What was your husband doing, walking that way that night?" Gilda asked and Deidre flashed her a frown.

"Checking the fence line, of course. He was worried some of the cattle had got through."

"Does that happen often?"

"Often enough."

"Can I ask you something?" Roxy said, and Deidre turned with wary eyes upon her. "How do you feel about the idea of the Moody property becoming a music festival site?"

Deidre seemed to fluster then, padding down her apron and stepping back into the kitchen. "Oh, you'd have to speak to my husband about that. I don't get involved in that kind of thing."

Then she swiftly shut the door on them both.

CHAPTER 23

As they followed the patchy grass towards the boundary fence line, Roxy snorted. "She doesn't get involved? Yeah, right! You can tell Deidre hates the whole idea, and why wouldn't she? If she thinks Moody Views is noisy now, just wait until they start running music festivals every month."

"Yes, but what's that got to do with Sunny Forrest?" When Roxy didn't answer, Gilda stopped and turned back to her. "You're thinking of Jed now, aren't you? You're thinking the Holloway couple have a pretty good motive to stop the man in his tracks."

Roxy shrugged and kept walking.

Gilda caught up to her. "You do know we're looking into *Sunny's* death, not Jed's, right? I did make that bit crystal clear?"

"Yes, yes, but it doesn't mean we can't make a few enquiries. I mean, they could be related. Did you get a look at that shed we passed? Plenty of electrical gear in there. The old farmer must be pretty handy in that department. They're not like city folk. Don't call the local electrician when things stuff up."

Gilda thought about this. "Okay, just say you're right and

the old couple did somehow rig Jed's amp, to try to put an end to the festivals; you do realise that Annika is still alive and kicking. She may still go ahead with it. You don't know whose idea the festivals were in the first place. In any case, how does it connect with Sunny's death? How would killing Sunny be of any benefit to Ma and Pa Kettle back there?"

Roxy shrugged again. She couldn't answer that. She knew she was grasping at straws, but she could definitely sense some tension in Deidre Holloway. She didn't say much, but what she did say spoke of envy and regret. Deidre clearly missed her old neighbours, and why wouldn't she? Judging from the family portraits, she came from good old-fashioned farming stock. The "pop star" blow-ins must have been quite a culture shock.

Did Deidre and her husband somehow instigate both deaths in an effort to scare away the nouveau riche neighbours? Roxy gave her brain a shake. It was a preposterous idea, she decided. She was no longer grasping at straws, but rather, she had her head stuck in the entire haystack.

"Sorry, Rox, but if Sunny's death turns out to be murder, I just can't see that old couple doing it. Makes no sense. Oh look, there's the gate."

Gilda strode forward and cranked it open then Roxy followed her through, securing the gate firmly behind her just as a hand-painted sign on the fence instructed her to. From the fence line, the forest had been allowed to flourish and it was hard to see beyond the trees, although they could hear the sound of bubbling water not far off. It didn't take long to reach the creek, which clearly ran close to the boundary line, just on the Moodys' side at the edge of the rainforest.

No sooner had they spotted the creek than a makeshift memorial site came into view. The women stopped and surveyed the surroundings silently for a few minutes, taking in the small wooden cross that had been wedged into the side of the bank and the faded clusters of plastic flowers that were wrapped around it, a few fresh wildflowers strewn nearby. It looked a little tacky and it surprised Roxy. It didn't seem like Sam's style, but then what would she know? Losing a sibling could probably turn even the toughest cookie into a crumbling mess.

The creek, now more a benign trickle than a raging river, looked as harmless as a puddle. Neither woman could imagine anyone drowning in it, let alone a local girl familiar with the lay of the land.

"Must have had a lot of rain that day to turn it so deadly," Gilda said.

Roxy nodded. "They do get more than their share of rain during the wet season apparently—hence the name *rain*forest. When did she die exactly?"

"Last January."

"That's the wet season, right?"

Gilda cocked her head to one side. "What am I? A weather girl? Wouldn't have a clue."

They looked around. Apart from the cross, there were no other signs of life, although on the other side of the creek, they could make out two separate paths leading in the direction of the Moody property. One was well worn and disappeared into the forest. That had to be the shortcut Annika was referring to. The other path was more overgrown and appeared to lead along the creek for a bit before also plunging into the forest. They squinted their eyes and could just make out what looked like a hut in the darkening shadows of a cluster of lillypillies. If they'd come any later, they would not have noticed it.

"Shall we take a closer look?" Gilda said, carefully stepping on dry rocks across the creek, making sure her boots did not get drenched.

Roxy followed a little less cautiously—her boots were old and waterproof and she was longing for an excuse to replace them. The two women proceeded to pluck their way past overhanging branches and through spindly cobwebs that had formed across the path.

"God, I hate nature," Gilda groaned just before an enormous grasshopper dropped down on her arm. She brushed it away with a shriek.

Roxy laughed. "You don't flinch at biker gangs, but you squeal at a bug?"

Gilda turned back to sneer at her. "Not all of us have turned into Steve Irwin overnight. I can't believe you're so chilled."

Roxy chewed on her lower lip. She couldn't believe it either. It was so unlike her to be relaxed around Mother Nature. She'd always assumed she was a rusted on city chick. This assignment had left her questioning everything she knew about herself. Was it possible to change this late in life?

"Finally!" Gilda said as they reached the hut, which turned out to be more of a hutch with three sides and a slanting tin roof.

There was a large thatched mat on the floor and several enormous cushions on top. A small wooden crate had been turned on its side and several candles stood, half burned next to an overflowing ceramic ashtray and a kerosene lamp. An empty bottle of red wine sat on the ground beside the crate and a silver goblet had been turned over next to it. Judging from the lack of spider webs covering the entranceway, the place had been recently used.

"Looks like a love nest," Roxy said, and Gilda nodded.

"'Blissful' and 'romantic'. Must be what Annika was referring to. Could be where Sunny and Jed met up, judging from the proximity to the creek." She looked around. "I wonder how far away the Moody house is."

Roxy stepped towards the ashtray and pointed at the cigarette butts. She could just make out the word "Marlborough" on the side of one that was only half smoked.

"Can you remember what brand Jed smoked?" Gilda asked, producing a plastic bag from her jacket pocket.

"Not off hand. But they *all* seem to smoke; must think musos are immune to lung cancer." She watched Gilda dump the contents of the ashtray into the bag and seal it up again. "You really think you're going to find some evidence this late in the game?"

Gilda stared at the bag. "These look recent to me, but it can't hurt to try. Quick clearly didn't bother." She looked around a little longer and then out to the skyline, or what she could see of it through the thick trees. "Listen, it's going to get very dark very fast, so we should make our way back. Farmer John might even be there now, thumping the table for his supper."

Roxy laughed. "Don't knock the old-fashioned way of life, Gilda. He farms the land and she keeps the home fires burning. It clearly works for them."

"Does it? Really?" Gilda looked appalled by the thought. "Thank God I'm not an old-fashioned girl then."

As they made their way back to the Holloway house, they found John Holloway standing by the property gate, clearly waiting for them, a grim look on his face. Holloway was dressed in a rugby jersey and moleskins. He had a large, balding head, and wore the heavily lined face of a man who had worked his whole life under a beating sun, a man who clearly thought sunscreen was for sissies. A large chunk of skin had been cut out of his nose and he had pale purple sunspots all over his face.

"Deidre shouldn't't've let you come this way," he barked as they walked up to greet him. Then he cleared his throat and said a little more gently, "Gets a bit rough is all."

"Oh, it's nothing we can't handle," Gilda said cheerfully, hoping to disarm him.

After he secured the gate behind them, he shook their hands and said, "So you're lookin' into the young lady's drowning then?"

"That's correct. Is there any more light you can shed on that?"

He shook his head firmly and leaned against the fence. "No light to shed. Poor girl risked it and she paid the price."

He spoke in a monotone, his voice low and croaky.

"You firmly believe it was an accident?"

"'Course I do. Everybody does."

"Her brother, Sam, doesn't," Roxy said defiantly, and he darted his watery grey eyes towards her.

He went to say something, stopped, swallowed hard as though trying to choke back tears, then tried again. "We lost a child once. Long time ago."

"Oh, I'm so—"

He brushed her off, impatient with her sympathy. "It's hard to let go. When it happens. It's hard..." He choked again then coughed away the emotion. "I was the first to find that poor lass, Sunny. There was nothin' suspicious there. She drowned in the creek and that's all there is to it. The family's just got to accept the verdict and move on." His tone had turned a little snarly again and, again, he seemed to check himself and soften his voice before adding, "Now if you'll excuse me, I'd better get back. Deidre's got lamb chops waitin'."

He nodded once then turned and walked shakily back towards the house while Roxy stood watching him, chewing madly on her bottom lip.

"Come on then," said Gilda, making her own way back. "Let's get out of here."

Roxy scowled. She felt bad for the old couple, really she did, but she also had a feeling they had more to share about Sunny and the day she was discovered. "They're hiding something," she said, catching up to Gilda. "At least I'm sure the old guy is. What a cranky bugger! Aren't you going to question him further? Surely he can tell you more than that."

Gilda shook her head. "You may well be right, Roxy, but not now, not tonight. If I know one thing about country folk, it's never come between a hungry farmer and his dinner, especially when the missus is serving lamb chops." She smiled. "Come on, there's something else I want to look into."

"Oh?"

Gilda stopped. "Remember that newspaper article we found in the files? The one with the picture of the creek bed." Roxy nodded. "I don't think that was an official crime scene photograph. At least the image wasn't amongst the photos we found in the file."

"You think someone else took it?"

"Looks to me like someone else was at the scene of the crime, and not long afterwards, either. They might have taken the photo from a distance then sold it on to the newspaper. But who would do such a thing?"

Roxy smiled again. "I know just the sleazebag for the job."

CHAPTER 24

Macker Maroney was not at his usual post, sucking on cigarettes and hassling innocent patrons, when the two women pulled up in front of the Goddess Café. However, Govinda was back at the front door and appeared to be closing up. There were two young children at her heels this time, and neither looked anything like the one Roxy had seen just days earlier. One was definitely a girl, in hot pink leggings and a rumpled white dress, sitting on the ground, playing with a Bratz doll. She had to be about five or six. Beside her was a smaller child, short black hair; muddy face; eyes wide and brown. That child was of indiscriminate gender but probably around the age of four.

"He's probably trying to persuade some poor Swedish backpacker to get her kit off for him," Govinda said when they asked after the photographer. She sighed. "I don't mean to speak ill, but he's got some *serious* karma coming his way, that dude."

"Does he live around here?" Gilda asked as Govinda slammed the front door shut and began to secure the padlock.

"Mama, I want lollie. Maaaama!" screeched the smallest,

dark-haired child, and Govinda sighed. She looked weary today, less bubbly than before. Perhaps Jed's death was taking a toll on all of them.

"Oh Destiny, I just locked up."

"Mama!!"

She sighed again, undid the padlock and pulled the girl up onto her hip before walking back inside the shop. The two women followed her in and watched as she reached for a bag of mixed lollies; opened them and handed them to Destiny.

"Heavenly Rose, you want some, too?" she called out and when the older child did not answer, she grabbed an extra bag anyway.

"I think he has digs at the old M.O. on Cooleys Shoot," Govinda told them as she made her way back outside.

"M.O?"

"Multiple Occupancy. It's a big property a whole bunch of folk share, a few kilometres back towards the highway. Big stone statue of Buddha out the front, you can't miss it. Here, Heavenly." She dumped the lollies in her daughter's lap and proceeded to lock up again, the other child still clinging to her hip, a red snake dangling from her lips.

"What do you know about Sunny Forrest's death?" Gilda asked and Govinda turned around with a look of surprise.

"Sunny?"

"Yes."

"You a copper?"

"Yes, a detective from Sydney."

"Oh, right." She said nothing more as she placed Destiny back on the ground next to her sister then stepped around them to check the windows, giving the shutters a good rattle to ensure they were locked in place. "Sunny Forrest," she said, turning back, her eyes a little watery. "The silly little kitten." She sniffed, rubbed a hand across her nose, causing her bangles to sing and dance. "Um, I don't know much, why, what do you want to know?"

"We just want to know the local goss," Gilda said.

A tiny frown formed between her eyes. "Sorry, not really

into gossip."

Roxy tried not to scoff. "Oh, come on, Govinda, you must have heard something. You told me the other day that everyone knows everyone's business around here."

Govinda hesitated again before finally saying, "Well, I know it hurt poor Sambo pretty badly. I mean, I feel dreadful for him, I really do. Just because his sister plays with fire, doesn't mean he should get burnt."

"Fire? What do you mean by that?" asked Gilda.

Govinda shook her dreadlocks from side to side. "I'm just saying karma can be a pretty nasty bitch when she sets her mind to it, doesn't matter who you are, how sweet." She jangled her way back to the front of the shop and scooped both children up, one on each hip.

"Are you saying you think Sunny was killed because she had an affair with Jed Moody?"

Govinda looked horrified at the suggestion. "What are you on?! I never said such a crazy ass thing. Nah, everyone knows the poor petal drowned. It was an accident!"

"But you did know about Sunny's affair with Jed?"

"Only after Sam came back and was all hysterical about it, ranting to anyone who'd listen that Jed had been messing with his sister and must have killed her and blahde blahde blah. Just wouldn't let it go, and now the entire village knows what went on." She smiled sadly. "Foolish man."

"That must have been hard for Annika to hear."

Govinda shrugged. "Wouldn't be the first time."

"Oh? Who else has Jed been playing up with?"

She shook her head firmly again and gave Gilda a sly smile. "Like I said, I'm no gossip. I hear stuff, can't help it at this place, it's like a magnet for gossips." She crinkled her nose up. "But I never pass it on. That's not my energy, man. Not what I'm into."

"Bad karma?" Gilda suggested, smirking.

Before Govinda could reply, the youngest child began yanking at her mum's top screaming, "Mama, milkie! Milkie!"

Govinda sighed heavily and began to undo the top buttons of her blouse. That wiped the smirk off Gilda's face.

"Right, well, we might leave you to it then," she announced, quickly turning away.

Roxy suppressed a giggle as she followed the detective back to the car. "Got a problem with breastfeeding in public?"

"No, I do not. It's breastfeeding in front of me that freaks me out. And isn't that kid, like, *four*?"

They both turned to glance back at Govinda who was now walking towards the back of the shop and along a pathway that led to a weatherboard house half hidden in the shadows of large gums. Roxy had not noticed it before. The youngest child was still at her breast, the other clinging onto the other hip, her Bratz doll in hand, as though she were incapable of walking.

"How does she manage that?" Gilda said, both appalled and in awe, and Roxy laughed.

"I'm telling you the woman is the Queen of Multi-tasking." As she opened the car door, Roxy felt her stomach growl. "Pity she closed the shop so early today. I'm starving. Shall we go get some dinner somewhere? I doubt Bindi has anything to offer."

Gilda nodded, pulling out her mobile phone. "Let's head back to Tweed and see if we can't talk a certain blue-eyed copper into joining us."

****

From a distance, a man was watching. He'd been watching them closely for some time, and he didn't like what he was seeing. Not one bit.

What were those two snoops up to? He wondered.

What did they hope to find?

And how could he stop them without it turning violent this time?

CHAPTER 25

Detective Inspector Brent Wiles had not changed a jot since the last time Roxy had seen him. He was still sharply dressed; his Italian suit out of place in the laid-back Tweed Heads pub, and his goatee was so perfectly clipped, from a distance it looked like it had been sketched on with a black marker pen. When he stepped through the front door, various faces turned to stare at him, but he seemed not to notice, simply glanced around nonchalantly, then, spotting Gilda and Roxy at a side table, strode across as though he had all the time in the world. He was a cool customer, Roxy decided, and it must be a great trick when dealing with nervous criminals.

It was now Friday night and the hotel was bursting with noisy patrons, mostly blue-collar boozers and shaggy old guys. The jukebox was belting out a Midnight Oil track, and several patrons were whooping at a football match being broadcast on one of the three television sets buzzing above their heads. It felt a million miles from the Byron hinterland and Gilda couldn't have been happier.

"Much better this way," she told Roxy. "No locals around to eavesdrop, and too noisy even if they were."

The two women had chosen a table just behind the billiard table, and were already working their way through their second glass of red wine (as cheap and rough as the pub) when Wiles walked up.

"Gilda Maltin, you didn't waste any time getting up here," he said, his whole face lighting up as he took both her hands in his.

"You remember Roxy Parker?" Gilda said. "From the—"

"Gordon Reilly case, yes I do." He reached across the table and shook Roxy's hand. "You get around."

Gilda laughed. "That's our Roxy, always in the right place at the wrong time."

"I'll just grab a beer. Would you ladies like another wine?"

They shuddered in unison. "It's like paint stripper," said Gilda. "We'd better ease up or we'll pay for it tomorrow."

After Wiles had fetched himself a schooner of lager and the three of them had placed orders behind the counter they got down to business.

Wiles said, "You decided to dig deeper into that drowning death then?" Gilda nodded and he asked, "First impressions?"

"There's something a little off but I can't quite get my head around it yet." Now he nodded. "I haven't got long, though, so I have to get cracking tomorrow. How about you? How long do you think the Jed Moody case will take?"

He glanced across to Roxy and back to her. "You know I can't say much in front of a civilian, Gilda, especially a civilian who also happens to be a witness."

"Of course, Brent. I wasn't—"

He held a large palm up, his expression softened. "I just have to talk in generals, that's all. I'm getting Vonnie from FSG up first thing in the morning."

"The big guns, then." She turned to Roxy. "Vonnie works for the Forensic Services Group. They're the state specialists in fingerprints, DNA, that kind of thing. Vonnie's one of the best."

"She is *the* best," Wiles said before scowling. "They made a mess of it. Moved the body too damn fast—didn't even get a photographer in, would you believe? And at least one of the attending officers put his paw prints everywhere. There's no clear time line for the DNA evidence. It's a shambles." He smiled, unperturbed. "But we'll sort it out. You able to lend a hand or will the other matter hold you up?"

"I'd love to help you. It depends what I find and whether Houlihan wants me to pursue it. If not, I'll see if I can hang around, help out."

He paused as the waitress brought their meals over then said, "That'd be good. Quick's not a bad bloke, but I'm not sure how useful he's going to be. Before you called I was trying to organise a meal with him, wanted to get up to speed, but he wasn't having it. Said something about needing a surf, would you believe." Wiles's frown suggested what he thought of that. "It's the beginning of a murder investigation. You'd expect a little more dedication at this point."

"Quick by name, not be nature?" Gilda said, and Wiles shrugged without replying.

Roxy felt heartened by all of this. Wiles was being diplomatic, but it was clear he hadn't the least amount of faith in the local commander, and it justified Sam's so-called "hysteria". Despite what the likes of Govinda and Houghton claimed, Sam had been right all along. Whether Sunny had drowned accidentally or not, it was obvious that the investigating officer had not done his job. He was lazy and disengaged, Wiles had practically said as much.

No wonder Sam was such an angry man.

Roxy debated then whether to tell Wiles of the close relationship she had witnessed between Annika Moody and Detective Quick but decided to hold her tongue for now. Perhaps she had over read the situation; perhaps Quick was just a touchy-feely kind of guy, a rare sympathetic cop. In any case, she could tell that Wiles was not much of a gossip, probably preferred to work with cold, hard facts, so she kept that to herself and thrust a hot chip into her mouth instead.

Later, though, as she perched on the windowsill in Gilda's room back at Bindi's, watching her friend prepare for bed, she realised that most of the night had been free of "shop talk" and she hadn't learnt any more than she already knew. She blamed herself for that.

"I should have opted out. Should have left you guys to mull over the details in privacy."

Gilda disagreed. "It's still early days. Wiles only just got here, and you heard the man. Quick's been about as useful as a dinghy in the desert. He wouldn't have that much more to tell me." She placed some moisturiser in her palms. "Once they get Vonnie up and start sifting through the evidence, they'll know more. I'll have a chat with him on my own then." She massaged the cream up and down her arms. "You know, the public always thinks murder investigations happen at lightning speed, and I guess on TV they do. But most of the time they take weeks and weeks to unfold, sometimes months and years, especially if you're dealing with DNA. Wiles hasn't even interviewed the witnesses yet."

"I'm on the list for tomorrow, remember? He wants to see me at the Moody house first thing."

"You okay with that?"

"It's not like I haven't been grilled by wily Wiles before."

"Oh, he's all right. A fair cop, I reckon. Bloody great spunk, too. Pity he's married. All the good ones are." She sighed dreamily. "How about those eyes of his?"

Roxy laughed. Like Quick, Wiles had startling blue eyes, another attribute that likely helped when grilling nervous suspects.

"Just tell him everything you told me," Gilda continued, "about the conversation you overheard inside the house with Annika and that mystery man. Oh, and the animosity that Alistair Avery seems to have with the guy."

"Isn't that just gossip? I get the feeling he's not much of a gossip queen."

"He's not, but that's for him to decide. Give him all the

info you have and let the cards fall where they may."

"And what if they fall at the feet of poor Sam?"

Gilda stopped massaging her arms and stared hard at her friend. "Then poor Sam will deserve everything he gets."

"I know, but—"

"Listen, Roxy, this is really important. Sam may have worked his charm on you, but Wiles is a professional and will see through all of that. If he did this thing, if he zapped the life out of one of Australia's biggest rock stars to avenge his sister's death, then Wiles will hold him accountable. And so he should. Cute dog or no cute dog."

Roxy shrugged, pretended like she didn't care, when the very thought of Sam Forrest being taken into custody again made her insides do an unsettling somersault.

CHAPTER 26

Detective Inspector Wiles had set up a command post at the Moody residence, in what was clearly once Jed's office, or perhaps Annika's. There was a large teak desk in the centre and an absurdly large black swivel chair behind it. In front, several smaller chairs sat looking across the desk and out through white shutters to a bright fern view.

"Thanks for coming in so early, especially for a Saturday," Wiles said as Roxy took one of those chairs in front of him. They had prearranged the 8:00 a.m. meeting the night before and the early start didn't bother Roxy today. She was looking forward to returning to the Moody property and having a word with Houghton about the book. One way or the other she needed to know whether it was going ahead.

"You're just lucky I didn't have that third glass of paint stripper," she told Wiles and he laughed.

It was a lovely laugh, rich and deep, and it reached his eyes, which sparkled crystal blue in the morning light that was now filtering through the shutters.

"You can blame me for that. I suggested the place. Wanted a watering hole close to my hotel, but I think I'll give it a miss tonight." He took a breath, hesitated then said,

"Listen, about Gilda. Is she——?"

He never got a chance to finish that question because the door swung open and Quick marched in, his thick boots pounding heavily on the bare floorboards. He nodded at Wiles and ignored Roxy completely as he strode across to the window and perched on the wide frame, his arms and legs crossed over in front of him. He looked defensive and uncomfortable.

"You know Detective Sergeant Quick from the Tweed Byron Local Area Command, of course," Wiles said to Roxy, and she gave Quick a polite smile. He returned it with sullen silence. "Quick will be sitting in for the interview which I'll be taping, for reference purposes only." He pointed to a digital recorder in front of him and she nodded, unperturbed.

Doing regular interviews herself, Roxy wasn't as suspicious of recorders as the average Joe tended to be. They were useful devices, enabling the interviewer to focus on the questions and the interviewee to be sure their answers would not be misquoted.

"So where is the lovely Detective Gilda Maltin today?" Wiles asked now as he positioned the recorder closer to Roxy at the edge of the desk and placed his finger over the "Record" button.

"She's gone back to the Tweed office, taking another look at Sunny's file."

Quick made a sound then, deep in his throat, and both Wiles and Roxy looked across at him, Wiles's eyebrows raised. The local detective had a grim look on his face and his eyes were staring intensely at the wall on the other side of the room.

Without missing a beat, Wiles turned back to Roxy and said, "If there's anything to be found, Detective Maltin will find it. Okay, let's hear your story then." He promptly pressed "Record".

And so they returned to the night of Jed Moody's murder. In clear, concise details, Roxy repeated the statement she gave Quick, this time making sure to include the mysterious conversation she had overheard between Annika and a mystery man in the living room that night. She also repeated what Alistair had said about Jed that morning.

"So there's some genuine animosity between the band members then," Wiles said, but before she could respond, Quick spoke up.

"The guys are good mates, actually " He stared at Roxy. "How long did you interview Al for? What, half an hour? An hour tops?"

She shifted in her seat. "About two hours."

"And you think you know someone in that time, do you? You think you suddenly know the whole dynamics of a band who've been together for decades, in just two hours?"

Roxy couldn't help blushing. She wasn't expecting such open animosity and she glanced at Wiles who remained silent.

"I'm just telling you what Alistair told me, that's all. He called Jed an asshole and a selfish prick, his words, not mine. I have it all on tape."

He tsked. "You got him on a bad day, that's all. I've known the guys for a lot longer than you and they've always got along. Best mates."

"Not according to the band's publicist, Harry Houghton. He pretty much confirmed there'd been tension between them for a long time, off the record, of course."

"*Of course,*" Quick said.

Wiles cleared his throat. "Let's move on to the electrician, Sam Forrest, then." His eyes switched from Quick back to Roxy who wondered whether Wiles found his colleague's aggressive style as unhinging as she did. So much for thinking Quick might be a sympathetic cop. "Did you see Mr. Forrest, or anyone for that matter, loitering on the eastern side of the house, anywhere near the bar stairs, at any time before Jed Moody got on stage that night?"

"Near the fuse box, you mean?"

He didn't reply, so she shook her head.

"And when Sam Forrest came to talk to you that night, about helping him with his sister's case, from which direction had he come?"

She tried to think. "I don't know. I mean, he was standing on the stairs when I came out from the bar, so I can't be sure."

"The stairs near the bar."

And the fuse box, Roxy thought. "Yes, but everyone had access to that—"

He cut her off: "And where did he go between the time you finished talking to him and the time that Jed Moody began to play?"

"Um, again, I'm not a hundred percent certain."

"Oh, your memory suddenly fails you now," Quick said, and again Wiles ignored him, keeping his eyes on Roxy.

She tried to ignore him too, but was feeling increasingly riled. Quick sounded more like a prosecutor than an impartial investigator and she didn't know what he was playing at. Was he angry that she had brought in her good friend to look over a case he'd clearly botched up? Was this more about his close relationship with the Moodys? Or was he always like this?

She took a deep breath, trying to collect her thoughts again. "Let's see, Govinda called us over to dance and Sam said something about hating hippies and then went inside, to the bar I assume. I went to the bonfire—but did not dance." She glanced at the recorder, not sure why she needed that to go on the record. "I can't be certain where Sam went after he went inside. I did see him in the crowd after Jed was killed though."

Wiles indicated some papers on the desk. "I have a witness who says Sam Forrest assaulted you the day you arrived. At the Goddess Café."

"Whoah!" she sat forward in her chair. "Sam did not assault me. He was just angry, had obviously heard I was writing Jed's autobiography and wondered how I could do it."

"He thinks Mr. Moody had something to do with his sister's death."

It wasn't a question, but she nodded. "Well, maybe. He seems to think it was never *investigated* properly."

Now it was her turn to glare at Quick, but he stared back, unruffled. It was clear he was not apologising for that.

She turned back to Wiles. "Sam is angry about what happened to his sister and it's completely understandable. She was barely twenty-one and having an affair with a married man, twice her age. He introduced them, he feels some guilt."

"You're talking about Jed Moody?" Wiles said.

"Yes. Jed and Sunny had been seeing each other before she died. But it wasn't just the affair. Sam was upset that her death didn't seem to make any difference to Jed, life kept moving on for him."

"Upset enough to kill him?" Quick asked.

Roxy shook her head emphatically without shifting her gaze from Wiles. "He's angry, sure, but I'm not convinced he's a killer. He's just not the type."

"So that little bust up with Macker Maroney at the Goddess Café the other day, that was just friendly banter, was it?" asked Quick.

Roxy swept her eyes to him. "Actually, Macker started that. He was saying some unforgiveable things about Sam's dead sister. What would you do?"

He ignored this and asked, "Is it true you're having an affair with Sam Forrest?"

Yet again Roxy was caught off guard. She blushed beetroot red and stared at him, aghast. "No! Who told you that?"

Quick was smirking now. He'd got the reaction he was after. "You were seen entering his property on several occasions. You stayed over one night."

"I was there looking after his dog while you had him locked up in jail!" *My God*, she thought, *the gossip here is extraordinary!* Turning back to Wiles, Roxy took a few deep breaths. "Look, Sam and I have become friends, that's all there is to it. He helped me get away from that sleazebag photographer the other day and we got chatting about his sister. I told him Gilda might be able to help, and that's what she's doing. That's all there is to this." When Wiles didn't say anything, she added, "I don't know whether Sam Forrest had a hand in Jed Moody's murder. Intuitively, I doubt it, but I guess you guys will find out one way or another. I'm just telling you what I feel and what I know. That's all. Unlike some people, this is not personal to me."

Now it was her turn to stare accusatorially at Quick.

Wiles had had enough of all of this. He switched off the recorder and got to his feet. "Thank you for your time, Ms Parker. I trust you'll still be around, should we have further questions?"

She assured him she would, then also stood up and made her way to the door. As she opened it, she glanced back to find Quick looking at Wiles with a smug look on his face. Whatever his agenda, she realised then that his little performance was all about discrediting her in the eyes of the senior cop and, most likely, discrediting her friend Gilda by association. She just hoped Wiles was smart enough to see through it.

In any case, it sent a small shiver down Roxy's spine. Whether Sam was guilty of Jed's murder or not, it was clear Detective Sergeant Quick was determined to place the blame firmly at his feet. The question was, *why?* Was this simply about a bruised ego after failing Sam's sister so badly, or was there something deeper and more sinister behind it?

CHAPTER 27

Roxy was so deep in thought after leaving the interview that she nearly ran straight into the arms of someone who was standing a few meters away. It was Sam.

"Oh my God!" she said, stepping back and blushing again as she recalled the conversation she'd just had with Quick. She wondered how soundproof the door was.

"You okay?" He held onto her arms to keep her from toppling over.

"Yes, I'm … I'm fine." She tilted her head towards the office. "Just been given a grilling by Quick." She tried to smile. "Your turn next is it?"

He nodded. "He still trying to pin it on me?"

"Afraid so. I don't know what you did to him in a past life, but he's gunning for you."

Sam's face broke into a wide smile. "Ah, but he's no longer in charge. I'm not worried."

You should be, she wanted to tell him, but instead she said, "Listen, they seem to think you and I … well…"

"Well?" His smile had turned a little cheeky, he clearly knew where she was going with that and she frowned back at him.

"Can you just explain, please, *very clearly* to both detectives that you and I are just friends, that's all."

"So we are friends, then?"

"Of course." Her expression lightened. "I don't babysit just anyone's dog, you know."

The door creaked open again and Quick peered out, his eyes settling on the two of them and his smirk returned. "When you're finished with Ms Parker, we'd like a word, Mr. Forrest."

He disappeared back inside and Sam did a mock salute and made his way towards the office before turning back. "Speaking of Lunar, he misses you. Big time. Want to pop over for a barbeque tonight? It can be our thank you present."

Roxy went to say yes, then reconsidered. "Oh, I'm not sure, Gilda's still around and…"

"Bring Gilda. Why not? We're just friends, after all, right?" Then he gave her a cocky smile as he, too, disappeared into the office.

"Oh, there you are Roxy!" She swung around to find Houghton peering out from the living area, his scruffy hair flying about his face. "Got a sec?"

Roxy nodded, took a few calming breaths of air, then made her way through the room and out to the veranda. Houghton was taking a seat back at the long wooden table, which was now clear of debris except for his mobile phone and laptop. He pulled a chair out for her then clicked something on the screen and turned back with a grin.

"So, we have liftoff!"

"Sorry?" Roxy's head was stuck somewhere between Jed Moody's murder and Sam Forrest's coy grin, and for a moment she had forgotten all about the book. She snapped out of it quickly and said, "Really?"

"Yep, it's good news, Annika has seen the light and the lads are eager to get the book happening, too. So, can we get cracking straight away?"

"Sure, of course. You'll have to speak with my agent—"

"Just did." He tapped his mobile. "We've nutted out an agreement, which I'll e-mail to him now, but he's asked if you can give him another call if you can find the time. Maybe use the landline here, hey? He's having a bit of trouble getting through to your mobile."

She reached for her phone in the bottom of her bag. There was only one bar showing and even that disappeared as she stared at it. "I don't know why I bother."

"Try out in the car park near the studio, or the eastern corner of the veranda, just over there." He waved his phone. "Seems to be the magic spot for most people. But as I say, feel free to use the landline again. There's a bunch around the place, one by the bar, another in the kitchen. Annika won't mind." Roxy arched her eyebrows. She was whistling a different tune today then.

"Now, listen, here's what we're going to need. Not a huge amount, it'll be mostly pictorial, but a chapter on each band member, some info on Jed's background, some feel-good stuff about his marriage."

"Oh? I'm allowed to discuss that now?"

He chuckled. "Well, his fans can't hold it against him anymore."

"And Annika really is fine with all of this?"

"Yeah, yeah, she came round, like I knew she would. She knows we've gotta strike while the iron's hot."

"Will she let me interview her?"

"Says she's looking forward to it. She's meeting with the detectives in about an hour, but you might be able to catch her before then if you're lucky."

Roxy glanced at her phone. It was just after 9:00 a.m. "I had better chat to Oliver before I do anything else," she told him. "If you'll excuse me."

Returning inside, Roxy located the hand-held phone that was perched on the corner of the bar beside a cluster of liquor bottles, and picked it up. There was a man's voice on the other end, which confused her for a split second before she realised someone else in the house was using the phone. She heard the words, "—not *here*! I told you, pigs are everywhere, we'll get busted—" The voice stopped abruptly, sensing her on the other end, and said, "Who's there?!"

She dropped the phone back onto its cradle as though it were made of burning lava, and felt a rush of guilt followed by a shot of anxiety. Was that Alistair? Doug? She couldn't quite place the man's voice, but he sounded stressed.

He also sounded shifty.

She glanced around furtively. Was the caller using the kitchen phone? Half of her wanted to stride in and see who was talking, the other half—the smarter half—told her to mind her own business and get the hell out of there, and so she did, dashing back out to where Houghton was still tapping away at his laptop. He blinked at her.

"You look like you've seen a ghost."

Roxy slipped into the chair beside him and tried to smile. "No, no, I'm fine."

"Did you call Oliver?"

"Not yet." She grappled for her mobile. "I think I'll try my luck with my mobile." She tried to warm her smile up. "So, who else is around today, apart from Annika?"

He shrugged. "The boys are out in the studio going through Jed's files. Cook's here, too, slapping together some brunch for Annie, I think, why?"

"Who's the cook?" She tried to keep her tone nonchalant, wasn't sure she'd pulled it off.

"Oh, just a guy from the shop, Hans someone-or-other."

Roxy immediately remembered the man with the sinewy body and the black bun from the Goddess Cafe. "Come here often, does he?"

He shrugged. "Comes in occasionally and whips up a few meals to keep Annie happy. She was going to let him go, actually, she doesn't really have the budget for that kind of extravagance anymore but, well, now that Jed's gone... I guess she's not up to pulling dishes together at this stage. Plus she's got us buggers to feed, hey?" His eyes narrowed.

"Why do you ask?"

Roxy shook her head. "Just curious. So where's this magic spot then?"

Two minutes later, Roxy was leaning out across the veranda balustrade, her iPhone in one hand, the other holding onto the railing for dear life. "Olie? Is that you?" The signal kept cutting in and out.

"Oh … *(crackle, crackle)* the great … *(crackle)* Parker finally … *(crackle, crackle)* call!"

It might have been a bad line, but Oliver's sarcasm was clear as a bell. "Sorry, Olie. I've been busy with Gilda."

"Gilda? Tell me … *(crackle crackle)* there."

"What?"

"She's *there?*"

"Yes! She came to see if I was all right and is now staying to do some investigating work."

"What?!"

Roxy leaned out even farther to get a better signal. "She's looking into Sam's sister's drowning! The one I told you about yesterday!"

"Don't yell, I can hear you perfectly well." Roxy relaxed a little. "You two," Oliver continued. "You're like Tintin and his fluffy white dog."

"I'm hoping in this analogy of yours that I'm Tintin and not the dog."

He laughed. "Hey, you're the one with the canine fixation at the moment. Speaking of which, how is our friendly murder suspect? Still behind bars?"

"No, he is not." Although she wondered how long that would last. Would Sam even be free for a barbecue at his place tonight? Not if Quick had anything to do with it, she decided, then shrugged the thought away and changed the subject. "So, Houghton tells me the book is back on."

"Yep, great news for you, I have to say. I'm finalising the deets with him this morning and we should have a proper contract to you to sign by lunchtime. I'll get Shazza to e-mail it to you when it's done. Read through and let me know if you're happy with the terms and conditions. I negotiated a better word rate, but they seem to want fewer words now than the original book, so it evens out in the end, I'm sorry to say. Still, it's a pretty sum for a few days work."

"It'll be fine, Olie." She was happy to hang around.

"How's the investigation into the poor bugger's murder going? It's all over the press here. All anyone wants to talk about. In fact, your friend Maria called."

"Maria Constantinople, from *Glossy*?" Roxy pictured the overweight, over-cursing magazine editor and shuddered a little. "What did she want?"

"She wants you to write a story about Jed Moody and his murder, of course."

"Great! I could do with the extra money, although I don't exactly know the full story yet."

"I told her as much. Plus there is the small matter of the confidentiality agreement you signed before you flew up."

Roxy deflated. That's right. It seemed a lifetime ago now, but she recalled signing the contract in her agent's office the week before. It was standard stuff. Every ghostwriting contract included a confidentiality clause to ensure that anything seen or heard during client interviews remained at the client's discretion. And it made sense. As a ghostwriter you were invited into a person's inner sanctum and often saw and heard things that the client wished you hadn't. As they were footing the bill for the book, you abided by their wishes and promptly "unsaw" and "unheard" whatever they asked. This was not a biography. It was an authorised autobiography, and that's how the process worked.

Now she wished it didn't.

"Surely that doesn't cover Jed's death? I mean, there were loads of people there. It was practically a public event."

"Doesn't matter. The agreement covers everything that happens during the time you were employed to ghostwrite the book. His death included."

Fair enough. "It's not like I would have written anything

awful," she said, but let it drop. *Glossy* magazine would have plenty more stories where that came from. She hoped. "Okay, I'd better fly. I want to see if I can grab Annika before she disappears again."

Roxy had just spotted the widow walking around the side of the house, from the direction of the stables, her dog Coco nipping at her heels.

"Okay, but before you go," said Olie and she stiffened, afraid she'd lose the line again.

"Yes?"

"Be careful around that Sam guy. You may think he's innocent but, well, just keep a wide berth, okay?"

Why do people keep saying that? She thought moodily. "I'll be fine," Roxy told him, knowing she would be doing exactly the opposite of what he was advising, and not caring in the slightest.

CHAPTER 28

Annika Moody might have given the go-ahead for the Moody Roos book, but she wasn't about to help kick it into motion. "I really don't have the energy for that right now," grumbled Annika. "Plus, I have to see that detective with the lovely blue eyes. He has questions, apparently."

Roxy wasn't sure if she was referring to Quick or Wiles. "I didn't think you were meeting the detectives for another hour."

Her eyes narrowed. "Yes, and if it's all right with you, I'd like to have some breakfast first." She sighed resignedly. "Come back later today or tomorrow. I might have some time then." She went to walk off, then halted. "Where have you moved to? Houghton tells me you've cleared out of the bails."

No thanks to you, Roxy wanted to say but said, instead, "Oh, I decided to give you guys some space. I've booked into Bindi's Hideaway, not far from here."

Annika considered this for a moment, then shrugged and swept past her, yelling out, "Coco, come!"

Houghton had been watching the exchange and cringed. "Sorry about that, Roxy. You could head over to the studio, bail up Al, I'm pretty sure he's still there."

She glanced at the time, picked up her handbag and recorder and said, "I might leave Al for now. I spoke to him the other day so he's not my first priority. I might try the drummer instead."

"Whoops, no can do. You just missed him."

"Really?"

"Yeah, sorry, while you were talking to your agent, he cleared off, back to his beach pad. He's rarely here if he can help it." His eyes lit up. "You could follow him down, he's probably not doing much." He scribbled an address onto a slip of paper and handed it across. "If he's not there he'll be on the surf, out the back of his house. One way or the other you'll track him down." His eyes swept out to the lawn and a flicker of annoyance crossed his face. "Isn't that your copper friend? What's she up to?"

Roxy followed his gaze and spotted Gilda striding towards the house, from the direction of the thick forest that lay between the Holloway and Moody properties. Dropping her things back onto the table, Roxy skipped down the steps to join her friend out on the lawn, close to the sooty patch where the bonfire had burned so brightly just three nights earlier.

As she walked, she noticed the stage was still cordoned off with police tape, but Jed's guitar and amp were no longer there. Wiles must have taken them away as evidence.

"Morning, Missy!" Gilda called out as she approached. "How'd your grilling go? I hope Wiles was gentle as a lamb."

She rolled her eyes. "It's not Wiles I worry about. Quick is the one who bites. Really, the man's got serious issues."

Gilda laughed. "He knows he dropped the ball with Sunny Forrest and he knows you're the one who pointed it out, so he's never going to be your best friend, I'm afraid."

"I'm not." Roxy looked past her to the forest. "What have you been up to out there in the wild yonder?"

Gilda smiled mischievously. "I've been checking the pathway between the studio and the creek where Sunny was found. Did you know it takes precisely eight minutes to get from the studio door to the front of that *romantic* hutch?"

"Not too far for a muso to stumble in the dark then to meet his mistress?"

"Indeed. But that's not the interesting bit."

"Oh?"

"I found some jewellery at the hutch."

Roxy's brain ticked over. "Is it a Moody Ring?" It had to be Sunny's missing jewellery.

Gilda's smile dropped. "What? No, not quite." She produced a plastic bag from her jacket pocket and Roxy peered inside to what looked like a bit of string with tiny chunks of bright powdery rock attached.

"What is that?"

"That, my dear, is one of those ridiculous edible necklaces we used to wear when we were kids. Remember? They're made of candy and you hang them around your neck and chew away. Dentists must have loved those things. They probably invented them. Haven't seen one in years."

"I have," Roxy said, her brain ticking in a different direction now. "Where exactly did you find it?"

"Just outside the door of the hutch, under a clump of leaves. Easy to miss if you don't follow the line of ants that were making a quick meal of it. I had to flick them off first. That was no mean feat." She mock shuddered.

"Do you think it was dropped there recently?"

"Take a look at it. Any later than a week and the weather or the ants would have demolished the evidence. They're hard workers, those critters, but I thwarted them today." She looked impressed with herself, like she'd taken on vicious gangsters and won. Arching her blonde eyebrows, Gilda said, "Why? Where did you last see one of these?"

"I think I saw one hanging around the neck of a very young, very pretty blonde girl named Asha, who also happens to be the daughter of the local mayor."

"Really?" Gilda's eyes lit up.

"Really! Just the other night. The night Jed Moody was

killed. I can't be sure, but it looks similar to one she was chomping at."

"Veddy veddy interesting. Perhaps Asha was Jed's latest conquest."

Roxy glanced around. "Don't let Houghton hear you say that. He's adamant they weren't sleeping together, but the way he went on and on about it the other night, it makes me wonder."

"The man doth protest too much?" Roxy nodded and Gilda asked, "Could Asha and Jed have rendezvoused at the hutch before his gig?"

She thought about that. "I can't see how. She arrived with her dad quite late as far as I could tell. About fifteen, twenty minutes before Jed went on stage. I didn't catch her movements after that. If they had met up it would have to have been a quickie. Like I'm talking lightning speed." She did the maths. "Eight minutes there, eight minutes back. They would have had just a few minutes alone before he returned to the stage. Seems a bit illogical."

"Ah yes, but perhaps she had a taste for these, wore a different one that night. They could easily have met up the night before or the night before that."

"That's true. Jed was in his studio the night I arrived; he'd been there all the night before, too. Working late apparently. So, what? You think maybe Annika caught them at it and it was the final straw? She was certainly in a foul mood that night I arrived. After what had happened with Sunny, maybe she couldn't take any more." Roxy began clicking her fingers. "You know, I did see the mayor's daughter rushing into the middle of the crowd *after* Jed hit the stage, looking a bit flushed. He could easily have been staring at her when he dedicated the song to 'the love of my life'."

Gilda looked doubtful. "Really? A teenage kid is the love of Jed Moody's life? I find that hard to believe. The man's had his pick of women for several decades, and he settles on one who thinks candy necklaces are the height of fashion?"

Roxy cocked her head to one side. "Hang on a minute. I

thought you were focusing on Sunny's death, not Jed's."

"Ah, but maybe this necklace is the link between the two."

Before she could elaborate, Gilda gave Roxy a pointed look and pocketed the bag just as Houghton came stumbling across the lawn.

"You two look very intense out here. What're you up to?"

Gilda smiled. "Mr. Houghton, just the man I was looking for. I wonder if I can have a moment of your time?"

"Me? Why?"

"Just need to ask you a few questions about Sunny Forrest's death, if you don't mind."

His demeanor shifted and he began flicking glances back at the house. "Oh, well, sure, but I can't see what I'd have to say that could help you. I wasn't around when the poor girl drowned."

"Still. Shall we go back to the house?"

He mumbled something and led the way back to the veranda, and Roxy decided to join them, intrigued by what Gilda could possibly glean from the band's publicist. That's as far as she got.

"Thanks, Roxy. I've got it from here," Gilda said and Roxy frowned.

"Oh, of course, right." Damn it, Gilda was chucking her out. "I'll go and see if I can have another chat to Alistair while he's still around."

Houghton looked like he wanted to flee with her, and she couldn't help chuckling as she left him in the hands of the inimitable Gilda Maltin.

When Roxy got across to the recording studio, she found the front door partially ajar and tapped loudly a few times before slowly pushing it open. It was exceptionally heavy and twice as thick as a normal wooden door.

"Hello!" she sang out. "Anyone here?"

The place appeared to be empty and Roxy's voice was

swallowed up by the acoustics of the room, which were dull and flat. The air was musty and the place smelled like mouldy leather and stale tobacco. She glanced around. The space had been divided into two and there was an enormous Neve mixing console in one room, just in front of a wide window made of two panes of thick glass and looking out at the lush green forest. She looked through the window, wondering if you could see the hutch from here. If Roxy's calculations were correct, it had to be straight through those trees beyond.

An upright office chair sat in front of the mixing desk and behind it, a large, shabby black leather sofa with a small coffee table laden with music magazines, beer bottles and, surprise, surprise, an overflowing ashtray.

Both rooms were cluttered with musical instruments of all kinds, from tambourines to old banjos. She spotted at least twelve guitars, some hanging from the walls, others perched on guitar stands at various spots, and in the live room an enormous drum kit almost filled the space. She also spotted numerous amplifiers, speakers, microphones and what looked like a workbench against a wall with a range of tools including screwdrivers, an electrical hand tool of some sort, crimping tools and wire cutters. Above the bench she noticed a thin black telephone attached to the wall.

Roxy's eyes widened. Was that phone connected to the line in the main house? *Had the voice she overheard been coming from in here?*

"Rox!"

Roxy was caught by surprise and her heart nearly leapt out of her throat before she realised Gilda was standing at the studio door, ushering her across.

"I've just received word that Macker Maroney is down in Byron, at the local paper. I want to grab him before he takes off again. Feel like a drive?"

Roxy smiled. "Sure, there's a surfer dude I need to pop in on while we're there."

On their way through the hinterland down to the coast, Roxy took the opportunity to tell Gilda about the strange phone conversation she had overheard while at the Moody house. Gilda didn't seem nearly as excited by it.

"Most people are wary of cops," she said. "Someone telling his mates to stay away is not that unusual."

"Yes, but he said something about not wanting to get busted."

"So, they could've been talking about sharing a joint or something. These are musos, after all." Then, sensing Roxy's disappointment, asked, "Any idea who it was?"

"He sounded familiar. I've heard his voice before, but he didn't say enough for me to place it. I do know the two band members, Alistair and Doug, were there at the time, as was the man from the Goddess Café. Hans, I think his name is. He does some cooking for Annika, but get this…" She paused for effect. "He was getting the heave ho, apparently, before Jed died. Houghton reckons they could no longer afford him. Maybe it was Jed's idea to sack him, so Hans bumped him off."

"What? To keep his job?"

"Maybe he had grown accustomed to working in the big house. Didn't want to slum it down at the local café anymore. He does have access to the property, he's the cook, can come and go as he pleases."

"But can he rewire an amplifier so it electrocutes someone? He's just a cook, after all, right?"

She chewed mercilessly at her lower lip then said, "I know, I know. I'm grasping at straws again."

Gilda laughed and filed it away in her brain anyway, then said, "Houghton's a nervy character. I wonder what he's hiding."

"Could just be another person wary of cops."

"Touché!" Gilda responded, then flashed her a smile. "Do you know Mr. Houghton reckons he, too, knew nothing about Jed and Sunny's affair *before* Sunny showed up dead. Like Govinda, he insists he only found out about it after Sam showed up and starting making waves."

"Do you believe him?"

She snorted. "He's a publicist, darling! I don't believe a word that comes out of his mouth."

CHAPTER 29

The editorial office of the *Valley Times* looked exactly like what you'd expect of a small-town, small-time, free newspaper. Squashed into a few shabby rooms above a chemist on a side street, there were stacks of old newspapers against every available wall, desks crammed against each other and, despite it being the weekend, several flustered-looking newshounds madly typing away at aging PCs. The woman on the front desk looked as frazzled as the drudges, and completely unfazed by Gilda's badge.

"I dunno," she told her, barely looking up from her screen, a phone wedged to one ear, chewing madly at some gum. She nodded her head towards the inner sanctum of the office. "He's in there somewhere, help yourself."

"Thank you," Gilda said, and then asked Roxy, "Can you spot him?"

Roxy peered around the corner and smiled. "Yep, second desk along, got his head in a girlie mag, of course!"

Macker Maroney was the only person in the office who did not look busy. He had his legs crossed up on the desk and was slowly flicking through a copy of a sleazy men's magazine while the chaos whirled on around him. When

Roxy approached his desk, he looked up with a frown that quickly broke into a seedy smile.

"Wondered if you'd come good. Got something for me?"

She smiled smugly. "Yes, I do, as it happens. Macker Maroney meet Detective Gilda Maltin."

Macker also didn't look too perturbed by the detective's presence, simply shifted his eyes to her and said, "This about Jed Moody?"

She shook her head. "Sunny Forrest. Is there somewhere we can talk?"

He slammed the magazine shut and dropped his legs to the floor. "Sunny? Sam's sister? What about her?"

"Is there a meeting room somewhere or would you prefer to chat right here?" Gilda glanced around at the staff, all of whom had ceased typing and were now openly watching this exchange.

Macker stood up, snatched his cigarettes from the desk and turned towards a man two desks along. "Hey, Gazza! Just buzz my mobile when the proofs come back, yeah?"

Without waiting for a reply, he strode out of the office, past the receptionist and down the stairs to the street, his scrappy ponytail swishing behind him. Gilda and Roxy let him lead them to a café called Hobo just half a block down from the chemist. He was clearly a regular because he simply held a finger in the air and the barista nodded then raised his eyebrows at the women.

"Two large lattés, thanks," Gilda told him, then followed Macker back to a table on the pavement.

He sat down and instantly lit up, and Roxy stared at the generic cigarette box on the table but couldn't quite read the brand name.

"Do you mind if I bum a ciggie from you?"

He looked surprised by this, as did Gilda for that matter, then pulled a cigarette out and handed it to her before pocketing the box.

Roxy surreptitiously checked the brand printed along the butt. It was Marlborough. Now why did that not surprise her? She flashed a small smile at Gilda who was watching her intently and the detective nodded then turned to Macker.

"What can you tell me about Sunny Forrest's death?"

"You reopening the investigation?"

She ignored his return question and fired another one off: "Did you know Sunny Forrest personally?"

He dragged on his cigarette again and gave this some thought. "Sure. She used to hang at the Goddess Café. I got to know her a bit."

"Really?" This was Roxy now, sounding unconvinced.

He looked at her. "Sure, she was a pretty girl. Why not?" He turned his eyes back to Gilda. "You know, you're not bad looking yourself, you'd take a decent photo, if you wanted to. Got curves in all the right places." His muddy eyes lingered on those places and Roxy felt like jumping across the table and snotting him, but Gilda didn't flinch, just stared at him deadpan, her own eyes cold and unwavering. Despite this, he pulled a business card from his top pocket and placed it on the table in front of her. "Call me, we could work something out."

Gilda sighed now, as though bored beyond belief. "Did you ever see Sunny Forrest with Jed Moody? Maybe at the café? Maybe elsewhere?"

He smirked. "Nah, they weren't that obvious about it. I mean, he was an arrogant bastard, but he wasn't that arrogant. Annika would have killed him." His smirk deepened. "Perhaps she did."

Gilda waited for the barista to place their coffees down and leave before she said, "So how did you know they were seeing each other?"

His smirk dropped a little. He reached for his espresso and took a sip. "I have my sources."

Now Roxy shook her head. That old chestnut, she thought. It was the perfect "get out of jail" card for journalists and photographers alike.

"But you did know about their affair," Gilda persisted, "before she died?"

"Sure."

"You didn't happen to see them at any stage, did you? Maybe sneak up on them when they rendezvoused at the hutch."

He stared into his espresso glass, gave it a small whirl with one hand. "Don't know what you mean."

Gilda reached into her bag and pulled out a piece of paper. She unfolded it and placed it on the table in front of him. It was a freshly printed copy of the newspaper article, the one showing the soggy creek bed where Sunny's body had been found. He glanced at it and up at her.

"So?"

"So, how'd the *Valley Times* get lucky with this shot? It's the scene of the crime, and I know for a fact that the forensic photographer did not take that image."

He shrugged, took a second gulp of his coffee, finishing it off. He looked at Roxy's hand. "You gonna smoke that?"

Roxy was still holding onto the cigarette and she also shrugged. "Maybe later."

Macker watched her for a few seconds, looking slightly disquieted now, and Gilda decided to pounce.

"Mr Maroney, do I have to return to your office and have a word with your editor? I'm sure you gave her a nice neat spiel about getting approval from the investigating team or from Annika Moody herself. Do I need to make a liar out of you or are you going to save me the trouble and tell me what you were doing on the Moody property the day after Sunny Forrest died."

"How do you know that picture was taken the day after Sunny died?"

"Take a closer look at your handiwork, Mr Maroney. There's a couple of evidence paddles still in the ground." She tapped a long nail at the photo. "They get removed after the official photographer has come and gone, and I know for a fact that he came and went within twenty-four hours. Which means you did, too."

Macker still looked uncomfortable but his lips remained

shut, so she said, "Perhaps I should just go straight to Annika and see how she feels about the fact that you were trespassing on her land."

"Hey, I wasn't trespassing, no way!" Gilda stared at him, her knitted brows telling him what she thought of that comment, so he blurted, "It's true! I cut down through the creek. I'm allowed to, waterways are public property around here."

"I find that extremely hard to believe."

Macker's confidence returned then. He was in safer territory now. "Check it out with the local council if you want. Anyone can access a waterway, even when it goes through private land, so long as you don't go through that land while you do it. Who's to say I didn't clamber along the creek the whole way? I could've entered the creek from the main road. It cuts under the causeway there, just in front of the café."

Gilda narrowed her eyes further. He was good, very good. "How could you have walked in that way? The creek was flooded at that time, remember, that's how Sunny was supposed to have drowned."

He shrugged. "Wasn't flooded when I came along. Wasn't a problem at all."

"Still, whether you accessed the creek legally or not, I think you'll find taking photos on someone's private property, which is where that creek bed is, without that owner's permission is not legal."

"So, get out your furry handcuffs and take me into custody."

Gilda did not smile. "Here's the thing, Mr. Maroney, I'm not actually very interested in whether you were trespassing or even whether this shot was taken illegally. I'm more interested in what else you might have seen that day, or the days surrounding Sunny's death. I'm looking for evidence, that's all."

"Who's to say I was there any other time?"

She dropped her head to one side, making it abundantly

clear she neither believed him nor had the patience for his games. When he remained silent, she said, "This is a potential murder investigation, Mr. Maroney. I am currently looking through the evidence to decide whether to reopen the case. If I do, you could find yourself up on a charge of obstructing a murder investigation. Or worse, aiding and abetting a murderer."

"Hey, don't get your pretty knickers in a knot. I don't know anything about Sunny's death. I didn't see anything. I've got no intel that'll be any use to you." Still, he shot a quick glance at the cigarette that remained in Roxy's hand.

Gilda's patience had all run out. "I really don't have the time or energy for this crap, Mr Maroney, so let me spell it out for you. See that creek bed," she tapped her nail on the newspaper image again. "To the right of that, just out of the shot, is a small hutch. I know it and you know it. That hutch was a rendezvous point for Jed Moody and Sunny Forrest. I believe that you knew all about that hutch and that you snuck up on them, on at least one occasion, to take photos of their little trysts. Am I correct?"

He nudged his fat lips downwards. "You're delusional, that's what you are. Besides, you've got no proof of that. Where are these pictures, then? Where are these images I'm supposed to have taken? If I had these fantastic photos I'd be a rich man. I wouldn't be sitting here chatting to you. I'd be making money from them."

"Ah, but you were making money from them," said Roxy, who had been watching the exchange silently until now. "You were blackmailing Jed Moody, weren't you?"

Macker's eyes hardened. "What are you talking about?"

He had an edge in his voice now and Gilda, too, looked slightly taken aback as she stared across at her friend.

Roxy wished she'd worked it all out earlier, if only to give Gilda the heads-up, but it was just coming back to her now. She recalled the first time she met Jed, on the veranda of his house that night, and the cryptic conversation he had had with Houghton just before Annika appeared. He'd asked

Houghton if he'd given somebody "his marching orders". Houghton had been reluctant to discuss it in front of Roxy, yet Jed was not so reticent. He had said something like: *"I'm not giving that asshole one more cent. Tell him to go shove it."*

Was he referring to Macker Maroney?

She decided to take a punt. "You had pictures of Jed and Sunny together. You were blackmailing them. I know this for a fact, Macker. Jed and Houghton talked about it the night I arrived."

"That wasn't blackmail!" Macker growled. "Photos are a commodity, I wanted to see if I could find a buyer. Photographers do it all the time. Lock me up for that and you'll not only have to lock up half the photographers in the world, you'll have to close down every tabloid newspaper and gossip mag in existence. It's the way it works, yeah? You should know that."

She shook her head. "No, what I know is, any decent photographer asks permission *before* they take the photo, not afterwards, and they certainly don't blackmail people to stop printing it."

Gilda was not interested in a moral argument. "So it's true you do have images of Jed and Sunny together at the hutch?"

He hesitated again. "So, I had some pix of a married man playing up. It's not a criminal offence. They were taken the week before she died. Nothing to do with her death. She was alive and well when they finished up in the hutch. Had a big ole grin on her face, in fact." His eyes twinkled and Roxy felt nauseous.

"Having an affair may not be a criminal offence, Mr Maroney," Gilda snapped, "but it is a criminal offence to try to extort money out of Jed over it."

"Hey, settle down! No one was doing any extorting. Like I said, I just made a monetary exchange. Houghton offered to buy the pix in exchange for me not selling them on to a magazine. That's all there was to it."

Gilda sat back in her chair. Something was not adding up.

So, Jed was caught with his trousers down again. He'd been doing that for decades. It was hardly a revelation. In fact, hooking up with a young blonde was probably a feather in your cap when you were a middle-aged rock star. *So why did Houghton lie to her about it?* If what Macker was saying was true, Houghton clearly knew about the affair before Sunny died and was determined to hush it up. But why would Houghton care, she wondered?

She said as much to both Roxy and Maroney, adding, "Surely any publicity is good publicity."

Maroney shrugged. "I dunno, you'd have to ask Houghton that. Seemed bloody anxious to get hold of the shots, though. Swore me to secrecy. Made me delete the originals, the works. You're lucky I'm even telling you this. But that's all there is to it. End of story."

"I don't think it was the end of the story," said Roxy. "I think you got some more pix, just recently, this time of Jed with Asha Kidlong at the hutch. So you went back to Houghton to extort more cash."

He looked at her, smile widening. "Oooh, you're a clever cookie, you are. Keep trying, you're nearly there." He laughed, clearly enjoying himself. When Gilda sat forward looking like she was about to throttle him, he said, "Okay, so I got some more pix. But it's not what you think. These ones are a lot more incriminating."

"What do you mean by that?"

He shrugged. "I'm just sayin' these shots could land someone in very big trouble. But you're wrong about who it was."

"What do you mean?" Gilda repeated, more firmly this time.

"It wasn't Jed and Asha I photographed. That's all I'm saying."

"Who else was Jed with?" Roxy demanded and he clamped his lips shut, still managing to smile as he did so.

Gilda fumed. "We can subpoena the pictures, Mr Maroney. You might as well tell us now."

He shook his head defiantly. "Nope. No can do. As I say, have to protect my sources."

"Your income stream, more likely," Roxy snapped. "Are you waiting to get more money off Houghton?"

He stubbed out his cigarette then leaned forward. "Look, I don't know what any of this has got to do with Sunny's death. I had nothing to do with that. I feel bad, she was a good kid, sweet, you know? Sexy too. The day I heard about her death, I raced to the scene to get that one picture, then got the hell out of there. Went back along the creek. I didn't access anyone's land. I didn't tread on anyone's toes. It's just a friggin' photo."

"Not to Sam Forrest, it isn't," Roxy said. "That's the scene of his sister's death, it's sacred territory to him, and you went and splashed it all over the local rag."

Gilda cleared her throat. That wasn't really the point now and she'd had enough of Macker Maroney and his childish games. She would talk to Wiles about getting a search warrant for the photographer's camera and digital files and see what incriminating photos he was talking about. She stood up. "Okay, that will do for now. I'd thank you, Mr. Maroney, but I'm not sure there's any point."

"Let me make it up to you then." He nodded his head at the card she had left on the table. "Let me take your photo. I could really sex you up. We could both make a lot of dough."

When she ignored this and turned away, he called out, "Maybe a few shots of you wearing nothing but your handcuffs?"

Gilda didn't flinch. As she exited the café, she simply called back, "No, thank you, Mr. Maroney. I'd rather have my skin peeled off than spend any more time with you. Thanks for the coffees!"

"The hide of the man!" Roxy was saying as they made their way back to the main street where their car was parked. "I can't believe you didn't punch him out or arrest him for being an A-class slimeball."

Gilda shrugged. "Oh well, we left him with the bill for the coffee, that's gotta hurt a cheapskate like Maroney."

"But you're going to let him get away with that comment?"

"You think that's the first time I've heard that kind of thing? I'm a female cop, Roxy it comes with the territory. One of the many delectable ways lowlifes try to get under your skin, try to bring you down to their level. The trick is not to react."

"Still, what a scumbag."

Now Gilda laughed as they reached her car and she unlocked the doors. "Your mother would say I should be grateful anyone wants to take my photo at this stage of my life."

"Oh, my mother would have taken his card and begged him to photograph me, as well," Roxy said, then managed to laugh along with her. "So, are you going to try to get hold of his camera?"

"You bet. Maroney's obviously got a stack of photos that could bust this case right open, not to mention Wiles's investigation. He's clearly been sneaking onto the Moody property for years taking snaps. God knows what else he's photographed. He may not even realise what evidence he has. He could be sitting on a goldmine."

"What do you think he meant by 'incriminating' pictures? Maybe we should check Asha's age. Houghton said she was seventeen or eighteen, but maybe he's lying. She could be underage, for all we know. That's pretty incriminating."

"Except Maroney said the incriminating shots *weren't* of Jed and Asha, remember?"

Roxy groaned. "But can we believe anything that comes out of that slimeball's mouth? Isn't he in the same category as the publicist?"

"Oh, I think paparazzi are even lower on the Slimeball Scale. Still, I can't believe Houghton just lied to me about that. He clearly knew about Jed's affair with Sunny, so why keep it to himself? Like I keep saying, it's not illegal, it's no big deal." She paused. "*Or is it?* Maybe there's more to all of this than meets the eye. Maybe that's why Sunny had to die."

Gilda started the engine and turned back along the main street, heading south. She suddenly groaned. "It's not clicking into place. I mean, whether Maroney was blackmailing anyone with anything, I just don't think that's the issue. If he did have something on Jed or Sunny or whomever, then it should have been *him* lying in that creek or zapped with 240 volts, right?"

Roxy nodded. That made sense. "Maybe we're overthinking it and it all comes back to the jealous wife. Annika was really possessive of Jed when I first met her. I mean, viciously so. Seems to me, she's the obvious suspect. First she finds out about Sunny and kills her in a fit of rage. Then finds out about Jed and Asha or some other underage chick and realises it's never going to end, she's going to have to keep killing women until the cows come home, so she finally wreaks revenge on her ratbag husband instead."

Gilda glanced across at her, a tiny smile playing at her lips. "Dare I say it?"

Roxy shook her head. "Don't bother. I know, straws, straws, straws!"

Then she slumped in her seat despondently.

CHAPTER 30

A pungent mix of salt, sunscreen and mildew rushed up to meet Roxy and Gilda as they made their way through the scrubby palm garden at the back of Doug Campbell's beach house, a renovated 1950s' fibro shack. They had already knocked on the front door and called out his name, to no avail, so took Houghton's advice and decided to check the beach where Doug famously spent his time.

A bush turkey scratched around in the scrubby grounds that separated the house from the sand dunes and they watched it scurry away as they weaved their way along the leafy path towards the beach. At the top of the dunes, thick clumps of Bitou bush did little to hide the spectacular view of the achingly white sand and the deep blue sea beyond. They could just make out some surfers at the break when Roxy pointed.

"Could be him."

"Pity I didn't bring my bikini," Gilda replied. "Shall we leave a note and come back?"

"Oi! What do you want?" shouted a male voice behind them.

They swung back towards the pathway to find the

drummer, surfboard under one arm, weaving his way down a second pathway from the beach, one they hadn't noticed earlier. The two paths merged halfway along and they made their way across, closer to where Doug was now standing, dripping wet in a black Rip Curl wetsuit.

"Hi, Doug, it's me, Roxy Parker!" she called out and he stared at her for a second before his white Zinc-covered lips broke into a smile.

"Right, yeah. Sorry, didn't recognise you. Come down, I'll just wash up."

They followed him back to the house and waited while he rinsed himself and his board beneath a makeshift shower that had been erected below a wattle. He tugged his wetsuit off to reveal floral board-shorts and a surprisingly ripped body for a man in his forties—tanned six-pack, bulging biceps, chest-hair bleached from the sun.

Doug shook his hair out like a wet dog, then walked across to the house, leaned his board against one wall, and waved them towards a grey wooden deck under a mouldy shade sail. There was a faded outdoor setting and he pulled out a chair and sat down, so they followed, Roxy being sure to introduce Gilda as she did so.

"Gilda's looking into Sunny Forrest's death," she explained.

Unlike almost everyone else, Doug didn't bat an eyelid. "Oh right, good luck with that." He looked at Roxy. "And you're back on the book, yeah?"

She nodded. "You happy about that?" He just shrugged. "Look," Roxy continued, "I'm sorry to crash your pad like this, I was in town and I just wanted to drop by and see if we would set up a time to do the interview. It'll probably take about two hours, and then I can leave you alone."

"No sweat, I've got all the time in the world. Although if the surf's pumping you might have trouble catching me."

"How does 11:00 a.m. tomorrow sound?"

He nodded. "That'll give me time to get a surf in after breaky. Can I get you guys anything? Soft drink? Beer?"

They shook their heads. "We won't stay long," Gilda spoke now. "I just tagged along in the hope I can ask you a couple of quick questions regarding Ms Forrest."

He brushed his hands through his dripping hair and gave his head another shake, sending salty drops flying towards them. "Go on then."

"Did you know her at all?"

"Nope. Only heard about her after it all happened. Houghton told me."

"So you didn't know she was having an affair with Jed?"

He snickered. "Man, if I was to keep up with every affair Jed had, I'd have no time for surfing."

"He was prolific, was he?"

He shrugged but said nothing.

Gilda needed to get this straight. "Did you know anything about the photos that Macker Maroney took of Sunny and Jed together before she died?"

He stared at her blankly and shook his head.

She was not sure if she believed him. "What about Asha Kidlong?"

"Who?"

"The local mayor's daughter. We suspect Jed was seeing her before he was killed."

He shrugged again. "As I say, hard to keep up."

"Did you have any problem with him sleeping around like that?" Roxy asked.

"Why should I? It's his biz."

"What about his wife?"

He laughed. "Annika. She can't talk."

Gilda sat forward. "Mrs. Moody was unfaithful too?"

It was the first flicker of trepidation that crossed his face, the first time he looked like he had strayed into uncomfortable territory. He promptly backpedalled. "Oh, I don't know anything about that." He clamped his lips shut.

"What happens on the Moody property stays on the Moody property, eh?" Roxy said, and he just shrugged again.

"So Jed never mentioned Sunny before she died?" Gilda

persisted. "He never mentioned having trouble with a girl, maybe wanting out? Remember, we're talking about eighteen months ago now."

He shook his head more slowly this time, and Gilda decided he had to be lying. She leaned forward. "Listen, if you're trying to protect Jed, you're wasting your time. He's gone. I'm not interested in Jed's affairs as such; I just want to find out what happened to that poor young girl. Sunny Forrest was only twenty-one, you know? She had her whole life ahead of her."

Doug swished his lips to one side and appeared to give this some thought. Eventually he said, "Look, it's true, I kept out of Jed's shit. That was his business, Houghton's business, too. But I stayed right out of it. Didn't wanna know."

"Houghton?"

He sniggered. "It's his job to protect us from ourselves."

"Buuuuut?" Gilda prodded.

He hesitated. "But there was this one chick, right? I don't know her name, could've been Sunny, I can't say for sure. But she was persistent, man. I'll give her that. She kept calling Jed on his mobile, over and over. It'd been happening for, I dunno, months."

"One month? Ten months?" Gilda said.

"More like ten, maybe longer. Well before Sunny showed up dead, I know that much. Drove Jed freakin' nuts. You know, we're in the middle of recording, he'd get this text, suddenly he'd have to run off for an hour."

"Could it have been Annika?"

"Nah. She knew better than to interrupt Jed during a recording session. Besides, we'd have to keep playing while he was gone, so Annie would think he was still workin' away, when really…" He smiled at the thought of what Jed was getting up to.

"Did he meet this person in the hutch, near the creek? Do you know?"

"Dunno. S'pose he could've. He always took off out that

back door of the studio. It leads to the creek. I didn't ask, didn't care."

"How do you know it was a woman he was seeing?"

"What, you saying he was gay?" He chuckled heartily at this. When Gilda didn't chuckle along, he said, "Saw one of the texts once."

"And what did the text say?" *God, it was like pulling teeth!*

"Can't really remember. Just know he'd got a message, started swearing, threw the phone down and stormed out. I looked at the screen. I can't even remember the message to be honest, some shit like, 'I need to see you NOW' or something. But, you know, it had all that kisses and hugs crap at the bottom. Had to be a chick."

"Do you know if Jed happened to get one of these messages the day Sunny died? Were you in the studio working that day?"

She told him the date and he tried to remember back but failed. "There's no way these brain cells are gonna remember that shit, man. *Waaay* too long ago. I do know he'd been a bit moody around that time. I mean, the guy could be a dick at the best of times, but he was in a filthy mood after that chick was found dead by the creek. Then he went all kinda quiet."

"Quiet? How do you mean?"

"Recorded less, spent more time with Annika. I thought maybe he'd seen the light and realised life was short. Or some shit like that." He chuckled again.

"More likely he was feeling guilty," Gilda said to Roxy as they drove away from Doug's beach shack and back towards the hinterland. "Whatever happened to Sunny, Jed must have felt partly to blame. She was obviously there to meet him when it happened."

"Yes, but here's the thing," said Roxy. "That can't have been Sunny texting Jed every hour in the studio for ten months."

"Why not?"

"Well, for starters, Sunny and Jed only met each other about six weeks or so before she died. At least, that's what Sam says. He introduced them, after all. Plus, Sam told me his sister was 'pure as snow'. She only ate organic, never watched TV etcetera, etcetera."

"So?"

"So, she didn't own a mobile phone. Believed they gave you brain cancer. If that's true, there's no way she was calling and texting Jed every hour for almost a year. Nope, whoever was harassing Jed with those texts, whoever he was sneaking out to see behind the studio, I don't reckon it was Sunny Forrest."

Gilda groaned aloud. "So who the hell was it?"

"Asha Kidlong?"

"We're talking over two years ago! She would've been about fifteen then, surely not!" She shuddered at the thought. "Still, I have to wonder how long they've known each other, Jed and Asha. I should check that."

"Maybe Asha killed Sunny, to clear the way?" Roxy blurted, clicking her fingers with the excitement of a whole new suspect. "Then she killed Jed because he refused to leave his wife."

Gilda gave her a sidelong stare. "A teenage girl who wears candy necklaces and shows up to gigs with daddy dear is going to drown a grown woman in a creek, let alone know how to electrocute someone?"

"Yeah, yeah," Roxy muttered. "Straws, straws, straws."

"Come on," said Gilda, trying to cheer her up. "Let's head back to the café. There's a certain creek I'd like to take a closer look at."

CHAPTER 31

Govinda didn't appear to be working when the two women pulled their car into the lot at the Goddess Café, but they did find Hans at the back of the shop, this time doing inventory. He placed his clipboard aside when he saw them and made his way to the espresso machine, automatically assuming coffees were in order.

"No thanks," Gilda told him. "I'm all coffeed out."

Roxy was, too, but her eagerness to question the man won out so she ordered her usual then watched as he set about making it. Casually, she said, "So, I hear you do some cooking, up at Moody Views."

He glanced up at her quickly then back to the machine. "That's right."

"Did I see you there this morning? Thought I might have."

He didn't look at her this time. "Yeah, I was there." His voice sounded a little stiff, but then she might just have been reading into that.

"So Annika's still going to keep you on, even though Jed's gone?"

He looked at her properly this time and something

passed behind his eyes, but she could not read it. He slowly shrugged. "Not sure yet." His lips softened into a smile. "She's got a soft spot for my cooking so, maybe ... who knows?" He nodded his head towards the food display at the front of the shop. "Particularly likes my corn frittatas, her special favourite. You should try one."

Roxy declined but Gilda's eyes lit up. "I'll go for one of those lovely brownies. They look delish."

His smile widened, revealing missing molars up the back of his mouth. "Gluten free, is that okay? You eat gluten free?" He looked dubious.

"I eat anything as long as it's got chocolate in it."

"Grab one and I'll bring the coffee out."

Gilda chose the largest brownie she could see, wrapped it in a serviette and followed Roxy outside to a shady table.

As they took their seats, Roxy said, "What do you think about Hans?" She nodded her head back to the shop. "Bit dodgy?"

Gilda shrugged. "Don't know, but Annika's right about one thing. The man sure can cook. This is delectable. Want some?" She held the brownie towards Roxy who quickly declined.

"I'm saving myself for tonight, which reminds me, you're invited too." Gilda was already mid-mouthful, so simply raised her eyebrows in query. "Sam has invited us over to his place for a barbie, to thank us for looking after Lunar."

"Can't he just give us a bottle of wine like ordinary people?" she said, chewing away. "Doesn't need to drag us all the way out there again, does he? I'm not trying to be a killjoy or anything..."

"But?"

"But he is still a suspect in Jed's murder. Might be smarter just to keep your distance until we know what's what."

Roxy felt a wave of anger wash over her. "Are you worried I'm going to end up dead, or in his bed?" Before she could answer, Roxy added, "Because, quite frankly, if it's the latter then you're getting ahead of yourself. It's just *dinner*. That's all there is to it. Come along and you'll see for yourself."

Gilda was shaking her head now. "Wish I could, but I can't. I've got a hot date myself."

"Really?"

"Nah, not really. Our friendly Sydney detective wants to make up for last night. Take me to a decent restaurant this time."

"*Really?*" Roxy repeated, her eyes widening, and Gilda smiled.

"Now who's getting ahead of themselves? The man is married and I am simply going to compare notes and see how his investigation is going. Which is why you can't come this time. He'll be more candid without you around."

Before Roxy could respond, Hans was hovering over them with her coffee.

As he placed it down, Gilda asked, "Is Govinda about?"

He shook his head. "Not well today. Can I help you with something?"

"Maybe." She glanced around. "Is it true that the Wilson's River goes through this land?"

"Sure." He pointed to the far end of the car park where the trees looked thick and impenetrable. "It's more of a creek than a river. There's a small swimming hole down past the Coolamons. It's pretty rough, though. I can point you to some much better swimming spots."

"Not today, thanks. But if I *did* want a swim, could I access the creek quite easily?" He nodded warily. "Do you know if it leads through to the Moody property?"

Again he seemed to hesitate. "The Moody property?" She nodded. "I don't know, I can't say for sure." He diverted his eyes a little. "Why do you ask this?"

"Oh, no reason, just curious."

She smiled disarmingly at him but it didn't work. The man's eyes narrowed as he slowly backed away and Roxy wondered about him again. She was getting a strange vibe from Hans, but she had done enough straw grasping for one day so let it drop as Gilda turned her gaze upon the distant Coolamon trees.

"Now, if I was a good cop," she said, "I'd be trudging over there, sussing out that creek access for myself."

Roxy turned in her seat and looked out towards the creek. "I'll go along with you if you want. Haven't had a decent walk today, would do me some good."

Gilda thought about it then shook her head. "Nah. I don't think that's going to get me anywhere, well, apart from up a muddy creek in my fabulous city boots, of course. Nah, if I want to find out more about those pictures Maroney has, I think I need to go straight to the source."

"Get the search warrant?"

"Yep. Check out Maroney's files and see what these incriminating photos are all about. Hopefully wipe the smug smile off his ugly face."

A polite cough caught their attention and they turned back to find Hans hovering again. This time he had a brown paper bag in his hands. "This is for you," he told Roxy, holding it out.

She looked at him curiously then slowly took the bag. Inside she found a steamy corn frittata. It smelled sweet and delicious.

"You don't need to eat it now," he told her, his gaping smile widening, "but when you do, you will be in heaven!" He glanced at Gilda. "You want one, too?"

She patted her belly where the brownie had now disappeared and smiled. "I'm already in heaven, thanks, Hans. Will be there in a second to pay the bill."

"No hurry. Stay as long as you like."

As Hans trotted off, stopping at various tables to clean away used cups and plates, they both watched him silently for a while. Gilda said, "I'm not so sure he's such a bad guy, Roxy."

"Why? Because he tried to bribe us with free frittatas?"

"God, no! I mean, if he'd offered me free chocolate, we'd

be in business, but … No, I just can't see it, that's all. Plus, again, there is the small matter of how a cook knows how to string up an electrical instrument to kill someone."

"We don't know his background," Roxy suggested, but Gilda was already shaking her head and staring at her watch.

"No time to think about it now. I've got a handsome detective I need to pry for gossip."

"Is that what they're calling it these days?"

Gilda threw her scrunched up serviette at Roxy as they finished up.

CHAPTER 32

When Roxy pulled up in front of the old cottage, she spotted Sam standing off to the side of the property, just beyond the cottage kitchen. He was standing in front of what looked like a homemade brick barbeque, his wave getting lost in the plumes of smoke that billowed out from underneath a metal plate. She felt surprisingly pleased to see him and tried to dampen her smile a little as she grabbed the green bag that was sitting on the passenger seat beside her.

This is just a social call, she told herself, *a simple thank you dinner. That's all.*

Stepping out of the car, Roxy remembered not to lock it this time and made her way across to the barbeque where Sam was jabbing at something with long silver tongs, an open beer in his other hand.

Lunar came bouncing towards her, tongue hanging out and she reached down and gave the dog a pat, then held out the bag to Sam.

"I come bearing gifts. I have a large tub of organic coleslaw and a corn frittata, courtesy of Hans, as well as some Nimbin cheese and crackers and two bottles of Merlot."

"Planning on getting sloshed, are we?"

She laughed. "I'm replacing the one Gilda and I pilfered the other night." She looked at the grill. "What is that?"

Now it was his turn to laugh. "Kangaroo meat, but don't worry, it's not road kill. I got it from the local butcher."

"That's a relief."

"Ever tried it before?"

"Yes I have, thank you very much. Kangaroo steaks are *de rigueur* in Sydney restaurants these days in case you hadn't noticed. Just don't tell the tourists."

"I know, they freak out, huh? They can't believe we eat our own mascot! Little do they know, farmers hate the animals. Kangaroos can be a major pest out in these parts. Bit like the Moody Roos!" He chuckled softly at that. "You're gonna love this. I've marinated it in red wine. Not Merlot though, you cleaned me out of that."

"Hence the extra bottle." Roxy retorted.

"There's also garlic and rosemary in the marinade, and my own secret ingredient."

"Oh?" She asked.

He nudged his eyebrows up. "A tip from my mother, but I can't tell you. Family secret. The Forrests would rather die than let it out." He seemed to realise what he had said then and his smile dropped, his eyes looked away.

"I'll pop all this inside," Roxy said, holding the bag up again.

"Help yourself to a glass while you're there. You know where the good crystal is."

She laughed as she made her way to the house. Once inside, she noticed that Sam had already set the table and placed a small bowl of wild flowers in the centre, a few mismatched candles around it. She felt a sliver of anticipation, followed quickly by a stab of caution.

Just take it easy, Roxy. She told herself again. *This isn't a date.*

Yet the way the table had been decorated, the effort Sam had gone to with the meal, she couldn't help feeling it was more than a simple barbecue.

Back outside, mug of red wine in her hand, Roxy found Sam placing several cobs of fresh corn on one side of the grill, and she watched him work for a few minutes, sipping her wine and stroking Lunar's head. She felt a wave of contentment wash over her. Here she was in the middle of a murder investigation, again, and she was strangely relaxed. It had to be the peaceful setting, she decided, the stillness and the serenity.

"You cook much at home?" Sam asked, looking back at her through wisps of smoke.

"Not as much as I should. I've got some good Indian and Thai restaurants around me. You get a bit lazy in the city."

"Yeah, well, that's the thing about the country, nobody willing to deliver Laksa all the way out here. Closest eatery we've got is Govinda's, and that's no fun unless you're a tofu-chomping vegan, of course."

"Hey, I'm expecting big things from that frittata." She sipped her wine. "Everyone calls it Govinda's rather than the Goddess Café. I gather she owns it, not Hans?"

"Hans? Nah, he's just the latest man in her life."

"Oh? They're going out?"

He nodded. "Been shacked up for a while now. So, yeah, Govinda's dad set up the place years ago. Had a mechanics business first, saw the potential of people standing around waiting for their cars to be fixed, started a shop, then a café."

Roxy recalled the old signage for "Trev's Motor Mechanics". "So what happened? To Trev?"

"Cars got too fancy for the poor bugger. He used to do it all on his own. Govinda helped out occasionally where she could, but it got too tricky for them both. The newcomers take their shiny BMWs and Mercs to Lismore to be serviced these days. Not so many old bombs that need working on now. Trev up and left about two years ago, but Govinda keeps the store going. Even the rich folk round here need bread and milk, even if it is soy."

"What's Govinda's story? She has so many kids."

"Yeah, she's got a stack of girls, that's for sure. At least four, although I lost count a while back."

She whistled. "Bloody hell. She doesn't know when to stop. Who's the dad? Hans?"

He sniggered. "What makes you think there's just one?" There was a slight edge to Sam's voice and then his eyes clouded over. "I don't know Govinda's whole story, but I do know there's been a bunch of blokes over the years. She's got an older daughter, I think, who's living with her dad. For all I know, each kid could be from a different father." He glanced up at her and then back away again. "Not that I can talk. Mum was just the same. The women around here aren't exactly the faithful types."

"Or maybe it's the men," suggested Roxy.

"You can't blame 'em, just look at the name of Govinda's café. That's what some of them expect around here, certainly women like Govinda and Annika. They want to be treated like goddesses, put up on pedestals. I don't know why. They're no more special than anyone else."

The bitterness in his tone surprised Roxy and she wondered if a *goddess* had hurt him in the past. Govinda, perhaps? She vaguely recalled the first time she had met the woman, at her café, how she had mentioned "soothing" Sam over the death of his sister. Was that a euphemism for something more intimate? The very thought left her feeling prickly and somewhat irritated, and it wasn't helped by Sam's obvious hypocrisy. If anyone was thrusting anyone on a pedestal, it was Sam with his sister Sunny. Big brother seemed to act as though little sis could do no wrong, yet if she really was so pure, why was she sleeping with a married rock star in the first place? And why did she end up alone and dead in a creek on the Moody property?

Was it karma as Govinda had suggested? *Had she brought it upon herself?*

"What are you thinking about?" It was Sam, watching her silently, platter of food in his hands now. She shook the dark thoughts away.

"Oh, nothing. Can I take that inside?"

"Thanks. I'll douse the flames and join you in a sec."

Roxy took the large, chipped platter and returned to the cottage to pop it on the table. She added her goodies to the mix, then replenished her cup and placed an empty mug at Sam's plate, in case he wanted to join her in the wine. Lunar had followed her in, staring eagerly up at the meat platter and she laughed.

"Not my job to feed you tonight. You'll have to talk to Sam about that."

When Sam appeared, he whistled for Lunar and pointed to the door. The dog immediately backed away from the platter, giving it one final, woeful look before slipping outside again.

"He's already been fed," Sam explained. "Just being greedy."

"Well, you can't blame him, this smells delicious! You're a whiz on the barbeque."

"Hey, can't be an Aussie bloke and not know how to pull off a good barbie. They take your citizenship off you, you know."

Roxy laughed, relaxing a little now. She couldn't remember the last time anyone had cooked for her. Max wasn't much of a foodie, preferring to dine out at his favourite Indian haunt, and both Oliver and Gilda probably hadn't stepped inside their kitchens in years. Probably didn't know where to find them. The only home chef she knew was her step-dad, Charlie, but even then, she'd been away so much she hadn't eaten at her mum's place in months.

"Hook in," Sam said as they picked up their cutlery.

He had put on a jazz CD and lit the candles and for a moment Roxy forgot why she was there at all, but then Sam broke the magical spell.

"So Gilda couldn't make it tonight?"

"Sends her apologies."

"Sure she does!" He laughed. "She doesn't like me much,

does she?"

"Oh, she's just being protective, that's all."

"Do you need protecting?" The catch in his voice unsettled her and she pretended she didn't hear it.

"She is a detective. Can't help herself."

He considered this for a few moments. "So how is she going on Sunny's case?"

"Slowly," Roxy said. Truthfully, she was now more interested in Jed Moody's death and there were still so many unanswered questions regarding that, especially concerning the man sitting across from her. She needed to sort a few facts out in her head, so she said, "Do you mind if I ask you a few questions about the other night?"

"Which night?"

Which night?! "The night your nemesis got fried."

He placed his knife and fork down neatly on his plate, as though preparing himself for an onslaught. "What about it?"

"Why did you never tell me you were an electrician?"

He cast her a wary glance. "I didn't deliberately hold that from you, if that's what you're getting at."

"I'm not getting at anything. I just want to know the truth."

"The truth is, I had motive enough as it was. I guess I was just worried that if I mentioned it, you wouldn't have helped me. That's true, isn't it?"

She frowned. "I don't know. But you have to be honest with me, Sam, if I'm going to help. Full disclosure, okay?" He nodded. "Where did you go after we spoke?"

"What?"

"The cops keep asking me this. After we spoke on the steps outside the bar, after you told me Jed needed karma to come bite him on the bum, where did you go?"

He folded his arms over his chest. "Not to the fuse box, if that's what you're thinking."

"You've got to stop second-guessing me, Sam." She pushed her plate away, no longer as ravenous. "If I really thought you'd killed the guy, do you think I'd be out here, all alone with you?"

He thought about this and then said, "You're not alone; Lunar will protect you." His lips broke into a smile but she didn't smile back. "Okay, let me tell you what happened, and what I told Wiles and Quick. You and I spoke then I went inside, got a beer then came back out. I didn't slip around to the fuse box, I didn't tamper with Jed's amp."

"Did you notice Annika when you went inside? Did you hear her?"

"Yeah, I did."

"Really?" She sat forward.

"She was with that mad Greenie, they were just coming out of one of the rooms."

"Greenie?"

"Yeah, you know, the councillor."

"You mean Mayor Kidlong?"

"No, not him, his lackey. The one who's always attached to his hip. Younger bloke, dodgy ponytail... Don't know his name."

Roxy sat back in her chair with a thud. That's not what she'd been expecting. She tried to think back to the night of Jed's death, to picture the man who had walked in with the mayor and his daughter, but nothing had stuck.

She said, "But it sounded to me like Annika was flirting with someone and I thought the Greens Party guys were against her and the whole idea of the music festivals."

"So? Annika flirts with anyone who's got what she wants, and what she wants is permission to run a bunch of festivals at Moody Views."

"But it sounded *really* flirty, like they were having an affair."

He laughed. "That's her M.O. You've seen her with Houghton, surely? The way she carries on with him you'd think they were lovers."

"Yeah, I had noticed that. Obviously they're not?"

"You serious? Houghton and Annika? She wouldn't stoop so low, but she likes him to think she will. Keeps him hanging on, keeps Jed a little jealous, or as jealous as he could get with that giant ego. She works men, you must have realised that. Got no time for women because she can't flirt with them, at least not all of them. But she sure knows how to twist a man around her little finger, gets them just where she wants them."

"Does she do that with Alistair and Doug?"

"Probably."

"Could she have convinced someone to kill Jed for her?" *Or even Sunny*, she wondered to herself.

He gave her question some thought. "Maybe, but then she's ballsy, that one. If Annika wanted someone dead, I reckon she would've enjoyed doing it herself."

Roxy felt a small shiver race down her spine. She'd got that impression from Annika herself. "So she could simply have been flirting with the councillor that night, to help get the festival approved. Nothing more than that?"

She recalled how the councillor had been worried they would get caught together in the house—"He'll have my balls if he knows what we're up to," he'd said. Roxy had assumed he'd meant Jed Moody; now she realised he could easily be referring to his boss, Mayor Kidlong. There goes that theory, she thought glumly.

Sam was pouring the wine now and watching her. "Why this fixation with Annika? Do you think she killed Jed?"

Roxy told him she didn't know, but explained that spouses were always prime suspects. "Who do you think did it?"

"It's more like who I *don't* suspect."

"Really?" This made a nice change. Max would have dismissed that question and promptly changed the subject, never much of a fan of Roxy's mind games. Sam seemed happy to play along and was already ticking names off with his fingers.

"So, Annika, sure. She's a likely suspect. Had the best access to his gear and the fuse box, of course. And plenty of reasons to want him dead."

"But could she have pulled it off?"

He sat back. Shrugged. "Not sure she's got the know-how, that's true. She's good at managing a band, but tampering with the electricity? I've thought about it, and it wasn't just the gear that was messed with, the earth had to have been lifted somewhere in the circuit for it to work." Roxy looked at him confused and he smiled. "Just take my word for it. Next, we've got any number of women he's treated like crap over the past twenty years, but again, do any know their way around an electrical circuit?"

"No idea," replied Roxy.

Sam continued reeling off his list of suspects. "Alistair Avery, now he could pull it off. Been around electrical instruments long enough to know how to mess with one."

"Surely Doug would be the same?"

"Nah, Doug's as thick as three planks. No way he could pull it off. Plus, he's just the drummer, no electrical know-how required. But Houghton…"

"Really?" Roxy's eyes widened. "He has electrical knowledge?"

"Maybe," he replied. "Again, he's been around it long enough, plus he did play lead guitar back in the late eighties. Maybe he was handy on the soldering iron."

"Soldering iron?" she asked.

"Oh it's just like a hand tool you use to melt metal, fix your electronic gear, that kind of thing. Jed probably has a few lying about."

Roxy vaguely recalled seeing something like that recently. "Okay," she said, "and Houghton is a musician as well? I didn't know that." She took another good gulp of her wine. "He never mentioned that to me."

"Well, he wouldn't, would he? It's a sore subject." He placed his wine down and explained. "His band had a minor hit, if you count a bit of airplay on public radio. But then the lead singer went and got married and it kinda tore the band up."

"Bit of a Yoko Ono, was she?"

"Annika's been called worse names than that."

"Annika? What are you talking about?" Suddenly the penny dropped. "Do you mean Jed's first band, Horror Story? Was Houghton in that band?"

"Yeah. It didn't last long, but he had his fifteen minutes of fame. More like fifteen seconds, but you know…"

"So why did the band break up?"

"Apart from the fact they were crap?"

"That never stopped anyone before."

He thought about this. "As I say, I think it had a lot to do with Annika and the other band members, there were something like six in all, they even had a saxophonist." He laughed. "Gotta love the eighties. Anyway, I gather the rest of the band loathed Annika. She hadn't learnt how to hone her charm at that stage, so they all pissed off and left Jed holding the mic. He didn't waste time, set up the Moody Roos with a whole new lineup. And the rest, as they say, is history."

"How do you know all this?" Roxy asked, picking up her cob of corn and sprinkling a little salt onto it. Roxy was enjoying herself again. Pointing the finger at people was great fun.

"Jed and I were mates for a long time, remember? I once asked him why Houghton worked so bloody hard. He doesn't get paid that much, you know. Tiny percentage of sales, commissions when they score gigs, that's about it. Sometimes I swear that guy was more desperate for the band to succeed than they were. Anyway, Jed said Houghton was just living through them vicariously now. Missed opportunity, that kinda stuff."

"Why didn't he join the Moody Roos? Play guitar for them?"

"Dunno. Maybe he wasn't good enough. Or maybe he was too good—wouldn't want to steal Jed's thunder. Who knows? Perhaps he just wanted to be behind the scenes after that. You should ask him." Sam glanced towards the door. "All right then, you can come in now."

Lunar appeared from behind the front door and trotted in, tail wagging, eyes sparkling, and made his way under the table, beside Roxy's feet. Sam laughed.

"You traitor. One night with Roxy and you're hers forever."

Roxy laughed, too, felt a warm glow in her belly, then shook it off and focused on the conversation at hand. "But why would Houghton want to kill Jed? Sounds to me like he had a vested interest in keeping him alive."

"Not necessarily. I mean, there's only so many reunion tours you can pull off, and I heard this was going to be their last. Maybe he's hoping to cash in on the boost to sales now Jed's dead. Their Best Of album is already racing up the charts; merchandise is probably selling through the roof. There's nothing better than death to keep a band alive." He paused. "Or it could be less mercenary than that. Maybe he'd just had enough of trying to keep the band together, of Jed always putting himself and his crotch first." Again Sam's face clouded over and it was clear his sister was back on his mind. He didn't look keen to keep playing now, and Roxy decided to give him a break. She stood up and began clearing the plates.

When he stood up to join her, she said, "Don't even think about it. You cooked, I'll clean up." Then she nodded towards Lunar. "Besides, looks like you've got some making up to do."

CHAPTER 33

The croissant crumbled into buttery flakes in Roxy's hand and she slathered more homemade jam onto the final piece then popped it into her mouth. It was delicious, so, too, the fresh coffee and fruit platter that Bindi had placed on a sun-dappled table near the chirping frog pond.

Roxy had been enjoying breakfast for half an hour before Gilda joined her, dark glasses on, a scowl denting her forehead.

"Big night, eh?" Roxy asked as Gilda dropped into the seat opposite her and scowled even deeper. "When did you get back?"

Roxy had knocked softly on Gilda's door around 11:00 p.m. when she had returned to the B&B but got no response. She had assumed Gilda was fast asleep; her obvious hangover now suggested otherwise.

"I don't know," Gilda croaked, wincing as though the simple act of talking hurt. "It was well after midnight, I know that."

"So Mr. Wiles can throw 'em back, eh?"

She cringed. "Worse than that."

"Oh?"

Gilda reached for the coffee plunger and began to pour herself a cup. "I made a bit of an error of judgment."

Roxy looked confused. "What happened?"

Gilda added a little milk, a teaspoon of sugar and then took a tentative sip. "Might have ... well," she hunched over. "I might have ... accidentally, um, ended up ... in bed with him."

Roxy sat forward, surprised. "Really?! With Detective Wiles? Isn't he married?"

She hunched even further. "Yeeees."

"That's not like you."

"I know, but he said he and his wife are kinda going through something at the moment." When Roxy gave her a skeptical look, she quickly added, "I know, I know. I'm an idiot. You can blame the bloody restaurant. It was a really lovely Italian jobby with exquisite red wine, none of your cheap plonk. Then we moved on to dessert wine. It was all downhill after that."

"So the wine made you do it?"

"More like those dreamy blue eyes."

"You wicked woman!"

"I know, I know." Gilda reached for a croissant, went to take a bite, then appeared to reconsider and dropped it onto her plate. "I've always had a secret soft spot for the guy. And then when he told me he's not getting on with the wife at the moment, that they're probably going to separate, well..."

Roxy stared at her. "They always say that. Did he mention how she just doesn't understand him anymore?"

"Oh, don't give me that, Roxy. I know it was evil of me. But it's been bloody ages, I'm practically a born-again virgin, we don't all have gorgeous hunks throwing themselves at us, you know."

Roxy tsked. Poppycock, she wanted to say. Gilda was a stunner, turned heads everywhere she went. Hell, just yesterday she'd had a photographer begging her to pose for him (albeit a sleazebag paparazzi, but that was beside the point). Gilda may be pushing forty-five, but she had the youthful good looks of a woman half her age, her blonde, wispy hair and petite, hourglass figure adding a kind of sexy pixie look that lured men in droves.

Roxy sighed. Moral grandstanding was never part of their relationship, so she grinned and said, "I hope he was worth it at least."

Finally Gilda looked lively. "Oh my God, he was fantastic. I mean, really fantastic." She buckled over again. "I'm going straight to hell."

Roxy couldn't help laughing now. "Well, you're both grown-ups, I guess you know what you're doing. Anyway, I couldn't care less about that. Did you at least get some goss on the Jed Moody investigation before you locked lips?"

"Yes, thank you, I did! But before I get into that, what happened at Sam's place?" Her eyebrows nudged north from beneath her glasses.

Roxy said, "Unlike you, I behaved myself."

She half wished she hadn't. The dinner last night had been beautiful, the conversation effortless, yet she had torn herself away before she drank too much and ended up exactly where Gilda was sitting now. She had congratulated herself on her restraint, been impressed at the way she had avoided lingering eye contact with the man, and managed to flee before things got any cosier than they'd already become. She wondered now why she had bothered. Gilda, however, looked relieved to hear it.

"Good," she said. "Keep your distance there."

Roxy felt her hackles rise again. "He's not a bad guy, Gilda."

"Yeah, but you don't really know that, do you?"

"What's to know? He seems decent. He seems loyal and honest."

"Er no, that would be his dog."

Roxy glared at her. "You sound just like my mother."

"Well somebody's got to play devil's advocate."

"Why?" Roxy demanded. "Isn't this what you all accuse me of time and time again? What I was constantly getting wrong with Max? Never following my heart, always using my head."

"And your heart says him? Mr. Beard Guy who lives like a hermit in the bush? *Really?*"

"So *that's* what you've got against him? The fact that he has three-day growth and lives all the way out here, so far away from you and Sydney and Pico's wine bar. That's what it's about, isn't it? If Sam had a nicely trimmed goatee and wore an expensive Italian suit and lived in the heart of Sydney you'd be telling me to stop playing it so safe and plunge in."

"Exactly! But he doesn't wear a suit; he wears a checked shirt like some kind of country yokel. And he lives out here in *Deliverance* land and you don't even know the first thing about the guy. How can you be falling for him so quickly?"

Roxy screamed. "I'm not falling for him! How many times do I have to say that! I just had dinner with him, jeez!" She groaned loudly then took a deep calming breath. "Look, Gilda, I know what you're saying, but you're reading ahead. I just like the guy, I enjoy his company, that's all there is to it. I feel comfortable around him. Like … I don't know … like I've known him my whole life, or something. Is that so strange?"

"No," Gilda said, sighing. To her it sounded much worse than that. It sounded a lot like love.

They stewed in silence for a few minutes, neither woman meeting each other's eyes, and eventually Gilda said, "Well, do you want to hear what Wiles had to say or don't you?" It was a truce of sorts.

"Fine," Roxy snapped, trying not to sound too keen.

But before Gilda could tell her, Bindi came shimmying towards them across the lawn.

"Good morning!" she sang out and Gilda gave Roxy a quick head-shake, suggesting that they would continue the conversation later.

"Morning," the two women muttered back.

"How are we both feeling today?"

"Good, thanks," Roxy said, hoping she'd scoot off again just as quickly.

"Did we sleep well?"

Roxy nodded. "Yep, yep." *Clear off, please woman, I've got some gossip waiting.*

"You have, of course, missed the morning's yoga session with Chaitanya, but I thought you might like to know she does run individual classes, if you'd like to give her a call."

Gilda held a hand up firmly. "Not really our cup of tea, thanks, Bindi."

The woman looked slightly put out. "It would do you the world of good." Her eyes flittered across Gilda's washed out face. "She has an uncanny ability to cleanse your inner chakras. To help you unwind and clarify what's really important in life." She gave Gilda another pointed look then went to walk away when she remembered something and turned back. "Oh, Ms Maltin. You had a phone call, a few hours ago. I put it through to your room but you didn't pick up."

Gilda vaguely recalled an annoying ringing sound at some ungodly hour that morning. *So that's what that was.* "Did you take a message?"

"Yes, I did." She fumbled at a hidden pocket in her flowing yellow kaftan. "Someone called Macker Rooney, I think?"

"Macker Maroney, really?" Gilda flashed Roxy a curious glance. "What did he say?"

She located a slip of paper and handed it over. "He asked you to call him, please, as soon as you get a chance." She hesitated. "He sounded quite, er, anxious."

"Like, busy-anxious or needing-the-services-of-Chaitanya anxious?"

She gave Gilda a strained smile then bowed her head and floated off across the lawn, back towards the homestead.

"Interesting," Gilda said. "I wonder what he wants."

"Yes, fascinating, but get on with it. I'm on the edge of

my seat here. What did Wiles say?"

"What? Oh, well, Wiles is starting to gather a pretty good suspect list. Don't get too excited, your boyfriend is still up the top somewhere, but Wiles is looking at a few other suspects as well, which is a good thing."

Roxy's heart leapt, but she just said, "He's not my boyfriend."

Gilda smartly ignored this and said, "Wiles tells me the wiring work done on Jed's amplifier was so dodgy, it doesn't look like the handiwork of an experienced sparkie. Unless, of course, Sam was trying to shift the blame and deliberately did it badly." She sat back as though only just considering this. "There is that."

"No, no, I like the first theory. So who is Wiles looking at now?"

"He's got his eye on a few people. He's starting to consider the theory that Jed was killed to put an end to the festivals. Apparently there was a lot of animosity in the community about the plan."

"So I heard. Houghton told me Mayor Kidlong was dead against it."

"Yes, although Quick says the tide is turning on that. Apparently a new motion is being put forward at the next council meeting by one of the Greens councillors, and Kidlong may just get out voted."

"I think I know who that councillor might be." Roxy quickly filled Gilda in on the news Sam had told her last night, about the way Annika flirted to get what she wanted. "Sam tells me it was one of the young Greens guys that Annika was flirting with inside the house the night Jed died. Sounds to me like she was talking him around."

"She was certainly doing *something* to bring him round." Gilda shuddered visibly at the thought. "Okay, that makes sense. Anyway, it's not the tree huggers Wiles is looking at."

"Who then?"

"You won't believe it."

"Try me."

"He's looking at the Holloways."

"The farmers next door? Nooo!" This case got madder by the day. "Why?"

Gilda took another, more confident sip of her coffee. "Look, it's just a theory. One of many that Wiles is developing, and I don't think he's got a shred of evidence—"

"Get on with it!"

"Wiles has done some digging around and, well, they may play happy neighbours, but apparently the Holloways have been putting in endless complaints to council about Jed Moody, practically since he moved into the place."

"About the noise?"

"About everything. There are sixteen official complaints."

"Sixteen? You're kidding me?"

She shook her head and began ticking the points off with her fingers: "Noise, traffic, improper use of the creek, the main road, tree clearing."

"Tree clearing? You're serious? There's barely a twig on their property."

She shrugged. "The Moodys couldn't do a thing right. You name it, the old couple complained about it."

"They must have hated the festival idea."

"Oh yes, loathed that one big time. Were prepared to take them to court apparently. This is all according to the local council staffers. I think they've had a gutful."

Roxy eyed Gilda's croissant. "Speaking of which, you gonna eat that?" She shook her head, looked ready to throw up, so Roxy grabbed it and began smothering it in jam. "So why do the Holloways keep going over to the Moodys' place, acting all buddy buddy?"

"According to Annika, they rarely do go over, despite what it looked like. Wiles believes—and, as I say, he's still establishing the evidence, I shouldn't even be telling you this and don't you dare share this with *anyone*—but he wonders whether that's why they went that night."

"To get rid of their annoying rock star neighbour once and for all." Roxy replied, putting the pieces together.

"Exactly. They may have come back the next day, pretending to commiserate with the grieving widow, just to check they hadn't left any evidence behind."

"And let me guess, John Holloway has the know-how to fiddle with the wires?" Roxy asked, recalling the old work shed they passed when last at the Holloway property.

"Wiles believes so. Apparently Holloway repairs all his own machinery, generators, that kind of stuff. Wiles says he's got the happy trio—means, motive, opportunity. He's not a hundred percent certain, of course. It's early days and there is still the rather important matter of evidence. I'm not sure he's got any. Apart from all the nasty complaints to council."

Roxy took a bite of the pastry as she shook her head. "Still, it seems a little out there to me. I would never have picked it."

"You did, remember? When we met farmer John at the gate? You thought he was hiding something."

"Yes, but I didn't think he was a murderer." She chewed quickly. "How often do people bump off their noisy neighbours? Seems like an overreaction to me."

Gilda shrugged. "I've told you before, I've seen people kill for a lot less. Did I ever tell you about the time we arrested a guy for smacking his flatmate across the head with a cricket bat? Didn't kill him, but he came close. You know what his problem was? He hated his flatmate's taste in music." She paused. "Of course, the flatmate was a big fan of One Direction, so there was grounds for an appeal."

Roxy barely heard this; her mind was racing ahead now. Or rather, back, to the year before, to Sunny Forrest's death. "John Holloway was the one who found Sunny's body. Does Wiles think he killed her, too?"

Gilda held both hands up to stall her. "Don't get ahead of yourself, Missy. He knows nothing about that. I've found no evidence on that score, either." She finished off her coffee, poured another cup then offered the coffee plunger to Roxy who did the same. "I guess if you think really hard about it, which I'm trying not to do because my head is aching, big time, but if you think about it, Holloway could have killed Sunny in an attempt to put the blame on Jed. Or to try to scare him away..." Her voice trailed off, she didn't sound convinced.

"Or maybe," Roxy said, taking up where Gilda left off, "maybe farmer John had nothing to do with Sunny's death but finding the poor girl really touched a nerve. He did say he'd lost his own daughter. Maybe it was the final straw. Or at the very least it added to a litany of reasons he wanted to see the guy dead. He either felt sorry for Sunny—yet another Moody victim—or he'd just had enough of all the chaos this rock star had unleashed on the neighbourhood. There was no way he could afford to take Jed to court over the festivals. Maybe killing him was the only option." She sighed. "It must have been a very peaceful world before the Moodys moved in."

"Boring, more like it."

A distant cry caught their attention and they both looked back towards the B&B to find Bindi waving her hand frantically in the air. It looked like she was holding a telephone.

"Must be Macker again." Gilda struggled to her feet.

"I'll come with you. I'm done here."

The two women rushed across the lawn and Gilda reached for the phone but Bindi was already handing it to Roxy, who cocked her head to the side and said, "Hello? Who is this?"

"You have really got to get a better phone system!"

She smiled and rolled her eyes at Gilda. "Hi, Oliver, how are you doing?"

"How am *I* doing? You're the one I'm worried about. I had quite a time tracking you down. Does your bloody mobile ever work?"

"Not up here, it doesn't. I've told you that before." She didn't mention that she was quite enjoying being out of reach. "What's up?"

"Two things. First up, you never signed the contract."

"Sorry?"

"Hello? Are you smoking too much of that Nimbin weed? The Moody Roos book, Ms Parker! I need that contract back so we can get started on it. I e-mailed it to you yesterday. Is this ringing any bells? At all?"

"Sorry, I got busy with Gilda. Damn. I'll see if they've got a scanner here or fax machine or something."

"You do that." He paused. "You're poking your nose into Jed's murder, aren't you?"

"No, no, I'm not. Not directly, anyway."

"Look, you know you can't muck around with that. The band is paying for this book, but they're not going to want you digging about in the murder. It's supposed to be feel-good."

"Their lead singer just died. I'm not going to be able to avoid it."

"Just focus on the positive, please. Focus."

"Fine. So, what's the second thing?"

He growled. "Ring your bloody mother."

Roxy winced. "Been hassling you?"

"That's one way of putting it. She's back to her irate self. I don't mean to sound politically incorrect, but I swear that woman's got serious mental health issues. She can't get through to your mobile, seems to think you've been chopped to pieces, the usual stuff. Once again, please give her a call. I implore you!"

"I will, Oliver, I'll do it now."

"Good." He hung up and she turned to Gilda who was watching the exchange with a look of mild amusement.

"In the dogbox again?"

"It's not funny, Gilda. It's exhausting." She sighed. "I'd better make some calls and get some work done today or I'll be in more trouble. You're going to have to continue with Sunny on your lonesome, I'm afraid."

"That's not my biggest concern right now."

"Oh?"

Gilda nodded her head towards the front of the B&B. "I just spotted Wiles pull up."

Roxy's bad mood dropped away. "Oooh, that's *romantic*! Couldn't keep away, huh?"

Gilda responded with a death stare, then took a deep breath, ran a hand through her tussled hair and turned to face the music. Yet as Wiles strode through the front door, his lips set in a grim line, a solemn-looking Quick at his heels, it was clear romance was the last thing on the Sydney detective's mind.

"I need your help," he said to Gilda. "There's been another murder."

CHAPTER 34

Macker Maroney never knew what hit him.

Wiles and Gilda had a pretty good idea though. They found a bloodied axe not far from the dead man's feet, no doubt discarded by the killer who had somehow managed to bludgeon the photographer to death while he was enjoying his morning smoke.

His cigarette packet was on the dirt beside him, just outside the back door of the ramshackle house he rented at Cooleys Shoot. His ghoulish eyes stared up at them now, a half-smoked ciggie close by. Macker hadn't even had a chance to change out of his flannelette pyjamas and terry-toweling robe, and Gilda felt he looked quite pathetic lying there; his arrogant bluster vanquished for all time.

"I don't suppose we're going to find prints on that," she said, watching as Wiles placed the axe into an enormous evidence bag before handing it to Quick. Wiles shrugged. There was a wood-pile not far from where the dead man lay, and it didn't appear as though the killer had brought his own weapon. Was it a crime of passion, perhaps, or of opportunity?

"Who phoned it in?"

"A woman who lives up behind those trees there." Wiles pointed to a cluster of stringy gums. "Her teenage son found him, about an hour ago, he'd come down to give him some eggs."

"Eggs?"

"It's multiple occupancy, they share their shit, apparently."

"How cosy. Don't suppose this teenager spotted someone running off with a guilty look on their face."

He smiled thinly. "No such luck. Can you rush that to the Tweed lab ASAP?" he called out to Quick who was about to hand the axe over to a uniformed offer. "I want *you* to make sure it gets there. Tell them it's urgent."

Quick looked annoyed by this, and marched away to where his car had been parked, at the top of the muddy driveway.

"He's a joy to be around," Gilda said.

"Oh, he's okay. Mustn't be much fun having your territory pissed all over by a bigger dog. So, I wonder what this is about." He looked back at Macker's lifeless body.

"He left me a message this morning." Gilda said. "But I was still comatose, didn't take the call." She scrunched her face up, feeling pangs of guilt and regret.

"What did the message say?" Wiles looked at her, eyes wide.

"Nothing, just asked me to call him back. I'll question the B&B manager again. She said he sounded anxious." She groaned. "If only I'd been more *compos mentis*."

"Look, about last night—"

Gilda shook her head. "It shouldn't have happened and not only because you're married."

"But my wife isn't —"

"It was bloody unprofessional of both of us, we're in the middle of two investigations and now a man is dead. The same man who tried to reach out to me, maybe with some valuable information, before he was murdered. Arrgh! If only I had taken his call."

"Gilda, you know better than to beat yourself up about that. Nothing you can do about it now. You need to get over it and focus." His tone was harsh but when she looked up at him, Wiles's eyes were soft and sympathetic. "I could do with your help. Quick can't see beyond his own ego, no real use to me at the moment. Can you drop that other case for now? I can check it with Houlihan."

"I think my time's up anyway." She took the blue plastic gloves he was now handing her. "Rightio, then, let's see what we've got."

Back at Bindi's Eco Hideaway, Roxy was attempting to forget what she'd just heard about Macker Maroney and focus on the reason she was in Byron in the first place. It was no mean feat. She kept flashing back to Macker's ruddy face, his smarmy smile and sleazy innuendo. She hadn't liked the guy, loathed him, in fact, but he had been full of life, you had to give him that. She couldn't imagine him dead, couldn't even get her head around it yet. Still, if the locals were right and there was such a thing as karma, it had certainly come calling for Macker.

Suppressing a small shiver that tingled down her spine, Roxy began tapping into the B&B's WiFi and started trawling through scores of e-mails, mostly SPAM, to locate the relevant one from her agent.

She scanned through the contract as quickly as she could, printed it out down in the lobby, signed it, then enlisted Bindi to fax it to Oliver while she returned to her room to make some more calls. She took a weary breath and called her mum.

"Oh, my goodness me, she's alive!" Lorraine cried before calling out to someone, probably Charlie, "Call off the hounds, my daughter is alive!"

"Sorry, Mum," Roxy said, thinking those two simple words were so familiar they should form her epitaph. "My mobile has zero coverage up here."

"Oh, and they don't have landline telephones anymore?

The flower children not into that?"

"Yes, in fact I'm using the B&B's landline now, so I can't talk for long."

"B&B? I thought you were staying at that rock star's house, the one who was just *murdered*."

Lorraine managed to pack a lot of guilt and insinuation into that final word and Roxy winced. Did she really expect her mother would not have heard by now?

"It's a long story, Mum. I'm staying with Gilda at a place called Bindi's—"

"Gilda? Your police friend?"

"My best friend, yes. She's..." Roxy went to explain, thought better of it and said simply, "She's up here on police business." It was partially true.

"Is she investigating that rock star's murder?"

"No, she's not." As far as Roxy knew, this, too, was true.

"Well, now I think about it, that's good news. She can keep an eye on you."

It's Gilda who needed watching out for, Roxy thought, remembering what she'd been up to the night before. "I'm safe as houses here, Mum, don't worry about me." There was no way she was going to mention the latest murder; that would do her mother's head in. "What about you? Is everything okay? Oliver said you'd been hassling him again."

There was an intake of breath. "I was most certainly *not* hassling him. I called him once. Well, maybe two or three times. There might have been a fourth call, I can't remember. But that's not the point. I would have left the man alone if you had bothered to call me. I figured he'd know where my daughter was considering my daughter was too preoccupied to bother ringing her mother."

"Mum, I'm on assignment, and I've been out of Sydney what, six days."

"Six whole days, has it been that long? And you're already caught up in a murder, again!"

Roxy groaned to herself and said, "I'll give you this number should there be an actual emergency. You know the type? Someone's lost a limb, had a heart attack."

"Been electrocuted?"

Roxy winced again. "That has nothing to do with me."

"Well how do I know that? I hear it on the news, Oliver won't tell me anything."

"I'm fine, I promise you that!" She tried to soften her tone a bit. "Listen, I really can't call you all the time, Mum, not when I'm working."

Now Lorraine's tone turned to one of deep hurt. "I don't ask you to call me all the time, Roxanne. Just every now then would be nice."

Roxy ignored this, read out Bindi's phone number then said, "I'll call you in a few days. Give my love to Charlie, okay?"

There was a small huff. "Fine, start meddling in another horrendous murder while your poor mother sits here all worried about you."

"You have fun, too, Mum. Good-bye."

She hung up, collapsed onto the bed and pulled a pillow over her mouth to muffle her cries of anguish. They had always had a tense relationship, Roxy and Lorraine, yet it seemed to worsen after Roxy's father, Jacob, died. She was still a child when the cancer got him and she recalled now, walking back into their house soon after the wake, how their differences seemed to intensify without him around to hose things down. Roxy's father's death only compounded how little mother and daughter had in common. Yet they both endeavoured to keep the relationship going, if only out of respect for Jacob and a begrudging admiration for each other's wily determination to always be right. It had become a game of sorts between then, one that sometimes amused, sometimes grated. Sometimes left Roxy screaming into pillows.

She wondered now why she bothered, and why things seemed to get even harder as time went on. Wasn't her mother supposed to relax at some stage? After all, Roxy wasn't a child any more.

She sat up straight. No, she thought, I am *not* a child, and it's time to stop acting like one. She'd had just about enough of everyone telling her what she should and shouldn't do, and that included her best friend. She grabbed the phone again and stabbed in a mobile number she had somehow—oddly—learned off by heart.

"Hello?"

"Sam, hi, it's Roxy."

"Hey, Roxy," his voice softened. "We had fun last night, huh?"

"Not nearly enough," she replied. "Wanna meet again tonight?"

CHAPTER 35

Doug Campbell was not nearly as thick as Sam had made out. Simple was a better word for him, she decided. He just liked the simple life. Despite fame and fortune, all he seemed to care about was surfing his days away, smoking a bit of pot, and hanging out with his mates at the local pub. Drumming didn't seem to come into it, and, he admitted as she interviewed him that morning, he would have given up percussion a decade ago if it wasn't for the band's endless reunion tours and Houghton's persuasive powers.

"I guess Jed's death has put an end to that then?" she said as they sipped chai tea in the bright kitchen of his Byron beach house.

"Not if Houghton has his way," he replied, watching as honey slowly dripped from the teaspoon he was holding above his cup. "You want?" He darted a look at the honey jar and she shook her head. Some sugar would be nice, but the only sugar he could find was crawling with tiny black ants.

"The little buggers get into everything down here."

"No worries," she said, "I'll pass." He clearly hadn't yet heard about Macker's murder and she decided not to tell him. That wasn't the reason she was here. She would do as Oliver had asked and focus on the book. "So you were never as ambitious as Jed or Alistair?"

He laughed then licked the spoon before dumping it into the sink. "*No one's* as ambitious as Al. Nah, surfin's more my gig."

"What about a wife, kids?" He grimaced. "But you must have been tempted. Chicks used to throw themselves at you."

"Still do, occasionally."

She blushed. "Sorry, I didn't mean…"

He chuckled. "I've seen the grief Annika's given Jed and nope, no way, that kinda crap is not for me. Just give me a six-foot swell and a Thruster and I'm happy."

"You don't like Annika?"

He shrugged. "I don't *not* like her. Just wouldn't want one for myself, that's all."

They had spent the past two hours going through Doug's biography, Roxy ticking off all the basics—his date and place of birth, family background, early influences. They had then moved on to how Doug came to be in the band and she was stunned to learn his first audition had been in front of Annika, not Jed.

"Yeah, she'd placed an ad, looking for a drummer. I fronted up, she liked my chops and I got the job."

"It was up to *her*, not Jed?"

"Always has been, as far as I can tell."

"Can you remember where you saw the ad?"

He thought about it for a few minutes as he slurped his tea. "Nah, not off hand, sorry. Houghton'll remember, he was part of it from the start."

"Yes, I heard that he and Jed used to be in Horror Story before the Roos. Know much about that?"

"Not a lot. They never really talk about it. Bad blood between the band and Annika, something like that. That's why Annika got to pick Jed's next lineup, so we all got along. One big happy family." His tone suggested nothing could be further from the truth.

"Do Alistair and Annika get along?"

He cocked his head to the side and a sly smile crept onto his face. "That's one way of putting it."

"What do you mean?"

"Look, I just front up, do the love-ins, tick off the gigs, take the money and get out again."

"Love-ins?"

He chuckled. "God, I won't miss those."

"*Love-ins?*" she repeated.

"Annika insisted we all have a little powwow before each gig. You know, heads together, positive affirmations, that kind of crap."

"The point being?"

He put on a hippie-dippy voice: "Positive vibes, man."

Roxy laughed. "Sounds more like Govinda's spiel to me. Are they friends, those two?"

He looked shocked at the thought. "What? Annie and Govinda? What are you on? No way, man!"

"They seem to have lots in common."

"Too much in common, if you ask me."

"Both goddesses?" she suggested, remembering Sam's words from the night before and he chuckled.

"To say the least. Listen was there anything else you needed? I gotta get rollin'."

Roxy thought about how fortunate Jed's death was for the reluctant drummer—the end of relentless gigs. Could that be a motive for murder? She shook her head.

"Cool. Maybe just text if you think of anything else."

"Good idea, except coverage here is a bit patchy. Do you go up to the Moody place often? Am I likely to run into you up there?"

"Too far from the coast for me. But I guess I'll have to get up there sometime this week and see what's cookin'. Houghton has plans. Reckons we need to do one final memorial tour."

"You're obviously not keen."

It wasn't even a question, he'd already made his feelings crystal clear, but he gave it some thought as he walked her to the door.

"It's not that I don't want to do the tour, I don't really care, to be honest, just not sure it's gonna work without Jed. I mean, Al can moan all he likes, but Jed was *The Man*. The Moody Roos aren't much without the Moody in it."

Doug's words echoed in Roxy's brain the whole way back from the coast, along the winding hinterland to Jasper Road.

He was right, of course. Jed Moody *was* the Moody Roos, whether Al liked it or not. So unless Jed's death was done in the heat of rage—which it couldn't have been, not the way it was carried out—then whoever killed Jed had to be better off with him dead, not worse. Which seemed to rule out Houghton and Annika—they had both worked so hard to create this life for themselves, he was their cash cow, would they really destroy it all now? There were only so many Best Of albums you could sell, surely?

It did point the finger at the band, however. Wiles might be gunning for the Holloways, but Roxy felt like the answer to this crime had to lay closer to home. She wondered again about Doug. Could he have murdered Jed to rid himself, once and for all, of the monster on his back, to ensure he could get on with the quiet life he so clearly craved? Seemed a bit extreme, she decided, plus he didn't appear to have the enthusiasm for it. The guy just plodded through life, that much was clear. He was happy to go with the flow. He might be into catching waves, but he didn't seem the type to cause them.

Besides, couldn't he just say no to Houghton and tell him to find another drummer? Would anyone really have cared? Or noticed for that matter?

Which brought her back to Al. It was time to have another chat with the bass player. She glanced at the clock in the car. It was after one. Hopefully she would catch him up at the Moody house, her next destination. She was hoping

Gilda would be there, too. The small matter of Macker Maroney's murder was now wrestling its way back into her consciousness and would not be so easily ignored this time. She was keen to find out how the investigation was progressing and what, if anything, it had to do with Sunny and Jed.

CHAPTER 36

"**I** haven't seen that detective friend of yours," Annika told Roxy as she stood at the front door of her house; her feet bare, her hair in a tousled ponytail high on her head. "But I did hear about that paparazzi guy. Hans just told me. It's all over the village. Can't say I'm devastated."

"Yes, well, he was a bit of a grub, but I'm not sure he deserved that."

Annika cocked an eyebrow at Roxy. "You're a nicer person than me, then. Coffee?"

Roxy tried not to look surprised as she followed Annika down the long hallway, remembering to discard her shoes by the door.

"So, Hans is back?" she said.

"Just dropped off some fresh bread and milk. Deserted me again, though, got to run the café. Govinda's as good as useless these days, what with all those kids of hers. And another on the way."

"Another?"

Annika rolled her eyes as they entered the kitchen. "Apparently four daughters are just not enough."

She padded over to an enormous gleaming espresso

machine and started heating it up while Roxy took a stool at the floating kitchen bench and studied her. Now in her late thirties, Annika was still an extremely beautiful woman, elegantly dressed and statuesque, her high ponytail pulling her face back and making her almond-shaped eyes seem almost feline.

Roxy wondered what she would do now and asked as much.

"I'll get on with my life, of course! I did have one, you know, it wasn't *all* about Jed."

"Will you keep this property?"

"Absolutely, yes. In fact, I'm going to start running festivals here. It's such a stunning piece of land, really very underutilised. I'd like to share it more."

"What do your neighbours think about that?" Roxy already knew the answer, of course, and Annika's eyes narrowed further.

"The Holloways can get stuffed! They had their chance, a hundred years in this area and have barely made a penny. It's time for them to move on and let the next generation have a whirl."

"You think they're going to leave?"

She placed a cup under the coffee spout. "I'm hoping they'll accept my offer and clear off."

"You've offered to buy their property?"

"I've offered much more than it's worth. You saw the place, right? Scrubby, cleared land. It'll take me years to replant, get it back to something vaguely resembling rainforest."

"Do you think they'll accept?"

"Oh God, I hope so. That couple has been an albatross around my neck. You take milk, right?"

She nodded, wondering if Annika had any idea about Wiles's suspicions. It didn't appear so, and she felt a small flutter of concern. If Wiles was right about the Holloways, then Annika's life might also be in jeopardy, especially if she was still pushing ahead with the festivals.

"Will the council permit you to run the festivals here?"

"Don't worry about them," she yelled over the sound of frothing milk. "I've got them sorted."

So I heard, Roxy thought, flashing back to the night of Jed's death. She wondered how far Annika took her flirtation. Had she exchanged sexual favours with the ponytailed councillor for a "Yes" vote on her development application, or was it more innocent than that?

Annika handed her the coffee then got busy making herself a cup. When she was done, they headed back out to the veranda where Roxy noticed the stage was still taped up.

Following her line of sight, Annika tsked loudly. "It's a bloody nuisance. I just want to clear it away and get on with my life."

It had only been four days since Jed was murdered, Roxy wanted to tell her but instead she asked, "How are you holding up?"

"I'm fine," she snapped. "I'll survive. As I say, my life wasn't all about Jed Moody. I wish everyone would remember that!"

Roxy felt a sudden surge of impatience with Annika. When she'd first arrived, Annika had been so possessive of Jed Moody, lecturing her about keeping her hands to herself. Now she was acting as though he was little more than a passing fad. "Jed was a *huge* part of your life, Annika," she snapped back. "You obviously loved him deeply and you're *allowed* to be upset, you know. You don't have to pretend like it's all okay."

Annika glanced sharply over at Roxy and looked like she was about to slap her down when emotion got the better of her. Her lower lip began to quiver and she slumped onto one of the sofas, hunched over her coffee cup and began sobbing into it.

Crikey. Thought Roxy. She hadn't expected that. She dumped her cup on a side table and sat down beside Annika, gently patting her on the back. They remained like this for some time and eventually the widow swiped her tears away and tried to pull herself together.

"Arggggh!" she said. "He makes me so angry! I can't believe he left me, I just can't believe it!"

"He didn't leave you, Annika. He was murdered."

She sniffed. "I know … I know … It's going to take a while, that's all. We'd been together since I was seventeen, you know."

"Seventeen? That is young."

"He's all I knew, he's all I cared about." She sniffed again. "It's going to take some getting used to."

"Of course it is. Can I get you a tissue?"

"Inside, on the table by the gold lamp."

Roxy retrieved the tissue box and they spent a few more minutes in contemplative silence before Annika gave her nose a final blow and said, "Enough of all this. I guess you want to interview me? For the book?"

"Only if you're up to it, Annika."

"Let's just get it over with, shall we?"

They never got the chance. Just as Roxy was pulling her digital recorder from her carry bag, they heard the sound of cars pulling up at the front of the house and Annika gave a weary sigh, wiped two fingers under her eyes to clear away any running mascara, then got up and walked back through the house towards the front door, Roxy close behind.

She pushed it open to reveal Wiles and Gilda stepping out of an unmarked vehicle, two uniformed officers out of a second patrol car.

"Is Alistair Avery here?" Gilda called out and Annika frowned.

"Somewhere, yes. Why?"

"Where is he, Mrs. Moody? We need to have a word." This was Wiles and he did not look like he had time for chitchat.

"God, I don't know." She glanced around. "I guess he's in the studio. He's going through some files with Houghton, but…"

"Where is the studio?"

"I'll show you," Roxy said, stepping forward. "It's this way."

She shared a curious look with Annika then led the officers away from the house and back towards the tall timber building on the far side of the house. At the door, Gilda took her arm and held her back. "We'll take it from here, thanks, Roxy. Can you return inside? We'll see you back there."

She nodded. "What's going on?"

Gilda held a hand up. "I'll see you back at the house."

Roxy nodded again then slowly made her way along the path, glancing back to see Wiles banging on the studio door, the officers on either side of it. "Alistair Avery? Police! Open up!"

"What on earth is going on?" Annika asked, leaning against the veranda railing, her dog Coco now in her arms. Coco was emitting the occasional yelp but there was no sincerity in it. For her part, Annika looked genuinely worried and Roxy was feeling a little concerned, too. Did Gilda and Wiles believe Alistair had killed Macker Maroney? Or was this about Jed's death?

"I have no idea, Annika. Let's just wait it out, okay?"

It didn't take long. Five minutes later, Gilda and Wiles were trudging back down the pathway towards the main house, the two uniformed officers behind them holding Alistair, his head bowed. He didn't meet anyone's eyes, simply looked down at the ground, while Houghton appeared behind him growling something into his mobile phone. Annika rushed towards them, aghast.

"What are you doing? What's going on?"

Wiles didn't answer her, simply turned to the officers and said, "Take Mr. Avery down to the station, guys and put him in an interrogation room. I need to have a word with Mrs. Moody separately first."

"You can't interrogate him without his lawyer!" Houghton squeaked, waving the phone at the officers as they shuffled Alistair into the police car and closed the door. Houghton leaned down towards the window and yelled, "I'll get Harris here, Al, don't panic, and don't say another bloody word!"

Roxy gave Gilda a bewildered look and she raised her eyebrows but remained silent.

"We'd like to have a word with you, Mrs. Moody. Do you mind if we use your office again?"

Annika looked at Wiles with outrage for a moment before sighing melodramatically, then striding back through the house towards the office. Gilda began to follow, then hesitated and turned back to Roxy who was still standing just outside, her brain buzzing with questions.

"I'll explain it all later," she whispered. "Can you hang around? I really need to talk to you. It's about Sunny."

"Sunny?" *What did she have to do with any of this?*

"Later, I promise."

She gave Roxy's hand a quick squeeze then entered Jed's office and swung the door shut behind her.

The house seemed eerily quiet now, and Roxy slowly closed the front door, wrapped her arms around herself and returned to the kitchen to fire up the espresso machine again. What an exhausting couple of days, she thought, and so baffling, too. She closed her eyes and tried to make sense of it all, but nothing was falling into place.

Was Alistair being arrested for Macker's murder, or Jed's? And what, if anything, did all this have to do with Sunny?

"How're you doing? You okay?"

Roxy's eyes popped open to find Houghton standing at the kitchen doorway, one hand still clutching his mobile, a strained look on his face.

She tried to smile. "Oh, I'm fine. What's going on with Alistair? Do you have any idea?"

He frowned. "They found some bloody photos that paparazzi bastard took of Al. He's in the shit, big time." He glanced at his phone. "Where is this friggin' lawyer? So much for, 'Call me anytime'!"

"What kind of photos?"

"Huh?"

"You said Macker had some photos."

"Oh, right." Houghton hesitated. "Look, I'd better not say anymore at this point. Won't do anyone any good. You using that?" He pointed to the espresso machine and she moved out of the way so he could make himself a cup. She didn't have the energy right now.

"Has Macker been blackmailing you all again?" she asked.

Houghton glanced around, shooting a look at the doorway then back at her. "What do you know about that?"

"I know Macker had photos of Jed and Sunny together, at the hutch out near the creek, before she died. I know he was trying to extort money out of you. Was Alistair still angry about that?"

"Al? Nah, he couldn't give a shit. I took care of that. Always do." He turned back to the machine. "It's ancient history now anyway. We paid the bastard off."

"So why did you tell Gilda yesterday that you didn't know about Jed and Sunny's affair?"

"Because she told me she was investigating Sunny's death. I didn't need to give myself a motive for wanting her gone, did I? It would just confuse matters. It was all sorted a long time ago."

"But Macker was obviously trying his luck again," Roxy persisted. "The night I first met Jed, he said something to you about it. Something about not paying him another cent."

"Oh, that was a total scam! Macker had some new pix, some grainy shots he thought were of Jed and Asha together, but we laughed. It wasn't who he thought it was."

"Who was it?"

He turned back to the machine, clearly not willing to be drawn further. Roxy watched him at the machine for a few minutes. Several pieces seemed to click into place in her brain, but first she needed to get a few things straight.

"I'm sorry to harp on about it, Houghton, but I still

don't understand why you paid Macker Maroney for those photos of Jed and Sunny in the first place." When he looked back at her blankly, she said, "I mean, surely that wasn't big news, Jed sleeping around. Surely you didn't need to protect him from that."

His eyes darted to the kitchen door and back again. "Shhh! Just keep it down, okay. Like I said, old news."

That's when it hit her. "You weren't paying to protect Jed, you paid to protect *Annika*, right? To make sure she didn't find out."

He sighed and strode across to the fridge to retrieve a jug of milk. "And she didn't find out either," he said. "Not until bloody Sam Forrest came back and started telling the whole world. Might as well have taken out a full-page ad in the *Valley Times*."

"So Annika had no idea about Jed's affair until after Sunny died?"

"What do you think I paid Macker for? I made sure it stayed quiet. Nobody knew, not until Sam started banging on about it."

Roxy lowered her voice. "Sorry, Houghton, but I got the impression Jed was always unfaithful. This couldn't have been shocking news to Annika, surely?"

"Not shocking, no, but it could've been the last straw." His eyes turned watery then and he swept around to continue making his coffee. Softly, gruffly, he said, "Why Annie put up with that bastard for so long, I don't know. But she did. I was just trying to save her from one more disappointment. I worried that if she knew she'd finally crack. She'd been negotiating festivals here. I figured she'd turn her hand at that and kick him out once and for all, and I wouldn't've blamed her for it."

"Why do you care? Is this about the band? About your commission?"

He reeled back. "No! It was about protecting poor Annie. How much more was she supposed to take?" He paused. "But yes, okay, maybe I was protecting the band, too, but not because of any commission. I love the Roos, always have, and Jed was stuffing it up all over again. One more indiscretion and Annie would've walked, then that would have been the end of the band. Without Annie, there is no band. Everyone goes on about the great Jed Moody. It was Annika who made him great. Like I said, Horror Story was a horror story. We couldn't pull a sound, he could barely sing. She taught him everything he knows. She gave him the moves, got him singing lessons; even scored Al and his great songwriting skills. The Moody Roos would have fallen apart without Annie. I knew it. He knew it too, but couldn't keep it in his pants."

"Yet she stayed around, even after Sam told her about Jed and his sister's affair."

"Yeah." His brow furrowed, and it was clear he was surprised by that.

"You must have been worried then when Jed hooked up with Asha."

He stopped frothing the milk. "Asha?"

"Asha Kidlong, the mayor's—"

"I know Ash, I pointed her out to you, remember? What makes you think Jed was with Asha?"

She thought of the candy necklace at the hutch, of the incessant texts that Jed had received. "Wasn't he?"

"Bloody hope not. He promised me, he swore he wouldn't. I just don't understand why people keep saying that." He stared at her. "What do you know?"

"Nothing, really."

She shifted on her stool. The truth was she didn't have any hard evidence Jed had been seeing Asha. A candy necklace amounted to nothing in the face of it. Her brain was growing foggy again. Okay, she thought, let's get back to those incriminating photos Macker had taken. He'd boasted of incriminating pictures but insisted they weren't of Jed and Asha. Her brain cleared, she sat forward with a start.

"It wasn't Jed and Asha, was it?" He looked at her confused, so she said, "It was *Alistair* and Asha! Al was the one with her at the hutch that night!" That would explain why Alistair had got onto the stage so late at the jam, about the same time Asha had returned to the audience. It also explained why everyone thought Jed was having an affair with Asha at the hutch, because that's where he'd conducted his affairs with Sunny.

Macker must have taken photos of Alistair and Asha together at the hutch. Her brain stalled. "But … but what's so incriminating about Al and Asha? Is Asha underage?"

He shook his head. "She's eighteen next week. I just checked."

"So they're both single, both of age. What's the big deal then?"

Houghton didn't answer, but his frown returned as he finished making his coffee. The Moody Roos' publicist was keeping a secret, she knew that, and she wondered why.

CHAPTER 37

"Roxy, got a minute?"

She swung around to find Gilda at the doorway, nudging her head back towards the office. Anrika was just stepping out when they approached, and the look she gave Roxy was one of utter contempt. Roxy stared at her surprised. What had she done now? Did she blame Roxy for the fact that Alistair was in custody?

"He won't be in custody for long, at least not for the murder of Macker Maroney," Gilda told her as they took seats in front of the desk. "Wiles has gone down to question him, but after hearing what Mrs. Moody had to say, he'll have to let him go for that. Got an alibi, the lucky bugger. But he's still got some pretty serious charges to answer."

"Like what?" Roxy asked. "I'm really confused, Gilda, what's going on? Why would you even think that Al wanted Macker dead?"

Gilda leaned back in her chair and proceeded to explain everything. While searching through Maroney's house that morning, she and Wiles had uncovered a stash of his photographs, some poorly hidden in a file on his computer, others in the computer's trash basket.

"There were a few of Asha Kidlong at the hutch," Gilda said.

"Yeah, I know, with Alistair. What's the big deal, though? They're both of age. Houghton assures me Asha's eighteen. That's the legal age."

"Not when you're buying drugs, it's not."

"Drugs?"

She nodded. "Macker had pictures of Asha exchanging cash for what looks like a bag of tiny white pills. Ecstasy, probably. We'll know more when we speak to her. Quick is hauling her in now."

"Wow, okay, that explains it then. She wasn't there to get it on with Al, she was just after drugs."

"Maybe both. Anyway, the pix are pretty dark and grainy, and at first we thought it was Jed Moody handing the pills over, but we had them blown up down at the lab and it's definitely Alistair Avery, can just make out the bottom of his glasses."

"Okay, so he was selling drugs, and what? You think Macker was blackmailing him so he killed him?"

She groaned. "We thought that. Not anymore. As I said, he's got a bloody good alibi." Before she could explain, Roxy had already worked it out. Several more pieces of the puzzle were shifting into place.

"He was with Annika, right?" Gilda looked surprised for a moment, and then nodded. "How long have they been sleeping together?"

"She swears it's just since Jed died."

"So much for the grieving widow!"

"I know, but I'm not so sure; they could've been at it for years. It doesn't change the fact he has a rock solid alibi, if you'll excuse the dreadful pun. Judging from the fact that Maroney called me around 7:30 this morning, the coroner thinks he was killed sometime between then and 9:00 a.m. Annika swears she was having her merry way with the bass player in the stables all morning. Then she left him at about ten and returned to the house."

"Maybe she's lying. To protect him."

"Reckons one of the stable hands saw them both exit around that time. I'll go and check that out now. What I don't get is why she bothered hiding it. Why slum it in the stables?" Her nose crinkled. "Her hubby's dead. Why all the secrecy?"

"She wasn't hiding it from her hubby," said Roxy. "She never was. She was hiding it from Houghton."

"*Houghton?*"

Roxy relayed the conversation she'd just had with the publicist. "He confirmed what Macker already told us, that he did buy the photos of Sunny and Jed together before she died. But Houghton didn't do that to protect Jed. It was all about Annika. He goes on about the band, but I have a feeling it's Annika he really adores. Has probably loved her since the very start. Has been protecting her from Jed's antics ever since. Annika obviously knows it, has been working that crush for years. She probably didn't want to disappoint Houghton or scare off her faithful puppy dog. Who knows?"

Gilda sighed. "What a bloody soap opera this place is! Everyone sleeping with everyone else. Everyone trying to protect everyone else."

"And still no idea who killed anyone," Roxy added gently. Gilda groaned loudly again. "Any idea who would want Macker dead?"

"A sleazy paparazzi who extorted money from people and treated women like shit; nah, can't imagine who would want to bludgeon the man with the blunt side of an axe." Gilda shook her head. "We're still going through all his files with a fine-tooth comb, God knows what else we'll find in there. A lot of it was trashed, but we're in the process of retrieving it now. I think half the community will be shaking in their boots waiting for the outcome of that."

"And most of the people who showed up at Jed's last gig. There were plenty of drugs going around that night. If Macker was lurking in the bushes, he could have taken a lot of incriminating pictures."

"Didn't you say most of it was pot? I can't see the hippies killing him over photos of a few joints, which, by the way, look just like rollie tobacco on camera. Hardly hold up in court. Nah, I'm more interested in murderers than stoners, thanks very much, but we'll see what we uncover at his house."

"Any idea why Macker called you so early this morning?"

"Bindi insists he never said."

"How'd he know where you were staying?"

She lifted one shoulder. "I've been wondering that myself. He must have done a little sleuthing to track me down so early in the morning, which makes me think he must have been very keen to talk to me. Didn't want to wait until I got into the station. Maybe he had some new information on Jed's murder, or maybe someone had started threatening him over something, who knows? In any case, it now goes with him to the grave." She sighed.

"You're not blaming yourself, I hope."

"Nah, I won't be losing sleep over that guy, but I am disappointed with myself and my behaviour. Waking up with a hangover in the middle of an investigation is unforgiveable. Which reminds me. You're not heading back to Sam's place tonight, are you?"

Roxy rolled her eyes. *Oh, not again.*

"No, listen, Rox, this is really important. I have to tell you something, it's about Sunny."

Before she could continue, the door swung open and Quick appeared. Gilda tried to hide her frustration and said, "What is it, Rod? I'm in the middle of something."

Quick looked from Gilda to Roxy and back again. "Brent needs you down at the station, ASAP. He's got the Kidlong girl and her father in there, and he wants you in on the interview." He glanced at Roxy again.

Roxy got to her feet. "I'll leave you to it."

Gilda frowned and held a hand up to Quick, stalling him. "Listen, Roxy, this really is important. Can we meet up later?

Maybe get a bite to eat?"

"Sorry, busy!" She wasn't about to elaborate. Gilda was so anti-Sam, she didn't have the energy to get into another argument about him now. Nor did she want to give Quick the satisfaction. "I'll just see you tomorrow, okay, we'll catch up then."

Gilda sighed heavily, also darting glances at Quick. "No, I really need to speak to you before then. I'll try your mobile later."

Roxy smiled as she stopped at the door of the office. "Good luck with that. No network coverage, remember? See ya!"

As Roxy's footsteps echoed down the corridor, Gilda had a sudden desire to jump up and chase after her, crash tackle her to the floor. And if it wasn't for the fact that Quick was now watching her with wide-eyed curiosity, she would have done just that. Instead, she tried to focus on the fact that she was in the middle of a murder investigation and swallow down an encroaching sense of dread.

Something inside Gilda was telling her that her best friend's life might now be in danger, and she had just served her up to the killer on a platter.

CHAPTER 38

The fire was roaring away, a fresh bottle of Merlot had just been opened, and Lunar was diplomatically slumped midway between Roxy and Sam on the rug in front of the couch.

"I loathed the guy," Sam was saying as he swirled the red liquid around in his glass. "But I can't believe someone would go as far as to chop his head off."

"It wasn't that gruesome, he was bludgeoned, apparently. Still, you play with fire…'"

"Yeah, yeah, you get burned."

They both stared at the fire then, mesmerised by the flames. "Thanks for dinner, by the way," Sam said, looking across to her. "I haven't had anyone cook me a meal in a long time. Not since Sunny was around."

She smiled back at him and his eyes grew watery. She had come over two hours earlier, laden with a green bag full of bok choy, broccoli, ginger and chicken to make a green curry, and a fresh bag of white rice. She also brought another bottle of Merlot, and two chocolate brownies from the café for dessert, although the way Sam was looking at her now, she wondered whether they would even get to them.

"You know, I haven't *cooked* a meal for anyone in a long

time," she said, breaking the silence.

"So, no handsome boyfriend waiting for his dinner back in Sydney?"

She thought of Max in Berlin, felt her heart choke a little then said, "No."

"How did *that* happen?"

"There was someone. It's over. Can we leave it at that?" She didn't want to ruin what had been a beautiful night.

He nodded and reached down to pat Lunar. She did the same.

"What about you?" she said softly, her mind going to Govinda or some other curvaceous goddess with a loose blouse and jangling limbs.

"Not for a long time. Nope, it's just me and Lunar, hey, boy?"

The dog's ears twitched, but he remained still, basking in all the attention.

"I wish I had a dog of my own," she said.

"You can always share mine." Sam flicked his eyes from Roxy to Lunar and back again.

She blushed, then turned her eyes to the fire and they watched it silently for a few more minutes, the air between them smouldering like the flames inside the woodburner.

Eventually, keen to break the silence, Roxy said, "So how often do you replenish the flowers at your sister's site?"

He glanced at her, surprised. "Sorry?"

"The memorial site, by the creek?"

His surprise intensified. "What memorial site?"

She hesitated. "There's a small cross, a bunch of flowers near where she died. Sorry, I thought you must have put them there."

His face clouded over and his eyes watered up again. "No, I haven't been back since, well, for over a year. I hate the place. Gives me the creeps." He swallowed hard. "Jed probably did that. Or Annika. On a guilt trip."

She nodded. He was probably right. She tried changing the subject. "I really love open fires. Nothing better." She glanced at the diminishing wood pile by the fireplace. "Need me to chop some more? I reckon I could give it a whirl."

"No, no, that's okay."

"Really, it's no bother. In fact, I'm very impressed that you think that I'm up for the job. Most men would turn all macho on me."

She went to stand up but he was shaking his head emphatically.

"No!" he said, more forcefully this time. Then he blushed, glanced away and back at her. "Sorry, it's just that, well, I was thinking maybe we could… you know, keep each other warm?"

The smile Sam gave her then was a little wry, a little devious, and she couldn't help laughing.

"My my, is that an invitation, Mr Forrest?"

He blushed again. "Do you need one?"

When Roxy didn't respond, Sam moved his hand across Lunar's back and closer towards her fingers and she felt a shot of electricity as their hands touched, then intertwined. He leaned towards her and placed a very gentle, tentative kiss on her lips. Roxy hesitated just for a second before she leaned in closer and kissed him back, while Lunar thumped his tail on the rug below their feet.

Several glorious minutes later, Roxy was just starting to feel her shoulders relax, just starting to wonder what took them so long, when Lunar suddenly growled and leapt to his feet. They broke apart and Sam was about to joke that Lunar must be jealous when he, too, got to his feet.

"There's a car coming," he said.

Roxy swept around to look through the front window, but couldn't yet see it. She listened hard and eventually she, too, heard the distant sound of an engine cut across the property.

Lunar's ears were now twitching and he was stalking back and forth across the threshold. Sam tried to placate him, patting him with one hand as the other reached for the door. The second it was opened, Lunar shot off down the driveway towards the sound and Roxy joined Sam at the door, peering out into the darkness.

The outside light was very dim and the night was dusky black, but Roxy had a dreadful feeling she recognised the car that was now barrelling down the driveway half obscured behind the trees. Within seconds she knew exactly who it was and she exhaled loudly.

"I'm so sorry, Sam. I'll take care of it."

"What do you mean? Who is it?"

Before she could answer, Gilda's hire car was screeching to a halt out the front of the cottage, Lunar bounding along close behind.

"Is that *Gilda*?" Sam asked.

Roxy nodded. "She's checking up on me. I'll see if I can get rid of her."

"She's welcome to come in—"

"No!" Roxy said. She had enjoyed that kiss too much. "Just give me a minute, okay?"

He shrugged, then plunged his hands into his pockets and returned to the fire. Roxy strode towards Gilda who was now flinging her car door open and jumping out.

"Your timing's bloody dreadful, Ms Maltin," she began, but Gilda was already cutting her off, waving her closer with one hand and darting looks back to the cottage.

"I knew I'd find you here," Gilda was hissing, her voice barely audible. "You didn't answer my calls!"

"My phone doesn't work here, you know that. What's up?"

"Where'd Sam go?"

"I asked him to give us a moment. Why?"

Gilda looked relieved. "I'll explain it all later. Just grab your bag quickly, don't say a word, just get in the car and let's go."

Roxy took a step back, folded her arms across herself. "You're kidding me, right? This is some kind of joke?"

Gilda shook her head firmly. "Nope, I'm dead serious. You need to come with me."

When Roxy snorted at this, Gilda strode swiftly past her; pausing at the door to take a quick look around. Once inside she saw Sam standing by the fire, staring at her. He waved but she ignored this, spotting Roxy's handbag by the stereo and scooped it up before returning outside.

"Come on," she said firmly. "Let's go."

Roxy stood her ground. "I'm not going anywhere, Gilda. I don't know what you think you're doing, but you're behaving like a crazy person. You're going far and beyond what a good friend should do. If I want to stay here with Sam, I will bloody stay here. Just accept it, build a bridge and get over it."

Gilda sighed loudly then strode back to the car, pulled the passenger side door open, and flung Roxy's bag inside. She then strode back to Roxy and took her by the arm.

"Please, Roxy."

"No!" Roxy yanked her arm free. "You're being ridiculous. I'm a grown woman. If I want to sleep with this man, I'll sleep with—"

"This has nothing to do with that," she hissed. "This is about your safety. You need to get in the car, now."

"Safety? What are you on about?"

"Just trust me, please! We need to leave. I'll explain everything later."

There was something about Gilda's tone that made every hair on Roxy's body stand on end. She felt a prickle of fear, a wave of confusion, but before she could question her further, Sam appeared at the doorway, scratching his head.

"Roxy? What's going on?"

Gilda's frown deepened and she glanced behind her then back at Roxy who was now looking at Sam.

"I have no idea! Gilda's turned into a psycho Mother Hen. She's trying to force me to leave."

"Why?"

She shrugged just as Lunar began barking wildly again. The roar of a second vehicle could be heard coming down the driveway, followed closely by a third, and Gilda looked almost relieved.

"What the hell is all this?" Sam asked, his hands bunched into fists by his side.

Gilda turned back to him. "Please, Sam. If you have any decency, at all, you'd let me get Roxy out of here before it all turns to shit."

"Shit?" Roxy said. "What do you mean?"

Just then a dark grey sedan came screeching down the driveway and pulled in beside Gilda's vehicle. Brent Wiles was behind the wheel and Quick was leaping out of the passenger seat before the car had even come to a complete stop. He made a beeline for Sam. Right behind them a patrol car pulled up with two uniformed officers who also leapt out and started rushing towards Sam.

Quick had an unsettling look of deep satisfaction on his face.

Roxy glanced from Quick to Sam and then glared back to Gilda. "Gilda! What the—?"

Gilda was now pulling Roxy towards her car. "He's in big bloody trouble," she whispered. "Just get in!"

Roxy knew not to argue now. She shot Sam an apologetic look and dropped into the passenger seat, then buckled up as Gilda put the car into reverse and began to back out of the driveway. As she backed away, Roxy watched the horror play out in front of her. With the two officers nearby, Quick was strapping handcuffs onto Sam's wrists and mouthing something into his ear. Roxy saw Sam's expression turn from confusion to disbelief then horror.

Sam yelled something at Quick then turned to seek out Roxy's eyes as she swiftly disappeared back down the driveway.

And as the forest began to gobble up her view of the cottage, the last thing Roxy heard was Sam's voice, desperate and imploring: "Roxy, I didn't do it! Rooooooxy!"

CHAPTER 39

Gilda was stony faced as she straightened up her vehicle and turned out onto the main road. Roxy had dropped into a moody silence, confused about what was going on and not at all sure she wanted to know. It was clear Sam was being arrested, and she wondered what new evidence they had found. She felt an icy sensation run down her spine. Eventually she said, "I was having a really beautiful night, in case you were wondering."

Gilda nodded without looking at her. "Good," she said flatly. "Hold onto that."

Roxy frowned. "You want to tell me why you're arresting Sam? Or am I supposed to guess."

"He's not officially arrested. They're just taking him in for questioning."

"In handcuffs? By four police officers? Why?!" When Gilda didn't reply, Roxy said, "Can you at least tell me, is this about Jed? Is this about Macker? What the hell is this about?"

"It's about both of them."

Roxy cocked her head to the side. "You don't honestly think Sam had anything to do with either of those murders."

274

"Wiles does."

"Wiles is a fool! First he was pointing the finger at the poor old farmer couple then he was trying to pin it all on Alistair. Now he's got Sam in his sights. He might have dreamy blue eyes, but the guy's as blind as a bat."

"We've got good evidence this time, Roxy, for all three murders. I'm really sorry."

"All *three?*" Roxy's frown deepened. She stared at Gilda who was not meeting her eyes, just focusing on the road ahead, her hands tight around the wheel. "You don't mean…" She stopped. "No way! You can't think Sam had anything to do with his sister's death, do you? Surely not!"

Gilda finally slowed the car and looked deep into her sorrowful eyes. "Listen, let's get back to the B&B and I'll explain it all to you properly."

This was not a conversation Gilda wanted to have while barrelling down a bumpy road at seventy kilometres an hour in the dark of night.

Roxy was furious but sat in rigid silence until they found their way back to Bindi's Hideaway.

It was now 10:25 p.m., and Bindi was still up when they walked in. She could tell from their expressions that something serious was afoot and didn't bother with her usual platitudes, instead simply ushered them into the empty guest lounge where the open fire was still burning, and pointed them towards the sideboard.

"Help yourself to herbal teas and biscuits, ladies. If you need anything else, just ring the lobby bell. I'll stay up as long as you need me."

Gilda looked at her, surprised. "Thank you," she said. "That's very kind."

Bindi bowed her head and walked out, softly closing the lounge room door behind her.

As Gilda set about making them a peppermint tea, Roxy collapsed onto the sofa, tucking her legs beneath her, nibbling ferociously at her lower lip.

"Here you go," Gilda said, placing the cup on the table in

front of her. "It's not my favourite brew, but it's probably just what we both need. Calm the nerves a little."

Gilda chose the armchair across from her and sat down, taking a moment to gather her thoughts before deciding the best approach was a direct one. She said, "Sam Forrest has a clear motive for all three murders now, and no alibi to speak of. I'm sorry."

"Oh, so you *finally* agree Sunny's death was murder, do you?" Roxy's voice was laced with sarcasm, but Gilda let her get away with that. "If you'll recall, it was *Sam* who kept saying that to you, to everyone who would listen. Why on earth would he kill his sister then demand you all look into it? Huh? Bloody ridiculous idea, or have you all turned as stupid as Quick?"

Gilda sat forward. "I'm not the enemy here, Roxy. I don't need your attitude."

"Fine." Her tone softened. "Sorry. Just tell me what you've got."

She sat back again. "As you know, we did a search of Maroney's property yesterday. We found some photos."

"Yeah, yeah, of Asha and Alistair at the hutch, doing a drug deal. What's that got to do with Sam?"

"Well, we found some other photos too. I was trying to tell you about this yesterday but I didn't get a chance. Quick came in and I didn't want to mention it in front of him. He's smug enough as it is."

"Don't tell me, they were of Asha and Jed Moody, right?"

Gilda shook her head. "Once in Jed's dreams, perhaps." She stopped and explained: "Wiles and I interviewed Asha Kidlong late this afternoon with her father and a lawyer present. Daddy Mayor is fuming and I reckon Al better watch his back. So yes, it turns out Asha did buy MDMA— Ecstasy—off Alistair Avery. Had been buying it off him for months; apparently all the young girls do. Some in exchange for sexual favours in the stables, some just for cash."

"That's gross," Roxy said, now recalling the pretty redhead who had been shaking hands with Alistair outside the stables the day she interviewed him. That must have been a drug deal. She also recalled the shifty phone conversation she had interrupted in the house. It was most likely Al organising yet another sale. "I wonder if Annika knows," she said, then added, "So no pix of Jed and Asha together then?"

"No, and there wouldn't be. Despite the rumours, Asha tells us she was *never* having an affair with Jed Moody, or with Alistair, for that matter. In fact, she found the whole idea quite revolting, and I quote, 'Ewwegh! Are you, like, *serious*? They're so old and crusty!'" She half laughed. "Juicy Jed clearly wasn't as juicy as he used to be."

Roxy would have laughed along too, if she wasn't feeling quite so apprehensive. "So what other photos did you find then?"

Gilda's smile dropped in the face of Roxy's apprehension. "Macker had files and files of nude photos of lots of different women. It was a little sideline he had going. Sold them onto girlie magazines like *Picture* and *Ralph*. We found an e-mail trail."

Roxy crossed her arms over herself. "So, he was a sleazebag, that's not illegal, right? And what's any of this got to do with Sam?" Even as she asked it, Roxy knew she didn't want to know.

"Amongst his digital files, we found pictures of Sunny Forrest. Naked pictures."

Roxy stared hard at her. "Little Sunny? No way. I mean, I can understand her modelling, she was obviously very beautiful, but naked? You must be mistaken."

"There's no question, it was Sunny all right and in all her birthday glory. Turns out she did some modelling for Maroney, didn't get paid a lot, but then again there's not a lot of work around here."

"Surely she was coerced! He must have forced her—"

"She's smiling in them, Roxy. Doesn't look like coercion to us." She placed her hand on Roxy's. "I was trying to tell you this yesterday."

Roxy removed her hand and folded her arms back across her chest. "Okay, so, Sunny's not as innocent as everyone thought. I still don't understand what any of this has to do with Sam. The way he spoke about his sister, he clearly didn't know about the photos. He thought she was as pure as snow."

Gilda took a tentative sip of her tea then said, "Sam knew. A neighbour on Maroney's M.O. recalls overhearing the two men having a shouting match about the photos about a month before Sunny died. Sam demanded the shots be erased, Maroney refused."

Roxy picked up her cup and stared into it gloomily. "So? He's looking out for his little sis. That's normal. Max would do the same thing for Caroline."

"Would Max come back one night and throw a rock through Maroney's front window? Would Max threaten to kill him?"

Roxy dropped her cup back to the table, untouched. "Sam did that?"

"According to the neighbour, yes."

"Can we trust this neighbour?"

Gilda groaned. "You're missing the point, Roxy. You're letting your heart get in the way of your head. You need to think clearly now, just try and meet me somewhere in the middle, okay?" Roxy didn't reply, so Gilda said, "Here's what we… well, Wiles and Quick think happened. I'm trying to keep an open mind, but it's getting increasingly more difficult." She took a deep breath. "They believe Sam found out about the nude pictures around the same time that Sunny started her affair with Jed Moody. It must have crushed him, his innocent little sister, not so innocent anymore. Wiles believes that Sam overreacted and either killed his sister accidentally out of rage, or perhaps for what he saw as 'her own good'."

Roxy shook her head slowly. "This is extremely outlandish, you do know that, right?"

Gilda shot her a pleading look. "Just hear me out.

Whether he meant to hurt his sister or not, Wiles believes that Sam couldn't get over what he'd done and so he wreaked revenge on the two men he must have blamed for everything—Jed Moody and Macker Maroney."

Roxy was still shaking her head so Gilda said, "Can you imagine how much Sam must have hated those two guys? They both used and abused his little sister for their own gain, one for sex, one for money."

Roxy recalled the way Sam spoke of his sister, how he had put her so high on a pedestal. That pedestal must have made an almighty crash when it came tumbling down. "Okay, I get that he hated them," she said. "Horrendous human beings, both of them and I'm not exactly their biggest fans either. But that doesn't make me a murderer just because I despise someone."

"Sam threatened to kill them both, on several occasions. There are plenty of witnesses including you, I believe. Didn't he try to take a swing at Maroney just a few days ago, at the Goddess Café?"

"Hey, he was provoked! Besides, that's what makes it so ridiculous, don't you see? He did it all so publicly! Screaming blue murder isn't proof of blue murder, right?"

Gilda sat back. "It gets worse."

"Worse? What? You've got a smoking gun?"

Again her tone was dripping with sarcasm, but when Gilda flashed her a despondent look, she felt her heart plummet and her mouth go dry, so she simply sat there as Gilda told her what she knew: "The axe that was used to kill Macker Maroney belongs to Sam Forrest." Roxy stared at her blankly so Gilda continued. "We found his fingerprints all over the handle. We have a witness who confirmed it was his. There's absolutely no question." She leaned towards Roxy then. "I'm so sorry, sweetie. I know you really liked him. I know this is really painful. We only confirmed the axe was Sam's late this evening, but we knew about the pictures earlier. I was trying to tell you about it before Quick interrupted us. I would have stopped you from going over there if I'd known that's where you were headed. I tried to call you…"

Roxy wasn't listening to her now. She was recalling how Sam had been so reluctant to let her chop firewood earlier tonight. She'd thought it was a ploy to get her into bed. *What if the truth was more sinister than that?* What if Sam was trying to hide the fact that his axe was no longer at his property because he'd taken it to Cooleys Shoot and used it to bludgeon a man to death?

She dropped her head into her hands with a low, sorrowful moan. After a few minutes, she looked up at Gilda, eyes wide. "Who told you about the axe?"

"Sorry?"

"Who confirmed the axe was Sam's?"

Gilda hesitated. "I can't tell you that, I'm sorry. But there's no denying it. The fingerprints are his."

She frowned. "Why do they even have Sam's fingerprints on file?"

"Quick arrested him last year over the rock incident. Took his prints then. Of course, you can't easily obtain fingerprints from rocks, almost impossible, in fact, but Quick didn't know that." She rolled her eyes dramatically to show Roxy what she thought of Quick's IQ. "But you *can* take them from the handle of an axe, and I'm sorry to say, Roxy, they match perfectly."

"This is utter bullshit, Gilda. Someone's obviously pinched Sam's axe from his cottage and planted it there!" Her tone was turning feisty again. "He's obviously being framed!"

"Oh, *Roxy.*"

"No, I'm serious. You have to consider it, Gilda, you have to keep an open mind."

"That's extremely hard to do, my sweet, when everything points to Sam. Just try and think about it logically the way you think about every other case you come across. Keep your emotions out of it. Sam hated both men, he had access to their properties, knew how to play with electricity, his own axe was found at the scene of the third crime, for Christ's sake. He has no alibi for any of this. He's *the* prime suspect."

Roxy thought then of how she had scurried away from Sam's house last night. She wondered now, if she had stayed over, if she had been with Sam this morning, could she have provided his alibi for Macker's murder?

"*My* mind is open, Roxy," Gilda said. "It's yours that's closed. Can't you see that?"

"What about the Holloways? I thought Wiles was gunning for them. Maybe they set this whole thing up." Gilda stared at her, deep sympathy in her eyes, but Roxy ploughed on. "Maybe Macker got pictures of them tampering with the gear and that's why they killed him?"

"What pictures, Roxy? We have all his files. Where are these pictures?"

"I don't know. It's just that you're talking like Sam is some kind of psychopath, and he's not."

"You've known him for less than a week, Roxy. You need to wise up!" Gilda was feeling terribly weary and finally losing patience with her friend. "I've met a few psychopaths in my time, they're often the most charming person in the room. In fact, if I recall, you've met your share of psychopaths, too. You almost fell for another one, remember?"

Roxy's mind shot back to a previous murder case, to an investigative reporter called David Lone who had breezily murdered a bunch of writers purely to create a plot for his next book. It was true, she had almost fallen for the guy, been charmed by his slick exterior, but something had stopped her, something instinctual had warned her to be careful, to hesitate.

Why hadn't her instincts kicked in with Sam?

Because he's not a murderer! She wanted to scream. *He's not!*

But even as she thought those words, she began to doubt herself and wondered whether she really, truly knew him. Maybe when you spend so much time around killers and death, when you stick your nose in time and time again, you lose sight of the light and forget what innocence looks like.

Maybe she could no longer spot a killer standing in front of her. Or worse, she thought now, tears trickling down her cheeks, when he's kissing you so sweetly on the lips.

CHAPTER 40

Roxy awoke in the middle of the night with a panicked thought: *What about Lunar?* If Sam didn't get bail and found himself locked up for the terrible charges that he faced, who was going to look after the poor dog?

She fumbled for her iPad and squinted at the clock. It was 3:08 a.m. She groaned. How would she ever get back to sleep now? Roxy suddenly longed to call Oliver, to pour out her heart and her anger and her refusal to believe what Gilda so desperately needed her to believe. But even he, a classic insomniac, would be asleep by now. Besides, Roxy knew what Oliver would say, how he'd take Gilda's side without hesitation.

She stared hard at the clock again, doing the maths. It would be daytime in Berlin now. Perhaps she could call Max; chew over the case with him for a bit? She shook her head irritably. Her ex-boyfriend was never very big on chewing over the facts. The best person for that had been Sam. And now Sam was...

She grimaced, unable to finish that thought, and got up, wandered across to the window to look out at the white waning moon above the pond. Shivering, she pulled the duvet cover off the bed, wrapped herself in it and thought about how peaceful her night had been before Gilda showed up. She knew exactly where things were heading and she felt sick to her stomach now.

Had she been about to jump into bed with a murderer?

Shaking the thought away, Roxy tried to concentrate on the facts. Maybe, just maybe, she could imagine Sam lashing out at the low-life photographer, but could he really have killed the man who was once his best mate, let alone his own flesh and blood? Could he really have slaughtered both Sunny and Jed?

In Roxy's head it vaguely added up, but not in her heart, and she wondered now what was happening to Sam. Had he been locked away? Would he be denied bail? And how was Lunar coping, all alone at Grears Crossing, without his master and his newfound friend?

By the time morning arrived, Roxy was bleary eyed and bad tempered. She had managed little more than five hours sleep and tried to straighten herself out in a hot shower before quickly getting dressed and scooting across the hallway to Gilda's room. Another guest was just entering his own room and he looked at her, startled. Roxy realised she must look a horror but she didn't care. She knocked loudly on Gilda's door. There was no answer.

Downstairs, Roxy found Gilda finishing a cup of coffee in the lounge room, on her way out.

"Wiles wants me in straight away. They're questioning Sam this morning."

"So they kept him in all night?"

"That was the plan."

"What about Lunar?"

Gilda stared at her. "What about her?"

"Him! Lunar is a male dog."

Gilda exhaled loudly and decided to let that one ride. She understood that Roxy was hurting and would give her some wriggle room today. "I assume Lunar's still at the house."

"And my car? Can you at least give me a ride out there so I can pick it up?"

"You can't go back there now, Rox. Wiles is getting a search warrant. The place will be crawling with cops. How about I organise for an officer to get your car delivered to you here?"

She shook her head. "Haven't got time to wait around. I need to go and see Annika and Houghton first. Can you give me a lift there at least?" It was time to face the music and have another conversation about the doomed book. It was all becoming such a tangled mess, and with Alistair now facing charges of drug possession and sale, she wondered if it would all be called off again. And if she even cared.

"What will happen to Sam?" she asked. "Will he get released in time to feed Lunar tonight?

Gilda looked at her like she had finally cracked. "With all that's going on at the moment, you're seriously worried about a dog?"

"Yes!"

She sighed. "If Sam remains in custody, the attending officers will take care of the dog."

"What do you mean 'take care'?"

"They'll feed it. Give it water, all the basics."

"And what if Sam gets formally charged, doesn't get out on bail?"

"Then Lunar will be placed at the pound. That's all they can do, Roxy. I think Lunar is the least of Sam's worries right now."

"He loves that dog, Gilda."

She stared at her. "He probably loves his freedom even more. Stop stressing about the blasted dog!"

No sooner had Gilda dropped her at the Moody property, promising to call her later with an update, when she came face to face with Annika who was now standing at the front door of the house watching her approach.

"Oh, it's the ghost who talks," she said, a little perturbed.

"Annika, I'm really sorry—"

"So you should be!" she snapped. "We've had nothing but grief since you arrived. We were happy before then. Everything was going really well. Jed was finishing his latest album, the tour was kicking off. Now, well, now my husband is dead, Alistair is on drug charges and poor Sam is up for murder, which is ludicrous!"

Roxy was in a filthy mood herself and was about to remind Annika that this was *not* a happy house before she arrived—it clearly hadn't been a happy house for some time—when the woman's final words hit home.

"You don't think Sam did it?"

She snorted. "Of course he didn't do it! God, woman!" Annika strode back through the house and Roxy rushed to keep up with her, not even bothering to discard her shoes this time.

"But why? Do you know something I don't?"

"I know Sam, dummy!" Then she stopped and turned to face Roxy. "You know the world didn't start revolving when you turned up, Roxy Parker. I've known Sam most of my adult life. He was Best Man at our wedding, and he had been Jed's best friend forever."

"Not over the past eighteen months, he hadn't."

She scoffed. "Oh, Sam was getting over that. So, Jed slept with his little sister. He was moving past it. I mean, if I could forgive the bastard, he could."

Roxy squinted. "Why *did* you forgive him?"

"Love," she said, turning away again to continue down the hallway. "It's a bitch, right?"

Roxy stood still, stunned for a moment, before racing after her. "So you really don't think Sam's guilty?"

Annika laughed as she made her way into the living room and towards the bar. "Sam is all bark, no bite. Hasn't got it in him."

"He did throw a rock into Macker's house one night."

Annika snorted. "Says who? That idiot Quick?"

"I thought you liked Quick." She remembered how

friendly the detective had been that night Jed was killed.

She snorted again. "He's a sap! You know the first time we met him, he'd come to investigate Sunny's drowning and was more interested in getting Jed's autograph than anything else. Asked for a tour of the studio." She rolled her eyes. "How embarrassing is that? No, Quick's a fool. He couldn't even find Sam's fingerprints on the rock. The witness gave some vague description, could've been anyone. Everyone hated that Maroney character. There's a hundred people who wanted him dead, but there's no way Sam killed him." She reached into the fridge and produced a jug of homemade orange juice. "OJ?"

Roxy shook her head, so she poured herself a glass before saying, "Sam's just a big softie, always was. That's why his sister's death cut him to the core. No, the cops have got that wrong. *Again.*" She took a long sip of her juice, leaning against the bar. "What a pack of amateurs. They seem to be working through each one of us. They'll haul me in next." She smiled at Roxy. "Don't look so stressed. Your boyfriend will be out before you know it."

Roxy wondered how Annika knew about that but suddenly didn't care. She had never liked the woman as much as she did right then. She could have hugged her and, sensing this perhaps, Annika pointed her glass towards the veranda and said, "Houghton's at his usual spot. He'd like a word." She smiled more wryly this time. "You're lucky. He's barely speaking to me."

When Roxy stepped out to the veranda, she saw Houghton deep in conversation with Doug and Alistair. While Doug looked as relaxed as always, Alistair's face was deeply sullen, grey bags under his eyes, his jaw tense. Houghton, too, looked like he'd been to hell and back, but when he caught sight of Roxy, he pushed his chubby cheeks into a smile and waved her across.

"Hey, Roxy," he squeaked. "So glad you're here, we need to talk."

She nodded and said hello to them all, noticing that Alistair's expression remained tense. She took the seat Houghton was offering her and waited.

"About the book," Houghton began.

"Off again, is it?"

He blinked. "Nah, 'course not!"

Yet again this mob had managed to surprise her. Roxy glanced at Alistair who was no longer meeting her eyes.

Catching her glance, Houghton said, "Oh, Al's been a bloody fool, but wouldn't be the first time someone from the band was up on drug charges."

Doug cackled. "Yeah, I got done a few years ago, Jed before that. No biggie."

"Okaaaay," Roxy said, still feeling hesitant.

"We just don't want you to mention anything about Al and…" Houghton stopped, swallowed hard as though having difficulty digesting the thought, his face crinkled with disgust, "about Al and Annie. That stays right out of it, got it?"

So *that's* what all the tension was about! She nodded, but had a feeling the gossip would already be doing the rounds at Govinda's café by now.

Houghton said, "That's all Jed's fans need to hear, that Al's been playing up with Jed's child bride. They'll turn on Al like wildfire and we'll never sell a single bloody ticket, let alone a book. So it's a no-go zone, got it?"

Roxy stared at him, feeling grubbier than she ever had with Macker Maroney. The photographer was absolutely right. These celebrities and their entourage were even sleazier and more underhanded than he was. At least he hadn't pretended to be otherwise. She tried not to show it as she said, "Fine. I've just got one interview to go then, with Annika."

Houghton interjected, "Nope, she stays of it."

"What? I thought…"

"Just go with what you've got. We're running out of time. Let's just get this bloody book done. Annika's missed her chance."

Then he grabbed his phone and strode away to make a call.

Doug was chuckling now. "He's pissed at you, big time."

Al growled. "He can piss off. As if Annie was ever gonna end up with him. Jesus." Then he glanced at Roxy. "Don't give me that holier than thou look. So, I sold a few tabs. Hell, if they're gonna lock me up for drugs, they're gonna have to lock up half the friggin' shire, shut down the Goddess Café, hell, *Quick's* probably got weed in his backyard masquerading as a tomato plant. He's an old surfie, I know what they're like."

Roxy's brain needed to back up a bit. "Goddess Café?" she said. "What do you mean by that?"

He shrugged. "What? You didn't fall for their holistic bullshit? Hans has been harvesting a nice little crop down by that swimming hole for years. Sells bags of weed to the backpackers when they rock past. Very lucrative side business, I believe. So how come he gets away with it and I get threatened with the lock up? What's that about?"

Roxy wasn't listening to him now. Her mind was spinning again. *So that's why Hans seemed so shifty*, she thought. Could he be responsible for all of this? She tried to wedge the pieces into place. Maybe Sunny and Jed had come across Hans' crop; maybe Macker had been blackmailing him over it. Perhaps he had killed them to silence them or to protect Govinda and her business?

Taking Roxy's own silence for attitude, Al stood up with a huff. "Forget this shit!" Then he stormed off.

Roxy blinked and caught Doug's eye.

He looked mildly amused. "Might be time for another 'love-in'," he chuckled. "So, you don't need any more from me?" She shook her head. "Good, I'm getting out of here. Way too much tension, man."

Then he, too, walked away, and Roxy was left sitting on the veranda feeling confused but a little more buoyed nonetheless. If what Al said was true, then Hans and potentially even Govinda also had a motive for all three murders. But was it strong enough? Do people kill over a few pot plants?

"Arrrgh!" she said aloud, shifting in her seat. Sadly for Sam, even *she* wasn't buying that. So, Hans grew a bit of weed. Big deal. You rarely got a custodial sentence for that anymore. You certainly wouldn't need to kill three people because of it.

Her mind wandered back to Sam again. Was he now behind bars? Did they have sufficient evidence to deny him bail? She thought, too, of what Annika had said and felt a certain sense of relief. It felt good to have someone in her corner, someone who knew the man better than she did. She just hoped Annika was right.

"Roxy, phone call!"

She looked around to find Annika waving the portable phone in her hand, and jumped up to retrieve it. It was Oliver, of course.

For the first few minutes she let him rant about drug deals and murders and the number of corpses that kept showing up everywhere she went. It had become a catch cry from her agent, and she thought then of her mother and cringed. She'd better call her before she also heard the news. When Oliver was done ranting, he said, "The bloody book better still be on."

"It is. I've done the two main interviews. I've got enough to start writing it up."

"Good. Why don't you come home? You can write it from here. I'll organise a flight."

She couldn't do it, there was no way she was deserting Sam now. Roxy kept thinking of his gentle kiss, his puppy dog eyes. She knew she was being foolish and irrational, she knew they had known each other just a week, but she felt a connection to him she had not felt with any man—at least, not since Max Farrell.

Roxy didn't say any of this to Oliver, of course. Instead, she just said, "I'd better hang around, in case more questions crop up. These guys are hard to track down over the phone." It was a white lie of sorts, but she wasn't prepared to give up on Sam Forrest, not yet.

And so she spent the rest of the morning sitting out on the veranda, her laptop in front of her, transcribing almost four hours of interviews with Alistair and Doug. It was a mind-numbing task and one she usually abhorred, but it proved a lifesaver today. She didn't have the energy for much more than mindless tapping.

By lunchtime Roxy decided to take a break and phone Gilda. She needed to know where things stood.

Stepping back into the living room, Roxy spotted Annika lying on the velvet sofa watching a music video, Coco curled up beside her fast asleep. A provocative smile suddenly filled the screen and Roxy gasped. It was Jed Moody, larger than life.

"He was one sexy mother," Annika said softly, her eyes staring at the screen.

Roxy nodded and sat down in the chair beside her. They both watched for a few more minutes before Roxy asked, "Was that the concert at the Sydney Cricket Ground?"

Annika nodded. "Yep, 45,000 seats. Biggest gig they ever did. I wangled that. Houghton was convinced they wouldn't fill the SCG, but I knew Jed would. Had no doubt whatsoever."

"You always believed in him, didn't you?"

"Even when he didn't believe in himself, which was fairly regularly." Roxy's eyebrows rose enquiringly, and Annika added, "It's funny; everyone thought he had a huge ego, but he was actually very fragile. It just took one bad review, one tiny dip in the charts, and he could be down for weeks. I always managed to bring him round, pump him up again."

And if that didn't work, Roxy thought, there was always someone else—for the both of them, by the sound of it. "Why did you both bother?" Roxy asked, still watching the Great Jed Moody strut across the stage. "I mean, don't take this the wrong way, Annika, but yours wasn't exactly the most faithful of marriages."

Roxy knew she was treading on very dangerous territory here and half expected Annika to slap her into place, but she simply sighed. "Because, despite it all, I loved the man, and I believed in him." She glanced across at Roxy, her smile coy. "Despite it all, I'm his biggest fan."

"And Houghton is yours?"

Her smile deflated. "Not anymore. Your book will be the final chapter, Roxy. After that, he tells me he's leaving. He's washing his hands of us all."

Roxy nodded. She couldn't blame him.

Annika looked back at the screen and her voice was barely audible as she said, "I guess it's time."

CHAPTER 41

Roxy left Annika to worship her ghost and wandered into the kitchen to make another phone call. She glanced around, half expecting to find Hans hovering by the oven, corn frittatas in hand, but he was nowhere to be seen, so she picked up the phone, propped herself on a stool and phoned Gilda's mobile.

"I'm glad you called," said Gilda. "Wasn't sure how to reach you. Still at the Moodys?"

"Yep. Getting on with the book."

"They're *still* doing it? Really?"

"Yep, cash registers don't stand still for anyone. Listen, I need to know how it's all going with Sam. Please tell me you've realised you've got it wrong and are releasing him."

There was a pause. "No can do, sorry. Wiles has already read him his rights. Again. Quick is preening like a freakin' peacock and if I hear the words 'I told you so' one more time, I'm going to thump him."

Roxy bristled at hearing that. "Will he get out on bail at least?"

"Won't know until tomorrow. I doubt it."

"So what about his dog?"

"Roxy, I just can't be stressing about that bloody dog."

"Fine, I understand. Can I at least go and get Lunar? Keep him until Sam gets out."

"*If* he gets out. What are you going to do with Lunar, anyway? You can't take him back to Bindi's. You heard the lecture when we arrived. It's a native animal sanctuary, there's no way she's allowing a dog in there."

"Oh, don't worry about that," Roxy said, glancing back towards the living room. "I've got someone else in mind."

"Here? Really?!" Annika was not convinced she cared one iota for Sam Forrest's dog. "I mean, I feel bad for Sam, I told you that, but it doesn't mean I give a toss about his dog!"

"Please, Annika," Roxy implored. "I'll go over there and get him. I'll even bring his dog food and feed him for you. It's just for a night or two. Hopefully Sam will be released on bail tomorrow and it won't be an issue." When Annika still didn't look convinced, Roxy glanced down at Coco, asleep at her tummy, and appealed to her softer side, the one she caught glimpses of from time to time. "Poor Lunar is all alone out there and must be stressing about where Sam is. Just one night, please."

Eventually Annika relented. "One night!" she said. "And make sure you bring his food and bowl and all that crap. I don't want to know about it."

Roxy smiled jubilantly, then grabbed her bag from the veranda and headed out the front door to her car, which had been driven back and parked under the old fig tree earlier that day by a young police officer.

By the time Roxy got to Sam's cottage, Gilda had already phoned ahead and she saw the same youthful officer, this time holding Lunar by a lead, waiting for her at the top of the driveway.

"You can't come any farther," he said. "Detective Milton says you're to take her from here."

"It's Detective Maltin and she's a he, but thank you,"

Roxy replied, thinking, *how hard is it to get right?* "Did you bring his food?"

The officer looked confused and she waved him off as she got out and opened the door for Lunar who was chomping at the bit to see her. "Never mind. I'll pick some up at the shop. Thanks again."

By the time they got to the Goddess Café, Lunar had his head out of the car window, tongue dangling down, ears flapping in the wind. He looked happy to be free and Roxy didn't blame him. He must have been very confused about why his owner kept disappearing at random intervals.

"Here we are, Lunar. Now *stay*, and I'll fetch you some grub."

She got out and left Lunar staring after her, head still out of the window, ears now pricked high.

The Goddess Café had a few patrons seated at its outdoor tables, several of whom Roxy recognised from her brief time in the shire, but she looked past them all and strode straight into the shop where Govinda was busily frothing milk at the espresso machine.

"Hey, chook!" Govinda called out then sensing something in Roxy's eyes, said, "Is everything okay?"

"I'm fine. Please tell me you sell dog food."

She nodded her head. "You looking after Lunar again?" She stopped. "They haven't hauled poor old Sam back in, have they?"

Roxy nodded. She couldn't believe Govinda hadn't heard the gossip.

As if reading her mind, the shop owner said, "I heard something about that but refused to believe it." She sighed. "Still, can't say I'm too surprised."

"Really?"

She waved a jangly hand in the air at someone who was just entering the shop. "Chai tea? Sure, chookie, I'll bring it out, yeah?"

The patron nodded and walked out again. Govinda

turned back to Roxy. "He had such dark energy, you know? And it seemed to be getting darker by the day. Hans told me about the fight Sambo had with Macker the other day." She sighed again. "I guess it was only a matter of time before he couldn't contain his rage."

"He didn't do it, Govinda. There's no way Sam killed Macker."

She stared hard at Roxy, a small smile edging onto her face. "You've fallen for him, I can see that."

Roxy blushed. "What's that got to do… I mean, whether I *like* him or not is irrelevant."

"Why else would you be defending him, kitten, after what he did? You must have it bad. He's a killer, Roxy."

"Nothing's been proven yet, Govinda, so stop speaking like it's done and dusted." She could feel her temper rising. "So where is this bloody dog food then?"

Govinda gave her a sympathetic smile then waved her on towards the middle of the shop. "Just over there, before you get to hardware."

A few minutes later, Roxy returned to the counter with three cans of dog food and a bag of dog biscuits as Govinda was returning inside with a pile of empty cups. She dumped them in the sink behind her and turned back, rubbing her belly.

Roxy glanced at the swelling bulge. "I hear you're having another one," she said, and Govinda's face lit up.

"Yep, a boy this time." Her smiled deflated and she looked crestfallen for a few seconds before she said, "Look, sorry if I upset you before."

Roxy waved her off. "It's fine, really. I just feel bad for Sam, that's all."

"We all do! But if you play with fire…"

"Yeah, yeah, you get bloody burned." If Roxy heard that cliché one more time, she was going to do some burning of her own.

"Speaking of fire, how's Al?" Govinda was typing the

price of the tins into the cash register.

"He'll be all right. I think they're more worried about the effect on album sales than his reputation."

She smiled. "Oh, selling a few E's isn't going to hurt, especially around here. No biggie."

Roxy thought about this, considered questioning her about the marijuana crop Hans supposedly grew at the back of the property, but she knew she was wasting her time. All she was doing was trying to find other suspects—any suspects—to help shift the blame away from Sam.

"That's six twenty, thanks," Govinda said, giving her a curious look. As Roxy handed the cash over, Govinda said, "So did your cop friend say what's going to happen to Al?"

Roxy shook her head. "Although he might want to watch his back. Asha's dad is on the warpath, apparently. Furious with him."

Govinda shook her head. "Another young kitten who's lost her way. First she sleeps with Jed, then she hits on Al."

"Except Asha was never *with* Jed. And she was only with Al for the drugs."

Govinda blinked a few times, confused. "She never slept with him?"

"Nope. In fact, she was quite revolted by the thought; said Jed was too old and crusty for her. I guess he was losing some of his sex appeal."

Govinda turned to place the dirty cups in the kitchen sink and reached for the tap. "She was young," she said softly, her voice barely audible over the swishing of the water. "Too young for Jed. Who knew?"

As Roxy returned outside, she noticed Hans sitting under the shade of the large Poinciana, sucking on a small harmonica, the music now wailing mournfully across the yard. Several of Govinda's children were playing happily in the sandpit nearby. She spotted the older child, Heavenly Rose, and her sister Destiny, the one with the dark hair, and beside them, clutching onto a bright red spade, was the toddler with the wicked grin and the bright, sunflower eyes.

Hans waved one hand as Roxy walked past, and as she waved back she stopped and stared. There was something about the scenario that was eerily familiar. An icy shiver raced down Roxy's back. *Oh my God!* She thought suddenly. *It's been staring at me from the start!*

Hans stopped played. "Everything okay?" he called out and she blinked a few times as pieces of the puzzle began to chop and change in her brain all over again.

She realised now that she had everything the wrong way around; everything was back to front. Roxy kept staring for a few more minutes and it was only when Hans's eyes narrowed and he went to stand up that she snapped herself out of it and forced a smile onto her lips. Roxy raced back to the car and jumped in. As Lunar bounced up to her and licked her face, she pushed him away and grappled for her mobile phone.

Damn it, still no reception.

She threw the phone back into her bag, took a final glance towards Hans, who was now standing, hands on his hips, frown across his forehead, and cranked the car to life. She had to get out of there and find Gilda fast. The answer had been in front of her nose all along, and she hadn't even noticed. The pieces of the puzzle were finally in their correct place and Roxy knew exactly who had *dunnit*, and why.

There was just one question left to ask.

CHAPTER 42

When Roxy returned to Moody Views, Annika had deserted the couch and was now lounging on a creamy coloured hammock that had been strung up on one edge of the lawn, between two trees.

Roxy watched her from the veranda as she keyed Gilda's mobile number into the house phone then placed it to her ear. Gilda did not pick up and she cursed under her breath, then left a message: "Gilda, it's Roxy. I need to ask you something. I need to know who told you that axe belonged to Sam. It's *really* important. Call me on..." she paused, cursing again. "Just try me on the Moody home number, as soon as you get this." She repeated the number then hung up and continued staring towards Annika for a few more minutes.

"Hey, Roxy," Houghton said, his head poking out from the French doors behind her.

She jumped. "Oh! Hey, Houghton. Do you know if Hans is due up here today?"

"Hans, the cook?" He shrugged. "I don't think so. Why?"

She turned back to stare out at the lawn. "I'll ask Annika."

He held his pudgy hand out to stall her. "You should probably leave her alone right now, if that's okay. Been watching Moody Roos clips all morning, she's a bit weepy at the moment."

Still trying to protect her, thought Roxy. *Well, too bad.* There was no time to pander to Annika's mood swings now. Ignoring him, she took the portable phone and marched down the stairs and across the grass towards Annika who was almost completely hidden inside the large cloth hammock.

"Annika?" Roxy called out as she approached, but there was no movement.

For a sudden, horrific second, Roxy wondered if she was too late but then the hammock shifted and a manicured hand appeared, followed by a face, peering out at Roxy through dark sunglasses.

"You're becoming really annoying, you know that? What do you want?

Roxy got closer and knelt down towards her. "I need to ask you a favour."

"Roxy Parker, how many more favours do I—"

"Is Hans coming up today?"

"Huh? What?"

"Hans, is he coming to cook for you today?"

She groaned. "No, I can't afford to feed you bludgers all the time. Told him his services are no longer required."

"Damn it!" she said, and when Annika pulled her sunglasses off to stare at her, she said, "You need to get him back here. Fast."

"What? Why?"

"Please, Annika. Just trust me on this. I think I know how to help Sam, but I need you to do me this one last favour." She thrust the phone towards her. "Just call him now, he's at the shop. Ask if he can come straight up, maybe bring some of his corn frittatas or something."

"But why? I don't understand."

"I'll explain it all later, just do it, *please!*"

Twenty minutes later, Roxy smiled as Hans's dusty VW Kombi van pulled out from the parking lot of the Goddess Café. She waited a few minutes more then pulled her own car from the shade of the trees on the other side of the road and turned it towards the café and into the parking lot. Roxy quickly parked and got out. As she strode towards the shop, her eyes scanned the tables to see who was about. It was well before closing time but, apart from two of Govinda's children still playing in the sandpit, there was no one else there. She didn't know whether this was a good thing or not, but she didn't have time to worry about it now. It was time to sort out the fact from the fiction, and she'd had enough of all the lies.

Govinda's head appeared from the door of the shop and then she stepped out, her youngest child at her hip, a big smile on her lips.

"You're back!" she called out. "Did you forget something?"

"Nope, I need to speak to you actually. Got a minute?"

Govinda looked surprised. "Not really. I'm closing up, bloody Hans just took off and left me to it, so I'm shutting up shop early. Just cleared the riffraff. Maybe come back tomorrow."

"No can do, Govinda. This is important." Roxy then swung around and strode across to a table and sat down.

Staring after her, blankly, Govinda shrugged then followed her across, placing the child with the others in the sandpit.

"Heavenly Rose, keep an eye on Melody, okay?"

"'Kay, Mama!" the child sang out as Govinda turned back to meet Roxy at the table. She took a seat and shook her head a few times.

"What's going on, chookie? You look so serious suddenly."

"This is serious, Govinda. We need to talk about Sunny."

She groaned. "Oh God, are we still on about *her*? Must

we really talk about that little cow again?"

Roxy tried to hold her smile but her anger was creeping up on her. "We could talk about your daughter instead, if you like."

Govinda glared at Roxy. "My daughter? Which one?"

Roxy turned towards the sandpit where the toddler was now playing, holding the red spade close to her chest again. From a distance it could almost pass for a miniature guitar, a candy apple red Fender Strat, perhaps. "The youngest one, Melody. Want to tell me about her?"

"What's to tell?"

"She's Jed's daughter, isn't she?"

Govinda looked like she had just been slapped and she held up her hand to cover her cheeks which were quickly turning red. "What are you talking about?"

"Your daughter, Melody. She's Jed's, right?"

She swept her eyes to Melody and back to Roxy. "No, she bloody well is not! She's *Hans's* daughter. Hans is her papa." Her hand went to her belly and Roxy shook her head.

"You can keep saying it until the cows come home, Govinda, but it's becoming increasingly obvious. She gets more like her real dad every day." Roxy glanced back to the small child who was now giggling at something her eldest sister was doing, her sunflower eyes wide with delight. "She may only be young, but she's already got his smile and, wow, definitely his eyes." Govinda was now staring at her daughter not saying anything, so Roxy continued on. "How long had you and Jed been seeing each other before you fell pregnant with Melody? Months? Years? A decade?"

Still Govinda stared at Melody; her own lips now clamped shut. Roxy ploughed on. "You always believed that eventually he would leave Annika for you, didn't you? But when that didn't happen you decided to give him an extra incentive. The one thing Annika couldn't give him, a child." She glanced at Melody, too. "But it didn't work, did it? Or maybe it was about to work when that sweet little kitten came along and suddenly it was game over for you. Jed only had eyes for Sunny. And she was younger than you; blonder, more fanatical, and she could easily give the guy a child. Hell, she could give him six if he wanted. So you had to get rid of her, didn't you? You had to kill the competition."

Govinda leapt to her feet as though she had been stung but still she said nothing, so Roxy took another deep breath and continued.

"So you waited until big brother Sam had left the area, then you lured the poor woman to the creek. What, did you tell her Jed wanted to see her? That he would be waiting at the hutch? You hit her over the head, you drowned her and then you couldn't help yourself. You ripped her Moody Ring off her finger and went back to her cottage and destroyed all the pictures of Jed."

Roxy smiled wryly. "But it didn't work, did it? He had no idea who killed Sunny, but it made him realise life was short. It made him go back to Annika. So you decided to do the one thing you always do, the only thing you know how. You lured him back and got pregnant again." She stared now at Govinda's swelling belly. "You told him it was a boy this time, like that would make all the difference."

Govinda moved behind the chair and placed her hands on her belly as if for some sort of protection. But Roxy just kept going.

"And it did work didn't it? You knew he'd never had any respect for girls, the way he used and abused them, but a son! Now that would have buttered up his ego. A son and an heir to his great fortune – it seemed perfect! Finally, after all the years, he agreed to leave his wife for you. Was he going to do it after the final reunion tour, or after the book?"

Govinda was staring hard at her now, a dark look of contempt in her eyes, but Roxy continued. "But then that nasty little rumour started to circulate, didn't it? I don't even know who started it, maybe Macker? Maybe Hans conjured it up to protect you, to try to turn you off Jed again? In any case, you heard that Jed was sleeping with a new woman, even younger and blonder than both you and Sunny. Asha

Kidlong. You couldn't bear it! That must have been devastating. It must have infuriated you."

Govinda was shaking her head now and Roxy felt emboldened by her obvious discomfort. "You probably considered killing the poor girl first, but then it dawned on you. It was never going to end. You could kill a hundred Ashas and more would rise up." She smiled at her pun. "You must have been seeing red then. After everything you had done for Jed—you had his daughter, then fell pregnant with his son, even killed a woman for him. What more did he want? How much more did you need to do to prove your devotion to him? It must have delighted you to rig up his amp and watch him fry."

"Noooo!" Govinda finally exclaimed. She had a panicked look on her face, her smug smile all gone. "How on earth would I know how to do that? You're forgetting Sam's the sparkie, not me."

"Ah, but you did know your way around a soldering iron. You used to help your dad in his mechanics business. Sam told me that once and I didn't think anything of it. You could easily have pulled it off. I spotted a soldering iron in the studio the other day. You could have slipped in and fiddled with Jed's amplifier while that dreadful support band was on stage that night. There was a curtain up behind them, hiding the Roos' gear. You could easily have placed the faulty equipment back and no one would have seen you in the dark. Hell, most of the crowd were half stoned, they wouldn't have remembered it if they had. Problem was, just before Jed died, he called out to you, didn't he? He looked straight at you in the audience and told you in his own cruel way that he was finally leaving Annika, that he was going to be with you."

Her eyes flooded with tears.

"You screamed out 'No!' didn't you? I heard it, just before he was killed. You realised then that you'd made a fatal error, but it was too late. It was *you* who was wailing after he died. Not because he'd been murdered, but because he'd been murdered by *you*."

Govinda's cheeks burned red again "You are completely nuts! You know that? You are as crazy as Sam Freaking Forrest! He's been putting all this bullshit into your head, but it's not true, none of it!"

"Oh, but you're wrong about Sam. He pointed the finger at lots of people, Govinda, but never at you. He thought you were his friend. You used to rock up to his house and comfort him, didn't you? What did you do? Feed him brownies and make him feel better about his sister? Were you doing it to appease your own guilt? Or was it so you knew where he lived and could steal something to plant evidence on him, if you needed to. Evidence like his axe, perhaps?"

Roxy realised she hadn't yet heard from Gilda, but she had a hunch it was Govinda who had identified Sam's axe. Govinda knew where he lived, and she could have stolen it the day before while Hans was running the shop.

"But... but *why*? Why would I kill Macker? That's insane!"

Roxy sighed. "Another unnecessary death, Govinda. Yet again you jumped the gun. You thought he had incriminating pictures of you. You see, Hans was here the day Gilda and I talked about Macker's photos. He must have overheard us and repeated the conversation to you. Were you worried those pictures showed you having sex with Jed at the hutch? Or was it worse than that? Were you terrified Macker had photographed you killing Sunny or tampering with Jed's gear? In any case, you weren't taking any chances. You stole Sam's axe and snuck onto Macker's property and killed him. Maybe he caught you going through his files first and tried to warn Gilda about you? Who knows, but I do know you killed him and did your best to erase his files. You probably went through them first and couldn't find anything to pin it on you. Either way, you dumped all his photos, just in case. All except for the nude shots of Sunny. You needed the cops to find those, didn't you? You needed them to look right at

Sam. And, in case that didn't work, you planted the axe there, too."

"Nonsense, nonsense, nonsense!" Govinda shrieked, and several of her children looked up at her before returning back to their games. Only Heavenly Rose kept staring, a tiny frown crinkling across her forehead.

Roxy lowered her voice, hoping Govinda would do the same. "When did you first decide to plant it on Sam? Was that the idea all along, or did it just come to you after Hans told you about the incriminating photos?"

"Nonsense, nonsense, nonsense," she repeated, softer this time, no longer meeting Roxy's eyes.

"But Macker wasn't talking about you at all, Govinda. He had incriminating pictures of Alistair and Asha, not Jed and Asha, and certainly not of you. We didn't know it, Hans didn't know it, and you didn't know it either. Yet still you killed him, just in case. Another person murdered in cold blood to protect yourself."

"My children!" she screamed again. "I was trying to protect my babies. They deserve a father!"

"You *killed* their father!" Roxy snapped back.

"And he deserved it, too!"

"Mama?" Heavenly Rose was standing now, looking worried.

Govinda stumbled towards her. "It's okay, baby, go back to your play, Mama G's okay."

She moved away from the sandpit then, to a table at the farthest edge of the garden, just out of earshot of her children. It was still cluttered with old dishes, but she ignored them as she slumped into the chair and flung her upper body across the tabletop.

Roxy watched her for a moment, not sure whether to continue. She stood up and walked towards her slowly. Sensing her, Govinda looked up and met her eyes.

"He made me so many promises," she said softly. "Over and over he promised me. He said he would leave that bitch, and he knew she'd been sleeping with Alistair and whoever else she could get her hands on. But then he kept changing his mind. Said it would ruin the band, would ruin everything. Like Melody and I were nothing to him!"

"So you killed him."

"I gave him a second chance! I told him I was having another child, his son this time. He was so happy… deliriously happy. He promised he would leave her then. He just asked me to wait until the tour was over, he said it would be the last, but he… he…"

Roxy shook her head. "He was *going* to, don't you see? He called you 'the love of his life' that night, he wrote that song for you, 'It's time, baby, it's time.'"

"But… but everyone was talking about Asha… I thought… I thought…" Her eyes drifted away and she slumped across the table again so Roxy took another step towards her.

"He was never sleeping with Asha You got that wrong. You kept telling me not to listen to the gossip, but you *did*, didn't you? You believed that, and you killed him—all for nothing!"

"Noooo!" she screeched, leaping back to her feet, a steak knife in her hands now.

Roxy stared at it in disbelief. Then she giggled. Roxy giggled like a stupid schoolgirl. She should have been nervous, wary at least, but she couldn't help laughing at the irony of it all.

Am I really going to get stabbed with a steak knife at a vegetarian café?

Trying to pull herself together, Roxy took a step backwards and held up her hands. "Just calm down, Govinda. I'm not the enemy here."

Govinda lurched towards her. "Yes, you are!" she screamed. "You and that upstart yuppie copper! You've been poking your nose into my business from the minute you got here! Why couldn't you just leave us alone?!"

"What? To kill more people who got in your way?"

"I would never have killed Macker if it wasn't for you.

It's all your fault!"

Roxy felt her shock turn back to anger, red and hot. "Don't you dare blame me for that! You think everyone else is to blame but yourself. No one told you to have an affair with a married man or drown poor Sunny in the creek that day! No one told you to electrocute Jed or smash Macker over the head to protect yourself. You pretend to be all spiritual and enlightened when really you're just a psychopathic groupie!"

Govinda's face contorted into a mask of rage, and any beauty she once had vanished as she lunged towards Roxy, the knife darting out in front. But before she could reach her, someone was yelling out, "Nooooooo!"

Both women swung around to find Hans rushing towards them, arms out. They had not even noticed his van return.

"Stay out of it, Hans!" she screamed back at him. "This is between me and Roxy!"

"No, Govinda, it is between you and your higher self!" He yelled back. "It is time to put the knife down, my angel. It is time to stop all this killing." He pointed to her belly. "Do it for the little one. Do it for Jed's baby."

Her face paled and she gulped back a sob. "You know?"

He nodded. "Of course, my darling. But it's okay. Don't you see? It's okay."

He was at her side now and was slowly peeling the knife from her hands as she collapsed into his arms. Roxy, too, dropped down into a seat; her whole body shaking as the sound of police sirens began wailing in the distance.

As Hans held Govinda tightly in his arms, Roxy looked back towards the sandpit where the children were now standing, staring horrified and wide eyed towards their mother, clearly shocked by the outburst.

All except for Jed's daughter, that is. Melody was staring at Roxy, watching her keenly with a wicked glint in her yellow and green sunflower-coloured eyes and a wide, slouchy smile.

CHAPTER 43

A flash of white broke the dark night sky and Roxy looked up to see a Tawny Frogmouth sweep low across the lawn at the back of Bindi's Hideaway. It had something in its mouth, a field mouse perhaps, and she felt a sliver of unease as she watched it swoop back up and out of sight.

"Are you okay?" Gilda asked, watching her keenly from across the pond where they both dangled their feet. Roxy nodded, then reached for the bottle of Merlot they had smuggled in earlier, and took a good long swig.

Her nerves were still rattled, but she was starting to feel calmer now that all the pieces had fallen into place. Still as she thought of that mouse, she realised that she, too, had nearly fallen prey to a predator who had been right under her nose all along.

"You *were* pretty lucky," Gilda agreed. "If it wasn't for Hans, who knows what might have happened. Good thing for the kids, too, they didn't need to watch their mother attempt to stab you."

Roxy shivered again and handed the bottle to Gilda. "But how did he know?"

"Hans was coming to see me when he left the shop, not

heading back to Annika's place to cook her dinner like you'd demanded. We ran into each other not far from the freeway turn off." Gilda took a big gulp of the wine then gave Roxy an eye roll. "What were you *thinking*, woman?! Luring Hans away so you could be alone with that mad woman?"

"I didn't realise I'd be all alone! I thought there'd be other people at the café, I just needed to get Hans out of there. I couldn't be sure if he was in on it with Govinda, and I worried that he'd be the one attacking me, not her."

"It's a pity he didn't speak up sooner. He'd started to suspect Govinda a while ago, apparently. She had told him that Melody and the new bub were his, but he had his doubts, the way she kept sneaking off at all hours and firing off secret texts, it got him wondering."

"He only had to look at Melody's face to know he wasn't the father."

"True. But I don't think he wanted to believe it, not until he heard Govinda tell Wiles that she was with him the morning Macker was killed. That's when he finally accepted the truth. He went along with Govinda but he knew she was lying, had seen her sneak off very early that morning and he finally had to admit she must have killed Macker. Then left the axe there to implicate Sam."

Roxy shivered. "She's pure evil."

"Masquerading as a goddess," Gilda added, handing the Merlot back to her friend. "Hans must have loved her very much to protect her for so long."

Roxy sneered as she took another sip. She'd had enough of protective love. It seemed to be the escape clause for all of them. Everybody was trying to protect everybody else and hurting each other in the process. Houghton had loved and protected both Annika and Jed his whole adult life despite all their indiscretions, manipulation and deceit. Or was it his income stream he really loved and wanted to protect?

Even Sam had come dangerously close to being locked away for being too protective a brother.

"How is Sam?" she asked, and Gilda cringed a little.

"Not talking to me, that's for sure." She nudged a toe towards Roxy's. "I'm sure he'd love to see you, though. They've released him, of course. He's back at his place now. Quick even organised for that bloody dog to be returned to him, he feels so bad."

"So he should!" She hesitated. Would Sam even want to see her after everything that had happened?

As if reading her mind, Gilda said, "He knows you had nothing to do with it, Roxy. He knows you've been barracking for him from the start." She helped herself to more wine then said, "Go on then, don't waste time with me, go to him."

Roxy stared at her. "I thought you didn't like him."

"It's not *him* I don't like, silly! It never really was. It's the *idea* of him that got under my nose. The fact that you might stay here with him and desert me in Sydney."

"Who says I'm going to stay here with him?"

Gilda gave her a sideways look. "That's the whole reason I never trusted him, Roxy. I realise now that it's not because I thought he was a killer. It's because deep down I realised you were falling for him, and I didn't want you to. I was just being a selfish cow."

Roxy half smiled. "So what's changed now?"

"Maybe I've done a bit of growing up myself. Or maybe it has something to do with my own blue-eyed guy."

"Wiles? So what about the wife?"

Gilda's smile lit up her face. "She moved out the day he caught the plane up. Had nothing to do with me apparently. He was telling the truth when he said they were at breaking point. She's always loathed his career, had had enough. So we're going to… well, we'll see how it goes."

"Good. You deserve happiness." Roxy paused. "And so do I!" She pushed the bottle towards Gilda and stood up.

"Back to the ranch?" Gilda asked, beaming up at her, and she beamed back.

"Oh yeah, it's time, baby, it's time."

****

Roxy heard Lunar before she saw him. A deep, loud "woof!" echoed through the trees followed by a swish of black and white as the dog came racing down the driveway towards her.

Roxy slowed the car and came to a stop just as Lunar approached, then leaned over and opened the passenger side door so he could jump inside. He bounced towards her, licked her face, then settled into the seat and stared out through the front windscreen, as if to say, "Okay, then, let's get going!"

Roxy laughed and closed the door, then continued on until she reached Sam's cottage, which was now lit up like a Christmas tree. She spotted Sam waiting at the front, a goofy smile in place, and she stopped the car and opened the door, waiting for Lunar to sweep past her before she, too, stepped out onto the drive.

Sam remained in the doorway, hands in his pockets, shy smile on his face. "I was hoping you'd come," he said, before glancing behind her. "That crazy cop friend isn't on her way too, is she?"

Roxy laughed and stepped towards him. "She's officially banned."

"Good. She's a classic case of 'be careful what you wish for'. She nearly got me locked up for life!"

"I think that was more Wiles and Quick's doing, but anyway, you're out now. You're okay."

"Thanks to you." He pulled his hands from his pockets, stepped towards her now. "You're the only one who had any faith in me."

Before Roxy could say anything, he wrapped his large arms around her and pulled her into a deep embrace. The horror of the past week evaporated in that moment, and she felt an overwhelming sense of calm. It was as though she had finally found her place, had finally come home.

"I'm so sorry about your sister," she whispered as they

continued holding onto each other.

"You play with fire…" Sam began, but she pulled back and stared into his eyes.

"No way!" she said. "That's just Govinda's crap. 'Hippie' my foot! She's the biggest fraud I ever met; there's not a spiritual bone in that woman's body. Listen to me, your sister did *not* deserve to die. No matter what she did, she did not deserve that."

He nodded, fat tears filling his eyes. He cleared his throat and brushed them away. "I can't believe it was Govinda. For eighteen months I've been unloading to her. I never knew." He shook his head. "She played me, big time."

"I don't know about that, Sam. Maybe she did it to assuage her guilt. She was probably the one who made the little memorial at the creek where Sunny died, kept replenishing the flowers. Maybe it's been eating her alive all this time. If there is such a thing as karma, Govinda knows she's in for some major strife. In any case, she got the ultimate punishment—she killed the only man she's ever loved. *She* did that. She has to live with that for the rest of her life."

"I wonder what will happen to those poor kids."

Roxy shrugged. "Who knows? Hopefully Hans will step up, take care of them all. Although I wonder whether Annika will try to get custody of Jed's girl and the unborn child. I'm not sure she should though. Be nice to keep the siblings together."

He nodded and stepped back. "Are you coming in? I make a mean coffee, you know."

She laughed. "Yeah, I think I will. But I'd like more than coffee this time." She hesitated. "Are you up for that?"

His face lit up, his smile widened. "Up for it? I've been waiting for it since the day you arrived, since I first saw you sitting at Govinda's Café, tapping away at your stupid iPad looking all beautiful and innocent."

"Really? You liked me then?" she laughed. "Wasn't that the day you abused me about protecting a killer?"

He smiled. "The way you handled that, the way you looked at me with those big green eyes of yours, I just knew I had to see you again. Why do you think I was at Jed's gig that night? Certainly wasn't there to watch the Moody Roos, that's for sure."

She blushed. If only she'd known, but then again, maybe she had known. Maybe that's why she had felt so comfortable with him, had so readily agreed to watch over Lunar the next day. Deep down she had known all along.

"Then you went and kidnapped me, if I recall." She laughed again. "You sure have a funny way of showing a girl you like her."

"How about this then." He took her face in his hands and kissed her long and hard on the lips. When he had finished, Roxy's head was spinning and she wasn't sure she could feel her feet anymore.

He smiled knowingly and said, "Come on, then, you look like you need that cuppa."

Then he took her hand and led her across the threshold while Lunar followed close behind, wagging his fluffy black tail with pure delight.

ABOUT THE AUTHOR

C.A. Larmer is a journalist, editor, teacher and author of multiple crime series, stand-alone novels and a non-fiction book about pioneering surveyors in Papua New Guinea. Christina grew up in PNG, was educated in Australia, and spent many years working in Sydney, London, Los Angeles and New York. She now lives with her musician husband, boomerang sons and their very cheeky Bluey on the east coast of Australia.

Sign up for news, views and giveaways:
calarmer.com

www.ingramcontent.com/pod-product-compliance
Lightning Source LLC
Chambersburg PA
CBHW031214120726
47905CB00002B/338